WHEN HELL
STRUCK TWELVE

WHEN HELL STRUCK TWELVE

A Billy Boyle World War II Mystery

James R. Benn

Published by Soho Press, Inc.
227 W 17th Street
New York, NY 10011

Library of Congress Cataloging-in-Publication Data
Benn, James R., author.
When hell struck twelve / James R. Benn.
Series: A Billy Boyle World War II mystery ; 14

ISBN 978-1-64129-192-7
eISBN 978-1-61695-964-7

1. Historical fiction. 2. War stories. 3. Mystery fiction. I. Title
PS3602.E6644 W46 2019 813'.6—dc23 2019012964

Printed in the United States of America

10 9 8 7 6 5 4 3 2 1

These verses believe; they love; they hope; that is all.
—Arthur Rimbaud

For Debbie, and all that we believe.

O childhood, the grass, the rain, the lake water on stones,
the moonlight when the hell struck twelve. . . .
The devil's in the tower right now.

FROM HELLISH NIGHT, BY ARTHUR RIMBAUD

PART ONE

FALAISE

CHAPTER ONE

THE FALAISE GAP, NORTHERN FRANCE
August 1944

THE GROUND WAS a carpet of gray corpses. They lay on the hillside in scattered clumps and on the valley floor below like a river flowing in from hell itself. Blasted by shells and bombs, ripped and torn by strafing aircraft, remnants of the once-mighty German army in Normandy were dead or dying in droves as they tried to escape the trap closing in on them.

Those desperate enough were struggling to flee the carnage, and the only way to do that was to drive us off this goddamn hill. Hill 262, according to the map. Two hundred and sixty-two meters high, it towered above the eastern road from Falaise and the green meadows littered with German dead, their field-gray uniforms coated in swirling dust and caked crimson with blood.

Across the valley, somewhere to the south, General Patton's Third Army was advancing on a long end run to slam the door on the German escape route. Patton was drawing near, but not fast enough to stop the stream of surviving Krauts from fighting their way out of the slowly closing trap. The enemy was in a tight spot, backed up on the road for thirty miles or so to the west, stuck in a shrinking pocket enveloped by Allied armies. But the pocket wasn't zipped up tight, not yet. We were in the right place, but not strong enough to lock it up. Patton's tanks were strong enough, but too far distant.

Even so, the valley was a shooting gallery filled with burning vehicles and men dying as they made their way forward on foot. Everything from long-range artillery to tank shells hit the valley floor with explosive bursts, churning up earth and igniting fuel tanks, plumes of yellow flame and black smoke dotting the roadway for miles. The rancid odor of death rose up on the blisteringly hot winds from the valley below, clawing at the back of my throat.

"Anything, Captain Boyle?" Lieutenant Feliks Kanski asked, as I hunched over the radio in the back of my jeep, which was parked next to a shell-shattered tree trunk, camouflaged by tangled limbs and dying leaves. There were few safe places within the square mile we possessed on this hill, and I was glad of what cover it offered. I shook my head as I gave my call sign over and over again, broadcasting on the frequency we'd been assigned.

"Keep at it, we need ammunition," Feliks said. His face was gaunt, his skin pale under the filth of three days on this hilltop. Sweat poured down his temples under the distinctive British tin pot helmet shading his eyes. Feliks was with the Polish 1st Armoured Division, as was everyone else on Hill 262.

Well, not everyone. I was here, along with my buddy Kaz. Lieutenant Piotr Kazimierz, that is. Kaz was a member of the Polish army-in-exile, but he wasn't with Feliks's frontline unit. He and I were part of a different outfit. We worked for General Eisenhower and wore the shoulder patch of the Supreme Headquarters, Allied Expeditionary Force. SHAEF. We'd arrived yesterday as part of a Canadian supply column that had run into bad luck in the form of a couple of Panther tanks who got us in their sights and took out all six trucks. We'd been in a jeep, and either they didn't spot us or felt we weren't worth a high explosive shell. After that, Hill 262 had been surrounded. Tanks and German paratroopers attacked on one side, fanatical SS troops on the other.

I gave Feliks my canteen. There wasn't much left, but he needed it more than I did. He took a sip and handed it back as static crackled, and I finally heard a voice. In English, thankfully. It was the 4th Canadian Armoured, and they had good news. I acknowledged the message and signed off.

"Supply drop at 0900," I said, which meant the planes were close. Feliks grinned.

"Good," he said. "I will pass the word. It is about time. We're down to fifty rounds per man. Some of the tanks have only a few shells left."

The Poles had been fighting for days. That hadn't been part of the plan. By now the northern and southern pincers should have linked up and had the Krauts trapped within a deadly embrace. Instead, Hill 262 was on its own and struggling to hold on.

Struggling in more ways than one. Every Polish soldier knew what surrender to the SS meant. Execution. With elements of two SS panzer divisions attacking from the west, trying to pry open an escape route for their pals inside the pocket, there was only one choice—fight to the death.

Every Pole on this hill knew about the Warsaw Uprising. The Polish Home Army had revolted and fought the Germans, expecting the Soviet army to liberate the city. But the Russians had not come to their aid. They halted, allowing SS troops to pour in and put down the rebellion. Tens of thousands of civilians were massacred as the Russians waited for the Nazis to wipe out the Home Army, which they considered a potential threat to Soviet rule. No Polish soldier would expect any mercy from the SS. Or give any, not after Warsaw. Not after five years of ruthless occupation and that last terrible bloodbath.

Shells exploded on the hillside, a reminder that the Germans in the valley still had deadly hardware and could use it effectively. Artillery sounded from the north, the 4th Canadian Armored boys trying to fight their way through the Kraut paratroopers to get to us and having a tough time of it. Small arms fire crackled along the line, but it was impossible to tell who was shooting at whom and with what effect.

I dashed over to Kaz, shells falling closer and closer. He was in a trench near an old hunting lodge, the only building on the hill. It had been pressed into service as a hospital and was crammed with wounded, Pole and German alike. Outside the lodge, several hundred prisoners were huddled together, guarded by Polish soldiers who'd been bandaged up but could manage guard duty.

"Did you get through?" Kaz asked, removing his steel-rimmed spectacles and cleaning them with the spotless white handkerchief he had managed to produce from one of his pockets. Monogrammed, no less, with his initials and family crest. Kaz may have been a lowly lieutenant in the eyes of the army, but he was a baron of the Augustus clan, and probably one of the few Polish nobles left alive.

"Yeah. Our Canadian pals said an airdrop of supplies is on the way. These guys giving you any trouble?"

"None at all," Kaz said, putting on his glasses and gazing out over the sullen prisoners sitting on trampled grass, his Sten gun resting on the lip of the trench. It might have been the submachine gun, or the terrible scar that cut across the side of Kaz's face. Both were frightening enough. "I think most are glad to be out of the war. Or in shock from the experience in that valley."

I unslung my Thompson submachine gun and leaned against the trench wall. Kaz was right. By the looks on their faces, these Fritzes had had enough. They'd come through the valley of death and been captured by Polish tankers. Lucky to have survived both, few of them saw any percentage in making a run for it. If they weren't killed outright, all they had to look forward to was more fighting and a high likelihood of dying on the dusty road to Paris.

Everybody wanted to get to Paris. GIs dreamt of it, a magical, near-mythical place of life, joy, wine, and women. French Resistance fighters wanted it for everything it meant to their nation still in chains. Germans wanted it for the safety it promised, or perhaps as a last chance for glamourous living and loot to carry back to the Reich.

I had my own reasons for getting to Paris.

"Still no SS?" I asked Kaz, after a quick survey of the POWs.

"No," Kaz replied. "No SS prisoners. They fight to the end. As do our men. We are in France, but between Poles and the SS, it is still Poland. It is still Warsaw."

"Fine by me," I said. "Last thing we need are die-hard Nazis talking these boys into making a break for it."

The POWs were the reason we were here. One of our jobs in the SHAEF Office of Special Investigations was prisoner interrogation. Well, one of Kaz's jobs, to tell the truth. He was the one who spoke half a dozen languages fluently and a bunch of others passably. When we had nothing that needed actual investigating, our boss put us on this detail. Which had only extended to receiving the prisoners when they were brought back from the front lines. But Kaz couldn't wait. He wanted to catch up with his Polish brethren, Feliks in particular. Feliks had intelligence contacts with the Home Army in occupied Poland, and Kaz had recently discovered that his younger sister Angelika was still alive, which was a very good thing. But she was working with the Polish underground, a very dangerous thing.

With the Warsaw Uprising and the slaughter of Polish civilians and fighters by the Nazis, Kaz was desperate to obtain whatever information he could. So, we invited ourselves along on that supply run. The brass wanted prisoners, especially officers, to interrogate about Kraut plans to defend Paris. That was the next stop in this campaign, once we bagged the remnants of the German army in the valley below. Which I'm sure had looked a whole lot easier on paper.

The Poles had a good haul of prisoners but no place to hold them. Our role should have been a walk in the park. Bring in the supplies and drive out the most senior POWs in the empty trucks. But war had a way of making even the simplest plan an unimaginable mess, and here we were smack in the middle of one. Feliks hadn't heard a damn thing about Angelika, the trucks were blown to hell and gone, and we were battling enemy forces intent on overrunning our position and hightailing it to the City of Light or wherever the Krauts were planning on making their next stand.

"Do you hear it?" Kaz said, nudging me as he kept one eye on the prisoners. I did. The low rumble of C-47 cargo planes approaching. Shouts and cheers went up from the Poles dug in around us. Even the German prisoners looked happy, understanding with a soldier's intuition that this sound meant chow and cigarettes. "There!"

Kaz pointed to the north as the sound of twin-engine aircraft grew in intensity, becoming their throbbing engines louder and more insistent. Then the first planes appeared, drawing closer as parachutes fell behind them, blossoming against the bright blue sky. Dozens of canisters floated beneath the white canopies as the flight of C-47s banked away from the anti-aircraft fire rising from the valley floor.

I kept my eye on the parachutes. They were too far away. The first ones landed far short of our positions, close to the Germans at the base of the hill. The rest drifted, snarling their cords in the trees on a ridgeline a quarter of a mile or more away. A groan went up from the men dug in around us. Even the prisoners looked disappointed.

"That's where we left from yesterday," Kaz said. "They dropped them to the Canadians, the fools."

"They'll break through to us," I said, trying to sound confident. "And they'll bring the supplies. It won't be long."

"We should have been back by now, interrogating these Nazi

officers," Kaz said, swinging his Sten gun to take in the prisoners sitting in the grass. Some of them ducked. Others laughed disdainfully at this unseemly display of nerves on the part of their *Kameraden.* "Perhaps we should start. We have a major and several captains here."

"No," I said. "We need to separate them. A guy won't snitch if he knows he's going to be tossed back in the clink with his pals. Too dangerous." That was one of the first things my dad taught me back in Boston. He was a homicide detective, and he had started training me to follow in the family business before I was in long pants.

"Yes, I see," Kaz said. "Besides, some of them may believe they will be freed after the next attack. They may have guessed we are low on ammunition."

As if on cue, mortar rounds sailed over our heads, exploding around us. This time, everyone ducked. I told Kaz to stay put and ran low as another flurry of explosions dropped in among the entrenchments.

It was another attack. We were dug in deep, so mortar rounds weren't much of a threat unless your foxhole took a direct hit. But it did tend to make you keep your head down, which was a problem if a few hundred pissed-off Krauts were advancing in your direction.

I ran by tanks, camouflaged by leafy branches and hidden in the rocky terrain. There was no activity on the hillside facing the valley road, just the ceaseless *crump* of distant artillery punishing the Germans below. I scuttled along behind the men, dug in all along the ridge. Nothing sounded other than the occasional rippling rattle of rifle fire.

On the northwest side of the hill, it was much the same. I dove into a foxhole already crowded with Poles manning a machine gun as another round of mortar fire sent shrapnel flying. I risked a quick glance above the logs protecting the gunners. Off to the left, a gulley ran down the hill, dotted with the bodies of Germans who'd tried to break through. These were the SS trying to loosen our hold on this hill so their pals could get out of the trap. By the twisted tangles of corpses, I didn't see them trying that route again.

On the right flank, the ground sloped gently downward, a line of trees and shrubs to the side obscuring my vision. I strained to see any sign of movement through the greenery, but no dice. One of the Poles used his binoculars and shook his head as he let them drop to his chest. Nothing.

My gaze wandered to the grassy field in front of us. Between the gully and the trees, tall grasses browned by the August sun bent as a warm gust brushed against them. No sign of Krauts.

Then I saw it. Clumps of grass that didn't bend with the breeze. Camouflage stuck on helmets. The enemy crawling silently forward on their bellies as we looked in all the obvious places.

"*Szkopy*," I said, nudging the gunner. He nodded, having just spotted them. His loader lifted the belt of .30 caliber ammo from the metal box and held it up. He had less than fifty rounds. There were a lot more *szkopy* than that. Kaz said it meant castrated ram, and the free Poles had adopted it as slang for the SS.

"I'll get more ammo," I said, and rolled out of the emplacement. I ran back to the tanks, ignoring the explosions that were becoming less frequent. That was not good; it meant the castrated rams were getting closer.

"Krauts!" I yelled to Feliks, who was up in the turret shouting into his radio. I told him where and that we needed .30 caliber ammo.

"We are out, damn it!" he yelled, throwing down the receiver. "The relief column is still held up. How many?"

"Hard to say. Couple hundred at least. They're crawling up the grassy slope, going slow. They don't know we've spotted them," I said. "The machine gun covering that ground is down to their last belt."

"We can't depress our guns to shoot downhill either," Feliks said. "If they break through, it will be a slaughter. But we still have these." He patted the big .50 caliber machine gun mounted on the turret. It was mainly for anti-aircraft protection, and the way it was set up, the gunner would have to stand exposed to enemy fire to use it. Risky, but with the *Luftwaffe* absent from the skies, there was a lot of ammo left.

Feliks signaled to one of the other tanks, and their treads spat dirt as they turned and rumbled off to the ridgeline. Feliks and the other tank commander held onto their guns, feet braced on the tank's hull as they moved forward. I ran ahead to the machine gun pit, where the gunners were nodding their heads. They'd heard the tanks, felt the ground tremble as they approached, and knew help was at hand. I prayed it was enough.

The Germans, crawling on their bellies, must have felt the tanks coming as well.

They rose up, running and screaming, firing as they came, all pretense of stealth abandoned as they made for the thin line of trenches dug in along the ridge. The gunner squeezed off a few rounds, aiming carefully. Men fell, but more came on. Bullets thumped into the logs and sandbags, zinging through the air above out heads and kicking up stones and dirt all around us.

The gunner's head snapped back, a bullet above one eye. His loader pushed the body away and fired, going through most of the ammo in his rage.

Where was Feliks? I could hear the roar of the Sherman's radial engine, but no firing.

I fired my Thompson as the gunner finished off his ammo. He grabbed a rifle and began firing. Up and down the line, men shot at the advancing SS with slow, deliberate volleys, each man counting down to his final bullet.

There were too many of them. Some dropped dead, others

rolled in the grass clutching wounds, but far more pressed on, faces blackened with dirt and gunpowder, snarling screams fueled by doses of Schnapps, fanaticism, and hatred for the subhuman Poles.

They came closer. The man next to me fired his last bullet. I handed him my pistol as a grenade exploded, showering us with dirt. I tossed my last grenade down the hill, screaming for Feliks as the Krauts got close enough to make out the SS runes on their collar tabs.

An engine roared directly above us, the Sherman's treads halting inches from my head. The .50 caliber machine gun spewed fire, Feliks's enraged screams loud enough to be heard between bursts. The rounds shattered the Germans, the second tank joining in with a crossfire that caught the SS in the open, ripping into flesh and bone, turning men into plumes of pink mist.

The machine guns were loaded with tracer rounds, bullets with a pyrotechnic charge that lit up and helped gunners aim at moving aircraft. Hitting men at this range, it set their clothing and flesh afire. The tracers ignited the dry grass, the wind fanning the flames as the SS tried to fall back, bullets striking them, sending up sprays of blood, severing limbs, slamming the dead and wounded into the burning earth.

"*Warszawa! Warszawa!*" The chant rose up from along the line, men standing and shaking their fists as Feliks and the other tanker unleashed their orgy of death. The grass burned. The dead and wounded burned. Shrieks of pain overcame even the chatter of the machine guns, which finally ceased for lack of targets.

I stood as well, listening to the Poles shout their revenge for the massacres in Warsaw. In the midst of all the yelling, I heard a familiar voice, and saw Kaz join us. He chanted *Warszawa* with the rest of them, tears streaming through the dirt and dust on his cheeks.

The last shots and shouts faded away as the Poles stopped,

stunned at their victory. Feliks jumped down from his tank, pistol at the ready. But there was no need. The smoke-filled field held only the dead and dying. Several SS troopers tried to drag themselves through the fire, their uniforms smoldering. Their cries and screams died as they did, bleeding, choking, and burning before us.

"Let them burn," Kaz said, his jaw clenched tight. "Hell is too good for them."

"*Niech płoną*," Feliks said, adding his agreement.

I found nothing in that sentiment to argue with. What strange creatures this war has made of us.

CHAPTER TWO

"I AM SORRY I have no news of Angelika," Feliks said. "But I will ask our intelligence people if there has been any word. After the uprising, radio contact was very difficult."

"Bury your dead and get some sleep," Kaz said. "But find out what you can when the time is right."

"I feel as if I may sleep forever, or never again," Feliks said, lighting a cigarette and looking out over the valley below. Explosions blossomed like a garland of black flowers across a distant field. A plume of sudden red and orange marked a fuel tank taking a direct hit. We watched the carnage, smiling.

Szkopy were dying and that was good. Fewer of them to face on the road to Paris.

The Canadians had broken through two hours ago. They brought ammunition and supplies and were busy evacuating the wounded. They'd even brought three hundred body bags for the dead. Feliks told them to get more.

"If you learn anything, contact Colonel Harding at 12th Army Group," Kaz said. "He will know where to find me." Harding was our boss in the small club that was the SHAEF Office of Special Investigations. Twelfth Army Group was the top American headquarters in France, not counting SHAEF's own advance headquarters, where General Eisenhower hung his hat.

"I will," Feliks promised as we shook hands. "Good luck with your prisoners."

"They're good and scared after that last attack," I said. "Nothing like a ringside seat at your own army's destruction to loosen tongues."

I got into the driver's seat of the jeep and waited while Kaz and Feliks exchanged a few private words. It seemed to me that Feliks had known Angelika pretty well back in Poland when they were working with the Home Army, as they called their underground. Feliks's identity had been blown and he had to go on the run, escaping to Sweden and eventually England. Each man had his own reasons for worrying about Angelika, so I left them to it.

In front of me a truck waited with our first batch of prisoners. One infantry major, a captain in the supply service, one lieutenant from an engineer company, and another from a signals unit. It wasn't hard to pick them out. The Germans used different colors on their shoulder tabs and caps to designate the branch of service. I took the major since he was the highest rank available. The supply captain might have some idea where supplies were being stockpiled, which would tell us where the Krauts might try to rally. Same thing with the engineer if he was involved in building defensive positions. And signals guys ran wire, which had to be hooked up to a higher headquarters. So that's how I ended up with these four representatives of the master race, all sitting glumly under the watchful eyes of their Canadian guards.

"Shall we?" Kaz said, taking his seat and holding his Sten gun at the ready. Not that I thought our prisoners were about to jump their guards and vault off a moving truck. Still, a little intimidation wouldn't hurt. I gave the high sign to the truck driver, and long after I had expected to, we left Hill 262 behind.

Sam Harding was waiting for us at the Canadian divisional headquarters at Saint-Gervais. HQ was set up in a forest overlooking the village. Camouflage netting was strung up, covering vehicles and tents beneath the trees. Colonel Samuel Harding was regular army, a veteran of the First World War, and a stickler for following orders. Even so, he was a decent guy. But he didn't look at all pleased to see us.

"What the hell did you two idiots think you were doing?" Harding demanded as the jeep rolled to a halt.

"Colonel, it was all my fault," Kaz said, exiting the jeep as he kept one eye and the barrel of his weapon trained on the prisoners.

"Lieutenant Kazimierz, it cannot be your fault since you went off with a superior officer. Right, *Captain* Boyle?"

"Yes sir," I said, getting up and standing at what might be thought of as attention. I liked everything about being a captain except for when it made me responsible for whatever trouble Kaz had led us into. He wasn't much for following orders either. Probably came from being a baron.

"You could have gotten Lieutenant Kazimierz killed on your damn joyride! You were to wait here for the prisoners, Boyle."

"Colonel, Kaz was looking for information about his sister. You remember Feliks, the guy with the Home Army contacts?"

"I don't give a good goddamn about Feliks," Harding yelled. He kept on yelling for a while, and I gave myself a mental kick in the pants for not remembering to simply say *yessir* over and over again when a senior officer gets himself in a snit. "I give orders for a reason, you two! Obeying orders is not optional, do you understand?" He jabbed a finger at both of us. I hadn't seen him this worked up in a while.

"Sam, come on, don't bust a gasket," Big Mike said, patting Harding on the shoulder. "It's not their fault the Poles got surrounded, is it?"

"Dammit, Big Mike," Harding said, shaking off the hand on his shoulder. It was a big hand. Staff Sergeant Mike Miecznikowski lived up to his nickname. He was broad in the shoulders, tall, and had a neck like a fireplug. But he was as gentle as a lamb when he wanted to be, and soothing words along with hands the size of ham hocks often served him well.

"Got a good haul of prisoners?" Big Mike asked, changing the subject as quickly as possible.

"We did," I said, telling Harding about the officers and the other prisoners following us. There was a POW cage nearby, and they could cool their heels in there while we interrogated our first four Fritzes.

"Okay," Colonel Harding said, his blood pressure seeming to return to normal. "You need to rest up before questioning these four?"

"We both could use some shuteye, sir, but we ought to get to these prisoners while they're still in shock," I said. It was true, and I also knew Harding well enough to know self-sacrifice appealed to him. "They've been through hell in that valley, and they saw the aftermath of an attack by the SS. Their pals got pretty chewed up. I don't want to give them time to get over it."

"Good," Harding said. "I'll get the Canadians working on the lower ranks while you get started on the officers. Anything to do with the Paris defenses is critical."

"How about this?" Big Mike said. "Billy and Kaz grab some joe and a quick bite while I take the Krauts and treat 'em real nice. Coffee and smokes, let 'em relax. Then I'll bring them to you one by one."

"Good cop, bad cop," I said. Big Mike was a Detroit patrolman before the war, so he knew the routine. He was blue through and through, still carried his shield. "We can make that work."

Kaz and I headed toward the smell of food. The mess was set up in a large granite barn with wide doors at either end open to the breeze. We loaded up our mess kits with coffee, corned beef hash, and biscuits. Hot joe and warm food never tasted so good.

After wolfing down my grub like a starving man, I sat back and surveyed the room. Lots of Canadians, of course, sporting their spiffy tanker's berets. A fair number of French Resistance fighters as well. Tough-looking fighters, their armbands marked FFI. The *Forces Françaises de l'intérieur*. French Forces of the Interior, but everyone called them fifis. Some armbands were also emblazoned with the Cross of Lorraine, the symbol of General Charles de Gaulle's Free France. But that was all the uniform they had. They were dressed in everything from a three-piece suit to a working man's blue coverall, or shorts with loose collarless shirts. And a handful of skirts and dresses as well. Women carried weapons along with the men; they were attired with a bit more flair, but just as deadly.

"Perhaps we could enlist the help of the fifis," Kaz said as he finished his coffee.

"I was thinking of the Poles," I said. My plan, such as it was, involved a threat to turn our prisoners over to the Polish troops, with Kaz playing the role of the heavy.

"That could work, but our prisoners are not SS. They would certainly worry about being delivered into Polish hands, but the Poles are still uniformed soldiers. Not so with the fifis."

"You're right," I said. Any Kraut who'd been part of the Occupation would have reason to worry about being turned over to the Resistance. Especially since they were civilians with no military control to speak of and a good number of Communists in their ranks. "Let's see if they'll play along."

Kaz nodded. He got a refill of coffee and stopped by a group of fifis. Kaz being Kaz, he selected the group with a couple of women, and soon he had them all at our table. The women had German MP40 submachine guns slung over their shoulders, while the men carried German rifles. None of them looked a day over twenty.

"Billy, this is Jules Herbert and Marie-Claire Mireille," Kaz said. "They both speak English. I've explained what we require and they are happy to help, along with Florent and Raymond."

"Maybe you give us one of the *boche*, yes?" Jules said, with enough of a laugh to show he was joking but would appreciate the gesture if we were so inclined.

"Sorry," I said. "But we work for General Eisenhower, and he wants these prisoners accounted for."

"Eisenhower?" Marie-Claire said, clearly impressed. She and the others chatted in French for a moment. "Have you met General de Gaulle?"

"No," I said. "But he is a great man." I wasn't sure about the leader of the Free French, but I figured it was what they wanted to hear. By the argument that broke out among them, I'd figured wrong.

"Yes, yes," Jules said, holding up a hand to stop the squabbling. "We all agree de Gaulle was right to not give up when the Germans occupied France. But some think he waits safely in London while we fight and die. Then he will come in and declare himself the head of the new government."

"And why should he not be in London?" Marie-Claire said. "He is the head of the army. This army, the FFI, and the French forces in uniform. Who else is there?"

I watched the other two men roll their eyes at what seemed to be a familiar argument. They didn't speak English, but I could tell they'd heard it all before. Shaking his head and grinning, one of them gave Jules a gentle shove.

"All right," Jules said, looking a bit embarrassed. "We will not bore you with our politics, Captain."

"Jules is with the FTP," Marie-Claire said. "The *Francs-Tireurs et Partisans*. They are the fighting arm of the French Communist Party. So, he has his opinions about General de Gaulle."

"And Marie-Claire is with the Catholic youth network *la Croix*," Jules said, laying a hand on hers. "She is very brave. And a good shot. But so *bourgeois*." This time it was Marie-Claire who gave him a shove and that got a laugh. It wasn't hard to see that these two young fighters were head over heels in love with each other, no matter their political differences.

"Are you a Communist?" Kaz asked Jules. "I understand not every FTP fighter is."

"Yes, I am, and proud as well," Jules said. "My unit is the Saint-Just Brigade, and we are all dedicated Marxists. We fight and have killed many *boche*. And lost many of our own."

"I applaud your courage," Kaz said. "But allow me to say it is easy to be a proud Communist when you have never had the opportunity to live under their rule. As a Pole, I know this all too well."

"But Stalin is helping to liberate your nation from the Nazis," Jules said.

"Be thankful the Russians are not liberating France, young man. They might overstay their welcome," Kaz said. "Now, enough of politics. Let us plan the farce we will play out for our German guests."

We had a tent, shielded from view by camouflage netting. Just right for giving the prisoners privacy, as well as getting them to worry about a lack of witnesses. Big Mike escorted the lead-off player in, aided by Raymond and Florent. Jules and Marie-Claire stood at the entrance, scowls of hatred directed at the *boche* paraded before them.

We sat the major down. He looked nervous. Big Mike stood outside with the partisans while Kaz went through a few basic questions with our guest. He was Major Wilhelm Fischer. Infantry, as was obvious by his collar tab. He kept up a stern face until Kaz explained that we needed information, and if he didn't give it to us, he'd end up giving it to the FTP.

Fischer protested, probably going on about the Geneva Convention and not being turned over to French civilians, Communists no less.

"Perhaps I should suggest my Polish friends," Kaz said to me. "They wear uniforms and are definitely not Reds."

I agreed. Kaz made his offer, which got Major Fischer all in a tizzy.

"*Nein, nein, bitte!*" He actually wept. Kaz talked to him in a calm voice, but he only got more agitated.

"What's the deal?" I asked.

"He says his men are all dead or captured. He doesn't know anything about Paris or the defenses there. His unit had no orders other than to escape and head in that direction. For the Seine River. Needless to say, he dislikes the idea of being given to the French or the Poles."

"You believe him?"

"I think so. I shall tell him we will give him to the French if we find out he's been lying when we talk to the other prisoners."

Kaz laid it out for the major, and by the look on his face I decided he was telling the truth. His story made sense. The Seine, which ran right through Paris, was the next logical defensive line for the Germans. In the chaotic retreat, there wouldn't have been time for more precise orders.

Big Mike took him away, and we repeated the process for the supply captain and the engineer lieutenant. The captain's supply column had been shot up and bombed. The engineer had been ordered to blow up a bridge over the Dives River but had no explosives. They were stunned and frightened at what had happened during the retreat through the Falaise Pocket. The threat of being turned over to the partisans scared them even more, but their expressions told me they'd have sung like stool pigeons if they had any information worth trading for their lives.

The last POW was our best hope. Unless he was a signals officer who hadn't seen a radio in weeks.

"Good news," Big Mike said, ushering in the nervous lieutenant who kept looking over his shoulder at the partisans outside leering at him with undisguised glee. "Heinz speaks English. *Ja*, Heinz?"

"*Ja*, I do," Heinz said. "Please, what happened to the others?"

"What others?" I asked.

"The other officers. The other three you took away."

"I haven't seen any German officers, Heinz. At least no live ones," I said, almost feeling sorry for the guy. Big Mike shoved him by the shoulders into a chair, where he sat hunched over, as if expecting to be beaten. "Have you seen any, Kaz?"

"Who keeps track of a few German officers here and there?" Kaz said. "So many people go missing in wartime, don't they, Heinz?"

"I do not know," he managed to stammer.

"Sure you do," I said. "Like all the Jews who went missing in Germany and then in France. And the hostages who were taken and shot by your people."

"I am not part of that," he said, sitting up a little straighter. "I transmit signals. I do not give orders."

"But you read them, orders coming in and orders going out," I said. "What do those orders say about the defense of Paris?"

"Paris? I know nothing about Paris. I have been there on leave, twice, but I have nothing to do with defending it." He looked back and forth between Kaz and me, struggling to find a sympathetic face.

"Where were you headed? Where was your unit going?" I asked.

"The Geneva Convention says I am not required to give that information," he said.

"That's right," I said, snapping my fingers. "I guess we need to find someone who hasn't signed the Geneva Convention. Any ideas, Kaz?"

"The *Francs-Tireurs et Partisans*," he said. "I am certain the French Communist Party did not sign."

"No, please," Heinz said, holding up one hand in supplication. "You do not understand. There were no orders. It was a retreat. Not organized. There is a word for it."

"Rout," I offered.

"Yes. A rout. We destroyed our equipment to make more room

in the trucks for the men. Then the *Jabos* came. Machine guns, rockets, and bombs. Those who lived walked. My commanding officer said to get across the Seine and then regroup. The last I saw him, he was in a ditch with his legs blown off. A rout, yes. That is the word."

Jabos. Kraut slang for the fighter-bombers that plagued their every daylight move. His story was the same as the others gave. Confusion, terror, desperation. As true as that was, one of these bastards could be hiding something. So I tried my last trick.

"Sorry, Heinz, but I don't believe you. It's time for you to take a walk in the woods with our French allies," I said.

"What? No," Heinz said, his mouth gaping open in fear. "You don't mean with the terrorists, do you?"

"*Une promenade dans les bois,*" Kaz said. "You must have picked up some French, Lieutenant. I am sure they will treat you with all the fairness you deserve."

"No, wait," Heinz said. His eyes darted back and forth as if he was reviewing every message he ever sent, searching for something of value.

"Your time is up," I said. "I hope you enjoyed your stay in France. It's about to become permanent."

"The terrorists," Heinz whispered, using the term the Krauts employed to describe those who dared to strike back at them. "I can tell you something about them."

"About the partisans?" Kaz said, glancing at Big Mike and the four partisans standing outside the tent. They weren't listening.

"Yes. But will that be enough? I know nothing about the Paris defenses, but I can tell you something of the terrorists—I mean partisans—if you will not turn me over to them."

"Okay, Heinz, it's a deal. Spill." He wrinkled his forehead trying to work that one out. "Tell us everything."

"Yes, I understand. The intelligence chief of my division often worked with the *Milice.* You know who they are?"

"Yeah," I said. We knew them all too well. French fascist militia who did a lot of dirty work for the Germans. They hunted the partisans and were often used to infiltrate their ranks. "What's your division?"

"The 91st Infantry. Colonel Schmid used the *Milice* to gather information on the partisans. But he also had his own contact with a partisan leader," Heinz said.

"A leader?" Kaz said.

"All I know is that this man led a group of terrorists and passed on information to my colonel," Heinz said. "I sent messages to army headquarters in Paris about it."

"What's the man's name?" I said. This was getting interesting.

"*Atlantik*," Heinz said.

"His code name," Kaz said.

"Yes, of course. He would not use his real name, even to his compatriots," Heinz said. "And the intelligence people use only code names. Is that enough?"

"Just about," I said. "What kind of information did he pass on?"

"Names. Names of other leaders in his group. He was with the *Francs-Tireurs et Partisans*. The Bolsheviks. Colonel Schmid once said *Atlantik* hated Russia and the Communists. Very much."

"Yet he served with them?" I asked. "Why did he betray them?"

"The French," Heinz said, giving a small shrug, as if that was the answer to this mystery. Or perhaps he'd never given it much thought at all. He was a radioman after all, just the messenger. It was up to us to make sense of it all and figure out who the hell *Atlantik* was.

CHAPTER THREE

"HEY, SAM, I think we got something," Big Mike said when we found Colonel Harding in his tent, standing over a map of the Paris area spread out on a table. A look passed between them, and I got the impression they knew something I didn't. Which was often the case, but Big Mike's tone told me the news of Heinz's story was even more important than I'd thought.

Harding looked up, irritated at the interruption, his finger still on the map where he'd been following one of the main routes into Paris. Most officers would have been annoyed at a sergeant calling them by their first name, but Big Mike had such a disarming way of doing it that Harding usually let it slide. Especially if no other brass was around. Besides, Big Mike was an excellent scrounger, and when you have a big, muscular non-com who can obtain whatever's needed without a lot of army paperwork, even a colonel will cut him some slack.

"What?" Harding said, giving Big Mike a discreet nod. I guess that meant he didn't need to hold back.

"One of the Kraut POWs told us about a Resistance leader who's rotten. He's been betraying his own men to the Germans. He might help move things along," Big Mike said.

"Help what along?" Kaz asked.

"I'll explain in a minute, Lieutenant, but first tell me who the guy is. Which Resistance group?" Harding said.

"We only know the code name the Germans gave him. *Atlantik*. And that he's with the *Francs-Tireurs et Partisans*," I said.

"Also, he hates the Communists," Kaz said. "But our POW could not explain why he was with the FTP given that hatred, since they are filled with Reds. He simply transmitted messages about him. It was the divisional intelligence officer who knew *Atlantik*."

"The FTP is everywhere," Harding said. "They're the largest armed Resistance group in France. Your German didn't know which FTP band this traitor is with?"

"No sir. But Heinz was a signals officer with the 91st Infantry Division. If we knew the area they operated in, that could narrow it down," I said.

"They've been all over Normandy," Harding said, checking another map. "We ran up against them at Utah Beach, then on the Cherbourg Peninsula. Lately they've been fighting to the west of here. Not much help."

"We could comb the POW cages for officers from the 91st," I said. "We might get lucky and find their intelligence chief alive. He might be persuaded to lead us to *Atlantik*. There's no telling how many deaths he's responsible for."

"Cruel deaths at the hands of the Gestapo," Kaz said. "He should be made to pay."

"Yeah," Harding said, barely listening as he stared at the map. "I need to call HQ. Wait here."

"That was interesting," I said after Harding was gone. We sat on empty crates while Big Mike grabbed the one chair. Fair enough, he'd probably crush the thin slats on the pine boxes. I rose to study the map and the roads leading into Paris, wondering what kind of fight the Nazis were going to put up there. They'd just destroyed Warsaw. Was Paris next?

"Yes," Kaz said, shaking out the crease in his trousers. Even though his uniform was stained with the dirt and blood of Hill 262, he wore it like a tuxedo. "There is much you and the colonel are not telling us, Big Mike. We are talking of bringing a traitor to justice. Something tells me you and he have another plan entirely."

"Sorry. I can't dish until Sam says it's okay. Need to know, ya know?" Big Mike said, enjoying his secret.

"And we don't need to know," I said, completing the refrain. "So, let's figure it out."

"I do like puzzles," Kaz said, sitting up even straighter. "Where do we start?"

"At the beginning," I said. "We're sent off to bring POWs back here for interrogation. Big Mike and the colonel stay behind. Why didn't this big lug come with us?"

"The colonel said it didn't take three of us," Kaz answered. "He was right. It shouldn't have. I did tell him I wanted to go because of Feliks and my fellow Poles, which he understood."

"Right. Then we jumped the gun, nearly got ourselves killed, but made it back with a haul of POWs. Then Harding blew his top," I said, trying to break things down and understand what happened every step of the way. It was a trick my dad taught me back when I was a rookie. He always did his best to show me the ropes. I didn't always pay attention, because I thought there would always be time to learn. Now I knew better.

But breaking things down stuck with me. Dad had said it was important to notice the little things and figure out why they'd happened, not just accept them at face value.

"The colonel was very upset," Kaz said. "He has lectured us sternly in the past, but today was different."

"Why?" I asked. Kaz was right. We'd taken tongue-lashings before, but this was different. Anger and impatience were normal, but Harding had been emotional, which was rare.

"He was concerned we would have gotten ourselves killed for nothing," he said.

"Or, he was upset because he would have blamed himself," I said.

"This is war, Billy," Kaz said. "People get killed. But you are right, there was something in how he reacted. And his response about *Atlantik* was odd."

"But not to him," I said. That was another thing Dad taught me. Unless you're dealing with a fool, which Harding wasn't, it was a mistake to write off unusual behavior as an unexplainable quirk. Find the motivation, and it won't seem so odd anymore.

"Yes, I see," Kaz said. "So *Atlantik* will prove useful in whatever plan the colonel is working on. The plan he is calling headquarters about right now."

"Deception," I said. "He's going to use this traitor in a deception campaign. How're we doing, Big Mike?" He made a zipper motion across his mouth, but by his barely stifled grin I knew I was on the right track.

"It must have something to do with Paris," Kaz said, standing to get a better look at the map and tracing his fingers on the roads leading to the city and the River Seine. "Ah, Paris. Beautiful in springtime. Not so much in August."

"Paris," I said, leaning over the map. There were grease-pencil marks on the roads leading to Paris, and other routes to the south. Lines marking the advance of Allied formations. But where were the German defensive lines? No wonder Harding was so desperate for information. He didn't have a clue where the Krauts were going to put up a fight.

"Everyone wants to get to Paris," Kaz said. "The Nazis, de Gaulle, all the Resistance factions, and every Allied soldier in Normandy."

Of course they did. So did I. Who doesn't want to go to Paris? Then I understood.

I knew who didn't want to go to Paris. General Eisenhower and the entire Allied army.

And I understood why Harding was so upset about our gali-vanting off to Hill 262.

"It's a ruse," I said.

"What is?" Kaz said.

"This whole quest for POWs who might know anything about the Paris defenses. Remember, one part of a good deception cam-paign is painting a believable picture. POWs, Canadians, the Poles, the FFI, us, we're all part of this effort to create the illusion we're frantic for dope on the Paris defenses."

"We are not?" Kaz asked.

"I'd say no. We've got the Krauts on the run. Whatever part of their army in Normandy we didn't destroy or bag in Falaise is hightailing it for Paris. The Seine is a natural defensive posi-tion."

"Paris is home to millions of people and some of the great art treasures of the world," Kaz said, thinking it through. "Yes, it would be a tremendous advantage for the Germans to fight there."

"So why not go around it? Our armor can chew up the retreat-ing Germans and leave the rest sitting in Paris. It'd be like one big fancy POW camp. We might even get over the Rhine before winter. Still zipped up, Big Mike?"

"Tight," was all he had to say.

"I am glad we were unhurt as a result of our unauthorized trip to Hill 262," Kaz said. "Colonel Harding never would have for-given himself for sending us on a mere deception errand if we had been killed."

"So thoughtful of you," I said. "Okay, Big Mike, let us in on the secret. How does *Atlantik* fit into this?"

He made the zipper move again.

"*Atlantik* is a traitor," Kaz said, tapping his finger on the map, marking the blank places where German entrenchments should have been. "Therefore, he can be useful. If he believes the story created for him."

"The story of the Allied plan to take Paris," I said, bending over the map for a closer look at the intersecting lines of rivers, roads, and ridges. "If the Krauts believe we're going after Paris, they'll fortify it. Bring in all the troops who escaped the trap at Falaise. Then we swing around and cut them off."

"If that is the plan, I see the military reason for it," Kaz said. "But what about the people of Paris? There are millions, with hardly enough food as it is. If this scheme brings more German troops into the city, they could starve."

"This is war, gentleman," Harding said, as he strode back into the tent. "We're here to defeat the enemy as quickly as possible. That's what Operation Frigate is all about."

"Sounds nautical, Colonel," Kaz said.

"This is strictly a land-based operation," Harding said. "But Frigates are fast ships, very maneuverable, so it's an apt name. Pack up your gear. I'll fill you in on the way back to Third Army HQ."

Harding looked excited, or at least what passed for excited when it came to his usually stony countenance. I almost said something about risking our lives for a deception campaign, but I didn't want to spoil his good mood. Besides, I had the feeling there were plenty more risks to come.

I knew a thing or two about ships. I'd walked a beat close to the South Boston Naval Annex, part of the big Boston Navy Yard. I'd seen the frigates they built there. Solid little ships, just right for dropping depth charges on submerged submarines. But lightly armed, and no match for the faster destroyers and cruisers lurking over the horizon.

And what was over the horizon to the east was a badly beaten, but still deadly, army.

CHAPTER FOUR

"PATTON'S MOVED UP to Saint-Hilaire," Harding said from the front seat, as Big Mike gunned the jeep and sent us careening down a rutted path. "There's a château outside of town where Third Army is setting up headquarters."

"Things are moving pretty fast," Big Mike said, glancing at me and Kaz as he rounded a bend, a meek glimmer of apology flitting across his face.

"Jeez, Big Mike, keep your eyes on the road, willya?" I said, gripping the side of the jeep. "Just because the Krauts didn't kill us, there's no reason for you to have a go at it."

"Sorry, fellas, but we don't have much time," Big Mike said, as he took a turn onto a wider country lane. "We've got a lot to set up."

"Colonel," Kaz said, tapping Harding on the shoulder. "I believe this road leads to La Fresnaye. Which is on the south side of the Falaise Pocket."

"It's the quickest route," Harding said. "Reports are this area has been cleared of Germans."

"Reports?" I said. I wasn't much for betting my life on an army report.

"Air reconnaissance and the French Resistance," he said. "Both report the tail end of the Kraut retreat passed through here a few hours ago. All that's left are dead, wounded, and maybe a few shell-shocked stragglers."

"Flyboys and fifis, huh?" I said, as I checked my Thompson for a full clip. "Let's hope none of those stragglers try to jump us for the jeep." If I was a straggler anxious to make it back to the Fatherland, a jeep would be just the ticket. I tried to stay alert and scan the thick undergrowth for signs of movement, but I was too damned tired and started to nod off.

Then the smell hit me. We'd been on a downward slope and Big Mike braked as we rounded a turn which emptied us into the open and flat valley floor. The road ran straight through fields and meadows flanked by ditches and overgrown embankments.

Bodies were everywhere. Tangled limbs and sprawled torsos displayed in every conceivable form of twisted agony. Burned bodies. Dismembered bodies. Bodies so untouched the men appeared to be sleeping. Beneath them lay bloated bodies, the unfortunates who were first to die on this killing ground, decomposing below the blanket of the most recent victims of our bombs and bullets.

Big Mike slowed the jeep to guide it around the rotting remains in the road, then gave up. There were too many on every yard of roadway, so he simply drove over them, avoiding the worst of the entwined dead, leaving them to their final embraces. Shot-up trucks and upended tanks smoldered with acrid fumes, oil and burnt flesh mingling into the perfume of mechanized violence.

"My God," Kaz whispered, holding a handkerchief over his mouth. "No wonder they were so desperate to get out."

"I had no idea," I said, the stink of the dead rising into my nostrils. We'd seen the artillery fire and fighter-bombers working over the roads from up on Hill 262, but it was all distant and removed, like watching a movie. Here, I could see the vehicles shredded by machine-gun fire, the bodies blown apart, the scorched and smoking wreckage of everything from tanks to staff cars and bicycles.

It was worse than I had ever imagined any hell to be.

"Hang on," Big Mike said, as he avoided a shell hole in the middle of the road. The jeep swayed as it jolted through the drainage ditch clogged with corpses.

I retched at the stench and the sound of cracking bones.

Big Mike drove grimly on, his hands white-knuckled at the wheel. No one spoke.

It was like that for miles. Finally, we took a turn on a narrow lane going south. It wasn't the direction the retreating Germans wanted to go, so it was nearly clear. We passed vehicles along the roadside, probably abandoned after they'd run out of fuel. A few dead Krauts lay outside one truck, pockets turned out, their weapons and boots gone.

"Watch for the *Maquis*," Kaz said. "That looks like their work. Or nearby villagers, if any are left alive. We don't want them mistaking us for the *boche*." *Maquis* was one of the all-purpose terms for Resistance fighters. Originally, they were young men who escaped into the forests and hills to avoid conscription into the forced labor service, which was basically slave labor. They were named after the scrub brush on the high ground and called *maquisards* after they began to arm themselves and fight the occupying Germans. Now, GIs called any French civilian with a weapon a *maquisard*. The actual number and variety of Resistance groups, spanning all ideologies and beliefs, was too bewildering to keep track of, so an all-purpose name came in handy.

"Slow down," Colonel Harding said, casually raising his carbine in the direction of the trees ahead.

"I see 'em, Sam," Big Mike said. A half dozen *maquisards* came out of the trees, pushing two German soldiers ahead of them. The Fritzes looked stunned, dirt and dust staining their faces, fear bleeding out of their eyes. The Frenchmen waved and laughed. They carried canvas bags, weighed down by whatever loot they'd taken from the dead.

"Stop," Harding said. He told Kaz to ask them if any other Germans were in the area.

"Not alive," Kaz said, after a back and forth with a guy toting a pistol and wearing a black beret and an even blacker mustache. "He says Saint-Hilaire is twelve kilometers down this road."

"Ask him what group he's with," Harding said. "Are they FTP?"

The man laughed when Kaz asked, the leader spitting on the ground before he answered in a torrent, thumping his chest at the end.

"They are not Communists," Kaz said. "He is rather adamant on that point. They called themselves the *Maquis* Henri, and that is Henri. They are from Saint-Hilaire."

"Tell Henri we will take the prisoners," Harding said. Kaz delivered the message, and Henri laughed again. He was having a good time today. I didn't believe for a minute they were real *maquisards*, not if they were still living in their village. They didn't have the look of men living rough in the woods. These were Johnny-come-latelies, eager to cash in on easy pickings and glory now that the Germans were gone.

Henri spoke again, waving his pistol in the air.

Then he shot each German in the back. They crumpled, and he delivered two more shots to finish them off.

"Henri says you may have them now," Kaz said, carefully adjusting the Sten gun he held in his lap, moving his finger closer to the trigger. "I think we should depart."

Big Mike didn't wait for the order. He drove off slowly, Kaz and I watching from the rear seat for any sudden moves. Henri and his men glared at us, probably wishing they could pull the boots off our feet as well.

"More like the local mafia than *Maquis*," Big Mike said once we were clear. "Maybe we should invite them to the show. They'll probably sell out to the highest bidder in no time."

"They're bums," Harding said. "Two-bit thugs who wouldn't know how to find a buyer outside their little village. But, we might as well get Henri there along with everyone else. You never know."

"Colonel, how about you fill us in?" I said. "What show, and who's invited?"

"There's a briefing scheduled for tomorrow at Patton's headquarters," Harding said, turning to face us. "We've sent out invites to all the Resistance leaders in the sector."

"Along with an offer of arms and supplies if they attend," Big Mike put in.

"Right. That'll guarantee the right people get there. Having it at Patton's HQ is part of the draw as well," Harding continued. "Everyone wants to catch a glimpse of Georgie Patton with his silver-plated revolver and cavalry boots, even the French."

"This briefing is part of the deception campaign, Colonel?" Kaz asked.

"Yes, the centerpiece. As you suspected, we've been advertising our desire for intelligence about German positions around Paris all up and down the line. There are enough pro-Vichy French still around that some might be tempted to tip off the Krauts."

"There's plenty who retreated with them," Big Mike said. "There's a chance their pals or relatives could get word to them about what we're after. Most of the telephone exchanges are working, so it wouldn't be hard to communicate."

The snarl of aircraft engines rose from over the horizon, quickly growing louder and more insistent. Big Mike pulled off the road, into the trees and under cover. We all instinctively ducked as four Thunderbolts roared overhead. From up there, we wouldn't look much different from all the other vehicles they'd bombed and strafed the past few days.

"So, we get the Resistance people together and brief them on their role in the upcoming attack," Harding said, scanning the sky through the branches. "Acting as scouts, protecting our flanks, guarding crossroads, that sort of thing."

"We make a big deal out of them helping to liberate Paris," Big Mike said. "But what you two came up with is the icing on the cake."

"Right," Harding said, tapping Big Mike on the shoulder to tell him to drive on. "We're going to put together a map and a set of phony plans and give our unknown traitor a chance to steal them."

"So," Kaz said, in a tone that barely disguised his disapproval, "you are going to trick our allies into thinking the liberation of Paris is imminent, allow a traitor to escape to the Nazis, and leave the people of Paris in the hands of the Nazis."

"Exactly," Harding said, apparently deciding not to take the bait. "We'll get everything set. You two get cleaned up and get some sleep. You deserve it."

Sleep?

After what I'd seen in the valley of Falaise I was afraid to close my eyes.

CHAPTER FIVE

WE PASSED A couple of shot-up trucks and a burned-out German staff car, with no gruesome corpses, a nice change of pace. Big Mike made a turn and we motored up a driveway over crushed white stone, plane trees planted like sentinels on either side. The entrance was so long it took a while for the château to come into sight. Three stories high, a short city block long, with a gray slate roof and too many chimneys to count. Apple trees dotted the gently rolling hills on one side as cows grazed in green fields on the other.

"Patton knows how to pick 'em," Big Mike said as we parked the jeep under camouflage netting strung up over the apple trees. He was right. Not a shell hole or broken window to be seen, with a view of lush hills and a gently flowing river. It was marred somewhat by the collection of army vehicles, tents, and stacks of supplies strewn about, but it was still idyllic compared to much of Normandy on this fine summer's day.

"I bet the Krauts who had to leave this place were sorry," I said, grabbing my pack as we climbed out of the jeep.

"They didn't get far," Harding said, leading the way to a row of tents set up in the orchard. "Those vehicles you saw out on the road? That was the German convoy. Ambushed by the Saint-Just Brigade, one of the larger FTP bands."

"Yes, we spoke to a young man, Jules Herbert, who is part of that unit," Kaz said. "A Communist, but he seems dedicated."

"They're good fighters," Harding said. "That's why I'm surprised one of them is a traitor. They hate the Germans almost as much as they despise the French fascists."

"There are many reasons for betrayal, Colonel," Kaz said. "But right now, I am more interested in cleanliness and cuisine. I assume General Patton has a decent officer's mess?"

"Chow's pretty good here," Big Mike said. Which for him meant there was a lot of it. As for me, our jaunt through the valley of death had put me off my feed.

"I think the general might invite a baron to dine with him," Harding said, cracking a bit of a smile. "Even if he is only a lieutenant." Or, it could have been a grimace. With him, it was hard to tell.

We found a sergeant who directed us to our tents. He pointed out the showers and suggested we get cleaned up, pronto. General Patton was a stickler for proper uniforms in the Third Army command area. Which meant ties, leggings, and helmets worn at all times. This guy was a fine example of Patton's GI fashion sense. His boots gleamed and his tie, or field scarf as the army insisted on calling it, was tucked neatly between the second and third buttons of his ironed shirt.

"Watch out for the MPs," the non-com said. "They'll fine you if they spot you looking like that." He waved a hand at us, as if we were hobos stinking up a ladies' parlor. "Fifty bucks for officers, twenty-five for enlisted men."

"You gotta be kidding," Big Mike said. "These guys just came off the line."

"I don't make the rules," he said, walking away. "But the MPs enforce 'em. I'm surprised they didn't stop you at a roadblock."

Probably we'd taken an unusual route, but I didn't feel like explaining myself. I didn't feel like much of anything, to tell the truth.

"Well, everyone here does seem well turned out, I must say.

I've never seen so many Americans with perfectly knotted ties," Kaz said.

"General Patton has his own way of doing things and he gets results," Harding said, stopping in front of a tent. "This one's mine. You three are next door. Your duffels were sent ahead, so get cleaned up immediately. Big Mike, dig out your field scarf and try to look sharp."

"Jeez, Colonel, them things are hardly big enough to go around my neck," Big Mike said. Nothing Uncle Sam made was ever big enough for the poor guy.

Harding told me and Kaz to meet him in an hour, and he'd review the rest of the plan for tomorrow over chow. We trooped into our tent and found three cots, each topped with our gear. The shelter had pine boards for a floor and room to stand up—luxurious by army standards.

"I gotta help Sam," Big Mike said, after he rummaged through his stuff and came up with a tie. "You guys need anything?"

"A valet," Kaz said. "But I shall endeavor to bathe and dress myself." Kaz had a way of acting as if nothing ever bothered him. Acting being exactly what he did, and he was a lot better at it than I was.

"We'll find the showers and get cleaned up," I said as I sat on my cot, a weariness hanging heavy on my bones.

"Damn tie," Big Mike muttered, as he mangled a knot and struggled to button up his shirt at the collar. Whatever his neck size, the army's wool shirts didn't come close. I stood up to lend him a hand and nearly fell over.

"Billy!" Big Mike said as he caught me. "You okay?"

"Sure, sure, just dizzy. Got up too fast. Probably need some water," I said, steadying myself with one hand on Big Mike's arm. I worked on his tie until it looked almost normal, then patted his arm and sat back down again. "There, now you look like a million bucks."

"Just so long as they don't nick me for twenty-five," Big Mike said as he made his way out of the tent, clapping his helmet on his head. "Thanks, Billy."

"Are you all right?" Kaz asked, taking a seat on his own cot.

"No," I said. "I mean, yeah, I'm fine. Just tired out, you know?" I unscrewed the cap on my canteen and gulped down the water that was left. It tasted like dust and death.

"Yes, I know," Kaz said, his head cradled in his hands. "I am tired as well. I think I shall be tired for a very long time. But now, I must wash off what I brought with me from that hill. Are you ready?"

"Not yet," I said. "You go ahead. I'll be right behind you."

Kaz stripped to the waist, grabbed his dopp kit, threw a towel over his shoulder, and told me I'd feel better after a shower. I said yeah and made believe right along with him.

Then I was alone.

I started to shake. First my hand, then my whole body was overcome with a trembling, a frantic quivering I couldn't control. I clasped my arms around my chest and fell to the floor, my knees on the rough pine planks. I was crying, weeping tears that spattered on the floor, tiny drops of unexpected anguish.

I don't know how long that went on. I made it back onto the cot and tried to get the shakes under control, afraid someone would walk in on me. What Harding would say, I couldn't even imagine. I held my head in my hands, the last of the welling tears soaking my palms.

Now, I'm not the crying type, so this frightened me. I'd seen a lot in this war, and nothing had got to me before, at least not like this. I'd had bad dreams, yeah. I may have hit the hooch hard a couple of times, sure. But what the hell was this?

What's wrong with me?

I sat still, waiting for my body to calm down. I couldn't take a chance on the shakes betraying me in front of Kaz and Big Mike.

They depended on me, especially when the lead started flying, so I didn't want them to think I wasn't up to it.

And I was. Wasn't I?

Why not? I'd been up to it since North Africa, Italy, and a half-dozen places in between. Since 1942, more than two years ago.

Maybe that was the problem.

I decided the best thing to do was not to think about it and go stand under some hot water. I tossed my filthy shirt on the floor, took my stuff, and went off in search of the showers.

Easier said than done. There were so many tents, guy-wires, and nets strung up that the place looked like a well-armed but disorganized circus had pitched camp around the château. I wandered along a line of twenty-man tents, some marked with the red cross, others doing business as supply rooms, radio rooms, and a mess tent.

Everything but showers.

Every other officer and GI was looking prim and proper in their neckties, not a speck of dirt or an unpolished button to be seen. Except for me, with a towel around my shoulders. I turned a corner, scanning the next row of tents and a line of vehicles parked under camouflage. No sign of Kaz. Everyone looked so damn clean there had to be *beaucoup* showers somewhere around here.

"Hey mac," I said to a corporal who'd just stepped down from a half-track. "You know where the showers are? I don't want Patton to see me and blow a gasket, know what I mean?"

"Sir!" The corporal said, coming to attention and giving a snappy salute. Given that I wasn't wearing a shirt with captain's bars, and my helmet didn't announce my rank for Kraut snipers to see, I wondered what was up.

I returned the salute and saw pity in the corporal's eyes.

Footsteps rustled on the ground behind me.

"Who the hell are you, soldier?"

I turned to face General George S. Patton himself. I automatically came to attention and nearly knocked myself over with the salute I brought up to the brim of my helmet.

"Captain William Boyle, sir."

Patton returned my salute, his mouth wound down with a sneer that reconnoitered the area around his chin. He looked me up and down while an aide stood a couple of steps behind him, clutching a map.

"You're a mess, Captain," Patton said, wrinkling his nose as he leaned close. He sure wasn't. He wore a helmet liner buffed to a glossy sheen, his burnished silver general's stars impossibly bright. Cavalry boots, riding breeches, and buttons polished into sparkling gold added to the dazzle. One hand rested on the butt of his famous ivory-handled Smith and Wesson .357 pistol, and he looked ready to use it. On me, maybe.

"Just came in off the line, General. I'm looking for the showers to get cleaned up," I said, hoping he'd grunt and wander off.

"Which of my units?" Patton demanded. "Where are your orders?" His voice rose and broke in a squeak that nearly made me laugh. Which would have been a mistake. I might have been losing my marbles, but I'm not an idiot.

"I'm with SHAEF, General," I said. "I'm here with Colonel Harding." Patton glanced at his aide, who quickly stepped closer.

"The Resistance briefing tomorrow morning, sir," the aide said. "This is the Captain Boyle I told you about."

"Oh. Ike's nephew, isn't it?" Patton's look softened, the sneer meandering into a smile. "You know, Ike and I go way back. We served together at Camp Meade. Commanded the Tank Corps, one after the other. You here to spy for your uncle, Captain Boyle?"

"No, sir. I mean, yes sir, General Eisenhower and I are related. Distant cousins, but I've always called him Uncle Ike. And I'm not here to spy on anyone."

"Tell Ike anything you want, Boyle, and give him my regards.

And it's good to see an officer from SHAEF who gets his fatigues dirty," Patton said. "Where did you see action?"

"Hill 262, General."

"With the Poles? Brave men. They did a hell of a job up there. Well, go get yourself presentable, Boyle. If I see you out of uniform again, you'll get a fine, Ike's nephew or not."

He brushed past me, moving off at a rapid pace, his aide scurrying behind. I still didn't know where the showers were, and I wasn't happy with Patton buttering me up because General Eisenhower and I were related.

I finally found them tucked behind a long stone barn bordering the apple orchard. I stood under the hot water, wondering if Patton went easy on me because of Uncle Ike. Probably. Everyone thought I had a direct line to him and could put in a good or bad word whenever I wanted. But it didn't work like that. And I wouldn't burden Uncle Ike—which I only called him in private—with personal requests or gossip on how Patton ran his headquarters. He had enough on his mind running the war, and if truth be told, one of his biggest problems, other than the Germans, was George Patton's big mouth.

I scrubbed, washing off the dirt and grit of Hill 262, the stink of death still lingering in my nostrils. It was hard to believe that a little more than two years ago I was a newcomer to all this, arriving in London a shavetail second looey, fresh from Officer's Candidate School and shocked at the events that had so quickly delivered me overseas.

Dad and my uncle, both Boston detectives, had served in the last war, along with their older brother Frank. He'd died in the trenches, and they never got over it. Especially since in our Irish Republican family, that war was fought pretty much to preserve the British Empire, and America had little reason to send so many boys off to die for that cause.

They didn't see this new war any differently, at least not when it came to fighting in Europe to save English bacon once again after Pearl Harbor. So, they hatched a plot to get a distant relative of my mother's, one Dwight David Eisenhower, to agree to take me on as a staff officer in Washington, DC. All of which sounded fine to me, until Uncle Ike was given command of US Army forces in Europe, and took me with him, happy to have a relative in tow who could serve as a military investigator.

The family may have oversold him on my detective credentials a bit. True, I'd been promoted to detective, making the switch from uniform to plainclothes at an early age. But a copy of the detective's exam had mysteriously made its way into my locker, so I did have some help. It's the way things work, and I make no apology for it. But it did make it tough when Uncle Ike assigned me to my first few cases. I'd had to rely on instinct and memories of what Dad had tried to teach me about solving murders. He'd been a good teacher, and I had the luck of the Irish, which is how I ended up here, I guess.

Which all makes sense, since I've never been able to figure out if the luck of the Irish stands for good fortune or if it's a sad commentary on our centuries of oppression. Either way, here I was, watching dirty water swirl at my feet, feeling like I'd never be clean again.

I shaved, scraping away stubble and soap, revealing a slack-jawed joe with bags hanging heavy under reddened eyes. I stared at him for a while, wondering who this new guy was. Once, my mom told me I looked like my father when he was a young man. I could see she was right. This is what he must have looked like in the trenches of the First World War.

CHAPTER SIX

"LET'S TAKE A walk," Harding said, after we'd washed out our mess kits. Patton might have been dining off fine china in the château, but we'd eaten in a crowded mess tent with dozens of guys, all chowing down macaroni slathered in some sort of meat sauce. It wasn't bad, and it wasn't good. Kaz sort of pushed it around his plate until Big Mike added it to his pile and wolfed it down.

Harding ate like he was on maneuvers, attacking his food from the flanks and mopping up the remnants. I managed to eat some, surprised at what appetite I had. Kaz looked exhausted, even cleaned up and sporting his tailored uniform.

"You okay?" I asked as we followed Harding and Big Mike outside.

"Well enough, but a trifle tired," Kaz said. "Nothing that a bath and soft bed at the Dorchester wouldn't cure."

Kaz's home was the Dorchester Hotel in London. A suite of rooms which he graciously shared with me. It was an extravagance, but one he could afford. Kaz's family was loaded, and his father had been one smart cookie. He saw what was coming in Europe and transferred the family wealth to Swiss banks before the war started. Unfortunately, the family itself was one step behind their dough, and they got caught in the squeeze between the Nazis and the Russians as the former enemies dismembered Poland. Now they were all dead, except for Angelika, victims of the Nazis and their savage extermination of the Polish intelligentsia.

Kaz kept the suite at the Dorchester because his family had come to visit when he was at Oxford, a couple of years before the war. They spent a Christmas together in those very rooms. Now he was a permanent resident of the hotel, where the staff treated him like royalty, and memories were draped like mourning shrouds in every room. He'd moved in as soon as he received his commission in the Polish army-in-exile. Originally, he worked as translator in General Eisenhower's headquarters, a short walk from the Dorchester in Grosvenor Square. He'd been given the job despite a weak heart, since it was no more strenuous than the work he'd done at Oxford as a student of languages. Many languages, which came in handy at headquarters.

But then I happened along and Kaz ended up as my partner. He'd toughened himself up, taking long, fast walks in Hyde Park and working out with dumbbells before dawn. Now he was wiry and muscled, with enough strength to see him through the worst this war threw at us, or so I hoped.

"Look, this deal with the phony plans is going to be a cake walk," I said. "We'll put on a show and do a lot of nothing, then head to London. Harding has got to give us a break after everything we've been through."

"It would be nice," Kaz said, the words riding a heavy sigh.

"Over here," Harding said, standing on a stone terrace at the rear of the château. He lit up a Lucky, clicking his Zippo shut as he glanced around. A few GIs wandered by, and a clutch of officers sat around a table drinking Scotch. We were safely out of earshot.

"We'll be in that room," Harding said, indicating a set of French doors that opened out onto the terrace.

"The salon, they call it," Big Mike added. "At last count, we had ten different Resistance groups coming. Plenty of people since they like to travel in hordes."

"Each group is getting a supply of weapons and ammunition," Harding said.

"Kind of like party favors for gangs," I said. "*Maquisards*, a few local homicidal maniacs, and a traitor thrown in the mix. I hope they don't start shooting at one another. Or us."

"Not every Resistance group is like the *Maquis* Henri," Harding said. "You know that. But it's impossible to separate out the bad from the good, so we need everyone we can get. Most of them agreed to come without the promise of supplies."

"Plus, they get to meet General Patton," Big Mike said. "He's agreed to say a few words. The man can draw a crowd, that's for damn sure."

"Okay, Colonel, what's the plan?" I said.

"We bring everyone into the salon at 0900 hours. General Patton will greet them and lay it on thick about how important this operation is, and the part they'll play in freeing Paris from the Germans. We'll have a detailed map of the area between here and Paris up on the board, showing where each group is to position itself at important crossroads and in blocking positions along our flank. It's marked TOP SECRET in red ink," Harding said. "What the map will also have are the routes our forces will take into Paris. It shows the French 2nd Armored Division under General Leclerc leading the way, supported by infantry units on either flank."

"The deception," Kaz said. "Leclerc's French forces are a nice touch."

"Yes. It's been in the works for a while, but you've given us a chance to deliver this misinformation right into the hands of the German command. I'm betting our traitor won't be able to resist," Harding said.

"The Germans will doubtless want confirmation," Kaz said. "I doubt they'd act merely on a verbal report by one man. Or woman, perhaps."

"We're going to provide the perfect opportunity. See that hill?" Harding pointed to a long hillside of lush green, topped by a small clump of trees, maybe a quarter mile distant. "An artillery barrage is going to strike that ground, just moments after Big Mike takes down the map and folds it up."

"I leave it on the table," Big Mike said. "Then we have more explosions, a lot closer."

"Engineers have charges set in that field," Harding said, nodding to the side of the château. "It'll look like the Germans are finding their range. We herd everyone into the basement shelter. They keep setting them off for a while, long enough to empty out the salon and give our man time to break away from the group."

"The lights go off, there's yelling and confusion, and an air raid siren begins to wail. It'll be the perfect time to swipe the map and run," Big Mike said.

"How do we know who took it?" I asked.

"If you stole a top-secret plan from a Kraut HQ, would you hang around?" Big Mike asked.

"No, I see what you mean. I'd take off," I said, thinking this charade might have a chance of working.

"We'll have men stationed out front and along the road, in touch by radio," Harding said. "You and Kaz will have a radio-equipped jeep, so all you need to do is tail him. But don't get close enough to catch him."

"Understood," Kaz said, nodding. "How long do we keep this up?"

"We'll play that by ear. I want to be sure he knows you're in pursuit. The Krauts can't think this was too easy, otherwise they'll smell a trap. Every MP within fifty miles is clued in, and they have orders to take their time checking identity papers but let the target through. They're connected to our radio net, so it should be fairly easy to track our quarry," Harding said. "Ideally, I'd like to have visual confirmation of him crossing over into the German lines."

"From what we have seen, the front is very fluid," Kaz said. "It may be some distance before an organized line of defense is reached." There was an uncomfortable silence. Kaz was being diplomatic. What he meant was we could easily stumble into a Kraut ambush.

"We need to know if this works," Harding said. "Keep him in sight, no matter where it takes you."

"I'll be a few miles behind you," Big Mike said. "In another radio jeep with a lieutenant from Third Army Intelligence who speaks French. He's the one giving the briefing tomorrow, after Patton's welcome. He's organized a half-track full of GIs from the reconnaissance platoon to tag along with us for added firepower."

"It should all work out," Harding said. "Any questions?"

Questions like *what are our chances of survival out in front of the American lines in a jeep headed for Kraut territory?* ran through my mind. But I kept my mouth shut. Harding was gung-ho on this plan, and I could see we had to keep up the phony pursuit right to the end.

Poor choice of words. Right up to the conclusion.

"Any chance of a week's leave after we wave goodbye to this turncoat?" was all I asked.

"See me when you get back," Harding said as he ground out his cigarette. "Now get a good night's sleep." He and Big Mike went into the château to check on last-minute details, leaving Kaz and me with the setting sun.

"He could have just agreed to the leave," Kaz said.

"Maybe he'll surprise us," I said.

"Or maybe we won't come back," Kaz said, the last rays of sunlight drenching his pale, drawn face. "Goodnight, Billy."

I watched Kaz walk away, shoulders slumped, and head bowed.

It wasn't his usual style, and I could see a weariness of body and soul weighing him down, the normally jaunty stride now more of an old man's shuffle.

I didn't feel all that chipper myself, but I wasn't ready to stretch out on my cot quite yet, bone-tired as I was. I might actually sleep, and then dream, and all the visions in my mind right now led down nightmare alley. So, I walked. Down the long drive and back again, meandering around the château and through the tent city sprawled around it and into the orchard.

I heard a familiar voice call my name, her French accent lilting and joyful.

"Billy, come join us!" It was Marie-Claire Mireille, along with Jules Herbert and another guy, all gathered around a flickering candle and a bottle of brandy in a tent with the sides rolled up.

"I will," I said, glad of the distraction. "I didn't expect to see you both again. You here for the big meeting?"

"Yes," Marie-Claire said. "My compatriots from *la Croix* will arrive in the morning, but I traveled with Jules and Bernard." Marie-Claire introduced me to Bernard Dujardin, leader of the Saint-Just Brigade. We shook hands, and I tried not to think of him as a potential traitor.

"*Bonjour*," Bernard said, passing me the bottle as I sat down. "Drink, eh?"

"*Santé!*" I said, slugging down the liquor. "You speak English?"

"A little," Bernard said, with a slight nod. "I learn from American comrades."

"Bernard fought in Spain," Jules said, "with the International Brigades. He knew many Americans from the Abraham Lincoln Battalion."

Jules spoke with awed pride about his leader's role in that terrible civil war. In the 1930s volunteers from all over the world had gone to Spain to help the government fight against General Franco's fascists. Germany and Italy helped Franco, and the Soviet

Union supplied the Republican government. It was an out-of-town run for the real war, and it got rave reviews in Berlin.

"I followed the news of the Lincoln boys," I said, feeling the booze warm my gut and relax me. My hand felt it too. Nary a shake. "They had an Irish Republican unit."

"*Oui,*" Bernard said. "Good men. They died well." He took a long pull from the bottle and gave it to Marie-Claire, who took a dainty sip. Bernard looked to be thirty or so, with the kind of worn face that comes with strife and worry. Gaunt, dark, and lined. Ten years ago, he probably looked a lot like Jules, fired up with an idealist's belief in his cause. Now, he looked haggard and worn.

"But you stood up to the fascists," Jules said. "If more had done so, you would have won."

"Well, they did not, and we lost," Bernard said. "But now, we can finish off the bastards, yes? We will have our victory."

"Peace," Marie-Claire said, as if uttering a prayer.

"Lucien!" Bernard called out, waving at another *maquisard*, and ignoring Marie-Claire's whispered plea. Jules squeezed her hand as the newcomer joined us. He wore a beret and a neckerchief knotted beneath a white shirt. A worn leather jacket, a pistol at his hip, and a cigarette dangling from one corner of his mouth completed the picture. He was a good-looking guy with a strong jaw who would have been at home on the cover of *Life* magazine as a dashing Resistance fighter.

"Lucien Faucon," he said. "*Le Commandant, Action de la jeunesse française.*"

"French Youth Action," Bernard said. "Lucien is a good Communist. He fought in Spain as well."

"Those days are gone, my friend," Lucien said. He spoke perfect English, with a clipped accent that told me he'd learned it from a British teacher at a good school. "This is the war we fight today. So, no more talk of Spain."

"*Oui*, I know it pains you to speak of it, forgive me. How was Brittany?"

Lucien explained he had been sent by the FTP leadership to organize forces in the province of Brittany and to assist Patton's drive to clear out the Germans and secure ports there. "Your General Patton is a reactionary, but he fights the *boche* well, so I hope to shake his hand," Lucien said.

"I am surprised so many Communists are eager to meet General Patton," Marie-Claire said. "I hear FTP units from all over are sending representatives."

"Oh, they come for weapons, too," Bernard said, taking another slug of brandy. "As well as to see the great Patton. What must he think of so many Red *maquisards*, eh? If he had gone to Spain, he would have fought for Franco, I am sure!"

"There you go, Bernard. Do you ever let an hour pass without bringing up Spain?"

"Yes. When I sleep, but then I dream of it." They reverted to French and began to argue the way old friends do when they revisit ancient grudges. Harsh words mingling with laughter amidst the scent of brandy and cigarette smoke.

I said goodnight, feeling like a third wheel. Marie-Claire left with me and took my arm as I walked her to a tent set aside for female *résistants*.

"Jules adores those men," she said. "His own father disapproves of him, and still supports Vichy, even after all that has happened. Jules looks to Bernard, especially, as a leader and a man who acts on his beliefs. Lucien, we have just come to know. The Communist Party sends him where he is most needed. Bernard and the Saint-Just Brigade are closer to where *la Croix* operates, him I know well. The Germans have done the impossible in our part of France."

"What's that?" I asked.

"Brought the godless Marxists and the devout Catholics

together, of course. We have cooperated to attack the Nazis and shared our intelligence. Before the war, we detested each other."

"What do you think of them? The *Francs-Tireurs et Partisans*."

"Oh, for the most part, as individuals, they are good men, those in the FTP. They are willing to fight. But if they come to rule France, I will be very afraid. The Communists did horrible things in Spain, as they do in the Soviet Union. They massacred nuns and priests and killed many on their own side who did not adopt the party line. Trotskyites and anarchists, for instance. To me, their differences were unimportant, but if anyone did not worship Stalin, it was the end of them."

"What does Jules think of that?" I asked.

"He admits there were excesses, but he cannot blame the Party. It means too much to him," she said. "But, I have faith. General de Gaulle will unite us, and then we can live our lives in freedom. Once the *boche* are gone, of course."

"And then you and Jules . . . ?" I asked, leaving the question open.

"Yes, then we will have to return to what we were. It will be hard to be ordinary once again. We do not even know each other's real names. Too dangerous. Isn't that strange? We have embraced *clandestinité* so long I wonder if we can give it up. Will we even remember the people we were? Ah, here I am. Goodnight, Captain."

She vanished behind the tent flap, leaving me alone in the moonlight. A walk with a pretty girl should have cheered me up, but all I was left with was the faint memory of who I'd been before this life of war and secrets.

CHAPTER SEVEN

"EVERYTHING ALL SET?" Colonel Harding asked Big Mike, as urns of steaming coffee were carried into the salon.

"Ready, Sam. The engineers have their explosives in place. I've got a dozen men ready to rush the room in a panic when the shelling starts. Our radio teams are in place, and there's a fully loaded jeep parked out front for Kaz and Billy."

"Okay, let's get the show started," Harding said. "Where's McKuras?"

"Here, sir," an officer said, entering through the terrace doors.

"Lieutenant Sean McKuras," Harding said, introducing us as Big Mike opened the main doors. "Our translator for the briefing."

"I'm hardly needed," McKuras said. "The colonel can *parlez français* just fine, but I'm happy to pitch in."

"Battlefield French from the last war," Harding said, going modest on us. "Lieutenant McKuras has a degree in French literature and studied at the Sorbonne. He'll be able to handle any questions much better than I could."

"Glad to help, and I'm looking forward to heading out with Big Mike," McKuras said, eagerness lighting up his face. He looked like his college days weren't too far behind him. Sandy-haired, blue-eyed, with soft, milky-pale skin, he was just the type you'd expect to find at a headquarters desk hunched over piles of paperwork. Overeager at the chance to prove himself.

"Have you been at the front at all, Lieutenant?" Kaz asked, probably wondering as I was if he'd be a liability for Big Mike. Not that trailing us and chatting with locals sounded all that dangerous.

"Not really," McKuras said. "Prisoner interrogation and liaison work with the Resistance. I've been shelled once," he added, as if it qualified him for a medal.

"Hey, I know you're an officer and Big Mike is a sergeant, but you need to listen to him when you're out there on your own," I said. "You'll be in no-man's-land, so don't start giving orders that will get you both killed, okay?"

"Don't worry, Captain. I admit, this is an exciting break from routine, but I want to come back in one piece, along with Big Mike. I want to see Paris again, after all."

"Very well," Kaz said. "*Qu'avez-vous étudié à la Sorbonne?*"

McKuras and Kaz yakked in French for a while as the crowd filtered in, most of them making a beeline for the coffee and the ample supply of sugar, which had been impossible to come by during the Occupation.

Jules Herbert came in with Bernard Dujardin and a couple of other rough types. Marie-Claire Mireille entered separately with another woman, older and well-dressed, along with a priest in his black robes.

I recognized Henri and his men, the local *Maquis* group we'd seen on our drive in. Thieves and killers, but likely not Reds, so I didn't worry about them other than pocketing the silver.

McKuras waved to a fellow flanked by a couple of musclemen who eyed the crowd with suspicion. They followed him as he made his way to us, not even glancing at the coffee. Bodyguards. This guy thought he was someone special.

Lieutenant McKuras introduced us to Marcel Jarnac, a member of the *Front national* executive committee, the organizing and political arm of the FTP. No wonder he traveled with protection. Jarnac looked about forty, tall and swarthy, with a long nose that could've given Charles de Gaulle's schnoz a run for the money. He wore a neatly trimmed mustache and a three-piece suit that made him look more like a judge than a Communist functionary.

"*Monsieur* Jarnac has been working closely with us, organizing arms and supplies for Resistance groups in the Third Army sector," McKuras said.

"Not just for the FTP," Jarnac said. "For all those who fight."

I was wrong. He didn't look like a judge. More of a politician, maybe.

"You must have been in great danger during the Occupation," I said, trying to get a sense of the man. Everyone I looked at here was a potential traitor.

"As we all were," Jarnac said. "Except for those who took refuge in London." He winked and laughed, showing he was just kidding. Such was the stature of General de Gaulle that even the slightest joke at his expense had to be delivered very carefully. "I began with the *Brigade Saint-Just*, fighting and building up a supply of arms. Now, I go to meetings. Bah."

One of the bodyguards delivered a cup of coffee to Jarnac, who gave a slight nod, indicating they could relax and take their turn at the sugar bowl.

"It seems you may still be in danger," Kaz said, watching as the two hulks waited at the coffee urn.

"Simply a precaution," Jarnac said. "Old habits are hard to break. Look, even Louvet comes with his guard of honor!"

McKuras knew Raymond Louvet as well, leader of the Gaullist Resistance group, *Corps Franc Nord*. Louvet had his own beefy men behind him, eyeing the crowded room with suspicion. No one had entered with rifles or machine guns, but there were enough revolvers and automatics in holsters, waistbands, and pockets to kick off our own gunfight at the O. K. Corral.

Louvet spoke no English, so McKuras handled the translation while everyone else sipped their hot joe. Turns out Louvet was a former policeman who'd hunted French Communists trying to cross the border to fight in Spain during the thirties, which was a violation of the non-intervention treaty France had signed.

"Now we are friends," Jarnac said, clapping Louvet on the shoulder. "All patriots. I would even forgive Louvet if he'd ever caught me." Louvet had a comeback suggesting Jarnac might have thought twice about that if he ever had caught him. Polite laughter followed. I wondered how friendly they'd be after the war, with the Krauts gone and a lot of automatic weapons lying around.

I glanced at my watch and excused myself from the group. I had about ten minutes before the festivities began, and I wanted to get a line on any other FTP people in the room. It wouldn't do to seem too curious in front of Jarnac, who seemed to be a careful and calculating kind of guy.

I said *bonjour* to Marie-Claire, who was with the older woman.

"Emilie, this is Captain Boyle," she said.

"Emilie?" I asked, expecting a full name.

"Just Emilie, until the Germans are gone or in their graves," she said. She was a little taller than I was, with long graceful fingers that lingered in my hand after I shook hers. Gray flecked her dark hair, and her slightly worn clothes looked like they had been elegant before the war.

"Father Matteu is fetching coffee for us," Marie-Claire said. "It has been some time since he had real coffee, having recently crossed over from the German lines."

"Where does *la Croix* operate?" I asked.

"We have agents from Saint-Malo to Paris," Emilie said. "Father Matteu oversees arms and setting up the parachute zones for delivery. Or did, I should say. Now our members are eager to join the new French army."

"Emilie ran a spy network and kept in touch with London via our radio operators," Marie-Claire said. "Until they were all captured after the invasion."

"Yes, it was very sad. We had two radio sets, and the operators had both survived for months. An eternity in this sad business. But when they were taken three weeks ago, we simply waited for the Americans to come," Emilie said. "It seemed to take forever, but then suddenly the Germans were all fleeing. One might almost feel sorry for them. I heard the slaughter was *très terrible*."

"It was," I said. "And I don't feel sorry for any of them. Except for a couple of stragglers I saw Henri execute yesterday."

"The *Maquis* Henri is little more than a gang of chicken thieves," Emilie said. "No one heard of them until the Germans retreated. They fired a few shots and looted what they could, and now proclaim themselves *résistants*. *Pathétique*."

"They are less than twelve men. We have over one hundred fighters," Marie-Claire said. "Not as many as the FTP groups, but enough to be counted. And *la Croix* has been active for over two years."

"You should be proud," I said. Marie-Claire's eyes shone with enthusiasm. She looked to Emilie with the same respect Jules had for Bernard.

"Marie-Claire has been invaluable," Emilie said. "She has been an excellent liaison with the Saint-Just Brigade. They are the largest FTP group in this area, and it has not always been easy to work with the Bolsheviks. Of course, love eases the way, does it not?" She smiled gently as she patted Marie-Claire's arm.

"I've met Jarnac, as well as Dujardin and Faucon last night," I said, steering the conversation to my proper duties here. "Any other FTP honchos around?"

"Honchos?" Emilie asked.

"Leaders, commanders. I don't know all the groups active in the area."

"Well, there is Olga Rassinier, of the FTP *Main-d'œuvre immigrée*," she said, nodding in the direction of a stout woman wearing a skirt and German boots, a pistol stuffed in her jacket pocket.

"It is a group made up of immigrants who fled the Nazis to take refuge in France. Olga is Russian and a charming woman, despite her looks and politics," Emilie said, with a mischievous smile. "Marcel Jarnac, who you have met, is a political leader of the FTP, and he travels all over France. He's lucky to have survived so long. And Faucon, who only recently returned from Brittany, is somewhere about."

"You're very well informed," I said.

"It is how I have remained alive," Emilie said. "One must pay attention to who goes where and how often, in order to understand when something is wrong. When the pattern is broken, the Gestapo is often close at hand."

Colonel Harding and Lieutenant McKuras walked to the front of the room, where Big Mike stood in front of a large map board draped in cloth. People began to quiet down and turn in their direction, abandoning their coffee cups and gossip. Everyone was eager to bathe in the glorious presence of General George Patton.

Kaz edged up to me as Harding called for everyone's attention. His battlefield French was actually pretty good. I understood a few of the words and was able to get the basic gist. They were great patriots, we were all comrades in arms destined to play a role in the liberation of Paris. That got a round of applause.

"See anybody suspicious?" I whispered to Kaz as the clapping died down.

"I saw no one wearing a Nazi armband," he said, his voice low. I gave him an elbow in the ribs as I caught sight of Lucien Faucon making his way into the room. He headed straight for the coffee, and I wondered if he and Bernard were fighting brandy hangovers.

Then he stopped short, staring at the front of the room. The French doors to the terrace opened and in walked General Patton, his khaki shirt pressed to attention, stars sparkling, riding boots buffed, slapping his riding crop against his leg. He scanned the room, and I was sure everyone, as I did, felt like he looked them straight in the eye. He conveyed an immediate sense of movement and barely restrained power. I felt his presence in a way I hadn't in our chance meeting last night. This was Patton at full force, ready to charm and intimidate in equal portions.

He ignored Harding and took center stage, right in front of the covered map. He surveyed the room again, a slight nod signaling approval of what he saw, gave his riding crop one final whack against his leg, and launched into rapid-fire French. It was too fast for me to understand, but I could tell he had the accent down pat. He sounded kind of snooty, like a waiter in a fancy restaurant who thinks you'd be happier in a diner across town.

He carried on for a while, winding up with his riding crop held high, shouting *vive la France, vive la liberté* to great applause. Then he lowered his arm, raising the riding crop to the assembled *résistants*, and spoke in almost a whisper.

"*Vive le Paris.*"

The room exploded in shouts and cries as the crowd surged forward, ready to embrace the general, hard-line Stalinists elbowing Catholics and Gaullists to get closer to Patton. Eyes glistened with tears, Patton's call to arms unleashing torrents of joy and passion.

Patton snapped to attention, halting the flow of the crowd. He raised his hand to his brow, saluting the gathered fighters, did an about-face, and strode ramrod straight out the terrace doors. It was a helluva performance. I knew it was all part of the deception, but the lump in my throat wasn't in on the secret.

Harding stepped in, telling the gathering that Lieutenant McKuras would start the briefing. As Big Mike pulled the sheet off the map board, I caught a glimpse of Harding checking his watch. I hoped we were on time.

"*Mon Dieu,*" Emilie whispered, her hand raised to her mouth.

"*C'est Paris,*" Bernard said, having moved closer as the throng moved forward.

Yes, it was Paris. The map showed all the roads heading east to the Seine River and the capital city. Paris. The name sent a shiver through me, and I wished it were true. Paris was more than a city to these people. It was the symbolic center of occupied Europe, and every Frenchman and woman in the room thought they were helping to set it free. All but one, that is.

Marie-Claire held both hands over her mouth, tears cascading down her cheeks. Her emotions were genuine and true. I felt ashamed to be deceiving her.

McKuras went over the assignments for each Resistance group, tapping crossroads and positions along the flank of the attack leading to Paris. There was a lot of cheering as each group learned of their role, and no one noticed Big Mike backing up a bit to give himself a better view of the hills visible through the terrace doors.

McKuras tapped his pointer on two red arrows leading to the heart of Paris. One went through the city of Saint-Cyr, the other south through Chartres and then Rambouillet, on the very outskirts of Paris. "*La deuxième Division Blindée,*" McKuras said. "General Leclerc."

At the mention of Leclerc's 2nd Armored Division, a Free French unit, the crowd erupted in another roar of approval. The French were liberating their own capital. It was too good to be true.

If only they knew.

"*Merci!*" Marie-Claire said, kissing me on both cheeks, then going for Kaz. Jules embraced her as Bernard and Emilie hugged each other in a frenzy of celebration. Jarnac grabbed Harding's hand and pumped it for all it was worth. Olga gave Lucien Faucon a bear hug, moving on quickly to others in her group. Lucien seemed stunned by the news, not as delirious and overjoyed as the others. Was he our man? Or was the moment simply too much for him? If the traitor was in this room, he'd probably be happier than anyone else with such prize information so tantalizingly close.

Harding glanced at his watch.

Shells screeched across the sky, exploding in the fields just visible through the glass doors. Another salvo arrived, peppering the hillside with fiery explosions, cratering the grassy pastures and shattering trees.

"Move away from the glass!" Big Mike bellowed as people edged slowly forward, curious and apprehensive at the same time. McKuras repeated it in French as the charges next to the château went off, melding perfectly with the distant artillery fire and creating the illusion that the Germans were zeroing in on us.

Half a dozen officers ran into the room from the terrace, holding their helmets down as they made their way inside, screaming about Kraut artillery fire. They played their role well, moving wide-eyed through the crowd and telling everyone to make for the air-raid shelter.

"*Dans la cave!*" McKuras shouted, telling everyone to take to the cellar. Big Mike led the way, waving his arm for everyone to follow. Another round of shells hitting the hillside got everyone going, just as the lights flickered. Kaz and I followed behind, ushering the crowd down a narrow marble staircase.

Everything went dark.

A few people screamed, until a sharp voice, maybe Jarnac, told everyone to calm down. A flashlight beam played on the wall ahead, and Harding urged people to follow him into the cellar. I could see Big Mike opening a thick wooden door, the shining light reflecting off rows of bottles in what was obviously the château's cavernous wine cellar. A ripple of laughter spread through the group as someone commented on the ready supply of champagne.

"Leave the door open for any others," Harding yelled to us. Also, to allow our man to get out, which could have already happened. The staircase had been wreathed in semi-darkness, and the large cellar itself was lit by nothing but the single flashlight. As we entered, I felt bodies brush by in either direction as excited chatter echoed throughout the stone chamber, confusion swirling the musty air.

A flow of GIs entered the cellar, mixing in with the French and pushing the crowd even farther in. I heard Kaz call for me as we were separated by the press of bodies. Then the flashlight went out and the cellar went black.

A single gasp rose from the mass of people jammed together. Then the frantic press of flesh as the crowd moved as one toward the faint light at the door.

"Kaz!" I shouted over the confused babble of curses and shrieks, as everyone tried to squeeze through the narrow doorway. Officers shouted orders to stay calm, which only eliminated any chance for actual calmness.

"Here," Kaz said, grasping my arm as we were pulled along by the flow of flesh, which was making its way to the door in unspoken agreement that aboveground explosions were preferable to the inky darkness below. Marie-Claire clung to his other arm, and I hoped this deception was worth the fear I saw on her face.

"It sounds like the shelling stopped," I said to her. "We'll be out in minute."

She nodded bravely, and we shuffled along in spurts and stops, bodies crammed as we neared the doorway. Shouts echoed from the stairs and the slow slog slammed to a halt.

"It sounds as if someone is hurt," Kaz said, standing on his toes to see ahead. I heard a GI coaxing someone to get up and figured there'd been a fall on the stairs.

Then came the scream. The kind of scream that didn't mean it was too dark, or too crowded, or someone had twisted their ankle. This scream meant blood and death, and it was filled with up-close terror.

"Lights!" I yelled over my shoulder, hoping Big Mike and Harding would sense that something was seriously wrong. Two flashlights snapped on, light playing on the walls before me. I pushed through the tightly packed throng, Kaz at my heels, still holding on to Marie-Claire. We made it up a few steps and saw folks standing in a circle at the landing, staring at the floor. Here, there was enough light to make out their faces, pale with unexpected horror.

"Who is it?" I said, pushing past Marcel Jarnac and Emilie.

Jules Herbert knelt by the body of an American officer, the lower back of his Ike jacket stained in darkening blood. Jules gently turned the body over, revealing the strangely peaceful face of Lieutenant Sean McKuras, who would never again see the spires of Notre Dame.

CHAPTER EIGHT

"SECURE THE AREA," Harding said, pushing through the crowd. "Get everyone back into the salon. No one leaves. Not the French, not our men."

Big Mike began to usher people upstairs. Harding intercepted a major and ordered him to organize the officers and GIs separately for questioning. Then he came back down the stairs, taking in the group still gathered around the body. Jules with his arm around Marie-Claire, and between Kaz and me, Jarnac, who stood with Emilie, whose face had gone white.

"He is dead, Colonel," Kaz said, feeling for a pulse on McKuras's neck as he knelt by the body.

"*Monsieur* Jarnac," Harding said, "would you please escort Emilie upstairs?"

"*Merci, mon Colonel,*" Emilie said, making the sign of the cross. "It is so upsetting to see the blood of the innocent spilled, even after years of war."

"Of course," Harding said, as Emilie put her arm through Jarnac's and gave one last glance at the corpse. Jules and Marie-Claire started to follow, but I took Jules by the arm and told him to stay. He let Marie-Claire go with reluctance as we returned to the body on the landing.

"Were you the first to see the body?" I asked Jules, keeping a grip on him and checking his hands for any sign of blood.

"I do not know," he said. "I was close to the front as people began to leave the cellar. It looked like someone stumbled ahead of me, and I saw *le lieutenant* on the ground. I thought he'd fallen and was hurt. Then came a scream, and I saw he was dead. I did not do this to him!" He yanked his hand away as he became aware of just what I was looking for.

"Is this how he lay?" Kaz asked, sweeping his hand along the body.

"I did turn him over, but yes, it was like this," Jules said.

"So, he was on his stomach, with his head facing the cellar door," I said. "He was stabbed from behind and most likely fell forward."

"He wasn't leaving the cellar then," Harding said. "He was coming down the stairs."

"With the killer at his back," Kaz said, standing and dusting off his knees.

"Sam, you better get up here," Big Mike yelled from the hallway above. Big Mike often used the colonel's first name, but seldom within earshot of so many people. Which meant something was very wrong.

"I'll stay with the body," I said, nodding to Kaz. He understood and left with Harding. Jules followed, looking worried and confused.

I knew the feeling.

I rolled McKuras over to see exactly how he'd fallen, cradling his head to avoid a final indignity on the hard marble. A small patch of blood stained the floor. He'd died quickly, likely from internal bleeding.

The slice through the fabric was thin and narrow. A dagger-cut right to the kidney. A quick kill with a twist of the blade, severing the major arteries and veins which ran through the organ.

Lieutenant McKuras was murdered by someone who knew what he was doing and had the right weapon for the job. Which included most of the people who'd been at this morning's gathering. The assassin was cool and collected as well. Two swipes of blood on the lieutenant's sleeve marked where the killer had cleaned his blade.

McKuras was the first casualty of this deception, and I hoped the commotion upstairs was all about the stolen map. But I feared otherwise. McKuras was killed because he saw something, and it wasn't the map being taken. That could've been explained away easily. If it had been me, I would have feigned outrage, saying I was simply safeguarding a top-secret document so rashly left in plain sight.

Two GIs with a stretcher finally showed up, and I told them to take McKuras to the morgue. They looked at me as if I was speaking in tongues.

"The field hospital then. Have your sawbones do an autopsy," I said, hoping that was clear enough. "Right away."

I went up to the salon. Harding already had MPs stationed at the doors, with people separated into four groups. Big Mike was quizzing the GIs who'd been present, while Kaz talked with a small group of French *résistants*. Harding had a handful of officers to one side. The largest group looked to be all FTP, and not a one of them looked happy.

Then I saw why. Against the far wall, near the coffee table, the body of Bernard Dujardin lay sprawled on its back. Harding caught my eye and snapped his fingers in the direction of the corpse.

I got to work. An MP stood close by, keeping an eye on the muttering pack of Communist fighters. This was one of their own, and the discovery of his body had soured the festive unity that bound these people together scant minutes ago.

"That's how he was found, Billy," Big Mike said, buttonholing a nervous corporal. "Be right with you."

I stood a few feet away from the late Bernard Dujardin. He lay on the floor next to the table with a scattering of cups and spoons at his side. The tablecloth had been pulled partway down in the struggle. This was different than McKuras. I knelt to inspect the body. Dujardin's wound was under his heart, a frontal assault with a dagger-like blade. The killer had looked Dujardin in the eye, possibly backing him up against the wall before driving the knife through his ribs and up into his heart. One of the coffee urns was overturned, dark brown stains spreading along the white tablecloth. Dujardin had gone down hard, falling against the table with only a few seconds to thrash about before his killer had him dead on the ground.

Efficient. Experienced. Lethal. Which fit a lot of people in this room, all of whom were still alive thanks to those very skills.

I stood, forcing myself to remember what this was supposed to be all about, and looked at the front of the room. The map was gone, nothing but one brass thumbtack and a torn shred of paper left hanging on the corkboard. This wasn't going at all how Harding had planned.

Deception plans were grand in theory, but a double murder right in front of me demanded attention. So, I got back to work and searched Dujardin's pockets. Nothing except for a pistol and a knife at his belt, hidden by the worn leather coat. The knife was a dagger, much like the one that killed him.

"Is that the murder weapon?" Harding asked from behind me.

"It's Dujardin's, but it was in a sheath. I doubt the killer took it and then put it back. But a dagger like this was used on both men," I said, handing it to Harding.

"Standard issue in arms drops to the Resistance," he said, hefting the blade. "The Special Operations Executive probably delivered thousands of these in the past two years."

"Meaning there's a fair number of them in this room," I said.

"Right. And we don't have much time to waste. You saw the

map is missing," he said, his voice a whisper. "We have to start acting like that means something."

"The murder of Lieutenant McKuras and Bernard Dujardin means something. That should be our priority. We don't even know if the map is connected to these killings."

"Of course it is, Boyle," Harding said, his voice a harsh whisper. "What else is worth killing for, especially with all these witnesses so close. Now focus. Where's the map?"

"It's not on Dujardin," I said. "My first thought was that someone saw him go for it and knifed him. But that doesn't explain why McKuras was killed."

"It does if Dujardin was killed because he saw who took it," Harding said. "Could McKuras have seen the confrontation and come to warn us?"

"Maybe," I said. "He couldn't have yelled for help with those explosions going off. He'd have to hotfoot down to the cellar."

"With the killer on his heels," Harding said. "But what the hell was he doing, hanging back like that?"

"Maybe he heard Dujardin cry out," I said. "Or maybe he was too curious for his own good. He was treating this like a school holiday. What matters most right now is who's not here. I doubt the killer hung around after stealing top secret plans and leaving two bloody corpses behind."

"Let's check with the FTP people. We had to separate them from the others once they saw Dujardin's body. Evidently their first thought was that it was a plot by de Gaulle's henchmen," Harding said.

"Colonel Harding," Marcel Jarnac said as we came closer. "I am sorry to say that one of our group is missing. Lucien Fassier is gone." One of the other FTP guys let loose a torrent of French, pointing at the other Resistance group, his face contorted in anger.

"Fassier?" I said. "I thought his name was Faucon."

"That is his *nom de guerre*, which means falcon. Fassier is his family name," Emilie said. "I learned this only a month ago but saw no reason to reveal it before." She was interrupted by an angry tirade from one of Jarnac's men.

"Lucien would never kill a comrade. Perhaps one of them killed him and hid the body," Jarnac translated, lifting an eyebrow in sympathy with the sentiment as the FTP man glared at the other groups.

"Two deaths and stolen battle plans are quite enough work for one man," Harding said. "I doubt there would have been time to kill a third and hide the corpse. And I mean no disrespect to you, but from what I know of the Communists fighting in Spain, there were many executions over points of Marxist doctrine. Were there any such arguments involving Fassier and Dujardin?"

Jarnac translated the question for the rest of the group and had to calm them with sharp words before they went silent.

"Yes, we can see there would not have been time, Colonel. And while we do not agree with you that such executions took place often, there were instances in Spain where enemies of the people were discovered, and justice had to be served. But, in the case of Lucien Fassier, we know of no such sectarian issues. Bernard and he were close friends, in fact. Lucien has been a busy man, sent to many places to better organize the struggle against the *boche*. I did not know him, but others speak highly of his character. In my work with the *Front national* executive committee, I heard him praised many times. However, I have no answer as to why he might have done this."

"I can't believe it," Jules spoke up. "But, he is gone. That much is true."

"I can speak for us all, Colonel," Jarnac said. "We will help you hunt him down. It is a point of honor."

"The most important thing is to carry out the plan for the liberation of Paris," Harding said. "We will find Fassier and stop him, but right now you all have your assignments. It is vital you carry them out and not become distracted by this tragedy."

"We can radio an alarm to MPs giving his description," Big Mike said, as if he just thought of it. "What was he driving?"

"A green Amilcar M2," Jules said. "An old model, with FFI painted on the doors. I will see if it is gone."

"An old automobile with FFI splashed on the door?" Jarnac said as Jules dashed outside. "There could be hundreds." He swept his hand through the air, taking in the breadth of the search. He wasn't exaggerating.

"We'll do what we can," Harding said. "Your people can help, but they need to stick to their positions."

"Then we must go immediately," Jarnac said, nodding his agreement.

"We need to finish questioning everyone," I said. "We haven't even started with the FTP."

"The priority is to get search teams out right now, and for the Resistance people to take their positions," Harding said, sticking to the script. "Boyle, you and Lieutenant Kazimierz take a jeep and begin scouting the roads leading to the German lines. I'll send someone out with Big Mike as well."

"It is gone," Jules reported, nearly out of breath. "Lucien's automobile. I still cannot believe it."

"We have seen many betrayals in this war," Jarnac said, as his eyes narrowed, his mouth set in a grim line of memory. "We will have revenge for this one, my boy."

"But someone here may have seen something," I said, as everyone began to move toward the door. "Something important."

"The theft of this *map* is important, Captain Boyle," Harding said. "These deaths are terrible, but we need to stay focused. Now let's find someone to head out with Big Mike."

"They were murdered, Colonel," I said, sensing that Harding was moving too fast. "And we don't know if the killer is done."

"There will be justice, my friend, do not worry," Jarnac said. "Now, Colonel, allow me to volunteer Jules if it is a translator you seek. Your sergeant looks quite capable, but Jules knows this area well."

"Good," Harding said. "Boyle, find out what Lieutenant Kazimierz and Big Mike have learned. Then be ready to leave in five minutes."

"Five minutes? We've got two corpses not even cold," I said, thinking like a cop and not wanting to leave the crime scene behind.

"Then make the most of the time you have," Harding said, turning to leave with an angry cloud across his face.

"I will," I said, drawing Dujardin's dagger from my belt. "Who has a knife like this?"

Jarnac repeated the question in French, reaching into his boot as he did and drawing out a similar blade. About ten others were held up in quick succession. SOE daggers, French stilettoes, and even a Nazi officer's blade.

"Enough of this foolishness," Emilie said, approaching the group. "Paris awaits. If any of us find the traitor Fassier, slit his throat. But we must go. *À Paris!*"

"*Oui!*" Jarnac shouted. "Spoken like a good Communist, if you don't mind my saying it."

"I shall take it as a compliment this one time," Emilie said pleasantly, her regal bearing giving away nothing of what she really thought of Jarnac. What would happen once the common enemy was gone, and these groups were at one another's throats again? Or had it already started?

Raymond Louvet joined the group, speaking with Jarnac, who nodded in agreement as he sheathed his knife.

"Louvet says he will put a dozen men into the hunt for Lucien Fassier," Emilie explained to me. "His *Corps Franc Nord* has many ex-police who tracked down Communists during the Spanish Civil War. He says it will be like the old days. As a joke, yes?"

"Jarnac isn't laughing," I said.

"He sometimes plays the loud fool, but he is very intelligent. He knows it is the best way to find Fassier," she said. "We shall handle this, one way or the other, Captain Boyle."

"Okay, just tell me this," I said, giving up on talking sense into Harding or any of these people. "Does Fassier have family nearby? Any place he might hide out before making for the German lines?"

"I only knew him as Lucien Faucon, his *nom de guerre*," Olga said, speaking for the first time and in surprisingly good English. "Only his closest friends would know his real identity and his family. And those friends are all dead."

"He told me his family name several weeks ago," Emilie said. "We were planning an action near his village and he said he hoped to see his mother soon. He made me promise to tell no one, a promise I now see no reason to keep." I made a mental note to check the name of the village, not that I thought he'd be stopping off for a home-cooked meal.

"Faucon escaped the Nazis last year when his group was ambushed. The only survivor," Jarnac said. "Or so the story goes. Then he was assigned to work with the Marxist youth movement, and more recently sent to fight in Brittany. I had never met him, but heard he was operating in our area. Whatever his name, he is more Lucien Faucon than whoever he was before the war."

"He fought in Spain. Wouldn't anyone know him from there?" I asked.

"Alas, so many who did are dead," Jarnac said. "Bernard knew him from those days, but I am afraid no one else can say that. As for the man he became, who knows?"

"You think he may have saved himself by turning traitor?" I asked.

Jarnac raised his hands, palm up. It was an unanswerable question.

"I knew him from the youth movement," Jules said. "I don't

think he betrayed any of our group. Some were killed or captured, but it was never a *grande catastrophe*."

"*Ne chie pas où tu manges*," Jarnac said. He moved away, his arm around Jules's shoulder, head bent close to his.

It made sense. You don't shit where you eat. Fassier wouldn't endanger himself by giving up a group directly under him. That would be far too obvious. But he'd be able to pass on dope about plenty of other groups, not to mention weapons drops, radios, and whatever information London was asking for. Invaluable stuff, much more important than nabbing a bunch of kids, no matter how well armed.

"Did you have many successes against the Germans?" I asked.

"Some, yes," Jules said, his face clouding at the memories of past combats. "But there were times when the *boche* were not there. Once an arms depot was empty. Did Lucien warn them, do you think?"

"We'll ask him when we find him, kid," I said. "Right, Colonel?"

"Get a move on, Boyle," Harding said. He couldn't even look me in the eye.

CHAPTER NINE

I WAS IN no mood to talk with anyone. We were about to let a murderer get away, all for the sake of a deception plan and that damned map. I stood by our jeep in front of the château, watching as trucks and automobiles, all with white-washed FFI and FTP markings, drove away. Each was filled with *résistants* who would soon be bragging to their comrades, wives, mistresses, and café owners about their role in the liberation of Paris. Harding didn't need a stolen secret map when he had talkative Resistance fighters and a working telephone exchange. Hell, if I knew anyone in Paris I could call them with a bit of patience and a helpful operator.

Dust from the departing column settled around me as I continued the check of our jeep, busying myself so I wouldn't fly off the handle if Harding came by. Our gas tank was topped off, and we had a spare jerry can of fuel. A SCR-694 radio was installed in the rear seat, which ought to give us a range of fifteen miles on a good day. Rations and water took up the rest of the back, along with a few cartons of Chesterfields, always useful for loosening tongues. Extra ammo and a bag of grenades. Everything we needed for a meaningless yet potentially violent jaunt through the French countryside.

I spotted Big Mike coming my way and pretended to check the radio frequencies.

"Billy, I got something," he said.

"Spare me," I said. "I don't need a pep talk. Let's just get this charade over with."

"Hey, don't take it out on me," Big Mike said. He stopped short, and moved to check his own jeep, outfitted the same as mine. "Who knew this guy would go nuts and slice up two people? It don't make sense. How could Fassier, or Faucon, or whatever he calls himself, survive this long as a double agent if he's that hot-headed?"

"Yeah, okay," I said. "It couldn't have been predicted, but that doesn't make it right, letting him go like this."

"That's what I'm trying to tell you, Billy. I might have a line on him," Big Mike said, his voice nearly a whisper.

"Okay, spill," I said, leaning against his jeep, on the lookout for Harding.

"Jules was talking with Jarnac when I told him we'd be leaving in a coupla minutes. It looked like Jarnac was puttin' the screws to the kid, but I couldn't make out a thing. So, I grabbed Kaz and told him to saunter by for an earful of French," Big Mike said, his eyes lighting up with the cloak and dagger stuff. It was nice to see someone was enjoying himself. "Turns out, Jarnac was pressing Jules on anything he might remember about Fassier. You know, just like a cop asking for the smallest detail that maybe didn't seem like a big deal at the time."

"Standard interrogation stuff," I said. As a Detroit bluecoat, Big Mike would know that better than most. "He come up with anything?"

"Yeah. Beaulieu. It's a village due east of here. Jules recalled that Fassier went there twice back when he first became part of his young Commie unit. Never said why, never went with anyone. But the first time he came back with a ham, then a wheel of cheese."

"The kind of thing you'd bring back from visiting family in the country," I said.

"That's what we're thinking," Big Mike said. "Of course, it could be he met his Kraut contact, and came away with chow for his troubles, but there's one way to find out."

"I'll check the map," I said, glad to have any kind of clue, and wondering what I'd do if it panned out.

"Thought you might," Big Mike said. "I don't like this any better than you do, Billy, but we can't let Sam know what we're up to. The brass is pressuring him for results on this one, and I don't want to get him into hot water."

"No reason to worry him," I said, giving Big Mike a wink. "And if Fassier disappears without a trace, the brass couldn't blame the colonel. It's a dangerous world out there."

"We're on the same page," he said. "One other thing. When I asked Jules what he and Jarnac were going on about, he didn't give up the story about Beaulieu. He claimed he still didn't really believe Fassier could be a traitor, and that's what they were arguing about."

"Seems like we can't fully trust him," I said. "He seems like a decent guy, but his loyalties might be to the FTP first and the rest of us second."

"Third," Big Mike said. "I'd put Marie-Claire first. He was upset about her going off with Emilie and *la Croix*. They had a bit of a fight and then made up with a big smooch."

"He's smart to put her in the lead spot," I said. "How're you going to handle him as your passenger? He might get suspicious with you not going off on your own after Fassier."

"I told him it was standard procedure. If the bad guy spots the first vehicle, he might think he outsmarted us and take to the road. Then we come along and have him boxed in."

"Might actually come to that," I said, looking around for Kaz and spotting Jules making his way to the jeep. "I'm going to find Kaz, then we'll head out."

I checked in the salon, which was empty except for a GI

scrubbing blood stains from the tile floor, mopping up red froth mingled with stale coffee.

Something caught my eye. At the corner of the table, one brass thumbtack. It must have fallen from the map when Fassier went after Bernard. It was the same kind of tack as the one still attached to a corner of the map. I picked it up, the GI lazily mopping up the last of the stain. I held it in my palm where it rattled around as the shakes came back to my right hand.

"Can I help you, Captain?" he asked, setting the mop in his bucket.

"No, you go ahead," I said, distracted as I tried to think through the sequence of events. Was Fassier clutching the map when Dujardin came after him? Or did he drop it so he could use both hands, one for the knife and the other to grab Dujardin and drive him against the wall?

The GI went to lift the coffee urn, the one that hadn't been overturned. A heavy *clunk* sounded when he moved it.

"Hold on," I said, motioning for him to set it down. I lifted the lid and removed the container that held wet coffee grounds. Inside the urn was a dagger. The tip, caked in blood, protruded a few inches above the last of the coffee.

"Holy," the GI said. "I was gonna drink some of that."

I told him to dump the joe before anyone else had the same idea. I dried off the knife on the tablecloth as I considered what this meant about the sequence of events. I'd assumed McKuras had seen Dujardin being killed and ran to alert us, with the killer catching up and silencing him. But the blade had been cleaned on McKuras's sleeve, and there wasn't much blood on him any-way. So why would the killer go back and hide the knife near Dujardin's body?

McKuras had to have been first. He saw Fassier taking the map. Fassier ran him down and went out through the salon, encountering Dujardin. Did Dujardin see the map? His killing was bloodier. Fassier was about to go out the front door to his vehicle, and didn't have time to clean the knife, so he just popped it into the coffee urn.

But why?

At that point, he was almost home free. He could have dropped it and walked out.

Maybe I had it wrong. Maybe he'd tried to clean the blade on McKuras, but it was too bloody. By this time, he'd be panicked. He'd thought all he had to do was swipe a map, but a few seconds later he'd killed two guys up close. That's enough to shake anyone. For whatever reason, he stashed the blade in the urn on his way out. It didn't make sense, but people do strange things during an unintended double homicide.

I left the odor of coppery blood and soured coffee behind and searched for Kaz. I spotted Harding in an office, field telephone to his ear. I ignored him, or he ignored me, it was hard to tell. I turned down a corridor and nearly bumped into Kaz, who quickly stuffed something in his pocket.

"Hey, where've you been?" I said. "We're ready to hit the road."

"I was visiting the medical section," Kaz said. "I wanted some aspirin." He patted his pocket, setting off a rattle of pills in tin.

"You feeling okay?" I asked, as we walked through the maze of hallways filled with scurrying clerks and earnest officers.

"A headache is all," Kaz said. "I've been tired as well. A rest would do us both good, don't you think?"

"Yeah. A soft bed and the absence of corpses would be a nice start," I said. "But are you sure you're up to this?"

"Certainly," Kaz said, as we stepped out onto the terrace washed with the summer sun. "It is not as if we will be exerting ourselves, after all."

"Big Mike told me about Beaulieu," I said, stopping to raise my face to the sun, letting the warmth wash over me.

"There may be some exertion then," Kaz said, a sighing weariness hanging off each word.

"We could accidently run into Fassier," I said.

"And not let him go," Kaz said. "That would give up the game. Big Mike agrees?"

"As long as it doesn't put Colonel Harding in the hot seat," I said. "What do you think?"

"I have managed to develop a callousness about death I never considered possible," Kaz said. "Having seen so much of it. But that does not hold true for murder. It is a crime against nature to murder a man in wartime. It robs him of the chance of surviving it."

"Okay. So, we roll into Beaulieu and see what happens. But if you're sick, maybe you should rest up. I could go out with Big Mike and Jules. Now that we have a lead, one jeep is as good as two."

"Just try to leave me behind," Kaz said, slapping me on the arm and giving me a crooked grin, the scar that split his face anchored in despair. It had been more than two years since the explosion that opened his face down to the cheekbone and killed his one true love. Daphne Seaton was never far from his mind, and some days it seemed he ached to join her. Less so now that he had hopes of finding his sister alive, but I'd grown so used to worrying about his hold on living and breathing that I was always on the lookout for the black dog of depression. Ordering him to stay behind and rest up was an option, but I preferred to keep my eye on him. The hope of his sister's survival was a damn fine thread to hold his life together. That had been my job since Daphne's death, and I wasn't about to relinquish it over a headache.

"Then take your aspirin. And you might want to hold on to this," I said. I gave him the dagger I'd discovered. "We might actually run into the guy who owns it."

I gave him the rundown on finding the knife on the way to the jeep and Big Mike's story for Jules about them tailing us.

"We may well run into *Monsieur* Jarnac and his men," Kaz said. "He was pressing poor Jules about any clue he might have."

"Well, poor Jules failed to tell Big Mike about Beaulieu, so we need to watch out for him," I said. "There might be something else he isn't telling us, which worries me." Right now, everything worried me. I worried about two dead bodies, a phony mission that might get us killed, acres of rotting corpses out in the Falaise Pocket, and my right hand, which quivered like the last leaf in a stiff autumn breeze.

We walked around the corner of the château to find the drive crowded with men and machinery. Staff cars and other vehicles were pulled in around our jeeps, and a crowd of enlisted men had gathered around a gaggle of officers on the steps to the entrance.

"It's General Eisenhower," one of the GIs said to us, a look of awe plastered over his face.

I spotted the general, standing near his car, hands in his pockets, chatting with Colonel Harding. He caught my eye and gave the smallest of nods. I stood back, waiting for him to move through the crowd, leaving the officers behind, giving the GIs his trademark Ike grin, asking where they were from, and getting a laugh when he asked if Georgie Patton was treating them well.

It was pure Uncle Ike.

He finally made it over to us, the rest of the men sensing he was done gabbing. He returned a sharp salute from Big Mike and asked him if he was having any trouble keeping me and Kaz in line.

"These guys? No problem, General," Big Mike said. He introduced Jules, whose eyes grew wide as Uncle Ike shook his hand and praised the work of the Resistance.

"Lieutenant Kazimierz," Uncle Ike said, grasping Kaz's hand. "I understand you were with the Poles on Hill 262. You must be tremendously proud of the stand they made."

"Yes, General. No disrespect meant, but it was good to fight with my own people," Kaz said, standing a little straighter. "And of course, Billy was with me."

"As I've been informed. I'm inclined to overlook your liberal interpretation of orders, Lieutenant, given the fight was being waged by your countrymen. But your captain here has no such excuse," he said, his eyes narrowing as he took in mine. "I need the both of you. You're vital to the war effort."

"Sorry, General," I said. "I honestly didn't know what we were getting ourselves into."

"Well, I'm glad you're both unhurt," Uncle Ike said, shaking a Lucky out of a pack and lighting up. "Walk with me a moment, William."

Uncle Ike had a way of being open with everyone and at ease in a crowd. As they did today, I've seen GIs gather around him, all laughs and delight, totally at ease with the most senior American officer in the European Theater of Operations. Even the way he stuck his hands in his pockets, in violation of strict army regulations on the subject, let guys know he wasn't about to go chickenshit on them.

But he could also close himself off. Like now, with his shoulders hunched and a smoke between his fingers, strolling beside me. Men melted away, sensing the public appearance was over and probably wondering who the hell this captain was whispering with Ike.

"I came through Falaise," he said. "I wanted to see Hill 262 for myself. On the way here, we stopped to walk through parts of the pocket. My God, William, I've never seen anything like it."

"Me either, Uncle Ike." I watched him draw on his Lucky like it held an elixir which might soothe his senses after the madness he'd witnessed.

"It was something out of Dante," he said. "It was literally possible to walk for hundreds of yards at a time, stepping on nothing but dead and decaying flesh."

He ground out the cigarette on the crushed stone driveway and immediately lit up another. I couldn't bear to tell him we'd driven over those bodies.

"We should be celebrating a victory," I said. "But it doesn't seem right somehow."

"If that scene is what our victories will look like, we need to end this war as soon as possible," he said. "Otherwise the entire continent will be laid waste. I shudder to think how many innocent French civilians were caught up in that slaughter. Whole villages were shattered and burned. I don't even know how we can clean up that battlefield before disease takes over."

"How many dead?" I asked, unable to put a number to the carnage I'd seen.

"Intelligence estimates from ten to fifteen thousand Germans killed in that valley of death," he said. "Perhaps up to fifty thousand captured. Massive losses in equipment. Those troops who did escape the pocket made it out mostly on foot, a demoralized, exhausted mass of men."

"Good. I hope they don't have a chance to regroup," I said.

"That's why I wanted to talk to you, William. I'm aware of the deception campaign Colonel Harding has put together. It's a nice little charade, and it may lead the Germans away from our intended line of advance."

"Around Paris," I said.

"Yes. Everyone and his brother wants us to take Paris. General de Gaulle insists upon it. But I'm not going there simply to satisfy French honor. If we can sweep around the city and smash the German forces before they regroup, it may hasten the end of the war. And if they retreat into Paris, then they'll have created their own POW camp for the next few months."

"But what about the civilians in Paris, Uncle Ike?"

"You saw what happened to civilians in the Falaise Gap, William! My God, they were wiped out. If we can avoid another scene like that on French ground, I'm all for it. The French in Paris may suffer hunger, but they won't be living in ruins, at least. There are no easy answers in this war, believe me."

I did.

"We'll do our best, Uncle Ike."

What else could I say?

"I know you will, William. It may seem a bit foolish to go after a spy *not* to catch him, but do your best to fail at it very visibly, okay?"

"Well, Uncle Ike, then I won't do my best," I said, giving the Supreme Commander a quick wink.

"That's the spirit, William. Now I've got to see Georgie Patton. Is my tie on straight?"

I wasn't in the mood for jokes, but I did laugh out loud at that one.

UNCLE IKE AND his entourage had gone into the château. Big Mike and Jules went in search of coffee and doughnuts to kill some time while we got a head start. That left me and Kaz.

Me, Kaz, and my guilty conscience.

Now I'd promised Uncle Ike I'd do my best to carry out the deception plan. I didn't have the guts to tell Kaz, so I had no idea what the hell was going to happen.

"Are we going anywhere, Billy?" Kaz asked from the passenger seat.

"Yeah," I said, giving him a glance. He rubbed his eyes and pulled down the brim of his service cap. His skin was pale, paler than usual. Out of the sunlight, ashen would have been the perfect description. "You ready?"

He waved a hand toward the road. I took that as a yes.

I started the jeep, noticing my right hand tremble as I took the wheel.

"We make the perfect pair for a false mission," Kaz said, looking at my hand, which I kept firmly clasped on the wheel. "You've had a shaky hand since we came off that hill."

"It's nothing," I said. "Like your headache. Forget about it. We're heading out on the road, like the Cisco Kid and Pancho."

"Who?"

"Western caballeros," I said, easing the jeep down the long driveway. "Didn't you ever go to the Saturday matinees as a kid?"

"My aunt took me to the opera in Warsaw often," Kaz said. "I don't recall any Spanish cowboys onstage."

"The Green Hornet and Kato?"

"That is somewhat better. I assume you are Kato the faithful chauffer, and I am the rich crime-fighter? You are driving, after all," Kaz said, his face almost relaxed. Maybe this little jaunt in the fresh air would cure his headache.

"Okay, you come up with a better duo," I said, slowing as three heavy trucks came down the road.

"Very well," he said. "I say Rosencrantz and Guildenstern. They were at least Europeans and embarked upon a mission for their king."

"That's Shakespeare, right?" I said, remembering English class back in South Boston. Sister Mary Gabriel had taught Hamlet like it was a lost book of the New Testament, and those names had always stuck with me. "What happened to them?"

"It is best I do not tell you."

CHAPTER TEN

THE MPS AT the HQ entrance had taken down the license plate of the green Amilcar, 7857 MZ. They'd radioed it to the other checkpoints, with instructions to confirm sightings and let the driver pass after a short delay, allowing us to draw closer.

Kaz navigated, skirting the southern edge of the Falaise Pocket on side roads that were little more than forested tracks. The wind gusted up about a half hour out and the stench of rotting flesh flowed over us, clinging to our clothes and skin, leaving a lingering scent of decay.

"Drive faster," Kaz said, sniffing his sleeve, then holding out his arms to the open air. I stepped on it, zipping along the dirt road between stands of spindly pines, feeling a bit like a kid on a joyride.

Then the snarl of a diving aircraft snatched the joy away. I took my foot off the gas and coasted, not wanting to brake and send up a telltale plume of dust. I steered off the road, bumping along on the rough ground until thick pine trees blocked the way. I didn't know if it was ours or theirs, as rare as *Luftwaffe* sightings were these days, but it didn't make much difference where the ammunition was made when it was hurtling in bursts straight for your head.

The prop wash from the fighter's propellers blew branches and pine needles around like a gusting nor'easter as we hunched over in our seats, waiting for the bombs and bullets that never arrived.

"Idiot," Kaz said, craning his neck to see between the branches. "He is coming around again. A Tempest, I think. Doesn't he know where he is?"

"There still could be Germans around," I said. "It's our fault for making dust. He might think we're Krauts making a run for it." The Tempest roared overhead, his wing dipping to get a better look at the ground as he circled. A rugged fighter-bomber, the British Tempest sported 20-millimeter cannon with bombs slung under its wings. If this guy decided to have a go at us, he'd leave a lot of kindling by the side of the road.

He gained altitude, soaring in a giant arc overhead before diving again, his nose pointed right at us.

"He's spotted us," I said, as he opened up with his four cannon, the staccato bursts coming nearer as he descended.

Kaz threw himself on top of me, my face shoved into the dirt. The Tempest rose skyward, dropping two bombs, deadly black dots of steel and explosive growing larger and closer. I felt Kaz tense as the bombs struck and detonated.

The ground shook, and the shock wave sent a blast of air and branches overhead. Then a secondary explosion sent a ball of flame skyward, maybe one hundred yards through the woods.

We hadn't been the target.

"Kaz, you okay?" I asked as we untangled ourselves, keeping one eye on the fireball.

"Yes," he said, brushing himself off. "I thought those bombs were meant for us."

"They could have been." I leaned in to look him in the eye. "And you could have been killed."

"I still may be if we do not investigate," he said, turning away and grabbing his Sten gun. "The jeep is well hidden here. Let's see what is ahead."

I grabbed my Thompson and followed, wondering what had gotten into him. I don't mind my life being saved, but having your best pal show he was willing to take a load of shrapnel for you was a shocker. I didn't have much time to think that through. There were Germans ahead.

We eased through the trees, one eye on the plume of smoke, the other on the lookout for field-gray uniforms through the green branches. The ground was soft with pine needles, our boots making no sound, the air filled with nothing but the snap of flames.

And one ungodly cry.

Someone was alive.

Without a word, we moved apart and crouched low as we worked our way forward, presenting less of a target in case any Germans were still alive and in better shape than the guy shrieking and moaning.

We came to a dirt track. The smoke came from around a corner, and we each took a side of the narrow lane, where tread marks were gouged into the rutted road. We both stared at the shattered trees, evidence of the Tempest's cannon fire. We edged around the corner and saw the carnage it had inflicted.

A German half-track was on its side, a smoking crater marking a near-direct hit. Bodies were strewn across the road, men ripped apart from the shredding 20mm fire. It looked like the half-track had tried to get off the road as we did, but a drainage ditch must have snagged the front wheel. The men riding in it had been sitting ducks. The strafing and bombs had accounted for a dozen dead Krauts.

And one barely alive, but nowhere to be seen. The rear of the vehicle was empty except for several unmarked crates. The front compartment was taken up by an officer with most of his head elsewhere.

"Here," Kaz said, appearing through the acrid smoke from the burning fuel tank. The side of the half-track was in the ditch, flames licking at the undercarriage from the fuel tank. Right by the screaming German.

He was pinned, his legs crushed by the seven-ton armored vehicle. Blood and oil stained his face, which was contorted in a grimace of horror and pain. The flames were already licking at his torso as his blackened hands slapped madly at the fire. If he saw us he gave no sign and had no words other than the scream of the damned.

Kaz put a burst of three bullets into his heart.

The forest went quiet except for the crackling of flames.

"There is a time for burning," Kaz said. "And a time for mercy."

I stared at the dead German. His face frozen in a rictus of pain. I tore my gaze away as a rattling sound demanded my attention. It was my right hand, trembling against the wooden stock of my Thompson.

We were both still up on that hill, and I didn't think we were coming down anytime soon.

I found Kaz riffling through the pockets of the headless Kraut officer. He hauled out papers and climbed down, reading them as I stood guard.

"This is an engineer detachment," he said, scanning the document. "The lieutenant had orders to deliver demolition materials to the commander of the Paris garrison and place himself at his disposal. They were sent from Le Mans and must have gotten lost."

"There were wooden crates in the back," I said, as flames lapped up over the side of the half-track and the implications dawned.

We ran.

I started the jeep as the explosions began, a series of concussive blasts that shattered the air and sent debris spinning off into the sky.

Driving by where the track emptied into our lane, I slowed to survey the remains. The huge half-track was nothing but a blackened and twisted hulk of smoking metal. All traces of the men were gone, replaced by a gaping shell hole. Trees were torn in every direction, as if a Kansas tornado had churned through the pines.

"What would the commandant of Paris want with such explosives?" Kaz said.

"That Tempest pilot saved our lives," I said, having no answer except to wonder how many other engineer units were heading to Paris with similar cargoes. "If he hadn't happened by, we would have collided with those guys, and it would have been us blown to hell."

"Yes, but not quite so spectacularly," Kaz said, adjusting his glasses as he unfolded the map on his lap.

"There is a crossroads ahead," he said, after a moment's study, "where the *Maquis* Henri are stationed. One road goes south to a small village, Tanville, the other east to Beaulieu. Unless Fassier took the long way around, he would have passed through the crossroad."

"But ahead of Henri and his crew," I said. "We'll check in with them anyway."

"There is an MP roadblock on the route to Beaulieu," Kaz said. "They should know."

The dirt road widened as it left the forest, carrying us out along a gently sloping ridge with a view of a valley graced with farmland and a scattering of houses and barns. The crossroad came into view as we crested a hill.

No sign of Henri and his *maquisards*. I slowed, and we craned our necks for some sign of the Frenchmen, thinking they might be dug in and camouflaged. All we saw were crushed cigarette butts and an empty wine bottle at the side of the road.

"They were here, but only long enough to smoke a few cigarettes," Kaz said, taking the binoculars from the back seat. He focused on the distant village of Tanville in the valley below. "There, a vehicle with FFI markings."

I could make out a faint white blur and the outline of a truck next to one of the jumbles of buildings grouped together along the road.

"Come on," I said. "Even though they're dogging it, we ought to warn them there are actually Germans in the area."

"Real *maquisards* would not need to be warned," Kaz said, as I wheeled the jeep around and descended into the village. Farms and barns surrounded a clutch of gray houses huddled by the roadside, like so many tiny hamlets scattered across the French countryside. A single truck with FFI in whitewash splashed across the door was drawn up outside a café. I pulled the jeep between the café and the next building, not wanting to leave an obvious target in the middle of the street.

Two men with Sten guns slung idly from their shoulders and cigarettes dangling from their lips lounged on chairs outside the entrance. One, a young fellow who looked semi-alert, stood and greeted us. His pal, older, unshaven, and with the heavy lids of a working drinker, pulled the kid's sleeve and got him to sit down.

Inside the café, Henri sat with half a dozen men, glasses of cloudy pastis at their elbows. The barman looked apprehensively at us, his eyes darting to the young girl carrying a jug of water to the table. The anise-flavored liqueur had to be diluted, and everyone had their favorite ratio, but these guys were more interested in the server than what she was serving.

Henri barked at us as he grabbed the girl's arm, asking what we wanted and a bunch more I couldn't catch. Kaz spoke to him calmly, and Henri responded with a brief silence, then laughter.

"I told him I wanted him to pay his bill, leave the young lady alone, and assume the post he had abandoned," Kaz said, watching as the girl scurried behind the bar.

Henri poured water into his glass of pastis, downed it in one gulp, and moved his hand to the pistol in his belt. Then he spoke.

"He says they will not pay this man who drank with the *boche*. That we should find our own woman, and that it is ridiculous to stand about on a deserted road," Kaz translated. "What do you say, Billy, should I shoot him?"

Henri and his gang didn't blink an eye. I knew that last bit was to see if they understood English. For the most part, anyway. "Let's wait," I said. "Tell 'em about the Krauts."

Henri wasn't impressed. Or too drunk to take the warning seriously. The café owner told Kaz they'd refused to pay, insulted his daughter Natalie, and he'd never seen them before, so how could they know if he drank with the Germans? Of course, he had to serve them, but he never raised a glass with them. And he was afraid for his daughter.

For himself, as well, I could tell by his nervous glances between us and the well-armed men. He was taking a chance on us leaving him alone with them.

"I am taking Natalie to her mother," Kaz said, after whispering with her and her father. "Their house is across the street." I took a seat as he left, my Thompson cradled in my arms, watching Henri. It was clear he was the leader, and his men would wait for him to make any move. So, he'd get it first.

Minutes later I saw a khaki blur flash by the window.

"Germans!" Kaz said, slamming the door against the wall and running back out. I followed, barely making it to the door ahead of Henri, who moved pretty damn fast for a stumbling drunk.

I followed Kaz around the side of the café, taking cover as he showed me where the road curved around the last of the houses and vanished into the rolling hills. Another Kraut half-track was barely visible, its camouflage blending almost perfectly with the line of trees at the edge of the cultivated field. The engine rumbled into life, and it jolted forward, a line of field-gray advancing on either side.

The young guy, who seemed the least inebriated of the lot, dove into the doorway of the café and aimed his weapon at the Germans. Henri made for the FFI truck, getting into the driver's seat and starting it up. Before half his men had climbed into the back, he floored it in reverse, knocking one guy over who didn't move fast enough.

The kid fired his Sten. He got off three short bursts before the Germans returned fire. A fusillade of lead spat from the machine gun mounted on the half-track, chewing up masonry and kicking up stone chips from the front of the café.

The men of *Maquis* Henri ran, the smartest, and most fortunate, making for narrow passageways between buildings. Anyone showing even the slightest hesitation was cut down, the rapid-fire machine gun slicing into flesh and bone like a butcher's blade.

Henri drove wildly, skewing the truck across the road in a vain attempt to turn around and gain speed. The German machine gun was faster. Rounds shattered the windshield, perforated the hood, blew out tires, and sent men twisting in agony over the side to fall dying in the dusty road.

I saw the kid raise his Sten, astounded he was still alive. Kaz hissed out an order in French, and he pulled back into the cover of the doorway. More Kraut soldiers came out of the woods as the half-track halted in the middle of the street, its machine gun swiveling, searching for any remaining threat.

Another half-track came through the trees, and the rest of the soldiers climbed aboard, carrying two wounded men with them.

"They haven't seen us," Kaz said. I remained still, thankful that the jeep had been hidden from view. I watched an officer shout orders, calling his men to regroup. Then he pointed down the road, away from the village.

"Another lost unit?" I whispered. "More demolitions?"

"Can you see their collar tabs?" Kaz said. I shook my head. Engineers wore black piping around their collar tabs and rank badges. But they were too far away. Kaz took a few steps to the jeep and returned with the binoculars, handing them to me.

"Engineers," I said, spotting the black piping. I watched as they eased down one of the wounded and laid him on the ground. He was dead. They gathered around him for a moment, then broke apart with angry shouts that echoed against the stone walls. The first half-track took off, away from us on the road heading west.

The second moved forward into the street, men standing up with their weapons aimed over the side. They machine-gunned the houses and threw grenades, casually, as if it were target practice. The heavy-caliber weapon shattered doors and shutters, evaporating glass and starting fires with incendiary rounds. It lasted less than a minute, and half the village was in shambles. The half-track turned around and roared down the road, its punishment meted out.

We came out from under cover. After the intense gunfire and explosions, the street seemed quiet. But then cries and moans rose up from within the houses, as crackling flames bit at doorframes. The kid stood with his Sten hanging by his side, his face streaked with tears and disbelief.

"*Je suis désolé*," he said. Over and over again.

"Tell him it's not his fault," I said to Kaz. "He doesn't need to be sorry. At least he fought back." Kaz nodded and spoke to the kid. Soothingly, with his hand on his shoulder.

People began to come out into the street. The café owner ran to his house calling out his daughter's name. A woman with bloody outstretched hands stood in front of a neighboring house, shrieking in a high-pitched, terrified voice.

"I told the boy that the Germans have done this before, without the slightest provocation," Kaz said. "But I think he will always blame himself."

"It was Henri's fault," I said. "If he'd kept his men at the crossroads, this fight wouldn't have happened."

Two men appeared, pulling an ancient fire cart with a water tank and hose. They pumped water into the worst of the fires as stunned residents gathered together. The café owner came out of his house alone and walked dazedly by us, mumbling Natalie's name, tears coursing down his cheeks.

"We need to report in," I said, trying to shake off the numbness that seemed to descend over me as I surveyed the carnage. "The checkpoints need to be warned and Harding should know about the engineers."

"Yes," Kaz said, his voice a sigh. "We cannot help these people." We turned to get in the jeep, and the kid followed us, asking a question I couldn't catch. Kaz spoke to him, then sat wearily in the jeep.

"What'd he want?" I said.

"He asked me what he should do," Kaz said. "I told him to bury the dead."

CHAPTER ELEVEN

WE DROVE BACK up the hill and parked where Henri and his pals should have stayed. Better reception on the high ground, and it got us away from the mournful village of Tanville.

I reached to flip a switch for our assigned frequency.

I couldn't. The shakes were back in my right hand, which quivered as I tried to work the dial.

"Do you need help?" Kaz asked from the front seat.

"No, all set," I said, using my left to set the frequency and grab the handset. I hoped Kaz hadn't noticed. He seemed lost in thought, rubbing his eyes and leaning forward. Headache, maybe.

My hand had been steady in Tanville, or at least I hadn't noticed a tremble. Which was a good thing, since it meant I'd be steady in a fight. Afterwards, well, who knows?

"King Two, this is White Rook, over." Big Mike was King Two. We'd gone too far to pick up Harding at Patton's headquarters, so he'd have to relay the report. It took a couple of tries, but I got Big Mike. I gave him our location, and reported on the engineers we'd stumbled across, their explosives, and the orders Kaz had found.

"Kaz, Big Mike wants you to go over those Kraut orders," I said. "Kaz!"

"What? Sorry, Billy, I think I fell asleep."

"You're one cool customer, Kaz. Here, review the Kraut orders with Big Mike, he wants details."

Kaz went through the papers, which instructed the officer in charge of the 318th Engineer Company, sent from Le Mans the day before, to report immediately to General Dietrich von Choltitz, military governor of Greater Paris. Duties unspecified.

"Those three half-tracks probably comprised a platoon," I said as Kaz signed off. "A full company means there's six or more still on their way to Paris."

"Big Mike is passing the information on and alerting the MPs at roadblocks. Of course, the rest of them may not be lost and are giving our lines a wide berth."

"Let's hope so," I said. "You need anything before we move? Some chow?"

"No, just some aspirin," Kaz said, tossing back a couple of pills and taking a slug from his canteen. He took a deep breath and exhaled, relaxing back in his seat. "Onward, then. I am looking forward to meeting Lucien Fassier."

"Purely by accident," I reminded Kaz.

"Of course. Beaulieu looks to be ten miles due west. We should find the MPs at Les Aspres, a few miles from here," he said, wiping his brow with his sleeve.

I drove on, keeping an eye on the horizon for any wandering Fritzes. Kaz seem content to nod off, a pretty hard thing to do in a jeep, even on this halfway-decent country road. It didn't take long to find Les Aspres, a small village straddling a crossroad, a stream, a few shops and not much else save the monument to the fallen of the previous war. There wasn't much room left on the granite, and I wondered how they'd handle the deaths and deportations of this latest war.

The MPs had the crossroads partially blocked by a couple of jeeps. A farmer's cart, pulled by a wizened horse that had somehow survived German pillaging and hungry winters, rolled through ahead of us.

"Your vehicle came through here about an hour ago," the MP sergeant informed us. "We checked his papers real slow like we was ordered to. He was driving a beat-up green sedan with FFI and FTP painted all over it. Pretty sloppy work at that."

"Okay, Sarge. You get the word about the Krauts?" I asked.

"The half-tracks? We did. I sent a jeep out to check the road south of here. They didn't see anyone. I think the locals are keeping their heads down until they figure out who's staying and who's going."

"Farmers are sensible people," Kaz said as we sped off, passing the cart with its small load of sugar beets. "Perhaps after we find Fassier we should emulate them."

"Do you have farmer's daughter's jokes in Poland?" I asked.

"Of course. The ancient Romans even had them, in only a slightly different form," Kaz said. "Have you heard the one about the eggs?"

I had, but not the exact version Kaz spun for me. He went on about folktales for a while. Apparently, his little catnap had revived him, and he seemed more energetic. If we did end up at a farm with a French maiden close by, I was sure Kaz would be as charming as ever. While he still carried a torch for Daphne, he didn't let that stop him from enjoying himself. There would never be another Daphne for him, I was sure. But the fact that so many women found him irresistible did occasionally focus his mind elsewhere.

Me, the only woman I could think about was Diana Seaton. She was Daphne's sister, and her death had bound the three of us in ways that only grief and revenge can manage. Kaz was protective of Diana, and me as well, for that matter. I felt the same way about her. Given that she was an agent with the Special Operations Executive and currently on assignment somewhere behind enemy lines, there wasn't much I could do in terms of protection. Diana and I were opposites, at least in the outward things. She was British Protestant upper class, a ride-to-the-foxes sort of English gentry, and I was an Irish Catholic working-class stiff from Southie.

We would die for each other.

And nearly had.

"But the first man disputes this because 'the man who told me you were dead is much more reliable than you,'" Kaz said, delivering the punchline to a joke I hadn't paid attention to.

"Funny," I said.

"Yes, fairly amusing for third century Rome, in any case. There, that must be Beaulieu."

I took his word for it as we drove down a lane bordered by the dappled trunks of plane trees. Beaulieu was more of a burg than the last two towns. Substantial houses stood back from the road, surrounded by low stone walls and iron fences. Further on, shops and cafés fronted a cobblestone street, the town untouched by bombs or bullets. People strolled on the sidewalks, the afternoon sun sending their shadows after them.

"*Police Municipale*," Kaz said, pointing to a sign above a brick-faced, two-story building with a small garden in front adorned by another monument to war dead. This one had room on both sides, for the Franco-Prussian War and the Great War. I guess they hadn't planned this far in advance.

"Café," I said, pulling in across the street. "I'm hungry, and we might learn more there than from the cops. You can say we're looking for a friend in the Resistance."

"Very well," Kaz said. "I wonder about the local police here. This is the first large town I've seen without FFI markings everywhere."

"Yeah," I said. One lone *V* for *victory* had been painted on a wall, but other than that, no crosses of Lorraine or FTP slapped on storefronts or vehicles. It was as if Beaulieu was too tidy to abide such crude expressions.

We sat outside at the café, where we soon were served a bottle of red wine and a mutton cassoulet. Kaz tasted the wine and complimented the waiter, but I thought I detected a brief wince. He had a delicate palate. I didn't, took a big gulp, and enjoyed it.

Kaz then played at suddenly remembering an acquaintance in the Resistance. "Beaulieu, isn't this where Lucien lives?" he asked me, and then described Lucien Fassier to the waiter, throwing in a whole bunch of French I couldn't understand. The waiter responded, and I heard him mention Fassier several times. Each pronouncement was accompanied by a sad shake of the head. Once, he gestured across the street, then went inside.

"Interesting," Kaz said, tasting the cassoulet. "Much better than the wine, I must say."

"What about our long-lost pal Lucien?" I asked, glancing at the door.

"The Fassier family is well known in Beaulieu. Lucien's father, Yves, was until very recently the *directeur de police municipal*."

"Lucien's old man was the chief of police? No wonder his kid turned commie. Where is he now?"

"Still across the street, but in a jail cell. Our waiter tells me many people in town are still sympathetic to Vichy, and many maintain their admiration for Marshal Pétain. Even so, the elder Fassier was so pro-fascist that the mayor and other luminaries decided he had to be arrested."

"To demonstrate their allegiance to the new order," I said.

"One could safely draw that conclusion," Kaz said. "But, it makes it seem unlikely that Lucien would make an appearance. The waiter says he has not seen him for some months."

"Which means he did come here before, when his old man was the top cop and probably working with the Germans and the *Milice*. So, why wouldn't he come now? Maybe he wants to see his father on the other side of the bars. Maybe he wants to comfort his mother."

"Perhaps. Madame Fassier is not well, my new friend informs me. It may be worthwhile to speak to both."

"After we eat," I said, scooping up another spoonful of white beans.

We decided to see Yves first, since he was right across the street and might be tarred and feathered at any moment. Inside the police station, it was like being in any cop house. A bleak entry room and a bored blue-uniformed officer on duty. Yellowing wanted posters hung off a bulletin board, some of them still bearing the swastika stamp of the occupier. Hey, maybe these guys were realists. The Krauts might be back. So far, Kaz and I seemed to be the sole representatives of the Allies, and no one was tossing any flowers our way.

Kaz asked to see the prisoner Yves Fassier as I showed my SHAEF identity card, which impressed the *gendarme* not one damn bit. He spoke into a telephone and cradled it with supreme indifference as we stood by his desk. Another cop called to us from the hallway and we followed him, his polished boots echoing off the tiled floor as he led us to the basement cells.

"*Le prisonnier Fassier,*" the cop said, coming to attention and producing the slightest of bows toward the man in the cell. Was he sympathetic to his old boss or was it nothing more than obedience to a habit of years? They were close to the same age, maybe fifty or so, and had probably worked together for decades. Our escort walked away, giving no further clue as to what he thought of his imprisoned former chief. Fassier set aside the Bible he was reading, looking at us with raised eyebrows, as if we'd interrupted his busy schedule.

"*Bonjour, Monsieur Fassier,*" Kaz began. He spouted some more French but Fassier stopped him with a wave of the hand.

"We can speak in English if it is easier for your American

friend," Fassier said, rising from his single chair and facing us through the bars. He was tall, dressed in his blue police trousers and a soiled white shirt. He had graying hair, a few days' growth of beard, and the posture of a military man, managing to look haughty despite his situation. "I learned to speak it as a child, and I was a liaison officer with the British Army in the old war. That was the last time the *Anglais* did anything worthwhile for France."

"You are entitled to your opinion, sir," Kaz said, introducing us and telling Fassier we had some questions about his son.

"What son?"

"Lucien," I said.

"I have no such son. I once had a boy by that name, but he became a godless Bolshevik and betrayed our laws and faith by going off to fight in Spain. On the side of Stalin, can you believe such nonsense? So, I have no son. I have disowned him. If you have anything else to ask, please do so. Otherwise, leave me alone."

Fassier folded his arms and gazed at us with contempt. I was no fan of Lucien Fassier, and his old man didn't do much for me either.

"You're not curious as to why two officers have come to ask about him?" I said, avoiding his son's name, not wanting to set off another round of condemnation.

"It is of no consequence," Fassier said.

"It is understandable that you should have other concerns," Kaz said, barely disguising his insolence. "Being held prisoner where once you were the chief of police."

"I have done my duty, to the nation and to Marshal Pétain," Fassier said, puffing out his chest and daring us to contradict him. "I have followed the orders of my government, and the only reason I am here is that our coward of a mayor and his people hope to hide their own allegiances by persecuting me. I did what they wanted done, and now I am here, alone."

"That is often the way with politicians," I said. "I was a policeman before the war. I know what you mean. The politicians protect themselves, don't they?"

"Indeed they do, young man. I think there will be a very swift judgement against me, and once I am in my grave, no one will be able to speak for me or against them. I am sorry I could be of no help to you today, and I am certain I will be of no help to anyone tomorrow."

"Might Lucien speak for you?" Kaz asked softly, bringing us back around to the subject of our visit.

"You do not understand," Fassier said, drawing closer to the bars, his mouth twisted in an angry sneer. "In the course of my duties, I hunted Communists along with the other terrorists who threatened our national revolution. I shot them or turned them over to the Germans, glad to rid the sacred soil of France of their presence. I am ashamed to have sired one of them, and I hope another patriot has put an end to his existence. Yes, he once was my son, and for that I can only say I hope the end was quick. As for the two of you, I bid you *adieu*."

There was not much else to say. We went upstairs, and I nodded to Kaz as we approached our escort's office. The nameplate read Inspecteur P. Ribot. The inspector sat at his desk, reading through a file. Kaz knocked, thanked him for his time, and asked a few questions.

"I speak a little English. *Un peu*," Ribot said. "Let us speak in French, yes?"

Kaz spoke as Ribot leaned back in his chair, sighed, and then gave his answers. Once we were outside, Kaz explained.

The Fassier family had lived in Beaulieu for generations and were well-regarded. Young Lucien was an only child, intelligent and loved by both parents. As he grew older, his ideas became radical, and his father put it down to youthful naiveté. Lucien went to university in Paris to study law, and his father, recently appointed the chief of police, hoped the discipline of hard study would mature Lucien's views and bring him into a career in the justice system. Instead, Lucien volunteered to fight in Spain against the fascists. This was too much for the father who had doted on him and previously defended him against all criticism. The elder Fassier had always been conservative, but his son's betrayal had deeply offended both his political and religious beliefs, and the elder Fassier became a right-wing extremist. When France surrendered, he blamed the Communists and focused all his rage into stamping them out. Some of the police thought he was hunting for Lucien, perhaps to save him. Others thought he had become unstable. But all agreed he was very good at what he did.

In answer to the last question, he said he doubted very much that Lucien had ever come home to visit his father. His mother, that was another matter, since she was very ill. Perhaps. Had he seen Lucien recently? No, not for years.

"Did he give you an address for the mother?" I asked.

"Yes. It is a short way, we can walk," Kaz said, heading down the street. "What did you think of Fassier?"

"I thought the bastard was sincere," I said. "Did Inspector Ribot give an opinion?"

"He said Fassier had once been a good man, but his anger and shame led him to do things that were terrible. His thought was that Fassier was indeed searching for his son but was never aware of his own motivation."

"Police inspectors can be pretty smart," I said, as we turned a corner. "I wish I was smart enough to figure out if this was a waste of time."

"I can't see why Lucien would risk seeing his father at any point during the Occupation," Kaz said. "Even if they were not estranged, he would hate how his father was cooperating with the Germans."

"Olga told us Lucien had lost most, if not all, of his early comrades. That could have been due in part to his father, so I agree. But he might risk it to see his mother," I said, glancing over my shoulder as I caught a glimpse of movement, a shadow melting between two houses.

"What?" Kaz asked, stopping to look around.

"Keep walking," I said. "I don't know if I imagined it, but I thought I saw someone watching us."

"Perhaps Jarnac or Louvet," Kaz said. "We are not the only ones searching for Fassier."

"Yeah, except they don't know they're not supposed to find him," I said. I wished I didn't either.

"This house," Kaz said, pointing to a large house faced in granite, with a rose garden choked with weeds. We walked up to the front door, past the untended garden, and knocked. A young woman wearing an apron and a dishtowel over her shoulder answered. Kaz turned on the charm and asked if we could see Madame Fassier. The girl opened the door, saying nothing. She showed us into a parlor and went off without a word.

The windows were closed, and the room was hot and stuffy. I pushed a curtain aside and watched the street. Had I been seeing things? The white lace curtain quivered in my hand, as if a breeze were blowing. But there wasn't a breeze in this still room.

I let go and the fluttering lace quieted.

"How's your headache?" I asked Kaz, catching him staring at my right hand as I shoved it into my pocket.

"Monotonous," he said, flopping down into a chair. Kaz seldom flopped. He looked ashen and exhausted. But my attention was drawn back to the window as I spotted a guy strolling by, dressed in worn corduroys and a thin jacket with a suspicious bulge in the pocket.

"Someone definitely has the place staked out," I said.

"Jarnac or Louvet?" Kaz asked with a heavy sigh, sounding bored by the whole affair.

"No way to know," I said. "The big boys aren't showing themselves."

"*Venez avec moi s'il vous plait*," the girl announced from the doorway. We followed her down a thickly carpeted hall to a sitting room where a low fire burned in the grate, even on this warm day. Seated close to the fire was a thin, gray-haired lady, a shawl around her shoulders.

Kaz handled the introductions. Unlike her husband, she spoke no English, so I stood back and watched. Also, unlike her husband, her eyes widened at the mention of her son, and her hand went to her mouth in a clear display of concern for him.

I could make out Kaz telling her he wasn't the bearer of any bad news, and I saw relief flood her face. A face that was gaunt and pale, with heavy gray bags under the eyes.

It was a dying face. Madame Fassier didn't have long for this world, and I wondered why her husband had not uttered a single word about her. He certainly wasn't short on words when it came to his disinherited son. The lady had some steel in her, that was clear. She hadn't batted an eyelash when two strangers with submachine guns were brought into her sitting room. Only the mention of her son had produced a reaction.

She and Kaz kept on talking as I looked around the room. It was furnished nicely, with oil paintings on the walls and expensive-looking vases on display. Was Fassier well-off before the war, or had he found a way to enrich himself as part of his willing collaboration?

There was a portrait of Marshal Pétain in a gilt-edged frame, set on a lacquered side table in a place of pride, near a collection of family portraits. Lucien was not among them. Not many homes in recently liberated towns had the old marshal on display. Was Madame Fassier pro-fascist as her husband was, or did she simply not have the energy or desire to remove this reminder of the old order? Perhaps she thought her husband might still return home.

In this room, the curtains were open to allow the afternoon sun to filter in. At the rear of the house a vegetable garden filled the space between a small barn and a line of fir trees. Withered vines of beans stood on poles over turnip plants in the well-weeded soil. This was why the rose garden was untended. Who cared about roses when you need turnips and rutabagas to stave off starvation?

Madame Fassier wept. Kaz took her gnarled, bony hand and cupped it between his. Whispers passed between them, then Kaz rose, bowed, and I followed him out of the room.

"I'm going to look around outside," I said, as soon as we were in the hall. "Find the girl and see what she knows." I left Kaz heading for the kitchen and I went out the front door. As I shut it, I noticed two tiny holes in the doorjamb, right at eye level. Little nail holes almost covered by a glossy black paint job. Exactly where a mezuzah would have been placed. I remembered my pal Henry Resnikoff proudly showing me his when they bought a house on Blue Hill Avenue in Dorchester. It was a small case holding biblical passages, a daily reminder of faith and the presence of God.

This had been a Jewish home.

The house and furnishings had been confiscated after the chief of police deported the family who'd lived here. Then he took down the symbol of their religion and painted it over, leaving only tiny holes as evidence of who had lived here. I could see why he was in jail, and why his previous accomplices wanted to make a show of bringing him to justice. It would remove a living witness and take the heat off them, for their perhaps lesser or less obvious crimes.

I touched the empty space.

I turned away and circled around the house, trying to put away the helpless rage I felt at all the suffering this war had brought about, and how men like Yves Fassier took advantage of it for nothing more than thick rugs and nice paintings. I followed a side street and spotted the stand of fir trees that abutted the Fassier property. I kept walking, then turned quickly, looking for a shadowy movement behind me. Nothing. Either I'd been imagining things, or the watchers from Louvet or Jarnac were staying close to the house.

I walked across a narrow, arched granite bridge. The stream and the trees were to the rear of the houses I'd walked past, including the Fassier place. The road curved, following the stream past a few more houses and stores, leading me to an old garage and a busy bicycle repair shop. With hardly any fuel available during the Occupation, bicycles had become highly valuable. The Germans requisitioned most motor vehicles, so there was little work left for automobile mechanics. The garage was deserted, the sour hard-packed dirt on the path smelling of oil and rust.

Traces of bicycle tire tracks were etched in the soil of the path leading to the stream. A rough wooden bridge spanned it, and the path continued to the town center. A convenient shortcut. Through the pine branches I could make out the rear of the Fassier house just as a woman on a bicycle rattled over the bridge, giving me a nervous glance as she pedaled faster to pass me by.

I didn't blame her for being nervous. An armed man on a wooded path could be dangerous. No one would see anything unless they walked right by.

Wait. No one would see.

I turned and jogged back to the garage, where the people in the bicycle shop avoided looking at me. After years of occupation, I guess they were in the habit of not questioning armed men. I rattled a door on the side of the garage. Locked. I went around the front and tried the small door set inside the large garage doors and found that locked as well. The glass was grimy, the interior swathed in darkness. A sturdy padlock secured the garage door. I unslung my Thompson and made ready to break a window in the small door.

"*Attendez!*" shouted a guy in blue overalls, waving a ring of keys as he ran from the bike shop. Apparently, the loss of a window helped overcome his reluctance to get involved. As he fumbled through the keys we talked, and I figured out he rented the bike shop from the guy who owned the garage, and no one had used it in *beaucoup* months.

I stooped to enter through the door and blinked to get my eyes used to the dark. It didn't take long to spot the tarpaulin-covered automobile at the far end. I yanked off the cover and wasn't a bit surprised to find the green Amilcar with the 7857 MZ license plate and the FFI markings.

The bicycle guy shrugged. News to him, of course.

I figured Lucien was long gone. He'd ditched the car to hide his tracks, but he had to have some other transport. I doubted even a fascist turncoat would stay in his dying mother's house with half the Resistance on his trail. Maybe there had been another car hidden in the garage, but I had a hunch there'd been something closer to home. I hotfooted it back across the stream and found a footpath leading through the trees to the Fassier garden. And to their barn.

The side door was unlocked. Garden tools and a wheelbarrow were arranged neatly next to a chair with one broken leg. A workbench sat along one wall, tools scattered along it. An oil can was shoved beneath it, fresh oil gleaming where it had run down the side. A rag smelled of gasoline, a rare and valuable commodity.

I spotted the gas can, covered by a pile of burlap. It still held a gallon or so.

It had to be a motorcycle. Otherwise, Lucien would have taken the gas can, or used it to fill the tank. There, leading to the double doors, a line of tire treads marked the path where he'd pushed it out. Too wide for a bicycle. Now our quarry was on a motorbike.

I found Kaz out front and filled him in on what I'd discovered.

"The serving girl admitted Lucien had been here today and

departed on a motorbike. Which gives him many more options," Kaz said. "He can travel cross-country and avoid checkpoints."

"Right. It might have been his plan all along, in case he made a big score."

"He had found refuge with his mother before," Kaz said. "She said her husband had gone too far in disowning Lucien, and that he'd made several visits to see her when Yves was gone."

"That checks out with the story Jules told," I said.

"Yes, she confirmed she gave him food and hid him for a night or two. He was haunted by the war. Not this one, as it turned out, but the war in Spain. He had nightmares, she confessed."

"Spain," I said. "That keeps coming up. Louvet, Jarnac, and Fassier."

"It makes sense," Kaz said. "There are many in the Resistance who supported the anti-fascists. And some, like Louvet, who were involved in stopping them."

"Did she ask why we were looking for Lucien?"

"Yes. Of course, at first, she feared the worst. But I assured her we simply needed his help, and with his habit of underground activities, we were having difficulty locating him," he said. "She made me promise to find him and bring him home before it is too late."

"Before his father is executed?"

"No. Madame Fassier was quite clear on that. Her husband's crimes against his countrymen were more than she could bear, but his betrayal of their own son was even worse. She had no desire for Lucien to experience his father's last moments, because she is certain they would only be filled with hatred for him. No, it is her death she spoke of. She feels it is very close."

"Jesus," I said. "I'm glad she hasn't heard what he got up to this morning. Did you get anything else useful from the girl?"

"Just that she knew of Lucien's visits. She was always given the day off, so she would not be culpable if the father discovered anything. She readily told me about today's visit, which lasted only minutes. He must have gotten here ahead of all of us, since the people watching the house are still here."

"That house had been a Jewish home," I said, filling in Kaz on what I'd noticed.

"Yes, the girl told me," he said. "Madame Fassier does not like it mentioned, as if silence will cover the guilt. Lucien was enraged when he found out."

"Anything else?"

"Well, there is good news and bad news. Lucien told her where he was going. To his friend from university, Charles Marchand," Kaz said.

"I take it that's the good news?"

"Correct. The bad news is that his friend lives in Rambouillet. Which is on the outskirts of Paris, on the other side of Chartres."

"Behind the German lines," I said.

"Most certainly," Kaz said. "Although the situation is very fluid. We should contact Big Mike and get an intelligence update."

Intelligence. I could use some. Nothing was adding up, and I began to think we were the ones being deceived in this deception campaign.

CHAPTER TWELVE

BACK AT THE jeep, Kaz got on the radio to contact Big Mike. A sudden shout arose from inside the café, followed by loud cheers as people spilled out onto the sidewalk. Across the street, police donning their kepi caps flooded out of the station, all of them excited, smiling and slapping one another's shoulders, making a beeline for the café.

"*Quelle est la célébration?*" I asked a guy near me, hoping I got the words right.

"*Les flics de Paris sont en grève,*" he said. Paris cops are what?

"On strike," Kaz said, shouting from the radio. "The Paris police have gone on strike."

The street outside the café became a madhouse of cheers, toasts, shouts, and praise for General de Gaulle and the *flics* of Paris, and by extension, the hometown cops as well.

"We have new orders," Kaz said, elbowing his way through the boisterous crowd. "Charles Marchand and Rambouillet will have to wait."

"Hang on," I said. "I can't make heads or tails out of what's going on here." I waved to Inspector Ribot, who worked his way over. A bottle of wine was thrust into my hand, and soon there were cheers for the Allies as well as de Gaulle. Kaz had to shout to ask Ribot what exactly had happened.

"The police of Paris, they are *en grève*. No work, you understand? They take the *Prefecture de Police*. It is like a fortress," he said, pride spreading across his face.

"You are sympathetic?" Kaz asked.

"*Oui!*" Ribot said. "We are not all Yves Fassier. Now the police will have their *honneur* again."

"Does Fassier feel the same way?" I asked.

"It does not matter. He is dead," Ribot said. "By the neck?"

"Hanged?" I said.

"Yes, yes. Hang-ed, as you say. Of his own making, with the sheet from the bed. Now, I must go. *Au revoir*."

"One more thing, Inspector," I said. "There are men watching Madame Fassier's house. Are they your men?"

"No. I will send officers to check. *Merci*."

"Suicide, really?" Kaz said as Ribot left.

"Maybe with *un peu* help," I said. "I don't think he'll be missed, but it would have been nice if he could have named his fellow collaborators."

"Much will be conveniently forgotten," Kaz said, "now that the French police have their honor back. And the Jews they rounded up have all been sent to death camps."

"What gives with the new orders?" I said, as soon as we were back in the jeep and clear of the crowd.

"We must pick up a French gentleman in Saint Christophe, about ten miles east of here, and return him to General Patton's headquarters."

"What? Are we a taxi service now? What about the phony pursuit of Lucien?"

"Big Mike says this is a high-priority task, according to Colonel Harding. We are closer to Saint-Christophe, so we must pick him up and Big Mike will meet us on the road back."

"This guy rates an escort? Who is he?"

"Big Mike said there could be no names over the radio. We are to meet an intelligence officer from the 4th Division in the town square. He's bringing this fellow in from the front," Kaz said. "Orders, what can we do?"

"Okay," I said, driving out of town. "At least this will be straight-forward. Then we can get back to not catching Lucien Fassier. Did you tell him about the motorcycle?"

"Yes, and I told him Rambouillet was his likely destination. He's alerting the MPs to watch for the motorcycle instead of the automobile, although he'd be a fool to go through a checkpoint when he could circle around cross-country."

"I wonder if he knows his father is dead," I said. "Or if he cares."

"You are still thinking about Yves?"

"I can't stop wondering why a son who evidently came around to his father's way of thinking didn't stop to see him," I said. "Especially knowing his execution was likely. His mother would have told him that."

"Perhaps Inspector Ribot lied," Kaz said, with little enthusiasm. Someone was lying, and someone was a traitor. I was beginning to think Fassier didn't fit the bill. But then why did he run? I let that one rumble around in my head while the road unwound before us.

Saint-Christophe was a small town gathered around a languid river and a small church opposite an ancient stone bridge. We spotted a truck and a jeep parked by the fountain in the center of town, GIs sitting on the stonework having a smoke. They told us our man was inside the truck.

"Major Hughes, Division G-2," a lanky officer said, jumping down from the back of the truck. "You Captain Boyle and Lieutenant Kazimierz?"

We agreed we were and Hughes signaled to a shadowy form inside the covered truck.

"Jean Gallois," the Frenchman said, jumping from the vehicle and shaking our hands with great fervor. He was sandy-haired and unshaven, dressed in a wrinkled, mud-stained suit he must have been wearing for days. There were bags under his eyes, but the pupils sparkled with energy and excitement. "I am chief of staff for the FFI in the greater Paris area. You will take me to General Eisenhower now?"

"We'll get you close," I said, casting a look toward Major Hughes.

"He checks out," Hughes said. "He's the real deal, just a couple of days out of Paris. Now get a move on, he's all yours."

"Any Kraut sightings around here?" I asked the major as we got back into the jeep.

"A few miles east, yeah. But Gallois made it through the lines, so they're spread thin. There're reports of German patrols and lots of lost units cut off and trying to find their way to the Seine. But organized opposition, no."

"We ran into an engineer company loaded down with explosives," I said. "Their orders were to report to the Paris commander."

"Then we must leave immediately," Gallois said, jamming himself into the rear of the jeep, beside the radio. "*S'il vous plaît.*"

"Hang on," I said, wheeling the jeep around and flooring it on the road out of town. It was dusk, but the long summer evening still left plenty of light to drive by. There might not be many Fritzes left wandering around, but I didn't see any reason to switch on headlights and tip off the ones that were.

"You've come from Paris," Kaz said, turning to speak to Gallois. "We just heard the police have gone on strike."

"Yes, and the Metro workers as well. Police forces are barricaded in the *Prefecture*, and the French flag is being hoisted throughout the city," he said. "But the situation is very dangerous. We need help."

"Who's in charge?" I asked, not wanting to get into what I knew of Uncle Ike's plans to skirt Paris, not liberate it.

"Colonel Rol," he said. "He is head of the FFI and controls all the armed forces in Paris. Not that we have that many arms. We need weapons, but most of all, we need Leclerc and his division to march on the city as soon as possible."

"Which is why you want to see General Eisenhower," I said.

"Of course. Already, many Germans are withdrawing from Paris. Most of the Gestapo left yesterday. Administrative units are leaving by the truckload. But there are still six thousand combat troops available to the commandant. And the engineering unit you mentioned worries me. He may be planning to blow up all the bridges over the Seine. It will be a disaster."

"Won't a battle in Paris be a disaster as well?" Kaz asked.

"Only if we waste time. A quick thrust would scatter the Germans before they dig in and destroy the bridges. And we have hundreds of fighters to strike at them as well. But you must hurry."

"I will," I said, pressing the accelerator to the floor. As for General Patton and Uncle Ike, they'd have to speak for themselves.

A few miles out, we saw Big Mike's jeep headed our way. He pulled over, turned around and waved as we passed. Jules craned his neck to check out our passenger.

"Ah, a young FTP fighter," Gallois said, spotting the FTP armband Jules wore. "Colonel Rol would be happy."

"He's FTP?" I asked.

"Yes. As are many of our fighters, even among the police," Gallois said.

"I assume that's his Resistance identity?" Kaz asked. "As is yours?"

"Yes, it would be far too dangerous for our families if our real names became known. Colonel Rol took his from a dear friend who was killed in Spain," Gallois said.

"Rol fought there?" I asked, sending a glance Kaz's way.

"Yes. Many of the FTP leaders did," Gallois said. "I think that is one reason they have fought so fiercely against the Germans. The Spanish Civil War hardened them."

"It was a war with many atrocities," Kaz said.

"As is this one," Gallois answered.

"Do you know an FTP leader named Lucien Fassier?" I asked, slowing to take a sharp curve. "He worked with a youth group."

"French Youth Action," Kaz added, when Gallois shook his head. "His Resistance name is Faucon."

"Ah, yes. Lucien Faucon. Very effective leader. He was sent to La Rochelle and then to Brittany to organize FTP youth groups. Has something happened?"

"We just met him at General Patton's headquarters," I said, avoiding the murders and the reason for the meeting. Gallois had a head of steam up and I didn't think the whole deception campaign would sit well with him, especially with his comrades rebelling against the Krauts in the very city the Allied High Command wanted to avoid. "He fought in Spain as well."

"Yes. There his *nom de guerre* was Harrier. A type of hawk," Gallois said.

"Another bird of prey, like the falcon," Kaz said.

"Harrier and then Faucon," I said. "I wonder why he changed it?"

"To confuse the *boche*, perhaps," Gallois said, leaning forward and grasping the back of my seat. "Our police certainly kept dossiers on those who crossed the border to fight in Spain. Too many such files found their way into the hands of the Gestapo."

"He does seem to favor birds who hunt their prey and attack quickly," Kaz said.

"Lucien had a reputation in Spain," Gallois said.

"For what?" Kaz asked.

"For doing what he was ordered to do. Some of us think the Party went too far in Spain, fighting amongst ourselves and our allies instead of against Franco and his fascists," Gallois said. "There were Russians everywhere, members of the NKVD." The Russian secret police.

"Are you saying he did their dirty work?" I asked.

"There was much of that, yes. Lucien Harrier was a fervent believer. He hated the anarchists as much as he did the fascists."

"But the anarchists fought against Franco," I said.

"Yes, well, the NKVD saw them as a threat," Gallois said, the admission of guilt and evil evident in the near-whisper nearly blown away on the breeze as we sped down the road.

"He was an enforcer," Kaz said. "An executioner. Which was why he didn't use his old *nom de guerre*?"

"It was a terrible war," Gallois said, avoiding the question and answering it at the same time. We rode in silence for a few miles, the darkening sky matching the mood.

"We have also met Raymond Louvet of *Corps Franc Nord*. He was a policeman who hunted those going over to Spain," Kaz said, turning back in his seat as he talked to Gallois.

"Yes, I know Louvet," he said, snapping out of whatever reverie had quieted him. "A good man. He did his duty then and does so now, even if he supports de Gaulle and his people in London."

"What do your people think of de Gaulle?" I asked.

"He gives fine speeches on the radio. From London," Gallois said. "But the war is here. The FTP fights, and many of us die. I fear de Gaulle expects to be anointed once he sets foot in a free Paris."

"What about Louvet?" Kaz asked. "He seemed very anti-Communist. Do you trust him?"

"I do," Gallois said. "Louvet may not favor the politics of the FTP, but we fight shoulder to shoulder with him. I respect that."

"Marcel Jarnac?" I asked. "He and Louvet seemed to get along well, although there was some tension between them."

"Jarnac is on the *Front national* executive committee," Gallois said. "Another veteran of Spain. He and Louvet were on opposite sides back then, but there is no hatred between them. We know that Louvet had to follow orders, and that France backed the non-intervention treaty. Every man did what he had to do. And women too. Jarnac lost his wife in Spain. But tell me, where did you meet all these people?"

"Our boss is responsible for liaison with Resistance groups," I said. "All in a day's work." I could hardly tell him we'd met them all within the last twenty-four hours as part of a major con job we were pulling on the Resistance.

It was dark when we pulled into Third Army HQ and found Colonel Harding waiting for us. We handed Gallois over to the Intelligence honchos who came streaming out of the château and surrounded the Frenchman. He took time to thank us and shake our hands before heading off. He gave me a look as he grasped mine, and I was afraid he'd felt the tremor against his own palm. But he said nothing, the look vanishing in the excitement of the moment.

I wished him luck, thinking about those high explosives in the hands of German engineers in the City of Light.

It was the Parisians who'd need the luck.

CHAPTER THIRTEEN

"SORRY TO BRING you boys all the way back here," Colonel Harding said, as we sat down to hot chow in the mess tent. All of us except Jules, who'd gone off to see if there was any news of Marie-Claire. The late-night grub was corned-beef hash topped with a fried egg, and it tasted like a rich man's meal at the Ritz.

"Gallois is that important?" I asked, pausing with a forkful of hash at my lips.

"Important, dangerous, it all depends," Harding said.

"If the uprising in Paris continues, it could be a disaster," Kaz said.

"In more ways than one," Harding said. "Right now, de Gaulle is against the uprising, and he's trying to halt it any way he can."

"Whyszat?" Big Mike said, chewing on a fistful of bread.

"Because if the uprising succeeds, the FTP will be in control," Kaz said. "Communists."

"Exactly," Harding agreed. "They want a seat at the table when a new government is formed. The policy of the Allies is to install a military government until things stabilize. Of course, de Gaulle is against both of those approaches and insists he alone is the head of state."

"If I get this right, Ike and de Gaulle don't want an uprising,"

I said. "So, the people actually fighting the Nazis are the ones out of line."

"When you mix politics and strategy, there's no telling where things will end up," Harding said.

"Then there is the matter of French honor," Kaz said. "Both the Resistance fighters in Paris and de Gaulle are eager to reclaim it by liberating their capital. It is their holy grail."

"The situation is fluid," Harding said, nodding to Jules who joined us, his plate laden with hash. "And very critical."

"Which is why you pulled us off the search to bring Gallois here?" I said.

"Yes. I needed him brought here quickly and quietly. You understand the need for secrecy, Jules?" Harding asked, as the young man dug into his food.

"*Oui*, Colonel. I have kept many secrets, and the name you mentioned, I have already forgotten," Jules said, smiling as he chewed. He'd obviously had no news of Marie-Claire.

"Good. Now that you've delivered Gallois, I need you back on the search. We have to find Fassier, and you are the only ones who have even gotten close," Harding said, giving a quick glance at Jules to remind us of the charade.

"Colonel, we need some sleep," I said, not happy with the notion of driving in the dark all night.

"You'll get it. There's a truck loaded with sleeping rolls. You can grab some shuteye on the way to Rambouillet. I have drivers for your jeeps, and you ought to be there before dawn."

"Isn't that in German hands?" Kaz asked.

"Reports are they've pulled out. There's been a few FFI patrols through the town and everything's quiet. Now finish up and get a move on."

Jules was the only one excited by the news. It was a great adventure for him, tooling around with Big Mike and eating army chow. Kaz looked bushed, his complexion pale in the dim lantern light. He popped a pill and rubbed his eyes. I was worried about that headache of his. I kept my thoughts to myself and my right hand in my lap.

We finished the meal quickly, and Jules sped off to check one more time for news of Marie-Claire. Harding motioned for us to remain as the kid left.

"I have a gut feeling things might change quickly," he said.

"You mean if Gallois is successful?" Kaz asked.

"Yes. If he gets Patton on his side, there's no telling what SHAEF may do," Harding said in a low whisper. "I can't say I like the idea of leaving the Paris Resistance in the lurch, and I suspect others may feel the same, even if it doesn't make strategic sense."

"What's that mean for us?" I said.

"There's a message ready to be sent out to SOE agents in Paris in case we decide to support the uprising. The Resistance has been begging for weapons drops near Paris for weeks now, and the SOE has held off. But if this turns into a real battle, they're ready to go," Harding said. "I'll radio you the same message if it happens. That means stop Fassier at all costs."

"Because with Gallois in play, there's an actual chance Leclerc's French troops will be the ones to fight their way into Paris," I said. Harding nodded, his mouth set in a grim line.

"Jesus, Sam," Big Mike said. "We never figured on this."

"That's the problem with deception," Harding said, slamming his palm on the table. "It has to be real enough to be believable."

"What is the message?" Kaz asked, his eyelids heavy with fatigue.

"Two lines from a poem," Harding said. "You know Rimbaud, of course?" There was no pretending that question had been addressed to me or Big Mike.

"Not quite to my taste, but yes, I know his work," Kaz said. "Arthur Rimbaud, a poet of the last century. Fiery, died young."

"*The moonlight when the hell struck twelve. The devil's in the tower right now,*" Harding said, adding almost apologetically, "it's from something called 'Hellish Night.'"

"Sounds it," Big Mike said.

"When you hear the first line, it means it's likely we will move hard on Paris. The second line is the confirmation," Harding said.

"So, we stop Fassier when you send the second line," Big Mike said.

"No. When hell strikes twelve, you stop him. Dead in his tracks," Harding said.

Kaz laughed. It was so unexpected, we all looked at him, wondering why he found that amusing.

"No," Kaz said, laughing even more as he took in the looks we gave him. "No, I don't find that funny at all. I just recalled another line from Rimbaud. *Life is the farce we are all forced to endure.*" He laughed some more, but it wasn't the kind of laughter you wanted to join in with. Frantic, almost crazed. I looked away.

"Hell, Sam, why didn't you pick a nice poem? Like one by that guy who writes about the woods and stone walls? Normal stuff," Big Mike said. "Robert Frost, that's the guy."

"We're in France," Harding said. "It seemed like a good idea to pick a French poet."

"A poet who died young," Kaz said, and laughed some more. This time I joined in, even though the joke might end up being on us.

"Colonel," I said, as we walked to the vehicle park. "I'm beginning to wonder if we're chasing the wrong guy."

"He ran," Harding said. "No one else did."

"Things just aren't adding up," I said, and told him about Lucien's father, Yves. "Estranged or not, if your old man was about to be executed, wouldn't you try to intervene, especially if it turned out you were both on the same side?"

"It's the losing side," Harding said. "Maybe he didn't think it would do any good."

"But he could have said his farewells and he didn't. He was a stone's throw away from the jail, and he just left town. That tells me he still held a helluva grudge against his father. Or he was there for some other reason and didn't give a good goddamn about his jailbird *père*."

"You and your father are close, aren't you, Boyle?"

"Sure," I said. "The whole family is."

"Not all fathers are the same. That goes for families too. Don't read too much into it."

"Okay," I said. "But maybe you could dig a little deeper into Lucien. Did you know he fought in Spain under a different name? He was known as Harrier and had a reputation as an enforcer for the Stalinists."

"I'll see what I can find out," Harding said as we approached the truck. Our jeeps were being topped off with fuel as GIs tossed wool blankets and sleeping bags in the canvas-covered rear of the truck. "But remember, it's hard to get info on these Resistance people, especially veterans of the Spanish Civil War. They've been hiding their identities for years."

"Exactly," I said. "What do we really know about them?"

"Get some sleep," Harding said, giving me a pat on the shoulder. "Then find Lucien Fassier."

A few minutes later we were riding along in the deuce-and-a-half truck, trying to sleep on bedrolls and scratchy wool blankets as we rolled down the main road, following our two jeeps. Jules had brought along a bottle of wine, and we passed that around for a while. Kaz laughed now and then, for no reason that we could explain to Jules, who took it all in stride.

Farce wasn't too far from it.

I AWOKE WITH the dry taste of red wine fermenting on my tongue. The truck had braked, sending me sliding into Big Mike, who barely noticed as he sawed logs, stretched out on his sleeping bag.

"We're here, Captain," the driver said, slapping the side of the truck. I saw by the luminous dial on my watch it was five thirty, or *oh-five-thirty* the way the army liked to say it.

Kaz stretched himself awake and Jules popped up with ridiculous ease. Big Mike gave a final snort as I kicked his boot and jumped down from the truck. The guys who'd driven our jeeps took our places and the truck rumbled off, leaving us in the town square with a thin slit of dawning light showing along the road that led east. To Paris.

"What now?" Kaz asked, as we stood by our jeep. "Knock on doors and wake up the good people of Rambouillet?"

"Coffee," Big Mike said, as he shuffled over to his jeep. He pulled a thermos from a knapsack and poured us all some hot joe. After a few sips, the fuzzy feeling in my mouth started to subside. "We can check in with the FFI down the road. I think it's Louvet's group. There's a crossroads to the south, and it's the furthest FFI outpost."

"Check in with Harding first," I said. "Let's see if we have any sightings."

"Then speak with the *Police Municipale*," Kaz said, looking at a nearby building with its blue-and-white sign and windows spilling light out onto the street.

Across the square lights appeared at the windows of a hotel, a three-story granite affair with a steep, dark-tiled roof. It was probably the staff preparing breakfast and brewing fresh coffee. A small-town hotel was always a good place to gather intelligence. But so were the cops, even though they wouldn't be serving pastries.

Big Mike was working the radio, so I told Jules to stick with him while Kaz and I spoke with the *gendarmes*. We slugged down the cooling coffee and made for the station. Rambouillet was a fairly big town, not quite a city but more than a village. The local cops were housed on a corner, in a squat building several stories high and covered in flaking mustard-colored stucco.

Inside, a narrow hallway led to an empty desk.

Slamming doors and shouts echoed through the building, followed by a flurry of footsteps down a stairway hidden from view. I heard a car start up around back as two uniformed cops dashed by us, muttering apologies and flying out the door.

Meurtre, one of them had said. Murder was a good reason to empty out a police station just before dawn. We walked out after them, catching sight of the cop car turning a corner with the two cops on foot giving chase.

"If we are going to talk to the police, we should go to the police," Kaz said, with impeccable logic. I signaled Big Mike, who'd taken notice of the tumult, and we trailed the cops as Jules stayed with the jeep. Turning the corner, we saw the car pulled over in front of a narrow two-story house halfway down the block, headlights illuminating the open door. Two cops in the street were talking with a man dressed in a blue worker's jacket and a wool cap. Flashlights blazed within the house as the other policemen stomped through it. Finally, one of the cops took notice of Kaz and me and asked what our business was.

Kaz spoke with him, mentioning the name of Fassier's friend, Charles Marchand. The cop's eyes narrowed at the mention of Marchand and he told Kaz to wait a moment. He whispered to his partner, who moved closer to us, one hand resting on the butt of his holstered revolver. The first cop went inside as our guard motioned for the man in the wool cap to move on.

I didn't like the looks of this.

Kaz took a few steps on the sidewalk and stared at the nameplate by the door. Under the German occupation, all French homes had been required to post a list of residents by the entrance. This sign bore one name. Kaz motioned me closer. I squinted to read it in the harsh glare of the headlights.

Charles Marchand.

No wonder the cop was watching us like a couple of thugs. If we weren't armed, he probably would've handcuffed us but instead he kept a steely eye trained on our slung weapons. Kaz began to chat with him, and his perfectly accented French seemed to thaw out the *gendarme*.

"It seems a fellow on his way to work saw the door to this house wide open. He knew Charles Marchand and called inside to see if everything was alright. He found Marchand dead in the sitting room, then used the telephone to call the police," Kaz said.

"They didn't detain him for questioning?" I said.

"No, they know him well, and besides, there was much blood. The fellow had none on him, except on the soles of his feet," Kaz said. "He says his superiors will want to know why we came here. A detective from the *police judiciaire* is on his way."

"Judicial police?" I said.

"Yes. In France, they are separate from the regular uniformed police. They operate out of the prosecutor's office," Kaz said.

"Have you been arrested in France? You seem to know a lot about it."

"There was an indiscretion in Marseilles once, but all was forgiven," he said, as a black Citroën Traction Avant pulled up to the curb. A young plainclothes cop jumped out from behind the wheel and opened the rear door. Out stepped a tall, gaunt man with a graying goatee and a sharp eye that took in the scene before him.

"We were expecting General Leclerc and his tanks," he said. "Not a lone American and *un officier polonais* so far from home."

"Sorry, sir, I can't tell you anything about General Leclerc," I said. "We're here looking for someone."

"So I understand, and I hear he is now lying dead upon his

parlor carpet. Please remain here, gentlemen, while I acquaint myself with the situation. *Inspecteur* Giles Dufort, at your service."

Kaz responded, giving our names and dressing it all up in a lot of French politeness. Perhaps picking up on Dufort's aristocratic bearing, he tossed in a reference to his title as a baron of the Augustus clan, and there was an exchange of slight, almost apologetic bows, as if it was bad form to mention it so close to a cooling body.

As Dufort made for the door, an officer rushed out, shoving him aside, and promptly retched in the gutter.

"*Un corps,*" he muttered, spitting out flecks of vomit. "*Un autre corps.*"

"It seems we have a rather distressing second corpse," Dufort said to us, with the calmness that comes from years of viewing what human beings do to one another. "You must remain here, do you understand?"

Kaz said he did, which was good enough for the inspector, who didn't bother asking me.

"I think we have gotten *Monsieur* Marchand killed," I said. "And maybe Lucien Fassier as well."

"How?" Kaz asked.

"Yesterday in Beaulieu, we learned about Marchand," I said.

"From the servant girl," Kaz said. "But if she told anyone else, that is not our fault."

"No, but we talked about it on the street while people were coming out of the café and celebrating. There was someone watching the Fassier residence, and they could have tailed us there and blended in with the crowd. While we were babysitting Gallois, they headed here, found Marchand, and killed him along with his houseguest."

"We don't know it's Fassier," Kaz said.

"I do."

"How?" Kaz asked.

"He was tortured for being a traitor. Cops don't puke like that unless it's something really bad. This is more than another double homicide."

Dufort stepped outside. I had him pegged for an experienced guy, maybe fifty plus a few years, which meant he'd seen a thing or two. His mouth hung open, and his face had gone pale. He shook a Gauloises from a pack and lit up, inhaling the strong tobacco like a soothing drug.

"This is a bad business, my friends," he said. "You must tell me everything you know."

"We're tracking a possible double agent," I said, figuring this fit well enough with the deception plan. "A man called Lucien Fassier, originally from Beaulieu, where his father was the chief of the municipal police."

"Yes, Yves Fassier," Dufort said. "Why do you say he *was* the chief?"

"Because he was arrested after the village was liberated and thrown in his own jail. Yesterday, he hung himself. Or somebody helped him end it all," I said.

"Interesting," Dufort said. "Few will miss him, now that the *boche* have gone. But what does that have to do with his son?"

"We learned in Beaulieu that Lucien had come here to hide. He's on his way to Paris with documents he had stolen from General Patton's headquarters," I said. I gave him a quick rundown on what had happened, and said we needed to view the murder scene.

"When did you arrive?" Dufort asked, a glimmer of suspicion in his question. I would have wondered about us too.

"Twenty minutes ago," I said. "We went straight to the police station to ask for help locating Charles Marchand and found everyone running here. Listen, Inspector, I was a detective myself before the war. I know this looks odd, but there are a lot of other people who were upset with Fassier. Resistance people."

"There have been armed groups about since yesterday," Dufort said. "Everyone is talking about the Allies taking Paris, with Leclerc and his men in the lead. But all I have seen are men and women with FFI armbands and the two of you, of course."

"Inspector, if you'd allow us inside, we need to determine if Fassier had a document with him. A map showing the planned advance into Paris," I said.

"Very well," Dufort said, grinding out the cigarette with his heel. "Prepare yourselves."

We entered the building, greeted by a narrow hallway and a sitting room on our right. Marchand lay on the floor, his feet sticking out into the hall. His chest was stained with dried blood, the carpet beneath his back soaked in it.

"Whoever is responsible did little to hide it," Dufort said. "The door was left open and Marchand's feet were visible from the street."

"My guess is he opened the door for the killer," I said. "Then he was pushed back, a knife run through his ribs, and left there."

"While the others searched for Fassier," Kaz said. Dufort gave him a quizzical look. "There had to be others, since Fassier would be quick to run at the first sign of trouble. He survived the Spanish Civil War and the Occupation, which means he was adept at survival."

"Ah," Dufort said. "He was with the FTP then?"

"Yes. I don't think they treat turncoats lightly," I said.

"No, the Communists are willing to spill blood, theirs and everyone else's. As you shall see. Come," he said, walking along the hall and pushing open a door. A single bare bulb lit a series of steep, uneven steps leading to a basement. He ducked his head, and even Kaz had to do the same in the cramped passageway.

Thick wooden beams carried the weight of the house above our heads. Shadows played across the cellar as we passed in front of the swinging light bulb. Something was hung from the rafter, something that once had been human.

That something had been Lucien Fassier.

Wire bound his wrists, his arms strung up behind his back, shoulders at a terrible angle. They'd been dislocated, his screams muffled by the rag gagging his mouth. His cheeks and lips were cut in several places, blood staining his clothes and dripping onto the hard-packed dirt floor. His feet were bound tightly by the wire, his trousers down around his ankles. Oddly, his eyes weren't marred or swollen shut.

My own eyes adjusted to the gloom, my mind trying to make sense of what I saw.

His genitals were gone, cut away and left in a small pile of red gore beneath his feet.

Kaz stumbled back, grabbing the wall for support as he took in the scene of torture. I stood my ground, my cop's pride on display, as I worked to stifle my rising gorge. I had to work the scene. One of the lessons Dad drummed into me was that a detective can't allow his emotions to get away from him, at least not at a crime scene or an autopsy. There was too much information to take in, and a guy who was swooning from the blood and guts was bound to miss something.

Later, he always said. *Later, at Kirby's Tavern, we can talk about it over a drink. But for now, focus. Focus on finding traces the killer left behind.*

"The gag tells me the killer wanted to take his time," I said. "And that he didn't need Fassier to say anything. This wasn't torture in order to obtain information. This was torture for its own sake. Revenge?"

"What do you make of the eyes?" Dufort said, studying me as I looked at the ruined corpse.

"He left them alone so Fassier could see what was coming. So he could see his killer clearly," I said, grasping why they'd been left unmarked. The area around the eyes can't take much bruising without swelling shut. "This was personal."

"Yes. Marchand was killed quickly and cleanly, because he was in the way. With Fassier, the killer took his time. There may have been other *complices*, but this was the work of one man. A man who desired that Fassier should suffer greatly," Dufort said.

"We need to search him," I said. Kaz, who was no stranger to blood, edged even farther away, grabbing the railing for support.

"You may," Dufort said. "But without moving the body. The coroner must examine it first, and he is known to take his time."

"Kaz, would you tell Big Mike to radio Harding? He needs to know what happened," I said. Kaz nodded weakly, and I was glad of the excuse to get him out of this awful cellar. Once he was upstairs, Dufort and I bent to our work.

Searching Fassier's trousers was unpleasant, the stench of what he voided mingling with the coppery, brittle smell of drying blood. Scratch unpleasant. It was repulsive. But nothing was in his pockets. His worn jacket held nothing either.

"His pockets weren't turned out," I said as we both backed away from the corpse. "It doesn't look like he was searched."

"My men are searching the house now," Dufort said, motioning to the stairs. "I think there is nothing else for us here."

I looked around the small space, almost empty except for spindly old chairs and a few tools, all covered with thick cobwebs. There was nothing to be found here except dust going to dust.

Upstairs, the place was being tossed by the uniformed cops and Dufort's young partner. A back door leading out of the kitchen showed signs of having been kicked in, splintered wood scattered on the tile floor. They'd come in hard at the rear, after Fassier had been alerted by the attack on Marchand.

"How many?" Dufort asked, sensing my thoughts.

"Someone to get Marchand to open the door," I said. "Maybe someone he trusted. A local? Then the guy with the knife, and another at the rear to block any escape."

"I would say their leader was a fourth. This was a well-planned operation, accomplished swiftly without attracting attention," Dufort said. "Whoever tortured Fassier made certain of that."

It made sense. The killer wanted Fassier all for himself, and based on what I'd seen, he'd want to be sure his quarry didn't get away. We continued through the house. Two bedrooms and a small bath upstairs yielding nothing but the debris of everyday life. Dirty laundry, a threadbare suit hanging in an armoire, and rough, yellowing sheets on a bed covered by quilts sprouting feathers out of tiny holes.

Downstairs, the nicest room in Marchand's place was opposite the kitchen and sitting room, a comfortable study where officers flipped through books and tossed them on the floor like so much garbage. Others pulled out desk drawers and rummaged through papers, flicking through documents once important enough to file and save, now nothing more than wastepaper.

I tested floorboards for loose slats, looked on the underside of drawers, rustled through the cold ashes in the grate, and helped one of the cops take cheap prints out of picture frames. Nothing.

"Marchand was a teacher," Dufort told me, after a conversation with his partner. "Forty-one years of age, unmarried, and possessed of poor lungs, which kept him from being sent for forced labor to Germany by the *Service du travail obligatoire*." The STO was a Vichy outfit that did the Krauts' work for them, rounding up Frenchmen for what amounted to slave labor. They were the best recruiting tool the Resistance could have hoped for. Thousands had taken to the woods and mountains to avoid their roundups. "He survived illness and the Occupation only to be slain because he gave shelter to the even more unfortunate Lucien Fassier. Tell me, what was their connection?"

"They attended university together in Paris," I said. "We believe Fassier was on his way there with the map."

"His pursuers knew this as well?" Dufort said, his eyebrow raised.

"We learned about it from a girl who works in his mother's house," I said. "They may have done the same, or we could have been overheard talking about it. We were detained, so they got here ahead of us."

"Unfortunate for these two men," Dufort said, idly kicking a book out of the way as we left the study. He had another chat with his partner, and then motioned me to follow him outside. I didn't mind leaving that sad and terrible house one bit.

Kaz had driven the jeep out front. The sun was up, casting long shadows in the street as people gathered around the police car. He looked paler than ever.

"Are you okay?" I asked in a low voice, not wanting to embarrass him. Cops are taught to act tough around scenes like that, but Kaz, after all, was still basically an academic at heart.

"Yes, I am fine," he said, with a weak smile.

"I have more questions for you, gentlemen," Dufort said, lighting another cigarette. "But let us find some refreshment. Follow me please, the Hôtel du Grand Veneur is around the corner."

His partner opened the car door for him and Dufort folded himself in, not looking back. It was nicely worded, and it sounded like there'd be coffee, but it was still an order. We followed the Citroën to the hotel; the same one we'd been left next to when the truck dropped us off.

That seemed like ages ago.

CHAPTER FOURTEEN

BIG MIKE AND Jules had driven off in search of higher ground, unable to raise Colonel Harding or anyone else on the radio network. Kaz and I sat at an outdoor table with Inspector Dufort, the day warming as the sun crept over the rooftops. His junior partner lounged against the Citroën, smoking and watching both vehicles. Dufort had told us to leave our weapons in the jeep, and we'd obediently stashed the Thompson and the Sten gun away.

More civilized, he said. Easier to cuff us, as well, if need be.

Dufort ordered and settled back in his chair with a sigh.

"This is not how I imagined the arrival of the Allies, my friends," he said. "The rumors fly about General Leclerc, but all we see is a dead Communist and you two. It is very strange. Tell me more about Fassier's treachery, and those who knew about it."

"It began early yesterday," I said, giving him the cover story about the meeting at Patton's HQ. "There was some shelling, and Fassier took advantage of the confusion to steal a top-secret map. In the process, he killed another FTP leader and an American intelligence officer."

"You were given the task of tracking him down?" Dufort asked.

"Yes. His description was also sent out to the Military Police," I said.

"FFI units assigned to protect important crossroads," Kaz

added, "also knew of Fassier and were on the lookout. He left his automobile with FFI markings in Beaulieu and took a motorcycle here."

"Where, through either your unwitting assistance or from the serving girl, he was found out," Dufort said. "Leaving me with the troublesome murder of a local resident as well as a victim of the *épuration sauvage.*"

The wild purge. We'd heard the term before. Revenge and retribution unleashed by the French as the Germans pulled out ahead of the imposition of a legal government. Old scores were settled under the guise of *la liberation*, most of them having to do with the war, some of them using the Occupation as an excuse.

The wild purge left men like Inspector Dufort with little recourse to investigate the numerous armed bands, some of them no more than mobs, acting in the absence of any legal restraints. The Germans with their iron-fisted control were gone. The Vichy state was discredited, and the fascist *Milice* had retreated with their Kraut pals. No one knew if the Allies were going to run France, or let de Gaulle set up shop. Or if the Communists with their powerful FTP army would declare themselves in charge, especially if they held Paris.

"It will be difficult to bring a murder charge against a *résistant* executing a traitor," Kaz said. The waiter appeared and set down three large cups of coffee. *Café au lait*, the way the French liked it, good joe swimming in steamed milk. Then plates of rolls, butter, and jam.

By unspoken consent, we feasted for a few minutes before continuing.

"Better," Dufort said. "I have always found murders to be discovered at inconvenient times. Is it that way in America, Captain Boyle?"

"The call always seems to come at the end of a shift," I said. "Or just before."

"Shift? Oh, yes, I see. Indeed, it is not my practice to begin the day so early. So, tell me. Who are the others in pursuit of Fassier?"

I went over the list. Marcel Jarnac, a member of the *Front national* executive committee, the political wing of the FTP. Olga Rassinier of the FTP *Main-d'œuvre immigrée*, the collection of immigrants and escapees from Nazi-controlled areas fighting in France. Raymond Louvet, leader of the Gaullist Resistance group, *Corps Franc Nord*. Emilie and Father Matteu of the Catholic *la Croix* network. And of course, Jules Herbert, who was with us. I told him about Bernard Dujardin and Sean McKuras, who'd been Fassier's victims.

"Those are the main leaders who were present at the meeting," Kaz said. "But they all had fighters with them. It could be anyone. No one appreciates a turncoat, but the Communists especially will go to great lengths to punish anyone who betrays the Party."

"Yes, yes," Dufort said. "But I think this was a betrayal of more than political beliefs. You saw what was done." He spooned jam onto his bread and bit into it eagerly. My stomach turned, and I looked at Kaz, who'd gone pale again. Was Dufort taunting us?

"Raymond Louvet is manning a roadblock just south of here," I said. "We could start with him."

"Perhaps," Dufort said, sipping his coffee. "But to make an arrest, I will need more. More men, more weapons. The FFI now operates in the open and is very well armed, thanks to the British dropping supplies throughout the countryside." He ground out his cigarette in the ashtray and finished the last of his coffee. "You mentioned the Saint-Just Brigade. They are FTP too, and the most extreme of all the groups. They would be a good place to start. And the woman, Olga. Is it not possible she was used to gain entrance to Marchand's house? There are many armed women in the FFI, but men still can be gullible in their presence. Or Emilie, the Catholic? One never knows."

"What do you mean, exactly?" Kaz said.

"I mean that you must find out who the murderer is. I will arrest the killer for taking the life of Charles Marchand, have no doubt. But I cannot get involved in a war with the FFI. That, I can only lose."

"We're both after the same thing," I said. "If we find the map, we find the killer."

"The map is your concern," Dufort said, shaking a smoke out of his pack and tapping it on the table to pack down the tobacco. "The killer is mine. And if you do not find him, Captain Boyle and Lieutenant Kazimierz of Supreme Headquarters, I will charge both of you with this murder and bring charges against you to your superiors. Am I clear?" He struck a match and watched us as he lit up and snuffed out the match.

"I understand you," I said. I sure did. Dufort was a wily guy, and he was handing off a hot potato to us. Nothing personal, but he needed leverage. Maybe the charges would come to nothing, or maybe they'd prove an embarrassment to the Allies. Which could mean there'd be a scapegoat, and I could tell who he had in mind for that job.

"Very well. Head for the *police judiciaire,* by the monument you passed coming into town. If you go left at the monument, you will come to the crossroads where Louvet and his men are," Dufort said, rising and dropping some coins on the table. "*Bonne journée.*"

"If I did not feel somewhat responsible for what happened to Marchand, I would be tempted to call his bluff," Kaz said, nibbling at a piece of bread.

"We're supposed to solve cases and make things easier for General Eisenhower," I said. "Getting involved in murder charges would not make anything easier for him." Or me, I should have added. Uncle Ike was such a straight arrow he'd make sure no special favors were granted to a relative in hot water.

"Then we proceed as normal," Kaz said. "We can radio Big Mike and have him meet us at the crossroads. If the killer has possession of the map, he may be headed for the German lines. We should find out where they are exactly."

"You fellas looking for Germans?" A figure slouched in the doorway, a cigarette dangling from his lips. He was an older guy in a billed cap, wearing GI khakis with a *US War Correspondent* arched patch on his shoulder.

"Looking to stay away from 'em," I said. "Who are you, pal?"

"Name's Ernie Pyle," he said, taking a seat. "What are you guys doing this far forward?"

"Ernie Pyle? The reporter?" I said. "My folks read all your columns. They're always asking why I don't get my name in print."

"Hey, we can fix that," Pyle said, pulling a notebook from his pocket. "Give me your names and tell me what you're doing here. Might be an interesting story."

"No, sorry, I shouldn't have said it that way. I wasn't asking for a mention," I said, backpedaling as fast as I could. The last thing we needed was a newspaperman in on this.

"We are lost, my friend is afraid to admit," Kaz said, turning on the charm. "It would be most embarrassing if word got out. That is why we were wondering about Germans. Are there any here?"

"Been nothing but reporters holed up in the hotel, and a bunch of crazy FFI types careening through the streets for the past two days. I've been waiting here to ride into Paris with General Leclerc, but where is he? I'm ready to pull up stakes. You boys have any idea what's happening?"

"Not a clue," I said. True enough. "But what about Krauts? Are they close?"

"Last I heard, there's an anti-tank gun dug in down the road a mile or so. Camouflaged in some trees, they say. Plus, a machine gun nest. They shot up an FFI car that got too close yesterday, so I don't recommend the direct approach."

"What about patrols?"

"I sure hope not," Pyle said. "I'd hate to be rousted out of bed by the German who had my room before me. I drank his schnapps. But if you want the latest dope, check back here tonight. Hemingway and his gang will have plenty to say. Some of it even true."

"Hemingway?" Kaz asked.

"The writer," Pyle said. "Ernest Hemingway. Big guy with a beard and pistol on his belt. You can't miss him. Booming voice and a bottle at hand."

"What gang?" I asked.

"Well, to hear him tell it, he's been authorized by the army to organize a force of fifis and gather intelligence. He's got a driver and some fool of an OSS officer along with him, and the local Resistance people love him. He's brought in jeeps loaded with arms and uniforms, God knows where from."

"But isn't he a war correspondent, like you?" I asked. "I thought you were prohibited from carrying weapons."

"Tell that to Hemingway. He claims since he only writes one column a month for *Collier's*, the rest of the time he's free to ply his trade as a guerilla fighter. He convinced the army, but I can't say the Germans would buy his story," Pyle said. "Anyway, drop by tonight. Before he gets really sloshed."

"When's that?" I asked.

"Oh, it's probably too late already," Pyle said with a grin. "See you boys in the funny papers."

"Funny papers?" Kaz asked as Pyle ambled away.

"The comic section of the newspaper," I said. "It kinda means he finds us laughable."

"Ah, I see," Kaz said, filing away another piece of American slang. "I think I know why he said that." He motioned in the direction of our jeep, where Pyle was giving our radio setup the once-over. After all, it's hard to get lost with a two-way radio in the back seat.

CHAPTER FIFTEEN

WE HEADED OUT down the road, leaving Ernie Pyle scribbling in his notebook, hoping he was as mystified at our presence as we were. Kaz radioed Big Mike, giving him our destination. We turned at the monument in front of the police station as instructed by Dufort, following the winding road through a small village hemmed in by thick stands of fir trees. I had to downshift to get the jeep up a steep hill, the gravel roadbed rutted and narrow.

We crested the ridge and came to the crossroads. Our road crossed a lane running along the hill, where a few houses huddled together, tucked under tall pines. The view was dramatic, stretching for miles in front of us, looking over farmland and pastures to the east, toward Paris itself.

There was a more surprising view as well. A gaggle of fifis gathered around a table and chairs set out by the door of one of the houses. Louvet, Jarnac, Olga, and Emilie looked up at us, hardly bothering to hide their good cheer as they drank champagne from mismatched glasses.

"What's the celebration all about?" I asked as I got out of the jeep.

"We have heard that Lucien Faucon has been found," Emilie said, draining her glass. "And that justice has been served."

"I never saw more bloody justice done," I said.

"We do not know the details," Jarnac said. "One of the *gendarmes* informed us not too long ago. A bad business, then?"

"Was it an FTP member who told you?" Kaz asked, not bothering to get out of his seat.

"What if it was?" Olga said. "Even those who serve the capitalist state can believe in the unity of the working classes."

"Oh, it may mean nothing," Kaz said with a diffident wave of his hand. "Or it may mean that someone on the police force knew Lucien was hiding there and informed his killers."

"Come, my friend, do not worry yourselves over this traitor," Jarnac said. "Have a drink with us."

"Was Charles Marchand a traitor?" I asked, watching for a reaction.

"Who?" Emilie asked. It was blank stares all around.

"The teacher who Lucien was staying with," I said. "He was murdered as well. But at least he hadn't been tortured like Lucien. Marchand died quickly. With Lucien Fassier, it took longer. He was kept alive as they cut off his genitals."

Emilie gasped. Louvet looked confused. Olga whispered a translation, but his stone face gave away nothing.

"Harboring a fascist traitor deserves a death sentence, I think," Jarnac said. "But perhaps one not quite so brutal. Tell me, did you find the map?"

"No," I said, studying their faces. Only Emilie had the grace to look stunned at the news of torture. Jarnac leaned close to Louvet, filling him in on what I'd said. Across the road, about a dozen of Louvet's *Corps Franc Nord* were dug in around a German machine gun covering the road. At least someone was doing their job around here.

"Louvet says if the map was not found, Fassier may already have handed it off to a contact," Jarnac said. "Have the *gendarmes* searched the house?"

"Thoroughly," I said. "If that's the case, the map may already be in Paris."

"Perhaps not," Emilie said, rising from her chair as if the company had become distasteful. "There have been German patrols everywhere, and they have a number of well-hidden flak cannon covering the roads. We lost fighters yesterday to them."

"Yes, the *boche* shoot at anything," Olga said. "There are not many of them to our front, but their positions are carefully camouflaged. Louvet learned that yesterday when he sent out patrols to keep Fassier contained if he were in Rambouillet. It will be no problem when Leclerc's tanks arrive, but until then . . ." She sighed, her gaze fixed on the faraway, dangerous hills.

"So why are you all here?" I asked.

"You have caught us out, Captain Boyle," Jarnac said. "We agreed to meet here to pool resources in the hunt for Fassier. Then we heard he had already been dealt with. So, we celebrate, eh? The good people of this house hid their wine well, but we know a thing or two about hiding, do we not?" He poured another round for everyone, asking Kaz and me again if we'd join them.

We declined.

They assured us all the roadblocks were still defended, and that their hunt had not taken any fighters away from their duty. And they asked again, where was Leclerc?

It was easy to feign ignorance.

I got out the binoculars and walked to where Louvet's men were dug in. The hilltops were swathed in trees, while the fields below were bare but for grasses and crops. Good positions for the dreaded German 88mm Flak gun, which could punch holes in our Sherman tanks. Which wasn't all that hard to do. Tankers had taken to calling them Ronsons, after the cigarette lighter, because they lit up so easily.

I searched the horizon, spotting a dark hulk that I thought might be a Ronson. As I focused the binoculars, I saw it was a burned-out automobile. I pointed it out to Kaz, who asked the *résistants* about it.

"An unfortunate encounter between an FTP patrol and a German machine gun nest," Kaz said, translating as three guys told the story at the same time. "Men of the Saint-Just Brigade went down that road even though they were warned of the danger. They were in high spirits, talking of Paris."

"They jumped the gun," I said.

"No, Billy, the machine gun jumped them," Kaz said, in perfect seriousness. There were occasional gaps in his understanding of American idioms.

"I mean as in a footrace," I said, "taking off before the starting pistol is fired."

"Ah, yes, I see. They jumped the gun indeed. They were foolish to think they could get to Paris," he said.

"Might have been a case of too much wine and not enough common sense," I said, as I heard a jeep behind us. It was Big Mike and Jules. The expressions on their faces couldn't have been any more different. Jules was smiling as he jumped out of the jeep and rushed to the Renault bakery van with FFI splashed on the side that had pulled up behind them. He helped Marie-Claire from the passenger seat, and they walked arm-in-arm to the champagne.

Big Mike didn't look like he was in the mood for celebration.

"The moonlight when the hell struck twelve," he said, sticking his thumb out toward the radio. "Came in about ten minutes ago."

Harding's signal that the advance on Paris might be on.

"You told the colonel about Fassier?" I said.

"Yeah, but he wants the map," Big Mike said. "His orders are to find it, and anyone Fassier may have talked to. Pronto."

"Okay," I said. "No second half of the message?"

"Nope. Sam said he'd confirm soon as he got word."

"The map could be anywhere," Kaz said. "Except for within the house where Fassier was found. It was searched thoroughly."

"Here's what we'll do. Big Mike, you and Jules go back into town. See if you can find Fassier's motorcycle. I didn't notice any kind of garage near Marchand's house. Maybe he stashed the map with the bike."

"Will do, if I can pry Jules away from his girl," Big Mike said. "We met up with this *la Croix* bunch coming to fetch Emilie from the powwow."

"Marie-Claire may stay with you, if you don't mind," Emilie said, having overheard the exchange. "I would like to hear first-hand what you learn of this killing. Although traitors must pay a steep price for their treachery, we should not become animals like the *boche* when we extract that payment."

"Sure," I said, glad to have another local to help Big Mike.

"Marie-Claire is quite resourceful," Emilie said, "and impetuous. But weren't we all once, Captain? *Au revoir.*"

I held back telling her the last time I'd been impetuous I was nine years old, and I jumped off my garage roof using a bedsheet as a parachute, expecting to gently float to earth. It didn't work out, and I spent the rest of that summer with my arm in a cast. So, I knew being impetuous in wartime was a shortcut to the cemetery.

"Thank you, Captain Boyle," Marie-Claire said, after Emilie had given her the news. "Jules and I have not seen much of each other."

"We're not on holiday," I said, trying to sound like Colonel Harding and not liking it one bit. "Stay on your toes and help Big Mike search for the map back in Rambouillet. There are still Krauts in the area."

"Toes?" Marie-Claire said, trying to translate that one.

"Stay alert," I said. "Like a dancer, or a boxer in the ring."

"*Les orteils*," Jules said, and they broke up laughing as they clambered into the jeep with Big Mike.

"What are you guys gonna do?"

"Talk with this crowd a bit more," I said. "Then follow up with the cop who tipped them off about Fassier."

"We should also speak to the gentleman who found Marchand's body," Kaz said. "Perhaps he saw someone on the street."

"Right. We'll ask to see the police report, if there is one," I said.

"Okay, I'll get you on the horn soon as we have anything," Big Mike said, and drove off with his gun-toting lovebirds.

Kaz and I went back to the table where Jarnac, Louvet, and Olga were polishing off their last bottle. He took a seat near Louvet and began to chat with him, while I pulled up a chair at the opposite end of the table.

"Emilie seemed distressed," I said. "Perhaps I shouldn't have shared the details of Fassier's torture."

"I have seen dear Emilie push the plunger on a detonator and blow up a bridge as a troop train crossed it," Olga said with a crooked smile. "I am sure many German boys lost their body parts as they crashed into the ravine. She is religious, yes, but no stranger to blood and bone."

"Every now and then it seems a bit much, don't you think?" I said, feeling the faint quiver of my hand on my thigh.

"It is sad," Jarnac said, twisting the empty glass in his hand. "I speak of the feeling of betrayal, when a man you trusted turns out to be false. It makes one feel the fool. And as for myself, that is something I hate. Therefore, I waste no tears on the fate of Lucien Fassier, or Harrier as he was known in Spain."

"Who do you think caught up with him?" I asked the two of them.

"Someone who wants the map," Olga said. "Otherwise it would have been left to be discovered."

"Perhaps," Jarnac said, rubbing his chin as he thought. "It also could have been someone from Beaulieu who knew him there. A friend of his and Marchand's, who would know where he lived and could expect a friendly greeting?"

"Not a bad idea," I had to admit. "Have either of you seen anyone suspicious since you've been here?"

They both laughed.

"Look around you, Captain Boyle," Olga said. "We are all suspicious people, that is why we still live."

"I should say out of the ordinary."

"Who can say? Nothing is ordinary," Jarnac said. "I hope to live to see an ordinary day."

"Well then, tell me when you both arrived here," I said, pushing my chair back and getting to the real point of this conversation. "Just for my report."

"About an hour after dawn," Jarnac said. "It was Louvet's suggestion we meet to work together to apprehend Fassier. He sent us messages last night, and we arrived this morning, only to hear the matter had been settled."

"Except for the map," I said.

"I am beginning to wonder about General Leclerc," Olga said. "Perhaps the map is of little importance after all."

"Louvet had no idea Fassier was here?" I said, ignoring her comment about the map. For the first time, it actually was important. They both shook their heads, and I wondered if Louvet may have invited them here to muddy the waters.

In the distance, a machine gun rattled away, echoing against the hillsides. We all rushed forward, craning our necks to see where it was coming from.

"There," Kaz said, binoculars already up to his eyes. He pointed to a few rooftops visible between the rolling hills. Rifle shots popped, and the machine gun kept up a steady rhythm of bursts, until a muted explosion marked the end of the encounter.

Kaz asked Louvet if his people were out that far, and he declared they were not.

"It may be Hemingway," Jarnac said. "The American writer and his men."

"We heard he was around here," I said. "I thought he was a war correspondent. What's he doing in a shoot-out?"

"He drinks more than he writes, so I hear," Jarnac said. "Some men love war. Hemingway loved it in Spain, but as a tourist. He darted toward danger, then darted away. Others did not have the pleasure of leaving the front when it pleased them."

"You knew Hemingway in Spain?" Kaz asked.

"Yes. That was enough for me. I do not need to know him in France," Jarnac muttered.

"But what's he doing running around out there?" I asked, as Kaz handed me the binoculars.

"He has a band of local *résistants* who met him on the road to Chartres. A leaderless group of young men who took to him," Olga said. "He managed to get them arms and uniforms somehow, and they race from village to village looking for Germans. I hear he reports back to the American division to our rear. He may do some good, or he may get those boys killed, who knows?"

"Look!" Kaz shouted, as Louvet's men cried out as well. A young guy, a kid really, maybe sixteen at most, ran up the road about a hundred yards out, waving his arms. Everyone waved back, and he turned, calling for someone to come forward.

A half dozen Germans in blue *Luftwaffe* uniforms became visible as they rounded a curve and trudged up the road. They were barefoot, hands held high, clutching their boots. Behind them marched another kid, even younger than his pal, his face almost angelic as he grinned at the marching prisoners. He too was armed only with a pistol.

"Smart of those boys to have the Fritzes carry their boots," I said. "Those uniforms might have drawn fire even with their *hände hoch*."

"And it is difficult to escape barefoot," Kaz added as Jarnac called out the boys' names. Kaz joined him as he went forward to greet the lads amidst the jeers and taunts tossed at the miserable-looking Germans.

"Saint-Just fighters?" I asked Olga as we watched the parade.

"It appears so. Marcel does not inform me of his movements and plans, Captain," she said, as Jarnac gave the two boys a bear hug and congratulated them. The prisoners were hustled off to the side and allowed to rest in the shade.

"The lads captured these *Luftwaffe* ground crew after their vehicle broke down," Kaz reported. "They were retreating from Chartres and put up no resistance. Sensible fellows, perhaps."

"If they make it back in one piece," I said.

"Do not worry, Captain," Jarnac said, looking cheerier than he'd been all day. "We will send them by truck back to your lines. Your intelligence officers may learn something of value."

Maybe. But they looked like a bunch of sad-sack mechanics to me. Still, they might have some scuttlebutt on the status of German aircraft.

"You learn anything from Louvet?" I said to Kaz as we stood apart from the others, watching the countryside, which bloomed with surprises today.

"No, his story matched what I heard them tell you. He suggested a meeting to be sure all the routes leading to Paris were covered to thwart Fassier's escape. He seemed genuinely surprised at learning of his death. But lies are simple things for those used to falsehoods."

"You're right," I said, my mind busy trying to sort out everything that had been said today. "Hey, without making a big deal of it, ask the guys manning the machine gun if Hemingway and his crew came through here today. Or if they knew what route he took."

Kaz nodded, making for the jeep first to grab a carton of Chesterfields. He stopped by the POWs, sitting on the ground and rubbing their bruised feet. He tossed one of them a pack of smokes. They smiled and said *danke*, happy for the small kindness.

I stared eastward as Kaz handed out the rest of the cigarettes. Louvet's fighters chattered with him as they lit up. Jarnac glanced back as he talked with the younger of the two boys, watching Kaz intently. Louvet snapped out orders about a truck for the *boche*, and then huddled with Olga, sharing a laugh. I didn't see much to laugh about. Wide-open country, hidden machine guns, mines, and death traps marking the path to the City of Light.

Where I had a hunch Diana Seaton was right now, doing whatever Special Operations Executive agents did in an enemy-occupied stronghold. She hadn't given a hint when she left so suddenly a few weeks ago, but it was all a big rush, and what was more important right now than Paris?

Everybody wants to go to Paris.

CHAPTER SIXTEEN

"THERE WAS NO sighting of Hemingway today," Kaz said as we drove away from the crossroads. "He did pass through yesterday in his jeep, followed by a truckload of local *Maquis*. Apparently, he talked a supply officer from the 2nd Infantry Division into providing uniforms and weapons."

"Well, I guess he does have a way with words. He sounds like the kind of war correspondent who makes his own story," I said, as the jeep strained to make it back up the rutted lane.

"Louvet's men seemed entranced by Hemingway," Kaz said. "They like that he always has a good supply of liquor and speaks French perfectly. For an American, that is quite a compliment from a Frenchman. But why your interest in Hemingway's comings and goings?"

"Because he's moving around out there, close to the German lines," I said. "I never figured a writer would get out in front of GIs, but he has."

"You think he may know a route through the German lines?" Kaz said, as we descended into the village we'd driven through earlier. Inquisitive heads leaned out of doorways and windows, perhaps checking to be sure we weren't Krauts here for a return engagement.

"Well, he sounds a little off his rocker, but he's got a bunch of locals to show him the back roads. He lived it up in Paris a while ago, so he's probably anxious to get back," I said.

Navigating an escape route between two armies was harder than it sounded. You can't just walk around with your hands up in the air, especially if you're a Frenchman trying to move through the Kraut lines. They'd shoot first and not bother asking questions. That meant the safest bet would be to sneak through, much like Gallois had done on his way out of Paris. Then announce yourself to some *boche* officer at a headquarters unit, far from too many nervous trigger fingers.

"Jarnac's men have been out as well," Kaz said, holding on to the seat with one hand and his wool cap with the other as I rounded a corner and headed back to Rambouillet.

"Those young kids? Not much of a patrol."

"I did wonder if they'd simply gone off on their own," Kaz said. "It is the kind of foolish lark boys excel at. They were lucky to have encountered such pliant Germans. But I didn't mean them, I was referring to the burned-out vehicle we saw earlier. That was the work of an FTP patrol, according to Louvet's men."

"That's right," I said. "Seems like there's more people out in no-man's-land than we thought." I made the circle around the monument by the *police judiciaire,* and wondered if Dufort was watching, and if he'd make good on his promise to raise holy hell with SHAEF if we didn't crack this case for him. I wasn't convinced it was anything more than a bluff, but we couldn't take a chance, especially since our interests coincided.

"This is the route Fassier would have taken into town, is it not?" Kaz said.

"Probably, unless he went around the long way," I said. "But I don't see why he would have. Even going cross-country, he would've ended up on this road. Why?"

"Perhaps he hid the map somewhere. He might have thought it too dangerous to keep with him at Marchand's house."

"Didn't help him much, but it's possible," I said. I pulled over by a row of shuttered shops, silent beneath their gray slate roofs. Normal life had not yet returned to this town on the knife's edge of advances and retreats, with cut-throat partisans on every road and death at the door.

We got out and walked, passing a café that was closed. Without knowing when Fassier had come this way—odds were after dark—it was impossible to tell what had been open or if people were even awake.

"There are trash cans in the alley," Kaz said, pointing down a narrow and smelly passage between the buildings.

"Too risky," I said. "They might collect the trash the next morning."

"Mail slots?" he said, gesturing to a brass hinged mail slot marked *Lettres*.

"Not unless the person on the other side of the door knew what they were getting," I said. We strolled along for a while longer, then admitted defeat and went back to the jeep.

"We need a break," I said. "Nothing makes sense. The torture, the missing map, all these fifis running around and getting themselves shot, it doesn't add up."

"What do we know for certain?" Kaz said, collapsing into the passenger seat and popping a pill.

"You still have that headache?"

"It came back. A lousy night's sleep in the rear of a truck with Big Mike snoring next to me didn't help. In any case, let us strip this down to the essentials. What do we know that is absolutely factual?"

"Bernard Dujardin and Sean McKuras were murdered," I said.

"Within a minute of each other," Kaz said.

"Then Fassier disappeared with the map."

"No," Kaz said, wagging his finger. "To a certainty, we know that Fassier, known as Faucon or Harrier before that, left in his vehicle. We also know the map vanished at the same time."

"Right, right," I said. Lack of sleep was affecting me too. "We assume he had the map, but we can't know it."

"We know Fassier was tortured to death," Kaz said.

"What else?"

"We believe Fassier did not visit his father, but once again, we do not know for certain," he said.

"Based on what his father and mother said, odds are he didn't. And Inspector Ribot would have known about it," I said. "I think we can chalk that up as a certainty."

"All right, I agree. Now let me ask you a question. Why do we think Fassier stole the map?"

"Because he ran," I said.

"And if he ran at the same moment the map vanished, but he did not take it, what would you call that?"

"A coincidence," I said, sinking down in my seat. I knew where Kaz was going with this. One of the things my dad drummed into my head was that in a murder investigation, there are no coincidences. Only undiscovered connections. "Okay, let's get back to work. Maybe Big Mike found something."

We radioed Big Mike, but he didn't answer. We stopped at the police station to get the address of the fellow who'd discovered Marchand's body. The cop who'd thrown up in the gutter recognized us and offered directions to where the witness, Maxim Renaud, lived out on the avenue de Paris, less than a quarter mile away. He worked at a lumber mill on the edge of town, and we found him trudging home from work.

He froze when he saw us, looking like he was ready to bolt. I figured it must have been a normal reflex during the Occupation to be leery of a military vehicle pulling up alongside you. Kaz spoke apologetically, and Maxim relaxed, even taking us up on the offer of a ride home. I drove slowly as Kaz asked his questions.

Maxim Renaud was in his forties, maybe older, or maybe simply well-aged after years of work. He wore the usual blue jacket that French workmen favored, worn corduroys, and a threadbare wool cap. As they talked, I wondered what he and Marchand had had in common. Fassier had known Marchand from the university in Paris, and Renaud didn't exactly look like a scholar.

I glanced at him in the back seat. He had a good build and callused hands rough from heavy labor. Some people who find a dead body are just plain unlucky. Others are the type of killer who can't resist returning to the scene and watching everyone get hysterical over what they've done. It's not always the case, but it happens often enough for me to always wonder about the first person to come upon a murder scene.

We dropped Renaud at his place, where Kaz gave him a couple of packs of smokes for his time. He left happy, unlatching the iron gate to a two-story stone house with a crumbling foundation and paint peeling from wooden shutters.

"What's his story?" I asked Kaz, as we watched Renaud unlock the door.

"Chess," Kaz said. "He and Charles Marchand played chess regularly at a café near the hotel. Maxim says there is only enough work for a half day and chess is a good way to spend the afternoon. Marchand didn't show up yesterday, so Maxim knocked on his door on his way home to see if he was unwell. He said he was sure he heard footsteps inside, but no one answered. He looked again this morning on his way to work and saw the door ajar."

"Chess. Okay, that makes sense," I said. "And it tells us Fassier showed up late afternoon sometime. Not much else."

"I wonder why Fassier stayed at all?" Kaz said. "Why not continue under the cover of darkness?"

"Too dangerous? He could have been waiting for word of a safe route," I said. "Or maybe he was holed up here for another reason we don't understand."

"The connection we have not yet made," Kaz said. "Ah, here is Big Mike."

Big Mike pulled up next to us, minus Marie-Claire and Jules.

"Where are those two kids?" I said.

"Jarnac sent that baby-face kid who captured the Krauts with a message for Jules. He needed him for a job, and of course Marie-Claire went along. Jules seemed to have a bad case of Paris fever, and we'd already found the motorcycle, so I cut 'em loose."

"Motorcycle? Where?" I asked.

"Behind some bushes by the house directly behind Marchand's place. It wasn't all that well hidden, but it would've been tough to spot in the dark," he said.

"You searched it?" I said, getting out of the jeep and stretching. The day was beginning to get the better of me. I needed food and sleep. And to think clearly.

"Yeah. I came up empty," Big Mike said. "But it wouldn't make any sense to hide the map anywhere on the bike. Might get pinched, and then you're done. You get anything from this guy?" He nodded in the direction of the house, where someone was peeking out from between lace curtains.

"He and Marchand were chess pals," I said. "Marchand didn't show for a game last night, and Maxim checked on him this morning."

"In other words, we got nothing," Big Mike said.

"Exactly," Kaz said, dropping heavily into his seat and mopping his brow. It was a warm day, but he was sweating like a field hand at harvest time.

"Let's head to the hotel," I said. "We'll get a room and see if Hemingway's back from his patrols." What he might have to offer I had no idea. To be honest, I was more interested in a soft bed and a bath. I wheeled the jeep around left-handed, my right hand in my lap, rustling against the GI fabric.

CHAPTER SEVENTEEN

THE STREET IN front of the Hôtel du Grand Veneur was awash with armed partisans hoisting wine bottles and shouting toasts to *Le Grand Capitaine*. It wasn't tough to spot their grand captain. Ernest Hemingway himself stood on the hotel steps, surrounded by fighters in a wild array of civilian clothes and uniforms. Some wore vests and suit jackets over GI wool shirts, others sported bright scarves worn over field jackets, and all were waving their Sten guns and American rifles madly as Hemingway took a swig of brandy. A couple of swigs, actually, straight from the bottle.

"Reinforcements!" he bellowed, catching sight of the three of us. He thrust the bottle at another war correspondent and stepped forward, the band of partisans parting before him, as did a gaggle of reporters. They all wore the War Correspondent patch on their shoulders. All except Hemingway, that is. He sported the 4th Infantry Division patch, although his heft and dark mustache marked him as anything but an infantryman. He cut through the noise around him with a clear and vibrant voice that managed to sound boyish and stern at the same time. "Who the hell are you fellows?"

"Hardly reinforcements," I said, and introduced Kaz and Big Mike. Hemingway was a big guy himself, and he squared himself up and puffed out a bit as he shook hands with Big Mike, sizing him up as if they were about to box a few rounds. He and Kaz exchanged greetings in French, and Hemingway grinned in approval. Me, he didn't find so interesting. "We're on the trail of a Resistance turncoat. We hear you and your men know every road and trail leading to Paris."

"You heard right, Captain. What do you need to know?" Hemingway beamed, whether from my flattery or the brandy, I couldn't tell.

"What's the best way into Paris?" I said. "What roads are the Germans guarding, and are there any left open? Maybe you could take a look at our map . . ."

"Your map?" he said, looking at the folded paper Kaz was clutching. "Come on upstairs, fellas, I've got a whole wall of maps."

Without waiting for us, he turned and bounded up the steps, a spry, burly bear of a man who didn't betray any evidence of drunkenness, save for the aroma of brandy that wafted in his wake like aftershave gone bad.

"Hey, General Hemingway," one of the correspondents yelled after him. "What the hell are you up to? The manager said you'd booked all the rooms in this joint."

"Shut up, Grant, and go back to Chicago," Hemingway said, barely breaking stride.

"Goddamn it, I'm talking to you. You don't run this place," the other man said.

"My fighters deserve a bed, which is more than I can say for a second-rate hack like you," Hemingway said, this time stopping to face Grant across the room. "I paid for the rooms and that's that."

"Second-rate? At least I'm not a first-rate hack like you," Grant shot back. The room went silent. Hemingway sneered at Grant, who let out a sharp laugh.

Hemingway launched himself at the other reporter and swung

his fist, landing a blow on Grant's jaw. Both of them tumbled to the floor and began kicking and punching like two grade-school kids. Grant was older than Hemingway, probably in his mid-fifties, but he gave as good as he got. Before there was any further harm done, a couple of correspondents pulled the two men apart, restraining them as they kept up the curses and taunts.

"Let's take this outside, Grant," Hemingway said through gritted teeth. He shook off the guy holding him back and stalked out of the lobby, not giving us a second thought.

"Come on, Grant," a round-faced kid with a mop of dark hair said, picking up the older guy's wool cap. "Forget about it. Hemingway's just a lot of hot air."

"No kidding," Grant said, and headed for the bar, along with a few other reporters.

"Hey, what are you guys doing here?" the kid said, giving us the once-over. "You with Hemingway?"

"No, just wanted to ask him a few questions," I said.

"Andy Rooney, *Stars and Stripes*," he said, his voice low as he glanced over his shoulder and motioned us out of the middle of the lobby and away from the remaining correspondents. "What's up? Are you scouting out a headquarters? Is Patton moving on Paris? I'm dying for some news here, Captain."

"Sorry, kid," Big Mike said. "We just went a bit out of our way because we heard Hemingway was here. It's not every day you get to meet a famous writer, you know."

"He's a jerk," Rooney said. "I've read his stuff but meeting him in person has ruined all that for me."

The front door slammed open, and Hemingway stood at the threshold. "Well, are you coming out to fight, Grant?" He stalked out again, yelling for Grant to come out and put up his fists.

"See what I mean?" Rooney said. "All Bruce Grant did was say what we're all thinking, and Hemingway flies off the handle. Grant's a damn good writer, too. He's with the *Chicago Times*, and he covers the war by writing about GIs, like Ernie Pyle does. Hemingway writes about himself."

"The French seem to love him," Kaz said, leaning against the wall and watching the celebration resume.

"They're kids," Rooney said. "He brings them guns and booze and tells them tall tales of Paris nights. He's not like any American they've ever seen. It's all a great adventure to them."

"Hell, Rooney, you're not much older than they are," Big Mike said, giving him a friendly slap on the shoulder.

"I'm twenty-four, and I've been over here for two years. Some of those fifis were still in high school when I was flying missions with the Eighth Air Force on assignment with *Stars and Stripes*," Rooney said. "They're brave, but they don't understand they're bit players in the Ernie Hemingway show."

"What do you know of their activities?" Kaz asked. "Are they really reconnoitering the routes to Paris?"

"Yeah, far as I know, they've gone several miles to the east. Farther than any regular troops I've seen, that's for sure," Rooney said. "And farther than any other reporter has gone, to be honest. Not that Hemingway's acting like a reporter. He's violating regulations by going out armed. He's already bragged about killing a bunch of Germans. No telling how much truth there is to that."

"All I want is a few minutes of his time," I said, as Hemingway's shouts calling for Grant grew louder. "We'll wait for him to calm down."

"I'm not buying your story, Captain," Rooney said. "What is it you're after?"

"Secret plans for the advance on Paris," I said. "Satisfied?"

"Okay, okay," Rooney said, holding up his hands in mock surrender. "No need to get all sarcastic, I can take a hint. Just take a seat and have a drink. He'll show up soon enough. Oh, and call him Papa. He loves it." Rooney returned to his reporter pals, and we grabbed the last seats in the lobby. I sure as hell wasn't going to call anyone "Papa," especially not this booming blowhard.

The angry shouts turned to laughter, and in a few minutes Hemingway came back in, surrounded by four partisans loaded down with grenades and carbines. He was grinning, seemingly over his temper tantrum.

"You boys still here? Come on up and I'll show you where we've been," he said, waving those big arms for us to follow in his wake.

"I shall wait here," Kaz said, stretching his legs out and sliding his cap down over his eyes. "I think two acolytes will be sufficient."

I always said Kaz was the smartest of our bunch.

Hemingway opened the door to his room and the *maquisards* trooped in, stacking a dozen M1 carbines and some sacks of grenades in a corner. Hemingway ushered them out, then turned to us with an expectant look in his eyes.

This wasn't a hotel room. It was an armory with a well-stocked bar. There were more rifles and ammo belts piled up by the bed, and half a dozen Thompson submachine guns laid out over full crates of grenades. Cases of wine were stacked up by the window along with bottles of cognac and whiskey.

"This is one helluva setup, Papa," Big Mike said, nodding his appreciation.

"That it is," Hemingway said, beaming at the compliment paired with his nickname. "What did you say your name was?"

"Big Mike," he said. "This is Captain Boyle."

"You can call me Billy," I said, offering my hand.

"You know, Big Mike," Hemingway said, not noticing or perhaps not caring about me, "we should arm wrestle, you and me." He stood toe-to-toe with Big Mike, his hands on his hips and a broad grin on his face.

"Nothing I'd like better," Big Mike said. "After you tell us about that map." He gazed at a series of maps taped to the wall, forming one large map of the area stretching to the outskirts of

Paris. As Hemingway turned, Big Mike gave me a quick wink. He knew how to size up a guy.

"This is our area of operations," Hemingway said, sounding more like a general than a reporter. "All the way from Chartres to Versailles. From there, it's just a hop skip to Paris."

"You and your men have been testing the German defenses?" I asked.

"What defenses?" Hemingway said. "There are plenty of Krauts out there, but it's hardly a defensive line. Too many of them for our small group, but we're more like cavalry scouts. Raiders, if you like. All we can do is give them a bloody nose, but if Leclerc and his armor would get moving, we'd all be having breakfast in Paris."

"Are you sending this information back to headquarters?" I asked, studying the red pencil marks around Rambouillet. I stuck my right hand in my pocket, beating the shakes to the punch by a couple of seconds.

"Damn right I am. It all goes up to the 4th Division. I've also sent a report direct to Leclerc, but I haven't heard a word back. The man's a fool if he doesn't listen to me," Hemingway said.

"What do these red lines signify?" I asked, tracing a route from the center of Rambouillet heading due east.

"That," he said, tapping his finger against the map, "is the god-damn road to Paris. It's wide open."

"How do you know?" I asked, studying the map and giving a glance to the stash of booze and the empty bottles Hemingway had by his bed, uncertain if his claims were real or alcohol induced.

"We ran into an anti-tank unit today and talked their lieutenant into coming forward with us to clear the road of mines," Hemingway said, puffing out his chest. "They had mine detectors and vehicles to clear trees off the road from where the Krauts dropped them. After they were done, we drove two miles farther on. No resistance. We just came back from another look. It's still open."

"It looks like a heavily wooded area. There could be Germans anywhere," I said.

"It's the Forest of Rambouillet," Hemingway said. "Used to be the king's hunting ground. And I'll tell you the same thing I told Marcel this morning. The Krauts and their damned mines are gone. All we need is to get some armor down that road and I'll buy us all drinks at the Ritz, damn it!"

"Wait, who's Marcel, Papa?" Big Mike said before I could.

"Marcel Jarnac, one of the FTP leaders. I knew him in Spain. Damn good fighting man," Hemingway said, clenching his jaw and gazing at his red-lined route. "He'd come for some Resistance confab and caught me before I went out with the boys."

"You saw Jarnac this morning?" I said. "Big, tall, long-nosed guy, about forty?"

"That's him," Hemingway said. "He had as many questions as you do. Come on, Big Mike, let's have a drink. Your friend too, if he can handle it."

Big Mike and I looked at each other for a second and made for the door. Hemingway stepped in front of us, a surprised look on his face. After all, he was used to people wanting to be around him, hanging on his every word.

"Sorry, Papa," Big Mike said, running interference and shoving me out of the room. "We gotta go."

We left Hemingway sputtering curses after us, surrounded by weapons, booze, and the aura of his own self-importance.

CHAPTER EIGHTEEN

WE THUNDERED DOWN the stairs, pushing aside reporters and partisans as Big Mike hollered for Kaz to wake the hell up. He stumbled groggily after us as we pushed open the doors and sprinted to the jeeps.

The radio was squawking. A gaggle of Resistance fighters gathered around, drawn by the noise.

"What has happened?" Kaz asked, gasping for breath as Big Mike picked up the receiver on his set.

"Remember Jarnac telling us he didn't want to see Hemingway again? Well, he'd already been here this morning asking about which road to Paris was clear."

"Marcel Jarnac is *Atlantik*, then," Kaz said.

"Yeah. He was the traitor all along. Now Hemingway's given him all the information he needs about a clear route through the Forest of Rambouillet."

"Not everything he needs," Kaz said. "It is still a dangerous route."

"Jules and Marie-Claire," I said, grasping what he meant. Big Mike looked up from his radio wide-eyed, I thought at the mention of the two young fighters. But it was something else.

"The devil's in the tower right now," he said. The second line of the Rimbaud poem. The clock had struck twelve and the Allied army was headed for Paris.

So was our killer, a traitor with a map worth thousands of lives. And two kids he was probably using to draw fire before it hit him. Jules would do anything Jarnac asked, and Marie-Claire would stick by him, no questions asked.

"Damn! How close is Sam?"

"That was him on the radio," Big Mike said. "He's about five miles out. He said Leclerc is taking the exact route that was on the phony map. This whole thing is FUBAR, Billy."

"Jesus Christ! Wait here for Harding," I said. "We'll take the road into the forest, toward the château." *Fucked up beyond all recognition* didn't begin to describe it if the Germans knew where to expect Leclerc's armor.

"I saw it on the map. We'll be right behind you," he said.

I started the jeep and gunned it down the road, taking a right after the hotel and heading for the local château, which was on the outskirts of town, right at the border of the forest.

"Are you sure?" Kaz asked as we took a corner too fast, barely missing a cart on the side of the road. The jeep skidded as I down-shifted, swerving until I finally regained control.

"Yeah, it all fits. Jarnac didn't want us to know he went to Hemingway to scout out an escape route. He has the map. As a matter of fact, I think he's always had it," I said, taking a deep breath and rethinking everything that had happened back at Patton's HQ.

"Then why did Fassier run?"

"I don't know why. I thought it was because of the map. We should have focused on what we knew for certain, instead of assuming too much," I said. We'd passed the last of the buildings now, and the road thinned out into a wooded lane. Civilians on bicycles rounded a bend, and I slowed to avoid taking half of them out.

Once past the cyclists, I floored it on the straightaway, my mind putting all the pieces together so that they finally made sense.

The knife. It hadn't been put in the coffee urn to hide it. It was there to hold the map above the coffee. The folded map was balanced on the knife hilt, keeping it clear of the coffee at the bottom. It had been Jarnac who took it. Jarnac who killed Bernard and ran down McKuras after he'd been spotted. Jarnac who plucked the map from the urn after it was all over and calmly drove away.

Maybe it was Jarnac who killed Fassier, but whoever had done it, that murder was over something else. Fassier was a convenient patsy, and even more so conveniently dead.

I explained it all to Kaz as fast as I could.

"Now that you mention it," Kaz said, holding on to avoid being spilled out of the jeep, "when Jarnac made a demonstration of showing his knife, along with all the others, did you notice anything?"

"Jesus," I said, as I replayed the scene in my mind. It had been there all along. "He pulled the knife from his boot, but he sheathed it at his belt."

"In an empty sheath," Kaz said. "He had two knives. Not so unusual for a man living a life *clandestinité*, but I should have seen the implication. It was done right in front of us."

"Goddamn. Right now, let's focus on finding Jarnac and those two kids." We roared past the château, a grand affair with four turrets and a front lawn the size of a football field. The road narrowed to a wooded lane, leafy branches overhead creating a tunnel of sunlit greenery. A truck rumbled down the road toward us, a red flag flapping above FTP splashed across the hood. I pulled across the road as Kaz flagged them down.

There were two men in the cab and four others in back, all of them eyeing us with suspicion until they recognized us from this morning's meeting. Kaz fired questions their way, telling them we needed to speak with Comrade Jarnac and it was *très important*. Had they seen him?

Yes, Jarnac had gone forward with young Jules and his

companion. Yes, they were in two cars, in case one broke down. No, they didn't know where they were going, it was all very secret. Jules was to return once Jarnac reached his destination. Yes, it was dangerous, but they'd been assured by *Le Grand Capitaine* that the road was free of mines and *boche*.

When? Just minutes ago, they'd seen them off at the edge of the forest.

I gunned the jeep, spitting gravel as we sped around the truck, Kaz grabbing his Sten, looping the sling over his shoulder and bracing it on the hood. The good news was we'd catch up with Jarnac soon, since he was likely lagging behind Jules and Marie-Claire, watching from a safe distance. Which was also the bad news, since they were his sacrificial lambs, out front to take fire on what they thought was a safe route.

I drove hard and fast, sending the jeep airborne as we crested a rise and the road descended into a rutted cascade of gravel and dirt. Kaz was holding onto his Sten with one hand and the side panel with the other, his feet braced to keep his body, and his aim, steady.

We hit a flat stretch of paved roadway as the woods began to thin out, and in the distance a vehicle appeared as it rose on the hilltop, vanishing as it descended.

"There!" Kaz shouted, pointing to a second vehicle as it followed the first. "Jarnac!"

I was hitting sixty, and the jeep wasn't about to go any faster. But I knew Jarnac was going slower, since Jules would have no reason to speed across the countryside, no matter what tale Jarnac spun for them about the road being clear of Krauts. And with Jarnac trailing them, I was sure we'd be on him in minutes.

We were out of the woods, driving through open rolling fields. The road began to curve here and there as it wended its way across the terrain dotted with copses of trees and stacks of freshly harvested hay. I had to slow up on the bends but gained speed when the road dipped and the ground evened out as we began to parallel a stream on our right.

Then Jarnac was right in front of us, driving an old Citroën coupe with no FFI markings. He was playing it safe every way he could. Ahead, Jules and Marie-Claire motored along, oblivious to what might lie around the next curve in the road.

"Take out his wheels," I shouted to Kaz. "I want him alive."

"If you insist," Kaz said, and settled in to take aim.

A machine gun shattered the air, the rapid fire of the German MG 42 sounding like a sheet of canvas being torn over and over again. An explosion, then a fireball erupted ahead.

"Damn him," Kaz muttered, and fired his Sten at Jarnac's auto, emptying the clip in one burst, any notion of taking him alive gone with the thought of the carnage Jules and Marie-Claire had driven into.

Slugs punctured the rear of the Citroën, the metallic *pings* sharp against the dull hammering of the Sten gun. Jarnac's car fishtailed wildly as Kaz dropped the clip and reloaded, and we both braced for the vehicle to crash into the ditch or roll over in front of us. I followed close on, desperate to keep Jarnac between us and the Kraut gunners ahead.

Finally, the Citroën lurched into the ditch, the passenger's door swinging open as the car tilted with its nose buried in the dirt. I got out with my Thompson, signaling Kaz to stay put and give me cover. I ran to the rear of the car, alert for any sign of movement.

I smelled gas.

A flame blossomed from the engine in a small *pumpf* as something ignited under the hood, just as the driver's door flew open.

Jarnac tumbled out, a pistol in his hand. I aimed the Thompson and was ready to tell him to drop it, or ready to squeeze the trigger, I wasn't really sure.

Before I could decide, the fuel tank exploded, sending up a

sheet of flame and blistering heat. I heard Jarnac fire, and then Kaz, as I was knocked away from the burning vehicle by the blast.

Through the hazy, shimmering glow expanding from the flames, I saw Jarnac run down the road, a white flag tied around his wrist and fluttering in the wind. I rose up, shaking off the shock from the explosion, and ran after him. I stayed behind the bastard, hoping that the Krauts were curious enough about a surrendering Frenchman not to fire on him. If they did, his body might slow a bullet or two, but it wouldn't stop them all.

The MG 42 fired again, chewing up the road on one side. They were staying away from Jarnac, and I wondered if they'd been expecting him. Another burst kicked up clods of dirt near my feet, and I vaulted forward, throwing myself at Jarnac and grabbing onto his leather jacket, pulling him down and rolling into the ditch with him.

More gunfire from the machine gun, and I realized they were firing on Kaz, keeping him down under cover. Jarnac and I rolled around, throwing punches and struggling for possession of my Thompson, which had been slung over my shoulder and now had both of our hands tangled in its sling.

I could hear Krauts yelling, and they didn't sound happy. Or that far away. Jarnac landed a punch square on my jaw, and I saw stars but kept my grip on the Thompson as he tried to jerk it away. I kicked at his knee, and we both lost our grip, the weapon falling into the thick, wet grass.

Jarnac was up and had the advantage. He kicked at my head and scrambled up the side of the ditch, his feet losing traction as he tried to climb out. I shook off another round of stars and launched myself at him, grabbing at his shoulders and coming away with a fistful of leather. More gunfire sounded, and I wondered who the hell was shooting at who.

More Germans screamed, a lot closer now. Jarnac threw me off and I fell back as he pulled himself out of the jacket, twisting away and yelling out in German to his pals. He went for me as I moved for the Thompson, and I heard him curse. He turned and ran, clutching his white flag, waving it high.

I watched a German potato masher grenade sail through the air in a high arc, headed my way. I threw myself to the bottom of the ditch, hearing a *clunk* as it landed in the road.

Then the explosion. Loud, sharp, and right above my head. I made myself move, checked myself for blood, and wiped away the dirt and stones that had showered down. The ditch had protected me from shrapnel and except for the ringing in my ears and a terrible sense of despair, I was just fine.

The lead was flying, tracer rounds zipping not far over my head, and I decided it would be best to stay cowered in this ditch and not to think about Jules and Marie-Claire, not to mention my failure at stopping Marcel Jarnac.

I was too late. Too late to save them, too late to stop Jarnac from getting away with the plans for the advance on Paris. Too late to stop the escape of a traitor and a murderer. *Atlantik* had beaten us.

The grass at the bottom of this ditch was cool and soft. I grasped it with my trembling hand and never wanted to leave.

PART TWO

PARIS

CHAPTER NINETEEN

I ROLLED ON my back and watched phosphorescent tracer rounds burn lightning hot above me, electric against the blue summer sky. It was like being in a dream, and for a moment I wondered if I was.

The ground trembled, and I knew it wasn't a dream. Giant tires appeared on the road above the ditch, dirt cascading over me as the vehicle braked hard and let loose with cannon fire. Armored scout car, part of my brain informed me. Fast, with a 37mm cannon and a .50 caliber machine gun. That's what chased the Krauts away.

Maybe it had blown a big hole in Jarnac's back. Maybe not. War is capricious.

The white tracers vanished, but the staccato chatter of the machine gun was still echoing inside my head, loud and insistent. The armored car let off another round, and the harsh crack of the cannon blew away the machine gun echoes dancing inside my brain.

I didn't want to get up. It was quiet for a moment, then a short burst from the machine gun sent shell casings raining down on me, red hot and trailing acrid wisps of smoke.

Boots appeared on the roadway. Black leather. That would be Kaz in his British ammo boots. I'd always meant to ask why they were called that. I felt Kaz's hands grab my shoulders, and tried to ask, but nothing came out.

Another pair of boots. Large brown combat boots. That was easy. Big Mike. He got his paws on me, and I was hoisted out of the ditch, still trying to form a sentence and not much caring that I couldn't.

Kaz and Big Mike were both making odd faces. I think they were trying to talk to me.

Almost upright, I came face-to-face with another pair of combat boots, spit-polished and gleaming in the sunlight. Colonel Harding stood on the hull of the scout car, one hand on the .50 machine gun. He jumped to the ground, laying his hand on my shoulder and leaning close.

He peppered me with words. They bounced off me like hail on a tin roof.

Big Mike put my helmet on my head and placed my weapon in my hands. My ears still rang, and I could barely hear the words spoken to me. Whatever they had to say didn't matter until I faced up to what I had done. I walked away, down the road, to where the price of my failures sat in a scorched and bullet-ridden wreck.

I glanced back and saw Harding order the armored car crew to scout ahead and look for any sign of Jarnac. The vehicle took off, taking a route through the fields to avoid sections of road that the Krauts might have zeroed in.

I felt a tug at my hand. I was still holding Jarnac's worn leather jacket. Big Mike loosened my grip on it and took it from me. I felt Kaz's presence at my side and wished he didn't have to see this. The explosion that had killed Daphne had been in an automobile, and this would only remind him of his loss. Not that he didn't think about it every day, but seeing a physical reminder of the devastating carnage which had taken the woman he loved would take a toll.

We both had to witness, each for our own reasons. To deny that would be to deny the very lives we mourned. And to deny responsibility.

We walked. Around a bend, down a slight incline, past a copse of trees by a meandering stream. It was in our nostrils before we saw it, the stink of burnt oil and flesh that was the perfume of the French countryside in this summer of 1944.

They'd driven a small Renault flatbed truck. It sat at the edge of the road, the cab blackened and stitched with bullet holes. Blistered paint traced a faint outline around the FFI lettering on the driver's door. Shattered glass crunched beneath our feet. Smoke curled from under the hood.

Marie-Claire and Jules sat upright next to each other in the small cab, terrible gaping wounds to their chests telling me at least they hadn't died by fire. It had consumed their clothes and seared their bodies, leaving them unrecognizable except for the color of their hair and the shape of their faces. I recognized a ring on Marie-Claire's hand. It was delicate, even after the fire had snapped at it.

I looked at Kaz. He stared at the bodies for a long time, his hand gripping the Sten gun as if Jarnac were already in his sights.

"The ground shall cover him," Kaz said, his voice barely a whisper.

This time I heard him just fine.

We turned away, the odor of death clinging to us as we walked back to where Big Mike and Harding waited.

"You okay, Billy?" Big Mike asked, as we drew near to the scout car. Not the first time he'd asked, by the look on his face.

"Yeah, fine. That grenade rattled me, that's all," I said, slinging my Thompson over my left shoulder and cramming my right hand into my pocket where it kept time like Jimmy Dorsey.

"How'd you know, Boyle?" Harding asked.

"Know what?" I asked, still feeling hazy. I was still in that ditch. I was still staring at the shattered bodies of two young kids. There wasn't much of me present to listen to whatever it was Harding was trying to say.

"About the map," he said, flourishing a folded paper. "It was hidden in the lining of this jacket."

"I had no idea," I said, staring dumbfounded at the torn shreds of the leather jacket at Harding's feet. "I was just trying to hang onto him. He shook me off, and I fell into the ditch. He pulled himself out of the sleeves trying to get away."

"Smart place to hide it," Big Mike said, kicking over the pile of rags. "Easy to keep tabs on the damn thing. Guess he thought it wasn't worth dying for once the lead started flying."

"Or necessary," Kaz said. "By now, he must have all the positions memorized. All he needs to do is recreate it."

"If the Krauts believe him," Big Mike said. I looked down the road in the direction Jarnac had run, passing Jules and Marie-Claire in the company of his German rescuers. I rubbed my hand against my face, trying to wipe away the grime and memories, the futile sense of loss and sacrifice. I had to think. I had to make sense of all this in the midst of senseless slaughter.

I took out my canteen and raised it to my mouth. My hand had steadied. Maybe my mind would follow suit.

"Look at what happened here," I said, wiping the moisture from my lips. "They knew he was heading into German territory. He sent those kids forward to announce himself and probably told the Krauts what kind of vehicle they'd be in."

"Kind of like a trip-wire," Big Mike said. "In case the Krauts didn't get the message."

"Yes, and it would not be difficult to arrange," Kaz said. "With telephone exchanges working, a message could easily be delivered across the lines."

"And he had that white flag tied around his wrist," I said. "A pre-arranged signal. The fact that we tried so hard to stop him will only reinforce the importance of his story." I leaned against the jeep, bone tired. Tired of the dead and their insistent demands to be remembered. All I wanted to do was sleep and forget. Forget about Jarnac and the people he'd murdered.

Bernard Dujardin, who was his comrade.

Sean McKuras, the translator who stumbled into the theft.

Jules Herbert and Marie-Claire Mireille, fighting patriots and lovers whose lives he threw away.

Charles Marchand, dead of a knife thrust for the simple act of taking in his friend.

Lucien Fassier, tortured to death for a reason I'd yet to fathom. I still had no idea why Fassier ran after the theft of the map, but it certainly left *Atlantik* with a convenient scapegoat. Not to mention a good reason for openly hunting down Fassier. Hell, if he'd confessed to killing him in that basement, half of France would have applauded him.

"Did you hear me, Boyle?" Harding said, gently placing his hand on my arm.

"Sorry, Colonel, what were you saying?"

"He has to be stopped," Harding said.

"He is headed to Paris, Colonel," Kaz said. In the distance, the *crack* of artillery echoed against the hills, reinforcing his point.

"German 88," Big Mike said, as the anti-tank gun unleashed another round. We waited for an explosion to mark the demise of the scout car. Instead, we heard the straining engine roaring back, straight along the road this time, coming into view and braking sharply as it drew alongside us.

The commander popped up from the turret hatch, glancing back down the lane.

"Two 88s, Colonel, dug in on a ridgeline about a half mile out," he shouted in an adrenaline surge. "They've got the road covered. Missed us by a couple of yards."

Harding told him to head back to Rambouillet, and he didn't waste a second saying so long. Couldn't blame him much; the high-velocity shell from a German 88 would have turned the lightly armored scout car into shards of scrap metal.

"At the risk of repeating myself, Colonel," Kaz said, "Jarnac is on his way to Paris. How are we to stop him?"

"We know exactly where he's going," Harding said. "Come on, there's not much time."

The only thing that made sense to me was that there wasn't much time. Because if knowing precisely where Jarnac was headed in German-occupied Paris was an advantage, the disadvantage was a shortened life expectancy.

CHAPTER TWENTY

HARDING HAD BROUGHT an I&R platoon—Intelligence and Reconnaissance—with him, and they'd conveniently set up an advance headquarters at the *police judiciaire*. Which was convenient for Inspector Dufort, who was waiting to complain about the intrusion of GIs and to demand an update on his murder investigation.

Harding looked confused, and I gave him the lowdown about Fassier and Dufort's vague threats to involve SHAEF.

"Do not misunderstand, Colonel," Dufort said, guiding us to his office. "I merely wished to enlist Captain Boyle in the pursuit of the killer, since he was already involved in hunting down Lucien Fassier."

"As were many members of the Resistance," Harding said. "Have you strong-armed them as well?"

"Strong-arm? Please, I do not understand," Dufort said, sitting behind his desk and gesturing to three chairs set before it. Big Mike leaned against the wall, arms folded. "But never mind, I think I can see the meaning."

"We don't have much time," Harding said. "All we can tell you is that the murder of Lucien Fassier is likely connected to a member of the Resistance who was secretly working with the Germans. I wouldn't advise you to make trouble where none exists."

"I understand you pursued Marcel Jarnac," Dufort said, ignoring Harding's warning.

"How do you know that?" Kaz asked. Dufort eyed him, and then turned his gaze onto me.

"The police have informers in America, do they not, Captain Boyle? It is the same here. I knew within minutes of your flight down the stairs from the room of *Monsieur* Hemingway."

"What of it?" Harding said, standing up and pushing back his chair, impatient with the delay.

"Nothing, except for the person I have waiting to speak with you," Dufort said. "A person with knowledge of Jarnac and his activities."

"Who?" Harding said. He didn't sit down, but he didn't make a move to leave either.

"First, you must remove your men," Dufort said. "This building belongs to the French government. Only General de Gaulle can commandeer it. It is a point of honor, you understand."

"I do," Harding said. "If you help us, we will find another site. What else?"

"Nothing," Dufort said, with a casual wave of his hand. "What is more important than honor?"

"Justice. Especially when it goes hand-in-hand with honor," Harding answered. Dufort sat silent for a long moment before he nodded in agreement. "I'll have my men move out as soon as we speak with whoever you have."

"Excellent," Dufort said. "And I will submit my report on the murders of Charles Marchand and his guest, killed by a fascist traitor. Which I will forward to my colleagues in Paris in due course."

"I'm glad that's all worked out," I said. "Now, who's this person of interest?"

"Olga Rassinier," Dufort said. "Russian. You already know her, of course, and her Resistance group of immigrant fighters. She is the most valued type of informant to any policeman. The spurned lover."

"She and Jarnac?" Kaz said.

"Yes, but I will let her tell you," Dufort said, standing. "Please use my office and let me know what else I may do to help."

In a minute he ushered Olga in and left us to it. I got up to give her my seat and leaned against the desk.

"It is true?" Olga asked, looking between us, her brow furrowed with worry. "Marcel is a traitor?"

"He was the one who stole the map. We got it back just before he went over to the Germans," Harding said, then told her about Marie-Claire and Jules.

"Oh, those poor children," Olga said, her hand raised to her mouth. "But even if you have the map, Marcel will know everything."

"That's why we must stop him. Anything you can tell us will help," Harding said.

"I cannot believe it. Marcel was a true comrade, he would never do such a thing," Olga murmured, as if trying to imagine the impossible. I could see Harding was getting impatient, but if this was a case of personal betrayal, she couldn't be rushed.

"You cared for him," I said, my voice soft and low. I reached forward and placed my steady hand on her arm. The clock on Dufort's desk ticked, filling the silence with the beat of a broken heart.

"We were in love. In Spain. And still here, but it was nothing like the old days. Nothing at all," she said, her voice catching in her throat. She looked out the window and seemed to gain strength from the green leaves wafting slowly in the breeze. "We were younger, and on fire with the purity of our beliefs. We wished to build a new society, do you understand? Fighters came from all over the world to join the International Brigades and fight for a just society. But here in France, it is different. We fight the Nazis, as any decent person must, but there will be no new society. We struggle, suffer, and die, but when it ends it will be the rich who come out on top, just as they were before the war. I am joyful when I see the Liberation come to each town and city, and sad, as well. Strange, is it not?"

"Olga, we have to catch Marcel, and quickly," I said, trying to bring her back. So much of this case went back to Spain, but we needed information in the here and now. "Can you help us?"

"Yes, I can. I can tell you where he will go in Paris. And I can tell you what happened between Marcel and Lucien Faucon."

"Fassier," Harding said.

"Yes, but I never knew him by either name. I had not seen him since Spain, not until he appeared at the headquarters of General Patton. He was known as Lucien Harrier, named for a hawk that swoops down and kills. He worked with the Russians, as we all did. But he also did the bidding of the NKVD."

"The Russian secret police," Kaz said. Olga wound her fingers together, her head bowed.

"Yes," she whispered. "There were many executions. Lucien killed more of our fighters than fascists. He was used by the NKVD to keep the various factions in line. To Stalin and his kind, the anarchists and communists who did not bow to Moscow were as bad as the fascists we all fought."

"What does this have to do with Jarnac?" Harding asked.

"His wife. Renée," she said, her words choked by grief. "She was an anarchist. A leader of the anti-fascist movement in Barcelona. She and Marcel argued all the time, and they could not stay together, so great were their passions. Still, they loved each other deeply. It may be hard to understand, but for us, our politics were our holy ground. Marcel and I, we believed in the same cause. We were proud Communists, and we believed in each other. But he loved Renée with a senseless passion."

"Lucien killed Renée," I said. It was the only answer, the only thing that made sense.

"She was executed by the NKVD, that much is certain. Did Lucien do it? Perhaps. Most likely, I should say, since she was found bound in his favored method. Wire tied around her ankles and wrists, pulled tight. Two bullets in the head. Marcel searched for him, but the Harrier disappeared. Until the other day, when he entered the room. I'd heard the name Faucon, but never knew it was him."

"He ran from Jarnac," Harding said.

"Yes. Marcel was mad to find him," she said, looking up at Harding as if she'd come out of a trance. "I have heard it was terrible. What Marcel did."

"It's over now," Harding said, skirting the issue. "You said you could help us find Jarnac."

"Yes," Olga said with a heavy sigh, laying her hands flat on her thighs and bowing her head as if in supplication. "He has a younger brother, Paul. He lives at number thirty-seven rue Ravignan, in Montmartre. Marcel traveled to Paris often, using false identity papers. He always visited Paul."

"Is Paul a Communist as well?" Harding asked, scribbling down the address on a piece of paper taken from Dufort's desk. "Will he be watched by the Germans?"

"No. Paul is a musician. A violinist. He uses his mother's last name to be safe. Lambert. He is nothing like Marcel, which is why, perhaps, Marcel always had a softness for him."

"Did Jarnac have any other regular stops in Paris?" Kaz asked, as Harding whispered with Big Mike, who left the room in a hurry.

"No, of course not," Olga said. "Marcel is too wily for that. He's stayed alive this long by never repeating his patterns. Except for Paul, and his visits were always unannounced."

"Thank you, Miss Rassinier," Harding said. "We hope to catch up with him before he can do any real damage."

"If you do," Olga said, standing up to go, "kill him. He is a traitor. Everything he was before, he is no more. Farewell."

She brushed past Harding, leaving the last of her passion behind, a final casualty of the Spanish Civil War.

Kaz leaned back in his chair, looking exhausted. It had been a long night and a long day. I clenched my fist to keep the shakes down as I watched Harding. He stood, walked to the window, and stared at the same tree Olga had found so riveting.

A pensive Harding was never a good sign. I nudged Kaz and threw a glance at Harding's back.

"Do we have any agents in Paris who could stop Jarnac?" I asked.

"We don't, no. The Special Operations Executive does, but there's not enough time to go through channels," Harding said.

"What do we have time for, Colonel?" I asked, knowing full well what the answer was going to be. After all, everyone wants to see Paris before they die, don't they?

"We now know the address of Jarnac's brother. We also know another address in Paris he's sure to visit," Harding said, his face still turned to the window.

"That would be the Hotel Lutetia, on the Left Bank," Kaz said, drumming his fingers on the arm of his chair. "A very nice hotel. I dined there once, in 1937, I believe."

"What? How could you know what hotel Jarnac is staying at?" I asked.

"Because the grand Hotel Lutetia now serves as the headquarters of the *Abwehr*," Harding said, finally turning to look us in the eye. "It's a good bet German military intelligence will be the first stop for our man *Atlantik*."

"Colonel, he's already got a head start on us, and he's most likely going in with a German escort," I said, standing and shoving my hands into my pockets. "It's impossible."

"What's not possible is letting Jarnac deliver that information," Harding said. "You heard the radio message. The devil's in the tower, and Leclerc is moving his division into place to move on Paris. By morning, his advance elements will be on the move."

"But Colonel," Kaz said, spreading his hands wide to encompass all the questions we had. "How shall we get there?"

"In here, fellas," Big Mike said from the hallway, ushering in two Frenchmen. Dufort brought up the rear, explaining something to the two guys that I couldn't quite grasp. They didn't seem happy and began to argue with Dufort. But he was the boss, and they calmed down fast.

I saw one of them look at my boots. His eyes brightened, and his entire disposition changed. He was about my size. His pal was smaller, wiry, like Kaz.

Exactly like Kaz.

"Don't tell me," I said, looking to Big Mike. He nodded. I sat down to take off my boots.

"We shall need identity cards," Kaz said, taking off his jacket and eyeing the worn suit of his counterpart with distaste. It was off the rack.

"Take your pick," Dufort said, emptying a file marked *Carte d'Identité* onto the desk. Twenty or so Vichy identity cards tumbled out. "Some are real, others are forgeries, but well done."

I put on my new dark blue trousers and stuck my feet into the detective's shoes. He was getting the better of the bargain. The soles felt like cardboard, which was par for the course in occupied France. Shoe leather was as rare as sugar. I pawed through the identity cards as Harding explained there was no time to take a photograph and match it up with the stamps overlapping the images. So, I looked for a guy who was close to my age and hair color. The closest I came was a *Milice* identity card with *Brigade Spéciale* emblazoned across it. Charles Guillemot looked sort of like me with some extra weight, thinning hair, and a lousy attitude.

"Very good," Dufort said. "The Germans may wave you through with that."

"What happened to Charles?" I asked.

"He is a *résistant*," Dufort said. "Several of these are his. We keep them safe for him."

"Here's one, Kaz," Big Mike said. "Looks sorta like you."

"Ah, that is a real one," Dufort said. "Jean Rey, who died when his train was bombed not far from here."

I took a look. Rey was thin, with a pinched face and a big forehead. "If you had an ugly older brother, this could be him," I said.

"Very well," Kaz said, knotting his tie. "Jean Rey it is. Contractor by trade, I see. I shall do my best to build rather than destroy, in memory of the large-headed Jean." Kaz buttoned his jacket and managed to make his dull, gray suit look almost fashionable.

The two detectives laced up their new boots and stomped out, dressed in wool khakis and broad smiles. Big Mike held on to my captain's bars and promised to take care of them. I looked forward to being reunited with them as soon as possible.

"You know your way around Paris, Lieutenant Kazimierz?" Harding asked as we left Dufort's office, donning our new fedoras. Mine was a touch too big, which I didn't mind since I could pull it down farther to hide my face in case anyone checked my identity card.

"Very well. I've not heard of the rue Ravignan, but it should be an easy matter to find it in Montmartre."

"Do you know the rue de Provence in the eighth *arrondissement*?" Harding asked, leading us outside to the jeeps where Big Mike started fiddling with the radio.

"That street does sound familiar, yes," Kaz said. "Why?"

"In case you need help, go to one-twenty-two rue de Provence," Harding said. "Ask for Malou."

"Malou who?" I asked.

"Just Malou," Harding said.

"There are no last names for the girls at the One-Two-Two,"

Kaz said, obviously knowing something I didn't. Which happened pretty often. "I will explain later, Billy."

"Okay, but how about someone explains what happens next?" I said.

"All set, Big Mike?" Harding asked, instead of answering me.

"Yep. There's a flight of Thunderbolts headed out. They'll hit the Kraut emplacements in thirty minutes," he said.

"Okay, let's move," Harding said, handing each of us a wad of money. "Take these *francs*. You may need some cash."

"And for you, Captain Boyle," Dufort said, giving me a small automatic. "It is a Ruby pistol. Only .32 caliber, but it fits nicely into a pocket. A member of the *Milice* would not be without one."

"Thanks," I said, hefting the small pistol. Not much stopping power, but if I had to use it, it would probably be close enough to do the trick. The grinding of gears and a sputtering engine announced the arrival of an old Peugeot. A really old Peugeot. One fender was about rusted off, and the rear window was broken. It was outfitted with big gazogene cylinders, designed to power the engine by burning wood in a container in the trunk. It wasn't elegant, but it made the wheels turn, which was a big accomplishment in occupied France.

"As you can see, it runs," Dufort said. "It will not be out of place in a town still under German control. The firebox is full, and it should get you to Chaville."

"What's in Chaville?" I asked.

"A railroad station, where you can board a train to Paris," Harding said.

"Here, I have drawn you a map," Dufort said, handing it to Kaz. "Many people from Paris take the train to the country in search of fresh food. It will be crowded, since everyone must be back before the curfew."

"It'll work," Harding said, with the enthusiasm of a guy who'd thought up a crazy scheme and wouldn't be around to find out if it actually worked.

"Okay," I said, as I slid behind the wheel. Kaz rolled his eyes and got in the passenger seat. Big Mike had to slam the door for him a few times before it stayed shut. He and Harding told us to follow their jeep as Dufort watched us leave.

"*Bonne chance!*" he said, waving his hand in farewell.

I had a peashooter pistol, a pocketful of cash, a wood-burning rattletrap, and a phony ID card. We'd need all the good luck in the world.

CHAPTER TWENTY-ONE

WE DROVE PAST where Marie-Claire and Jules had died. Their bodies were gone, thank God, but the burned-out hulk of their vehicle still sat as a reminder of the surprises the back-roads of rural France had in store. We halted at a bend in the road, and Harding went ahead to check the terrain with his binoculars.

"The Thunderbolts should be here soon," he said, signaling us to come closer. He pointed out twin knolls overlooking the roadway. "We gave them the location of the guns and orders to fly over the route to Chaville and shoot up any German vehicles or positions."

"You've thought of everything, Colonel," I said, trying to keep my expression neutral.

"Listen, this isn't a suicide mission," he snapped. "All indications are the Germans have no real defenses between here and Paris. There's a string of anti-aircraft guns in an arc around the city, and that's what those 88s probably are."

"The fighter-bombers are going to take care of them, don't worry," Big Mike said.

"If you see any other Germans, don't take chances," Harding said. "Get off the road and take to the woods. But make it to Chaville, that's important. You need to be in Paris before the 2100 hours curfew."

"Colonel, that doesn't leave us much time," I said.

"I know," he said. Big Mike handed around K-Rations, and we opened them on the hood of the jeep. I still had my concerns about this little jaunt, but I was hungry enough to forget about them for a moment and dig in. I devoured the biscuits, and ham and eggs straight out of the can, washed down with a bottle of wine Big Mike produced.

I'd just handed the bottle to Kaz when the drone of engines began to hum at the horizon. We craned our necks, trying to spot the speeding Thunderbolts, but the deafening roar of the low-flying planes was on us before we saw them. Heavy with death, they swooped overhead, their prop wash sucking up leaves and swaying heavy branches.

Two flights of four aircraft went after the German guns, each group breaking off to attack an emplacement. The German gunners fired, but the Thunderbolts came in too low and fast to hit. They carried rockets under their wings, and the planes each let loose in turn. Fiery explosions pock-marked the hills as the Thunderbolts soared away, circling for another attack.

"Look," Kaz said, pointing high in the sky. Above the attacking aircraft, another flight flew cover, circling over the battlefield.

The Thunderbolts returned, this time strafing the positions one by one. Each plane was armed with eight .50 machine guns spitting incendiary and armor-piercing bullets at a furious rate. Secondary explosions blossomed as German ammunition exploded, signaling an end to any possible resistance.

"Okay, go," Big Mike said as the fighters formed up and headed west, scouting out targets on the road to Chaville. I hoped at that altitude the pilots could tell the difference between our gazogene junker and a Kraut staff car.

"We'll meet you in the bar at the Hotel Lutetia," I said, with more bravado than I felt as I bent myself to fit in the rusty Peugeot. "After the *Abwehr* boys check out."

"Find Jarnac. Put a bullet in him. Wait for the cavalry to arrive. Leclerc will be a day behind you, two at the most," Harding said.

I waved as I drove off, the automobile straining to make it up a slight incline. I checked the rearview mirror. Big Mike looked worried, like he might never see us again. I felt the same way.

Descending, the Peugeot picked up speed. We cruised by the two hills, fires licking at the trees and sending gray clouds swirling into the sky. A solitary German soldier stumbled out of the burning woods, wisps of smoke curling from his uniform, his face blackened with burns and red with blood. His eyes gaped wide open, but he saw nothing, felt nothing, knew nothing other than to move away from the destruction, powered by the shock that would keep the pain at bay for a while longer. If I'd had more bullets, I would have saved him from the agonies ahead.

Instead I drove on.

"What do you think our chances are?" I asked Kaz as we drove by fields thick with grass, where cows or sheep once grazed before the Germans helped themselves to most of the livestock.

"Of getting to Paris? Oddly enough, good. The colonel is correct about the defenses being thin this far out. Mostly anti-aircraft units as he said. This is a no-man's-land, which is to our advantage. And we've heard about Parisians taking to the countryside to barter for food. The more crowded the train, the better our chances are," he said.

"What about finding Jarnac?"

"Of that, our chances are slight at best," Kaz said. "If he has a German escort to take him directly to his *Abwehr* contact, then I fail to see how we can intercept them and kill Jarnac with your little pistol."

"What if he doesn't?" I said, willing our vehicle to make it up a small incline without rolling backward. "Maybe those Krauts had orders to let him pass, nothing more. Jarnac figured he'd have his car to drive to Paris, so why would he need an escort?"

"Perhaps," Kaz said, scanning the terrain ahead. "If that were the case, he'd take the train as well. The Germans at the machine gun nest certainly took casualties from the colonel's armored car. They may not have been inclined or able to assist Jarnac."

"So, the best case for us is if he had to hoof it on his own to the nearest train station. Chaville?"

"I can't say from this map Dufort drew. It does show two turn-offs for other villages, and either could have a train station," Kaz said. "His note says trains depart from Chaville on the Paris line on the hour."

"Maybe we'll get lucky, and he'll be on the same train," I said, knowing that if luck had really been going our way, I would have kept hold of more than Jarnac's jacket.

"We should be alert to the possibility," Kaz said, as the chatter of machine guns reasserted itself, and four Thunderbolts glinted in the sunlight as they arced upwards into the sky after another strafing run.

Smoke rose up ahead of us, marking their target. A bright plume of flame blossomed and then faded. I slowed, which was not hard with our lumbering vehicle, and stopped as the destruction came into view.

A German truck lay on its side in a ditch, tires burning and sending thick, acrid, black smoke churning upwards as flames licked at the truck bed and swirled inside the cab. Two bodies sat up front, barely recognizable as human in the consuming fires. Around the truck, which was riddled with bullets, a dozen bodies lay sprawled, some missing limbs, some burning, all lifeless.

We drove around it, the heat from the conflagration shimmering against the late afternoon sky. Kaz rolled up his window. Two shots startled us, followed by more as I sped up.

"No one is shooting at us," Kaz said, looking back. "It is just their ammunition cooking off."

"Good. I'm done being shot at for today," I said. "How much farther?"

"Ten miles or so," Kaz said. "I wonder if those Germans were a patrol, or sent out to investigate the attack on the gun emplacements?"

"Probably checking for survivors," I said. That's what I wanted to believe, because it meant we wouldn't run into any more patrols. "Hey, tell me about this One-Two-Two place. Sounds like a whorehouse. How'd you know about it?"

"The One-Two-Two is a brothel," Kaz said. "A very high-class brothel with an illustrious clientele."

"Don't tell me you're including yourself," I said, giving him a questioning glance.

"I have been there, in the company of my uncle," Kaz said. "But I did not partake. He told me I was too young, but that I should come back when I turned twenty. In addition to the brothel, there is a restaurant and a salon, which is where I waited for my uncle to conclude his business."

"It must have been tempting," I said.

"Quite, especially since the waitresses wore nothing but high-heeled shoes and flowers in their hair," Kaz said. "However, I was young enough to be a bit frightened by my uncle's description of the higher floors in the mansion. As one ascends, the rooms are given over to whips and such. He said that at the One-Two-Two, the closer you drew to the sky, the closer you came to hell."

"Sounds like the perfect place for Nazis to relax after a long day in the torture chambers," I said.

"It also would be the perfect place to overhear a lot of interesting information," Kaz said. "In the salon as well as in the bedrooms. We should visit, even if we do not need assistance from Malou."

"Now that you're over twenty," I said. Soon we drew close to a crossroads, a sign pointing to Chaville, seven kilometers away.

"I owe it to the memory of my uncle, don't you think? Look, Billy, to the right."

A plowed field sprouted leafy greens. Turnips, probably. But a line of German soldiers was planting another crop. Mines. About twenty Krauts were advancing along the rows, digging holes for men behind them to bury anti-personnel mines. At the edge of the road, another group was clustering mines in the drainage ditch.

If GIs on the roadway came under fire, they'd dive into the ditches for cover and be killed by the mines planted there. If they went across the fields, they'd end up sitting ducks caught in the minefield trap there.

"Don't look at them," I said, keeping the speed of the Peugeot as steady as I could. The nearest men were no more than twenty yards away as we drove by. A German corporal stood up and took a long drink from his canteen, his eyes drawn to the car.

He looked straight at me. I nodded, and Kaz gave him a cheery little wave.

"This is a strange war," I muttered, as we drove past the work detail. Ahead, several trucks were parked in a grove of trees clustered around a bridge that spanned a small stream. Hidden just enough to save these guys from being worked over by the Thunderbolts.

"So far, we have seen more Germans than I expected," Kaz said.

"Laying mines is what you do when you don't have enough men to stop an attack," I said. "They know what's coming, and they know they can't stop it. But they can slow it down."

"Let us hope they are too busy to set up roadblocks," Kaz said, straining to see ahead along the meandering curves of the road. A farmhouse came into view, its gray slate roof sagging and in disrepair. An old man with a mustache sagging at a similar angle leaned on his hoe and watched us drive by.

He didn't crack a smile.

"The village is ahead," Kaz said, pointing to a church steeple. "Drive by the railway station so we can see what to expect."

The road narrowed to a cobblestone lane with houses and shops crowded along a thin ribbon of sidewalk. We drove into the town center, the church at one end and the railway station at the other. I cruised by slowly, looking for a spot to leave the car.

"There is a line at the ticket booth, and a train on the track," Kaz said.

"Any Krauts or police?" I asked.

"No. We should hurry. Stay close to me and do not speak."

I eased the car in alongside the church, tossed the key into the glove box, and gave Kaz most of my *francs*. I wouldn't know what to say when it came to forking out cash anyway. As we strolled down the sidewalk, my eyes darted in every direction. A few people sat chatting at a sidewalk café, two Kraut officers among them. They paid us no mind, more intent on their wine and eyeing a pair of pretty girls who walked by ignoring them with grave indifference.

Kaz stood at the end of the line, which snaked up several steps to the ticket window. I pulled the brim of my hat down, feeling like every set of eyes in town was glued to me. I wished someone would get behind me, and then became terrified of anyone starting up a conversation. I could make out a few words of French here and there, but everyone spoke so damn fast I had a hard time making sense of anything.

The line moved along, and we got to the top step. The whistle on the locomotive blew, and I could hear the hiss of steam as the boiler released excess pressure. We moved closer, and I saw Kaz counting out *francs*. I had no idea what the ticket cost, and I hoped he had a clue. Laying out too much dough wouldn't look right.

I heard footsteps.

I felt a presence at my back.

I heard German.

I saw Kaz's shoulders stiffen.

The line moved forward, and I listened to the Krauts chatter at each other. The two officers from the café maybe, since no other vehicles had pulled up.

The good news was I wouldn't be expected to understand.

The bad news was they might speak French.

We were almost to the ticket window.

I felt a tap on my shoulder. I turned, facing one of the officers from the café. He had a cigarette dangling from his lips, and he gestured as if he were lighting it. His pal laughed. He wanted a light, and they were both a little drunk.

I shook my head and turned away, like any self-respecting Frenchman would do. Now Kaz was at the window shoving cash under the grill and snatching up the tickets. I kept to his coattails and made for the train, like any guy in a hurry to get home.

The tipsy Germans were right behind me. Loud, like drunks often are. Especially drunks with pistols and the power of life and death.

It was easy to see the first railcar was crowded, so we walked down the platform to the next. Also packed. We went to another car, the bootheels of the two officers echoing in our wake. We got on board and worked our way toward the last two empty seats. Across from us sat an elderly couple, the woman cradling a basket covered with a towel. Eggs, maybe, or some delicacy from a local farm. Her husband held a string sack filled with potatoes. I wondered what they'd traded for the food. Family heirlooms from Paris were probably stacking up in the cupboards of farmers around the city. The food situation in Paris had to be bad to make this rail journey worthwhile.

The Kraut officers went past us, searching for empty seats. They found none and turned back, eyeing the passengers as if expecting them to give up their seats and doff their caps to the master race.

No one looked at them. It was the standard code of conduct

for most of the French when it came to daily interactions with the occupier. Curt politeness when required, aloof detachment when possible. Passengers quieted as the Germans strode down the aisle, their narrowed eyes as hostile and threatening as the slit in a concrete bunker.

They halted a couple of rows in front of us. I folded my arms, mainly to hide the twitching in my right hand, not wanting to give them an excuse to ask for my papers. Kaz yawned and covered his mouth.

"*Aufstehen*," the first officer said. I looked up, meeting his gaze. He beckoned with his fingers in a hurry-up motion. I couldn't move. His eyes darted back and forth, his face full of nervous energy.

The two men in front of us stood up and shuffled off down the aisle. The German's eyes registered relief. No matter that they were armed and lords over the men and women in this rail carriage, they were still outnumbered. They sat heavily on their seats, grunting the way people do at the end of a long day, relieved to be headed home.

I sighed, unaware I hadn't breathed since the German spoke. I glanced at Kaz, who raised an eyebrow, shrugged, and looked out the window. Nonchalant is his middle name.

The train lurched forward, and people began to pick up their conversations, a sense of relief flooding through the compartment now that the potential threat had passed. The locomotive cut loose with a shrill whistle as we picked up speed, leaving the town behind and traveling along a riverbed flanked by fields of crops wilting in the August heat. The countryside swam by, hills, fields, and forests in quick succession.

Kaz nudged me with his knee and arched an eyebrow toward the window. On the road paralleling the tracks was a convoy of trucks hauling the dreaded German 88 artillery pieces. Three of them, turning off the main road and heading into the fields beyond. Mainly an anti-aircraft weapon, the 88 was also deadly at long range against our tanks. We hadn't seen a lot of troop activity, but a few of these guns, well-concealed, could hold up an advance for hours.

Had *Atlantik* already delivered his traitorous message? Or were the Krauts simply moving what resources they had into position in front of Paris?

The train slowed as we rolled into another town. We stopped at the station where only a few people got off and more boarded. In seconds we were off, chugging toward Paris, the City of Light.

I'd seen London and Rome. Pretty impressive places. But no city stirred my imagination as much as Paris. Dad and Uncle Frank had told me about their adventures there while on leave during the First World War. If half their stories were to be believed, it was a helluva town. Of course, back then it hadn't been enemy territory. By the looks of the people on this train, it might be a touch threadbare. But it was still Paris.

The Germans in front of us were have a heated discussion, their heads close together, one of them shaking his head and waving his hand. Maybe they were debating which restaurant they'd miss the most when they left Paris. I could sense Kaz concentrating on their conversation as the door behind us opened.

"*Ihre Papiere, bitte,*" a voice announced sharply as the door slammed shut. Two Kraut soldiers, rifles slung over their shoulders, moved along the aisle, hands extended for the *carte d'identité* which every French person had to carry. These guys must have boarded at the last stop. It looked very routine, the Germans looking bored and impatient at the same time.

The officers continued talking, their argumentative tone fading into dismissive laughter. They ignored the oncoming soldiers. I did not.

One of them worked the left side of the aisle, his pal staying on our side. Behind me, a quarrel broke out between a young woman and her elderly companion. Glancing back, I saw the younger one hand her papers to the solider and turn to search the older woman's handbag. Had she lost her identity card? Finally, she came up with it. The German barely gave it a glance and moved on.

That was a good sign. Maybe he didn't think the old lady was a spy, or just didn't give a damn. The old couple opposite us got the same treatment, except their Kraut asked to see what was in the basket.

Eggs. The Kraut even said *danke* as she covered them up again.

It was almost our turn. Kaz had his card out. I kept mine in my pocket for the moment. The *Milice Brigade Spéciale* identity card was different from the standard card. It had the French national colors splashed across it in a red, white, and blue banner. It attracted notice, which was probably the point, but I decided to act as if I was undercover, hoping to keep it under wraps and avoid a close inspection.

The German stood next to me, the stock of his rifle banging against the seat.

Kaz held out his identity card. I pushed his hand back, looking the soldier straight in the eye. I withdrew my *Milice* card and held it down low, hidden from view of other passengers. I opened it, praying this would be quick, a quiver working through my hand as I held the jacket open to shield the card.

A frown creased his face. This was unusual, a break from the monotony of checking hundreds of identity cards. He squinted and leaned closer as I wondered if we'd be undone by a Kraut who needed glasses.

His partner took notice. He leaned in and gave me the once-over, his glance lingering for a moment on the *Milice* card. He patted the other's arm, a signal for him to move on. I made a discreet nod of thanks, one fascist to another. He moved on and offered a respectful nod to the officers, giving their travel documents a cursory check and handing them back. Maybe he bought the notion that I was a pro-Vichy agent tailing a terrorist. Maybe he didn't care about French collaborators and wanted a beer at the next stop. Either way was fine with me.

They proceeded along, a wave of tension ahead of them as they neared the front of the carriage. Papers were held up, inspected, and returned. No words were exchanged, and I had the feeling this was a common experience for everyone, Germans and French alike.

The train slowed, rounding a bend along the riverbank. The whistle blew as I watched a group of women weeding in a field. Potato plants, by the look of the leaves.

A man got to his feet at the front of the car, the German security guards six rows away. A young guy, he stood out among the older folks, kids, and women in the crowded compartment. He moved into the aisle, head down.

One of the officers shouted to the soldiers, pointing at the Frenchman.

The Frenchman ran, throwing open the door and slamming it shut. The Krauts ran after him, but before they got to the gangway between the cars, he'd launched himself off the train, tumbling and rolling down the grassy embankment. One of the guards fired his rifle, but the curving train hid the Frenchman from view.

Shots cracked from the carriage behind us. There were other Germans on the train, farther back, who'd had a better view. A submachine gun burst, then nothing but the clacking of the steel wheels and a sob from the old lady across from us.

The two soldiers strolled back into the carriage, mechanically picking up where they'd left off.

Ihre Papiere, bitte.

Had the Frenchman made it? Maybe. But how long could he survive without an identity card good enough to pass a security check? If he wasn't shot dead or wounded, and if he found a place to hunker down for a couple of days, he might make it.

Hell, his chances were probably better than ours.

The guards got off at the next stop, just outside of Paris, six of them remaining on the platform and staring into the carriage windows as we pulled out of the station.

The train chugged along, passing a boarded-up station with what looked like bomb damage. We slowed as the track continued through a built-up area with plain, stout buildings and warehouses on either side. A field of rubble rolled by, blackened brick walls standing amidst wrecked machinery. I didn't know we'd bombed this close to Paris. Or was this Paris itself, this neighborhood of smashed factories?

A sign hung crookedly above the entrance to a gutted brick building. RENAULT. I knew the company was working with the Vichy government to build vehicles for the German war machine. From the looks of things, they hadn't made any recent deliveries.

The train rumbled slowly on, finally crossing a wide river—it had to be the Seine—and moving into what looked to be the city proper. Then came a rail yard, where the train inched along before pulling into the station. It finally lurched to a halt, the sign on the platform telling me we were at the Gare Saint-Lazare.

Paris. I was in Paris.

I wasn't even scared.

CHAPTER TWENTY-TWO

SAINT-LAZARE WAS CAVERNOUS, a massive platform under a steel-girder glass roof, filled with hissing steam, Germans in field gray, and Parisians in their worn elegance. Exiting the train, I noticed German soldiers descending from the locomotive, watched by engineers with sooty faces and hatred in their eyes. A line of German officers was moving slowly aboard an eastbound train, each man weighed down with heavy suitcases. These were the lucky ones, getting out ahead of the Allies with all the loot they could carry.

Kraut guards walked two-by-two through the crowd, which opened and closed around them, the *Parisiennes* avoiding eye contact and the threat of their shouldered weapons. I followed Kaz to the exit, keeping close and watching for another security check.

A rattle of gunfire broke out, not close by, but echoing off the stone walls of the giant station. People jumped, startled at the noise, then returned to their orderly flow into the street. Even the guards did little more than exchange glances, as if this were a routine evening rush hour.

Kaz nodded toward the enamel sign on the corner of the building where we were waiting to cross. The rue Saint-Lazare followed by a right on the rue du Havre. Not that I'd remember, but it was the best way to show me the layout without speaking out loud. Down the street, he pointed to the Café Paul, a small place on the shady side of the road, with an empty table at the far end.

"No time," I whispered. He shook me off and sat, so I joined him. At least there were no Germans. The clientele was a mixture of guys in suits and workmen, some of whom were casting suspicious glances at each passerby. We sat, our chairs close and angled away from the others. Kaz signaled the waiter and gave our order.

"We have time," he said, glancing at the other tables.

"How do you know?" I asked quietly, trying to look calm. Hushed conversations always attract attention, so I crossed my legs and rested my chin in my hand. Your typical blasé Parisian.

"The *boche* on the train," he said. "They had been waiting for an agent to come across the lines."

"Jarnac?"

"They did not mention a name. But they said they had waited past the designated time, and would return tomorrow," Kaz said, leaning back as the waiter set down two glasses of white wine. He took a small sip, watching for the guy to go back inside. "It may well have been Jarnac. There may be other agents slipping through the lines along that sector, but how many would rate such a reception committee?"

"Then they're *Abwehr* agents themselves," I said. "What else did they say?"

"It was difficult to understand everything," Kaz said. "They joked about not being able to wait forever, and then argued about their boss. Evidently, he will not be happy when they show up without their man. One of them said he could handle it. Then they talked about where to eat, and how much they would miss French cuisine."

As if on cue, two bowls of potato soup were set down in front of us.

"I don't think Jarnac is going to wait a day," I said, taking a spoonful of soup and searching for the potatoes. A few odd bits of vegetable matter floated in the warm broth, and I felt jealous of the Kraut officers who were certainly dining better than anyone at this café.

"No. His information will have much less value tomorrow," Kaz said. "We can be certain he will get here tonight by any means possible."

"How far is it to the Hotel Lutetia?" I asked, sipping the cool white wine.

"About a thirty-minute walk," he said. "We shall stroll by the One-Two-Two first. It is only a few blocks from here, and on our way."

"Kaz, you're not planning on a stop there now, are you?" I said, smiling as I discovered a chunk of potato.

"Not today, certainly," he said. "But remember, we have a contact there in case of emergency. Should we become separated, you will need to know how to get there."

"Right," I said, polishing off the soup and glancing up with a start as gunfire sounded in the distance. Rifle shots, followed by a machine gun burst. A reminder that becoming separated could get both of us killed or wounded. "I wonder if that shooting is coming from the police headquarters? Inspector Ribot told us the cops had gone on strike and occupied the *Prefecture de Police*."

"The *Prefecture* is too far away," Kaz said. "The Germans mentioned something about a cease-fire, but I could not tell if they were referring to the police, the Resistance, or both."

"Sounds like somebody didn't get the message," I said, as a volley of fire sounded from a different direction. "Odd that no one here is panicking."

"I will ask the waiter about the cease-fire," Kaz said, signaling to him. I figured it made sense for anyone new in town to ask about all the shooting. The train station was close enough to this café that they probably served a lot of travelers. Not that there were many visiting Paris these days. Kaz chatted with the waiter, who grew more exasperated as they talked.

"There was a truce," Kaz told me. "The German commandant agreed to it along with representatives of the Resistance council. There were vehicles flying white flags with FFI and German representatives announcing the ceasefire. Germans were to be allowed to move freely, and the FFI could continue to hold their buildings and barricades."

"What happened?" I said, draining the last of my wine.

"The truce held for a time. Then some Germans who evidently did not receive word of it opened fire as they passed a barricade. The FFI retaliated. The Communists, who form the largest wing of the FFI in Paris, were never for the truce, so they called for more attacks against the occupiers. *A chacun son boche*, their slogan goes. To each his own *boche*."

"Is it safe on the streets?"

"He said in several neighborhoods it is quiet. In some places, the Germans still stand guard outside their buildings, sometimes in plain sight of the FFI at a barricade. Elsewhere, it is open warfare. He wonders if the Allies know how bad things are. Oh, and he apologizes for the soup."

Kaz settled up our tab and led the way. At the rue de Provence we hung a right and shortly ended up at number one-twenty-two. It was a plain, five-story structure with a stout wooden door and curtained windows.

"The club is known as the One-Two-Two," Kaz said. "Always said in English. If you become lost and need to get here, most Parisians will understand if you ask for directions."

"Let's plan on sticking together, Kaz," I said, pulling down the brim on my hat and covering my face as I spoke. I didn't see a *feldgrau* uniform in sight, but there was no telling if any of the men or women we passed on the sidewalk were *Milice*, otherwise pro-Vichy, or an opportunist who'd sell a couple of Allied agents down the river for a decent meal. Hell, I was carrying a *Milice* identity card myself, and any of the military-age guys within a few steps of me could be doing the same.

Kaz couldn't help pointing out the opera house, which was pretty impressive with its gilt copper statues lit by the early evening sun as it neared the horizon. Then we came to a wide street, which he told me was boulevard des Italiens, one of the four grand boulevards of Paris.

The street was empty, except for a single gazogene-powered Citroën that cruised slowly by. The sidewalks were full, crowds of people out strolling on a warm summer's evening. There was a buzz in the air, a sense of anticipation, as if everyone was on their way to a show but didn't know how to get there, or when it actually started.

We began to cross the boulevard, but the rough sound of a truck engine echoed against the granite buildings. Kaz pulled me back, and we moved off the road, taking cover in a doorway with half a dozen others. The crowds melted away as the truck neared us, like a school of fish threatened by a predator. It was full of German soldiers standing in the open back, rifles angled in every direction. A woman next to me turned her back and covered her eyes, while her companion stared at the occupants of the truck, hatred gleaming in her unblinking gaze.

One of the Krauts shot into a group of people huddled together on the pavement. They dove to the ground as the bullet ricocheted off the concrete. Laughter rippled from the soldiers as the truck rumbled on. No one was hurt, and people helped one another up, dusting themselves off and sending a stream of denunciation after the departing *boche*.

Within minutes, the street scene was back to normal, or what passed for normal in Paris during the waning days of occupation. A strange mixture of heady expectation, hatred, joy, and a smattering of tear-stained cheeks.

We crossed the boulevard and hustled down another wide road, the avenue de l'Opéra, Kaz informed me, which would take us back to the opera house and from there the One-Two-Two was a short walk. I told him I had my bearings and studied the buildings along this stretch. Lots of fancy shops, all closed. Big signs in German across the street, announcing a movie theater was a *Soldatenkino* and a department store a *Soldatenkaufhaus*. The pedestrians out on the broad sidewalks avoided that side of the road, even though there were no *boche* evident.

A few minutes later we spotted a group of Germans a block ahead, out in front of a building draped with red banners sporting the black swastika. Four stood at attention, guards at the front door. The rest looked like officers, their boots gleaming even at this distance. More men in *feldgrau* poured out the front door, milling about, aiming their rifles casually up and down the avenue. Civilians on the sidewalk ahead of us hesitated, some halting, some turning back. The crowd jammed up around us, people behind us colliding with those who'd stopped or started to flee.

Two young women held onto an older lady who'd lost her balance. I turned to see a gaggle of young men with tousled hair and rolled-up shirtsleeves, waving their arms and telling people behind them to go back. They had the disheveled look of *résistants*, their eyes gleaming with hatred as they glanced back at the Krauts piling out of the building. A few people shouted, calling out names of those they'd lost sight of, cursing and shaking their fists at the Germans who started to form up, their weapons leveled. In a second, the churning clutch of bodies moved, retreating from the *boche* and taking refuge down a side street.

The young men—boys, now that I looked at them more closely—stayed at the corner watching the Germans, stepping back, perhaps not believing the soldiers would fire. Kaz and I stuck together, the young women and their elderly charge shuffling along before us as we worked to keep the crowd from overwhelming them. Right as we made our turn into the side street, the Germans fired.

Bullets zinged against the cobblestones and one of the boys went down, then another. Screams raged through the crowd as they stampeded away, overturning café chairs and tables in the narrow lane. More shots echoed from the avenue, and one of the boys who'd been dragging his wounded companion to shelter was cut down as well. Shouts came from the avenue, pleas for help in French and orders in German, the words incomprehensible amidst the cries of pain and fear rising around us.

"Stay here," I said to Kaz, pushing him against the wall as I peeked around the corner. The gunshots had ended, but the Krauts were still formed up outside the building, maybe a headquarters or a barracks. I ran into the avenue, apparently low on common sense at that particular moment. I grabbed one kid by his collar and dragged him into the side street while he clutched at his leg, shattered by a Kraut slug. Kaz pulled him in and I returned to the avenue, helping another boy with his friend who'd taken one in the chest. He didn't look good, but he was breathing, short ragged gasps punctuated by pink frothy bubbles.

We brought him to safety as I glanced at the body of a kid spread-eagled in the street. He had the still limpness of death about him, not to mention the large pool of blood beneath his back.

"*Mort*," I said, grabbing the arm of the *résistant* who was about to dart back out onto the wide avenue. I shook my head, warning him about making a useless gesture as I glanced around the corner. He turned away with a finality that told me this wasn't the first death he'd witnessed at the hands of the occupiers.

Kaz was holding the kid with the wounded leg while one of his pals applied pressure to stanch the bleeding. A car appeared, flying a white flag with a red cross. A brace of *résistants* tumbled out, wearing FFI armbands and white smocks with hand-painted red crosses. They quickly patched up the wounded and placed them in the automobile, then jumped on the running boards as the vehicle sped away.

"Medical students," Kaz said, as the last of the crowd melted away into a warren of narrow lanes. All that was left was the body out on the avenue and the old lady with her two new friends, sipping wine at a nearby sidewalk café as the owner righted the chairs and tables strewn about. "Several have already been killed. As you might have been."

"It made sense at the time," I said, finding my hat and brushing it off. During the action, my hand was steady, as if it didn't want to betray me when it might get shot off. Now, in this quiet spot, the quiver began to work its way up my forearm. "What do we do now?"

The tromp of boots from the main avenue answered that one for us. The Germans were clearing the area, and this wasn't a place to linger. I saw the old woman wave to her young friends, who darted into the café, probably looking for a rear exit. Phony papers, most likely. She stayed put, finishing her wine. Real identity papers and the audacity of age, if I read the expression on her face correctly.

We took off at a good pace, winding through streets as Kaz guided us toward the Seine, which we had to cross to get to the Hotel Lutetia. We'd have to find a spot to stake out Jarnac, which meant a good hiding spot to avoid German guards, but one close enough to take a shot at him. A killing shot.

"Stop," Kaz said, thrusting out an arm. While I was thinking about plugging Jarnac, he'd been watching the street. A German staff car and a truck pulled over ahead of us. A half dozen Krauts went inside while the rest guarded the vehicles. The neighborhood was on the swanky side, with no rebellious youth in sight. A couple walking their dog stopped to chat, shaking their heads as Kaz spoke with them.

"Those officers were billeted in that apartment building," Kaz reported after they'd moved on. "They are taking all the furnishings and artwork with them. Apparently, it is happening in many of the finer Paris neighborhoods. The administrative troops are evacuating, taking with them what they wish."

We turned back, not wanting to be shanghaied into a moving detail.

Unfortunately, Kaz's sense of direction was off a bit. Paris reminded me a bit of Boston. The small, narrow lanes laid out with no special plan, winding through neighborhoods where the street names changed every few blocks. We found ourselves back at the avenue de l'Opéra, but on the south side of the military headquarters we'd encountered earlier. There were still Krauts gathered outside, but it was two blocks away, so we sauntered down the avenue like we belonged there. There wasn't much light left, even with the August sun setting late. As we passed rue Sainte-Anne, people spilled out onto the avenue, most of them glancing back over their shoulders. Not a good sign.

"*Boche!*"

Grinding gears and clanking treads told the same story as a half-track turned the far corner, unleashing a burst of machine gun fire into the crowd. But this time not everyone was unarmed. At the rear of the pack were FFI, weapons at the ready. They fired back with rifles and a few captured MP40 submachine guns as the wounded were spirited away. The dead remained behind.

It seemed most of this bunch were FFI, both armed and unarmed. We moved along with them, running to outpace the slow advance of the half-track. Then, from the southerly end of the avenue, a Tiger tank clanked into position, jolting to a halt and swiveling its turret toward the pack of *résistants*.

"This is a helluva ceasefire," I said to Kaz, as the fifty or so people around us moved away from the threat of the Tiger's

88mm cannon and toward the corner that would expose us to the half-track's machine gun.

Across the avenue, an apartment window opened on the third floor. A woman leaned out, waving and pointing to the wooden doorway below. A gray-haired fellow with a thick mustache opened it, revealing a small courtyard.

The choice was obvious. The pack surged across the broad avenue, running for the safety of the courtyard and the hope of escape beyond it. We joined in as two of the FFI stayed at the corner, firing their rifles at the half-track, hopefully buying us the time we'd need. Three men dashed around the corner under their covering fire, falling to their knees behind us, exhausted from their escape.

Machine gun fire came from the Tiger tank, spraying the street with hot lead. The shots peppered the building ahead of us. Lousy aim, or was the gunner reluctant to slaughter civilians? I saw chips flying from the stonework as bullets ricocheted, and I didn't much care what the reason was. Better the façade than me.

The first of the *résistants* to get to the door held it wide open, and the rest of us had to slow to make it through. The last FFI fighters at the corner ran pell-mell across the avenue, shepherding the three men ahead of them, one of them limping.

The Tiger's machine gun spat rounds again, this time finding their mark. One of the three men tumbled forward, his torso shredded. The two fighters grabbed the limping guy and ran him hard, practically lifting him across the threshold.

The door slammed shut behind us as machine gun rounds from the half-track stitched across it. Screams filtered out from the apartments as the gunner sprayed windows, shattering glass and sending residents spilling out the staircases. The guy who'd opened the door for us pointed to an interior doorway, sweeping his arm forward, telling us all to head that way.

"*Aux toits*," he shouted. I looked at Kaz.

"To the rooftops," he whispered. With this bunch, I didn't worry too much about being found out to be a Yank, but I didn't want to delay the getaway with a lot of backslapping either. So, we took our place in line as it snaked single-file up the narrow stairs. A few of the FFI lingered behind, tending to the guy with the injured leg. The firing from outside had died down, and I watched for any sign of the Krauts trying to smash through the stout wooden door. My guess was they were clearing the streets for troops moving through Paris on their way back to Germany. Or maybe they simply enjoyed being the boss in the big city and knew it was their last chance.

The FFI guys tried to lift the injured man up, but he waved them off. He sat on the ground, his back to us, head hung down low. Beneath the black beret was a thick head of black hair. He wore a white shirt with the sleeves rolled up, like a lot of these guys on this hot August night. But there was something about him.

I walked over and grabbed his beret.

Marcel Jarnac turned and glared at me, his dark eyes drilling into mine with undisguised hate.

CHAPTER TWENTY-THREE

"*TRAÎTRE!*" JARNAC SHOUTED, wasting no time. He pointed his finger at me, trembling as if in great fear of his life. Which was probably not an act.

Everyone was on edge, fingers on triggers and mistrust in their eyes. Jarnac was injured, a guy these FFI men had risked their lives to save. They were already on his side, if only unconsciously. I was some unknown guy in the crowd, while he was the first one to open his mouth, laying claim to the accusation of traitor.

I should have thought this through much better.

"*Américain,*" I said, tapping my chest, searching the sweaty faces for any glimpse of understanding. Jarnac accepted help getting up, and I could see he wasn't as crippled as he'd made out. Sure, he had a gash on his calf, maybe from a ricochet. But he'd been on the ground, bent over, to avoid us spotting him.

Now, he rose up to his full height, hanging on to the shoulder of a young *résistant*, further cementing their bond. He cut loose with a stream of denunciation, his bony finger aimed at Kaz, then me. I heard the phrase *Brigade Saint-Just* twice as Jarnac declared himself *chef*.

He was rapidly becoming the boss of this crowd. Kaz was trying to get a word or two strung together, but everyone was listening to Jarnac. One fighter poked Kaz in the gut with the barrel of his rifle, which convinced him to give up on the debate. We were grabbed roughly from behind, and the fifis went through our pockets.

This was not going to end well.

Kaz had most of the *francs*, which they found right away.

Then they found my pistol, which seemed to rile them up, even though carrying a weapon with all these Krauts around should have been considered sensible. I could have been one of them.

But the *Milice* identity card proved I wasn't.

Jarnac's eyes went wide, and the briefest of grins lit up his face. He couldn't believe his luck. Not only did his new friends believe his story, but I'd provided all the proof needed to seal the deal. There were only six FFI men left in the courtyard. But it was enough for a firing squad.

Kaz managed a few words, something about checking the identity card and looking at the picture. It didn't matter. The photo was close enough for this bunch, their rage and bloodlust running high. The guy behind me shoved me hard, forcing me to my knees. Then Kaz got the same treatment.

Jarnac stepped forward. The men went silent, watching him, waiting to see how the chief of the Saint-Just Brigade handled himself when it came to dealing with traitors. Behind us, I sensed movement, the shuffling of feet as the fifis edged away from the mess about to be displayed on the cobblestones.

"I am American," I said, looking straight at the guy nearest Jarnac. "My friend is Polish. We are Allied agents. Not *Milice*." I didn't know if he understood but talking to Jarnac was a waste of time.

He raised an eyebrow, a shimmer of curiosity on display. He looked at Kaz and placed one hand on Jarnac's arm.

A *clunk* echoed off the walls.

"Grenade!" I shouted, grabbing Kaz and shoving him toward the staircase door.

The German potato masher grenade rolled toward the main entrance as Jarnac and his pals dove for cover.

The explosion was fierce in the enclosed space, sending shrapnel zinging off the granite walls and leaving my ears ringing.

"Go!" I said to Kaz, pushing him into the vestibule, turning to check on who was watching us. He scrambled up the steps as a *résistant* advanced toward me, rifle at the ready. Two other fighters fired at a second-story window in the courtyard as another grenade sailed through the air. I scrambled into the staircase, hands up, with the FFI fighter following close. Another fifi slammed into us as we made a mad stumbling dash for the stairs. The grenade exploded, followed by a long scream. I raised my hands higher, blocking their view, as well as their aim, of Kaz scampering up the stairs.

Aux toits, my friend.

A rifle in my ribs got me going, my desire to give Kaz time for a clean getaway tempered by the notion of Germans coming after us as we climbed the narrow stairs, easy targets going up single file. I figured the Krauts must have come in through the windows, maybe hoisting themselves up from the top of the half-track and climbing in through the shattered windowpanes. By the number of guys behind me, they must have gotten a few of the fifis. And Jarnac? I could only hope.

But right now, I had a bigger problem. I'd been granted a stay of execution, but what I needed was a full pardon. From these guys and the Krauts. At the head of the stairs, a small door hung open on its hinges, the darkening sky beyond. On the roof, I waited, hands visible at my sides, not wanting to give my captors an excuse to shoot me while escaping. They spilled out, four of them, one grasping his arm, blood seeping through his fingers.

No Jarnac.

Shots sounded from below. In the apartments, maybe. Nazis taking their revenge on the residents for helping us escape. Or maybe they were taking potshots at people in the street. Either way, they weren't shooting at us. Cold comfort for those in the line of fire.

"*Avec moi,*" one of the FFI men said, the same fellow who'd taken my pistol. He wore a dirty white shirt and an FFI armband marked with the Cross of Lorraine. Since he didn't want to shoot me then and there, I decided it would be a fine idea to follow him and nodded my understanding.

"Roger," he said, which I took as a good sign, since executioners like to be anonymous. I told him my name was Billy but didn't offer to shake hands. I didn't want to push my luck.

He went first, running low along the spine of the apartment building, the gray zinc roof slanting off in either direction. At the next building, we had to make a small jump over a thin alley. It wasn't far, except for the way down. We grabbed onto chimney pots as we made our way across to the next rooftop, this one a full story lower. Roger hung down and let himself drop, clutching at a chimney and dancing around a skylight, barely keeping his balance. He called for one of his pals to come down next, which showed me he was still suspicious, or at least smart. After him, I dropped, and Roger caught me, passing me off to the other fighter, who kept his arm on mine. A discreet but unmistakable reminder that they wouldn't lose too much sleep tonight if they had to toss me into the road.

The wounded man was let down, the last *résistant* lowering him by his good arm.

We moved off, keeping away from the edge and being as quiet as possible, although I wondered about people in the attic apartments hearing us. Probably used to it, since it was an easy way to avoid patrols after curfew, or if you didn't have the right papers.

I looked around for any sign of Kaz, glad I didn't spot him, happy he got away, although it left me feeling lost without him. But this rooftop ramble kept me too busy to feel sorry for myself, since the next building looked like a killer. It went back up in height, and the roof was slate, pitched at a steep angle. I got dizzy looking at it.

A drainpipe at the edge of the building was the only way up. Roger grabbed hold of it and shinnied up, pulling himself onto the roof as something metallic gave way. There was a ping, and a small hunk of metal slid down the slate and vanished into the darkness below.

From our vantage point, the sky held lingering light, but below, the streets were pitch-black. Paris was still under a German blackout, but parts of the city glowed with faint lights, marking the boundaries of neighborhoods held by the Free French.

Roger beckoned me to come up next. I told myself it was a sign of trust, knowing full well that he wanted me—instead of one of his own men—to test out the drainpipe. I took hold of it, feeling the tremor in my hand and cursing the damned shakes. They'd left me alone when I was on my knees about to have my skull aired out, so why kick in now?

I inched my way up, making the mistake of looking down. Maybe the shakes were smarter than me. I went up, hand over hand, feet wrapped around the pipe. I felt Roger tap my shoulder and offer his hand. I took it and he pulled me up, grimacing as he moved back, keeping to the ridge, his legs straddling it. Nothing else popped off the drainpipe, and he signaled for the next man to climb up.

I took a deep breath and nodded my thanks. I inched backward, watching the wounded guy being lifted by two men. This was getting tricky. Roger leaned forward, his long arm extended to reach his friend's hand. He clasped it, grunting as he pulled him up. I reached over Roger, finding an elbow and pulling. We got him up and over onto the roof, and I scuttled back, out of the way.

Roger swung one leg over the peak, holding onto a chimney pot as he pulled the wounded guy along. He leaned forward, and I saw his body shift as he reached out for the next chimney pot. It was too late, his hand merely brushing against it as he slid down the slanted slate roof, trying to dig in his feet to halt the pull of gravity toward the dark cobblestones below.

I launched myself in his direction, one knee hooked over the peak, the rest of me headed down in the same direction, catching him by the wrist. His weight felt like it would pull my arm out of its socket, but I was more worried about my knee coming over the peak and the two of us taking a swan dive.

The wounded kid reached out with his good arm, but he had nothing to hold onto. Then he slid to the chimney pot, wrapping his legs around it and bending as far as he could in Roger's direction.

He got his other hand.

I felt the pull lessen on my own arm as he took some of Roger's weight. I caught a glimpse of another guy coming up and over the edge, and he joined in to pull Roger up. We laid against one another, breathing heavily, our bodies balanced on the thin peak, the dividing line between life and death.

For a moment. Then we were on our way, Roger in the lead, looking a bit wary, but still pushing ahead. The next building was lower, and we jumped to a wide ledge, then down onto the flat rooftop.

The tip of a cigarette glowed in front of us.

"*Bonsoir*," the voice said. It belonged to a man wearing a vest over his collarless shirt, sitting in a chair at the edge of the roof, next to a knee-high brick wall. He sounded like he expected us. The guy in the vest pointed to the street below, his cigarette dangling from his lips. It was a barricade, manned by dozens of the FFI, illuminated by lights shining from houses and cafés below. The gent nodded in the direction of his door, inviting us to descend through his apartment.

We were in a Free French neighborhood, which was better than a Nazi-controlled area. Except for the fact that it didn't necessarily mean *I* was free.

We descended the staircase. Armed and bloodied men didn't seem to alarm anyone, so I figured a lot of folks were taking the rooftop express. The barricade, which looked out over a four-way intersection, was built of paving stones, furniture, barrels, and sandbags. It looked like it would do a fine job of stopping a bullet and a lousy job of stopping a tank. Men, women, kids, everyone was strolling around like it was one big block party. Which, judging by the second barricade at the other end of rue Volney, it was.

A woman in a light blue dress, wearing a German helmet and a canvas sack filled with grenades over her shoulder, seemed to know Roger. She summoned help for the fifi with the bad arm, and a bunch of medicos wearing the same kind of red cross smocks I'd seen earlier scurried over. They sat him down and got to work cutting away his shirt.

Roger and the lady with the grenades had a talk, with a lot of gestures tossed in my direction. I figured my chances of not being shot out of hand were fairly good, but beyond that I had no idea what to expect.

"You say you are *américain?*" she said, tipping the helmet back on her head and studying me with narrowed eyes. She was maybe forty, with a round face and more curls than I'd ever seen under a Kraut helmet.

"I am. Sorry, but I don't speak much French. My name is Billy Boyle," I said, flashing a smile and trying to work up some boyish charm. But I didn't have much energy left for it.

"Mister Billy Boyle, why do you have this *carte d'identité* from the *Milice?* You are not Charles Guillemot, are you?" She studied the card again, glancing at my face and shaking her head. "Or perhaps you are, and it is a poor photograph?"

"No," I said. "I was shot down two weeks ago over Belgium. The underground smuggled me as far as Amiens, but they lost contact with the group that was supposed to get me through the lines. So, they gave me this and suggested I make my way to Paris and wait for the Allies."

"This worked?" she asked, slapping the identity card with her hand.

"Yes. It passed a security check on the train. And it almost got me killed, right Roger?"

Roger nodded. They whispered to each other while I tried to fill in my phony story about being shot down. I'd be a fighter pilot, maybe with a couple of kills to my credit. I didn't think it would help my case to lay out the whole story of Jarnac and the map, not after the way Roger and the others had acted around him. I couldn't tell if they knew him or just knew of the Saint-Just Brigade. Either way, I couldn't match that kind of clout.

"Then why did Marcel Jarnac call you *traître*?"

"I don't know," I said, giving my impression of a Gallic shrug of indifference. "Perhaps he knew of Charles Guillemot and thought I was him."

"Roger tells me he denounced you before seeing your papers," she said. This was one smart lady.

"I am sorry, of course. Yes, he did so immediately. I can't say why, although the man was in some pain. Whatever happened to him, *madame*?"

"Roger says he fled into the apartments, which was a bad idea, since the *boche* were there as well. I am Nicole Lalis, *Monsieur* Boyle, if that is your real name. Roger tells me you saved his life tonight."

"He was in a tight spot," I said. She furrowed her brow at that, so I explained what I meant.

"Ah, *oui*," she said. "That was good of you. Still, the leader of the Saint-Just Brigade would not make this *dénonciation* without reason. You will be our guest tonight. Jarnac may find his way here, since there are many members of the FTP in these streets."

"And in the morning, if he does not come?" I asked.

"We shall see," Nicole said.

"*Merci beaucoup, monsieur,*" a young girl said to me as she walked by. She wore a red cross armband, one of the medical team patching up the kid with the bad arm.

"For what?" I said, not even thinking. She looked puzzled and spoke to Nicole, who I was beginning to understand was the *chef* around here.

"She says you ran out under the guns of the *boche* to rescue a wounded man," Nicole said, eyeing me with what I hoped was newfound respect.

"I'm a fighter pilot, what can I say?" I tried the charm routine again, failing once more when Nicole didn't swoon.

"Roger will give you food. I will see to you in the morning," Nicole said, turning away and stepping up on a pile of cobblestones to peer out into the gloom. I was the least of her problems. There were a few thousand German troops in Paris who were a bigger headache right now.

"Excuse me, Nicole," I said, following her to the barricade. "You said there are a lot of FTP people here. Maybe some are in the Saint-Just Brigade? Could you ask them to put out the word that I'd like to speak with this Jarnac fellow? To set the record straight about who I am."

"I am FTP myself. But not of the *Brigade Saint-Just.* Tell me, why would you invite such trouble?" Nicole said, hardly taking her eyes off the intersection.

"I don't know how long it will be before the Americans get here, and I don't want a false accusation hanging over me," I said. Besides, I couldn't find Jarnac in time, unless I tempted him with some bait. Me.

"*Certainement,*" she said, after a moment's thought.

Roger tapped me on the shoulder and signaled me to follow him. I did, as Nicole called out to several of her people. A glance in my direction told me she was granting me my wish. Like the beat of jungle drums in a Tarzan movie, the message would reverberate among the FFI and the Reds, telling them an American was waiting to speak to Marcel Jarnac.

My guard, escort, or whatever Roger was, led me to a café lit by a few candles. There were no waiters or bartender. The place had been taken over as a mess hall for the fighters, doling out what food they had. We ended up with plates of boiled potatoes and mashed turnip, washed down with a couple of glasses of red wine.

"*Veux-tu aller?*" Roger said in a whisper, after slugging down the last of the wine.

I didn't get it.

"*Aller!*" That I got. He was offering to let me go.

"*Non,*" I said. "*Merci,* my friend, but I will stay for now. May I have my pistol?" I made a shooting motion with my hand and then mimed opening a paper. "*Carte d'identité?*"

"*Non, mon ami,*" Roger said. He was ready to let me slip away, but not to explain to Nicole where the pistol and papers had gone when morning rolled around. Fair enough.

On the wall behind us was a large-scale street map of Paris. I got up to look. It had the usual landmarks for tourists. The Eiffel Tower, the Louvre, the Arc de Triomphe, and Sacré-Coeur, the white-domed church on the hill in Montmartre. The map was marked in pen with German strongpoints as well. The Hotel Meurice, the Senate, and more.

"Moulin Rouge?" I asked, tapping the map in the area of Montmartre. Roger grinned at the mention of the famous nightclub with the naughty cancan dance. He pointed to the boulevard de Clichy, where Krauts had been lining up for years to see the dancers. In a few days, the crowds would be khaki, and the show would go on.

"Where are we?" I asked, pointing to each of us and then the map. Roger showed me rue Volney, tucked between two major thoroughfares. All the twists and turns on the pavement and across rooftops had led me back to within a block of the opera house. Which, I noted, was among the German strongpoints on the map. No wonder Nicole was keeping such a close watch.

Roger led me upstairs to a crowded apartment. *Résistants* were sprawled everywhere, weapons stacked against the wall. Some sleeping fighters lay with their arms curled around hard-won rifles. A kid of about ten handed us threadbare blankets and pointed down the hall. He was excited, having the time of his life sharing his apartment with the men and women of the Resistance.

Me, I was nothing but dog-tired. The room was a small study, with a young girl in the single easy chair, a Sten gun in her lap. Asleep, she looked about sixteen. Roger pointed to the corner and took a stretch of floor by the door for himself. Guarding the exit, after a fashion. He covered himself with his dusty suit jacket, laid his rifle at his side, and bunched up his blanket to use as a pillow. He pulled my pistol from his pocket and laid it next to the rifle. It was a small automatic, but still uncomfortable to sleep on.

I rolled up my jacket for a pillow and lay on half the blanket, pulling the other half over me. Roger said *bonne nuit*, and I followed suit. The girl murmured it back to us.

Strange how the normal patterns of life assert themselves in the most abnormal situations. It was almost soothing. But I would have felt a lot better if I knew I'd wake up before Jarnac stood in that doorway and said hello with a bullet.

I clenched the blanket, my hand quivering against my cheek as I willed it to calm down. I wondered where Kaz was. I wondered where Leclerc was. I wondered where Jarnac was, and if Kaz had been able to stop him. How he could have, I had no idea.

Me, I had an idea. But all I could do right now was try to stay awake. I dug my fingernails into my palm. I bit my lip.

The taste of blood was metallic on my tongue.

CHAPTER TWENTY-FOUR

I MIGHT HAVE fallen asleep, because for a moment I had no idea where I was. I made myself wake up. I had only one shot at this thing, a long shot, and it had to be taken now.

My eyes were gritty with fatigue when I pried them open. A damp breeze wafted through the room, and I could make out a drizzle of rain through the open window.

When was the last time I really slept? The previous night had been spent in the back of a truck, snatching a few winks as it rumbled through the dark, bringing us back from Patton's headquarters. The night before that was in a tent, on a cot, which wasn't bad as the army goes. Before that, in a foxhole on Hill 262, with German mortars serving up nightcaps and wake-up calls.

I shifted my position, careful to move quietly and not let my shoes scrape against the floor. My body ached with fatigue, but my mind was racing, sharp electric currents sending thoughts ricocheting inside my head.

I prayed it would keep me awake.

I heard a faint snort of breath from the girl in the chair as she tucked her legs underneath her and cradled her submachine gun like a teddy bear. She was out cold.

Roger was silent and unmoving, which might have been his style, or maybe he was having the same sort of lightning thoughts spinning through his brain. I lifted my arm slowly until I could read my wristwatch. Almost midnight. I'd slept a few hours, so maybe Roger was cutting logs in his own quiet way.

The hard floor was beginning to feel comfortable, so I had to make my move. If I woke up at dawn, it might be too late.

I rolled onto my side. Waited. Pushed myself up and noticed my right hand had stopped shaking. It was probably too tired. I waited for my breath to settle and got to my knees. The blanket muffled the sounds of my shoes as I got my feet under me and stood.

I went dizzy, or the room swayed around me, it was hard to tell the difference. One of us got our equilibrium, and I managed to stand, quietly, planning out my next steps. Literally. In two steps I'd be up to Roger, stretched out in front of the doorway. Then one big step over him and I'd be in the hall.

It sounded easy.

I slipped the phony identity card out of my jacket pocket but left the coat behind, not wanting to risk the rustle of fabric as I picked it up. I stepped away. One step, my shoe leather landing smoothly. Second step, and I was inches from Roger's arm, flung out at his side.

The pistol was by his elbow.

I knelt, slowly and quietly, reaching for the weapon. I got my hand on it just as a tremble started at the tip of my fingers and jiggled the steel barrel against the floor. I looped a finger through the trigger guard and lifted the pistol as I stepped over Roger's sleeping form, into the hall, not stopping until I got to the head of the stairs.

I stuck the two-bit automatic into my pocket and listened for any movement from the café. It was silent. I took the steps, careful not to let my heel fall too hard on the creaky wood. A couple of candles were guttering, ready to flicker out, giving the room a ghostly, shimmering light. I took one and carried it to the map, finding our neighborhood. I traced a route, circling around the German stronghold at the opera house, heading for Montmartre.

Once I found rue Taitbout, it was pretty much a straight shot up to the big boulevard de Clichy, which ought to be hard to miss. Then across, a left, another left, and a quick right would bring me to rue Ravignan. All I had to do then was find number thirty-seven, roust Paul Lambert out of bed, and kidnap him.

Or, if Jarnac was by any chance there, kill the bastard and leave Paul to bury him. But I doubted that possibility. Jarnac had something more important to attend to than visiting family.

So, grab Paul Lambert and bring him back here. While avoiding Krauts, of course. Not to mention trigger-happy *résistants* as I passed in front of their barricades. Then wait. Somewhere along the line I had to figure out what exactly to do with the kid.

I went through the kitchen and found a knife. Sharp, not too big. I stuck it in my belt and looked around for anything else that might come in handy. On a table I found a stack of armbands, the Cross of Lorraine and FFI nicely stitched. I put one on, swiped someone's beret, and decided I looked like a Parisian. In the dark, anyway.

I walked out the front door like I owned the joint. I went down to the far barricade, hoping the fighters there hadn't laid eyes on me being questioned by Nicole. There were a half dozen fifis on duty, leaning on the stacked paving stones and searching the streets for movement. I gave a jaunty wave and stepped onto the barricade and vaulted over, just another Resistance fighter on a mission.

"*Bonne chance*," one of them whispered as I scurried across the street, angling away from the approach to the opera house. I'd need all the luck Paris had to offer.

I didn't worry about the curfew. Germans were shooting civilians in broad daylight, so I figured the cover of darkness gave me an advantage. I cut into a side street, running from doorway to doorway, watching ahead of me for any sign of Krauts. I made it to the intersection as a car roared down the road, taking a corner at high speed and disappearing in seconds. German or French, I couldn't tell.

The misty rain soaked me, but it also hid me in the dark, foggy haze. Too bad it did the same for anyone else out there. There were no lights anywhere, which made it easier to see the flare of brightness as a match was struck at the corner ahead of me. A cigarette glowed, then disappeared.

It had to be a Fritz. Any Frenchman skulking around wouldn't give himself away like that. Behind me, I heard the faint tread of boots grow louder. A patrol, maybe. I hustled ahead, trying to make out any figures in the murkiness. I knelt behind a tree. I couldn't see a thing and hoped that it was because nothing was there. Maybe it was just a few Krauts coming home late from one last fling at the Moulin Rouge.

The boots grew louder and more insistent-sounding, and I knew I had to get out of there. I dashed ahead, darting into doorways and behind garbage cans, running broken-field style and hoping the Krauts didn't decide to double-time it.

I was close to the corner and caught a whiff of Kraut tobacco. It always smelled a little moldy to me. I froze, afraid to round the corner and run smack into trouble. The marching patrol drew closer, their hobnailed boots sparking harsh against the cobblestones. I made for the last doorway, hoping to hide in the shadows.

I slammed into a Kraut in the deep-set doorway. The brim of his helmet struck me in the forehead, my momentum shoving him against the door, his rifle clattering to the floor. Neither of us had expected this, but now we were embraced in a deadly, shuffling dance.

I shoved his helmet back, the strap catching on his throat and keeping him from crying out. He punched me in the ribs, hard, and I gasped for breath, both of us in the corner now, my hold on his helmet weakening as he hit me with a left again, sending me sliding sideways. I pulled the knife from my belt, his metal brim slipping from my grasp, just as he went for the knife sheathed in his belt.

I was faster.

The first thrust into his ribcage slid off bone. It hurt him, but he was still standing, flapping his hand at his side and trying to pull his blade. I stabbed him again, just where I'd been taught, right between the ribs and into the heart.

His arm dropped to his side, and he began to slide to the ground. I held him up to stop his body from falling right in front of the German formation coming my way. His head tilted forward, his eyes close to mine. They were blue. He blinked once, twice, as his last breath faded in the night air, a tiny *huff* marking the passing of life.

In a heartbeat—or in the time it would have taken his heart to beat if I hadn't shoved a length of cutlery into it—he became nothing but dead weight, and in an absurd flash of understanding, I knew where that term came from.

I crammed him into the corner of the doorway, jamming his rifle into his belt to keep him upright. The clatter of the hobnail boots echoed off the buildings, sounding closer and closer. I glanced around the edge of the doorway and made out the gleam of helmets headed my way.

"*Franz? Wo bist du?*"

The insistent whisper came from around the corner. Another guard, maybe, looking for Franz who'd snuck off for a smoke while on duty? I heard him call for Franz again.

"*Zigarette aus, Franz.*"

A warning. Maybe a non-com was on the prowl. The voice faded, searching for Franz in the other direction. I took a quick look around the corner, spotting the back of a Kraut guard, rifle slung over his shoulder. That didn't bother me as much as the sign above me.

Sicherheitsregiment.

I'd managed to walk right into a Security Regiment headquarters. Mere steps ahead of a patrol or maybe a changing of the guard. They'd sound the alarm as soon as they discovered Franz permanently off duty.

I pulled off my shoes and ran like hell, catching sight of a smoldering cigarette on the sidewalk, the smoke Franz never got to finish. It's glow followed me like an accusing eye as I bounded across the road, away from the guard and across the path of the oncoming patrol. In my stocking feet my footfalls were nearly silent, although my bursting lungs and beating heart made it sound like a stampede right behind me.

"*Halt!*"

Rifle fire cracked in the night, slugs hitting the cobblestones in front of me. If I had halted it would only have been to present the security troops with a stationary target. I sped up, stretching my legs and breathing in deep drinks of air. I made it across the wide road, sheltered from view by the building.

Another shot, this one whizzing by my ear. I'd forgotten about Franz's pal.

If I ran straight, he'd have another good chance at my back. If I took the right turn a few steps away, I might run into Krauts from the patrol fanning out. I ran across the street, angling away from the headquarters, hoping the mist and darkness would hide me. Besides, who in their right mind would expose themselves like this? A shoe in each hand, I ran hard, remembering my track coach back in Boston, who always told me that just because it hurts doesn't mean you have to stop.

It hurt, but a lot less than a bullet.

I caught the edge of a cobblestone with my toe and tumbled head over heels, tucking in my arm to take the hit. My body made a thudding sound and one shoe skittered away. I leapt up, unhurt as far as I could tell, and ran to grab my shoe.

Another shot, close enough for me to hear the whizzing sound as it passed by. Some Kraut with damn good hearing had picked up on the noise I made, and I could hear him shouting to the others.

More shots. I don't know if the rest of them spotted me, or if it was only a case of nervous Krauts firing into the dark. I kept running, putting in a few zigs and zags as I crossed a road that seemed as big as a football field. The rain had stopped, and a fog had begun to rise off the ground.

A motorcycle revved in the distance, the noise of its engine growing louder, as did the sound of hobnail boots converging from several directions. More shots came my way, not even near misses. Maybe they'd lost sight of me.

The motorcycle turned on its headlamp, the brightness blinding in the darkness. He came up the middle of the road, pinning me with his beam. A Kraut in the sidecar cut loose with his MP40, spraying the road with automatic fire while I tried to sprout wings and get to shelter on the other side.

The paving stones were slippery from the mist, and the motorcycle swerved a few times, but recovered. I kept running, thinking about the .32 pistol in my pocket. A foolish thought. I could do as much damage throwing it at them as firing it.

I spotted the side street I'd dart into. It seemed close, but my legs were wobbly and my lungs raw, each breath a searing pain.

More gunfire, lots of it, bullets zinging through the air all around me.

I was about to give up, fall to my knees, and take a few gasps of oxygen before they shot me. Then I saw it, and I did go to my knees. Flat on my face, as a matter of fact.

The gunfire was coming from the side street. From a barricade of sandbags, fifis were targeting the motorcycle, which took several hits and crashed spectacularly against a tree on the sidewalk. The Krauts out in the open beat a retreat, having no chance against the fighters shooting at them from under cover.

A handful of fighters ran out to grab weapons from the dead motorcyclists, and on the way back they helped me over the barricade, asking a million excited questions which I had no hope of understanding. But what I did understand, from the sign on the corner building, was that the football field I'd just crossed was the boulevard de Clichy.

I was getting close.

They gave me water, and I gave them my fighter-pilot impression, which seemed a fair trade. A few spoke a bit of English and gave me straightforward directions to rue Ravignan. I told them I had to get a message to a couple of Allied airmen in hiding and apologized for not being able to tell them more.

They shared their bread as readily as I shared my lies, and we were all happy with the arrangement.

"*Boche* no enter Montmartre," a girl of sixteen or so said, thinking about each word carefully as she spoke. "*Fin.*" She drew a finger across her throat, simplifying the translation.

A boy not much older than her came forward with a blue work shirt and handed it to me. The white shirt I'd been wearing since who-knows-when was stained with dirt, sweat, and blood. These fighters were all dressed rough, but I looked like a real bum, so I accepted gladly.

As I was about to leave, one of the crew brought out a cup of coffee from a café where they were gathered. Real coffee by the smell of it, in one of those tiny cups the French liked, which meant it packed a punch.

No one else had a cup. This was a gift, something special they were offering an American liberator. I thanked them and drank the steaming liquid, feeling the jolt to my brain.

"*Vive la France,*" I said.

"*Vive la liberté,*" came the response. Hard to argue with that.

As I left them their eyes were gleaming with pride and determination. Not a one of them looked over twenty, which meant they'd all grown up under the heel of Nazi repression. They were claiming their own new future, and I felt sorry for the next bunch of Krauts who tried to storm that barricade. And I worried about the kids taking foolhardy chances, since that's what kids do.

As I walked up the steady incline, I realized that *mont* meant mountain, and I was in for a bit of a climb. Just what my aching legs needed.

I stopped and heaved in a few breaths, bent over with my hands on my knees. I spotted the next turn and crossed the street, looking out over an unexpected view of the city. The darkness was tinged with fog and faint flashes of gunfire. Pools of light dotted the landscape, maybe pockets of working electricity, maybe burning buildings.

This was not the City of Light I'd imagined.

I trudged on. This neighborhood definitely was not the high-rent district. On the south side of the boulevard below, the apartment buildings were four or five stories high, built from granite, with balconies and high windows overlooking broad tree-lined streets. Here, stucco flaked off brickwork, and wooden shutters hung lazily on cramped, small buildings above narrow lanes. It was like ascending a hilltop into a country village.

I turned a corner and was faced with steps leading into the fog. A lot of steps. I kept a steady grasp on the iron railing, my thigh muscles feeling ready to snap. If my directions were right, the street at the top of the cobblestone stairs would be rue Ravignan.

It was, thank God. The blue enamel plaque on the corner of the building told me so. I wanted to kiss it, but I didn't have enough breath to pucker. I managed to walk, feeling almost weightless on the even surface. I found Paul Lambert's place easily enough. Number thirty-seven was a three-story joint with wooden shutters closed over the ground-floor windows. Vines covered the side, which stood adjacent to a small cottage at the end of the block. There was no concierge to guard the entrance, only a door leading to a small lobby strewn with old newspapers. There were four mailboxes. Lambert lived in 3B. More steps.

I wanted to rest. I wanted to sleep. But time was not my friend tonight, so I forced myself up the stairs, a grayish glow from a dirty skylight my only guide. I got to Lambert's, which was right next to 3A, almost knocking over a bicycle leaning close to his doorway. It looked like the top floor had been divided into two small flats, not that the apartment building was big to begin with.

I hesitated. I knew I'd have a problem if he didn't speak any English, but I figured we'd get around that somehow. It suddenly occurred to me that a knock on the door in the dead of night might be an occasion for concern in occupied Paris. I wished I knew how to say *It's not the Gestapo* in French, but failing that, I gave the door a few gentle, un-Nazi-like raps.

"*Monsieur* Lambert?" I said, trying to put a Continental lilt into my voice.

Nothing. I knocked again, a little louder this time. I called for Lambert once more, then pressed my ear to the wood and listened. I could make out the shuffling of feet, probably Lambert making his way from the bedroom. A sound like a door opening. Or was that from the other apartment? Then nothing.

Damn.

I ran down the stairs, fast, grabbing the bannister and whipping myself around at each landing. I burst out the door and ran to the side of the building adjacent to the smaller house. The rear window of Lambert's apartment was wide open. It was an easy jump to the roof of the neighboring house. If it had been the Gestapo, they'd have had that covered.

But Paul Lambert didn't know that, and now he was legging it to save his life.

Which way?

The street ended here, facing a small plaza. Too exposed. I took off down an alley behind the buildings, weaving between cans of garbage and spooking cats out for a midnight snack. It was his closest escape route, and one that gave him access to back doors and the twists and turns the residents of Montmartre undoubtedly knew well.

Then I heard a crash and a yell.

I ran closer and saw that a garbage can had done my job for me. Paul Lambert—it had better be him, after all this—rolled on the wet cobblestones clutching his knee and moaning. I trotted to a halt, holding out my hands to show him I meant no harm.

"Paul Lambert?" I said. "Do you speak English?"

That got his attention.

"*Oui*. You are not *boche*?"

"American," I said, giving him a hand as he got himself up. "I have a message from your brother."

"I do not have a brother," he said, looking around in a bit of a panic. "*Mon violin!*"

He scampered around the spilled garbage and came up with a violin case. He wiped the scraps of debris off with reverence, looking at me with unabashed pride.

"*Italien*," he said by way of explanation. "From the last century."

"That's swell, but aren't you curious about your brother Marcel?"

"What do you want?" he asked, holding the case to his chest like a baby. He was skinny, with a mop of dark hair curling around his ears. He had a few years on the kids at the barricade, but not many. Old enough to have been drafted for forced labor in Germany, and I wondered if Jarnac had traded information to keep his kid brother alive.

"I know your brother. Marcel Jarnac," I said, working to

convince him I was legit. Jarnac had probably drilled him on revealing nothing. "He asked me to bring you to him. He said the Germans had discovered he had a brother and were coming to arrest you."

"I have done nothing," he said, looking around as if Gestapo agents were hiding in the bushes.

"Right, but if the Germans have you, they will force your brother to give himself up. Do you understand?"

"Yes, I do. But why did he send an American? Are you with the FFI?"

"It's a long story, Paul. I was shot down, and the Resistance helped me. That's where I met Marcel. He couldn't make it to warn you, so he asked me to take you to a safe place," I said.

"Are the Americans coming?" he asked.

"Yes, they are very close. And General Leclerc as well. Tell me, how long has it been since you saw your brother?"

"A month, maybe longer," Paul said. "I did not know he was in Paris."

"His work is very secret," I said. True enough. And I knew by now he'd had plenty of time to get to the *Abwehr* at the Hotel Lutetia, assuming the Krauts he surrendered to didn't immediately put a bullet in his head. So, I had to get to him as soon possible.

"Where are you taking me? To Marcel?"

"No, Paul. To a safe place. You're going to love it, believe me."

I told him to lead the way to the Gare Saint-Lazare. He said all the trains had stopped running, and I explained that was just the general area. I couldn't tell him the actual destination in case we got picked up. Need to know, and he didn't need to know right now.

The route was a lot easier going downhill. We reached the boulevard de Clichy and hid in the shadows of a recessed door-way as I scanned the road and the buildings beyond. I couldn't make out much in the grayness but shuttered windows and garbage strewn in the gutter. The air was damp and sour, a faint mist floating in the darkness. I rubbed my eyes, raw with the grit of exhaustion, trying to see what awaited us on the other side.

I heard the rumble of an engine. Two engines, one running rough. A vehicle appeared in the distance, taking form as it came closer. Then another, close behind. Trucks jammed with armed men. Rifles jutted out at every angle as they passed us and faded into the foggy distance. Security troops? FFI? Germans retreating from the front lines? Vichy *Milice* making a getaway? It didn't really matter. Any of them would have been trigger-happy enough to gun down a couple of figures skulking in a doorway.

"Come on," I said to Lambert. He looked nervous. Smart kid.

We walked slowly. My theory was that running attracts more attention than a couple of guys out for a stroll, and given that we weren't being chased, it seemed the most sensible thing to do. If a Kraut had us in his sights, running at him wouldn't exactly calm him down. On the other hand, this slow pace would make it easy for him to take a steady aim.

Hell, since it didn't make much difference, I'd go with the walk. I was too damned tired to run.

Halfway across the boulevard, I heard shots. Pretty far away. I put an unsteady hand on Lambert's shoulder and told him not to worry. Mainly, I wanted a good hold of him in case he decided to run back home.

"Where is Marcel?" he asked, hugging the violin case to his chest.

"It's best for me not to say," I told him.

"You sound like Marcel," Lambert said, his pace quickening.

"Slow down and shut up," I said, disliking any comparison to his murdering traitor of a brother. Which wasn't fair to the kid. But then again, nothing that I was going to do would count as fair in his book.

On the far side of the boulevard we stopped, and I listened for any movement or voices ahead. Nothing.

"Sorry," I said to Lambert. "I didn't mean to snap at you."

"Snap?"

"Speak harshly," I said, pulling him into a doorway and glancing down the street. "It's just nerves. Don't worry, you'll be safe."

"I am nervous too," he said. "I have never been out after curfew."

"I think the *boche* are too busy to enforce it," I said. "But they're still dangerous. You aren't involved? With Marcel's work, I mean?"

"No. He made me promise I would attend to my studies. He said one life ruined by war was enough."

"He lost his wife in Spain, didn't he?" I said.

"You must be a good friend," Lambert said. "He never speaks of it. To anyone."

"We've become close," I said. Not close enough to suit me, but true enough. I didn't want him getting suspicious, so I tried to change the subject. "You're a musician."

"Yes, I study at the Sorbonne. I want to become a concert violinist," he said. "That is why I took my violin. It is the only thing I have of value."

"Okay, keep a good grip on it. You know the way to the train station from here?"

"*Bien sûr*," he said. "This way."

We scurried down a narrow street called the rue des Martyrs, which was a little disquieting, but it provided more cover than a lot of the monolithic blocks of apartments that I'd seen. The buildings were smaller here, rows of little shops with uneven facades, recessed doors, overhanging balconies, and a scattering of trees. Plenty of places to hide, at least in the darkness.

From there we moved through side streets angling off in different directions, taking us through a small park and around the back of a church. Then I saw the sign, the white letters easily visible. The rue du Havre, where Kaz and I had potato soup.

"This way," I told Lambert, who kept close to my side. I

wondered where Kaz was right now. If he'd evaded capture, he'd be fine. He always was. If not? A Pole with false papers wouldn't last a minute. But Kaz was a fast talker and fluent in German. I told myself to stop worrying. Kaz was smart and resourceful. Like giving me landmarks such as this café to get me to the One-Two-Two club.

We were about a block away. I heard a car door slam, loud and startling in the quiet night. We ran ahead to a covered archway. A department store, fancy shoes and dresses still on display. Last-minute gifts for the departing Krauts to buy their *fraus*.

It gave me a good view of the entrance to the One-Two-Two, but not of who was in the car. It drove off in the opposite direction, and the quiet settled in around us. Last customer of the evening? I hoped so.

I motioned for Lambert to follow and hustled across the street like a guy late to a party and worried about getting mugged in a strange part of town. In a hurry but trying to look nonchalant. I pulled off my FFI armband and stuffed it in my pocket as we approached the large double doors painted a deep burgundy red.

"Ask for Malou," I said to Lambert. "My French isn't so good."

"*Oui*," he said, agreeing readily as I knocked on the door. Nothing. I wondered if there was a secret knock, or if everyone had gone home. I raised my hand to give it another rap as the door swung open.

I'd expected a doorman. Or a bouncer.

Not two drunken Kraut officers.

They pushed past us as a staff car prowled down the street, a huge Mercedes-Benz that pulled over by the door, its engine purring like a leopard. Two Germans got out, one to hold the door open and the other to keep watch, submachine gun at the ready.

I got my foot in the door before it closed, keeping a tight grip on Lambert. One of the officers, a colonel, turned and studied

Lambert clutching his violin case. He began asking questions, first in German, then French.

The Kraut on watch quit scanning the street and focused on us, his MP40 swinging in our direction. The colonel pointed at the violin case and laughed. Lambert joined right in, nodding and chatting with the Kraut like he was an old pal. The colonel chuckled and waved off the suspicious guard, who shifted his weapon but not his eyes.

I kept my eyes down, taking a deep breath as we made it over the threshold. The door shut behind us with a reassuring solidity.

"What was that about?" I whispered, casting an eye down the hallway from the foyer where we stood.

"He reminded me to use the servant's entrance. Musicians should not use the front door, according to him. What kind of place is this?"

A woman walked down the stairs, her high-heeled shoes coming into view first. Then a bit of sheer gauzy material that didn't hide a thing. The next thing I saw was a surprised look on her face, her smile vanishing as she called for help, scurrying back up the steps.

"No Frenchmen today," Lambert translated. His neck craned as he followed her retreat up the stairs. "Is this *un bordel* for *boche* only?"

"Yes, but it's a safe place," I said, wondering if the joint was off-limits for civilians and keeping an eye out for muscle. The last thing I needed was to be thrown out into the street. "It's called the One-Two-Two."

"I have heard of it," he said, a mixture of reverence and worry in his tone. "They do strange things here, I am told."

"Relax," I said. "The whole world is pretty strange right now." Footsteps thundered down the steps. Not high heels. A sturdy fellow in a nicely-tailored suit made his appearance and snarled a few sentences between his teeth, the kind of thing you do when you don't want anyone else to hear how mad you are. He needed a shave and smelled of wine souring on his tongue.

"*Malou est ici?*" Lambert asked, as soon as he could get a word in.

"*Malou? Attendez,*" he growled, but there was a shift in his tone, the words laced with less threat than before. We obviously weren't clients, not dressed the way we were, but he didn't toss us out, so I figured our contact here had to be the real deal. We waited, as instructed, and in a couple of minutes he came down a few steps, snapped his fingers, and we went up.

It was on the next floor, which was good if what Kaz had told me about the shenanigans getting more risqué with the altitude held true. I didn't want Lambert running for the exits. We followed the guy to the end of the hall, where he pointed to a door.

"*Malou,*" he said, and left us, ascending the stairs at the rear to loftier heights and baser instincts.

CHAPTER TWENTY-FIVE

I KNOCKED, NOT sure what to expect. A Gestapo trap? Half-naked ladies? The door swung open and there stood the last person I expected to see in this high-class whorehouse.

Diana Seaton. The woman I loved. Dressed in a red silk dress cut low in the bosom and high on the thigh, her honey-colored hair pinned back to show off a ruby-studded choker.

"Hello, Billy. Who's your friend?" Diana couldn't hide the smile growing at the corners of her mouth, which only made me more confused. She didn't seem the least bit surprised to find me at her door, while my jaw was hanging open, my brain unable to get two words moving together.

"Paul Lambert," my companion said, his wits apparently unimpaired. "*Enchanté, Mademoiselle.*"

"*Entrez,*" Diana said, her hand on my shoulder as she pulled me across the threshold, her touch red-hot through my shirt.

"Diana," I whispered, finally able to speak.

"Malou, for now," she said, a finger to her lips. Lambert plopped himself down on a purple velvet chair that looked right at home facing a large bed with a red quilt matching Diana's dress. What there was of it. I'd encountered her working undercover for the Special Operations Executive before, but this put that notion in a whole new light.

"How did you know it was me?" I asked. I was having a hard time thinking this through. I was on the knife edge of exhaustion and wasn't entirely sure I understood what was going on.

"First, sit down," Diana said. "You look terrible."

"Haven't slept much," I said, collapsing on a couch, the soft cushions feeling like clouds. "Been dodging Krauts."

"Here," Diana said, pouring glasses of water from a carafe and giving them to Paul and me. I drank, then put the glass to my forehead, feeling the coolness against my skin. I set the glass down with a clatter and rubbed my hand to hide the quiver. "Paul is a friend?" She cocked a brow in his direction, inquiring about intentions and loyalties in one subtle movement.

"Can we talk? In private?" I said, watching Paul with the violin on his lap, his eyes taking in the room with its gaudy furnishings and flowery wallpaper. I nodded in the direction of a door that looked to lead to an adjoining room.

"It is best we all remain here," Diana said. "There are clients about. You were lucky to make it inside. Frenchmen are allowed only as guests of the Germans."

"The *boche* thought I was here to play," Paul said. "An officer who was leaving said I should have used the rear entrance."

"You are a violinist?" Diana asked, eyeing the case he cradled.

"Listen, we don't have time for small talk," I said. "I need your help."

"Then wait," she said, holding up her hand while nodding to Paul for his reply.

"Yes. I study classical music at the Sorbonne. I could not leave my instrument behind, it is the only thing of value I have."

"Then play for us, please. Can you do that?" Diana said, leaning closer to Paul. At that point, he was ready to do anything she asked. I finally realized what she was up to. Noise, to cover our conversation. They chatted in French for a while, and he decided on Beethoven's Violin Concerto in D. I almost put in a request for "GI Jive," since that was the big hit on Armed Forces Radio these days, but I didn't have the energy to play the wise guy.

Man alive, that GI Jive.

Diana turned off the lights and cranked open the window facing a small courtyard. She motioned for Paul to take his place. The breeze blew the curtains into the room, the late-night air shimmering Diana's red dress. Man alive, indeed.

"Go ahead, Paul," she said, patting him on the shoulder. "There are many important people who will hear you, although you will never know their names. The One-Two-Two is *très discret.*"

The first notes were mournful. Or maybe that was the mood I was in. Then the pace increased, the tune growing lively, Paul swaying and leaning into the music. The kid was good.

"Now, tell me what you need," Diana said, whispering as she sat on the couch.

"First, what's going on here? How did you know to expect me?"

"The name Malou, that's all. I had a radio transmission from SOE that you and Kaz would be in Paris ahead of the troops. If someone asked for Malou, it had to be one of you. The doorman is a loyal *résistant* and knew to bring you to me. I have many names here, Billy," she said with a cunning smirk.

"Of course. Sorry, my brain is moving pretty slow tonight. It's taking everything I have just to stay awake. What's with the outfit? Are you, you know, working here?" I glanced at the ornate bed.

She slapped me. Paul played on.

"There, that ought to wake you up. Now, tell me what you need. I don't have all night." The grin was gone.

"Sorry, I didn't mean it that way. I don't know what I meant," I said. "I had no idea what to expect, and then there you were, in that dress." I reached for the glass and gave up, my hand trembling too much to trust I could hold it.

"You don't look well, Billy," she said, her hand resting on my arm and her brow wrinkling with worry.

"I'm okay. I'm sorry about that remark, it was stupid. I need to keep this kid on ice for a day, that's all. And find Kaz."

"Has something happened to him?" Diana asked, her eyes wide with concern.

"We were separated. Got caught up in a Kraut raid and barely made it out. I thought he might have found his way here. Hoped he had, anyway."

"The situation in the streets is very fluid," she said. "In some areas there are pitched battles, in other neighborhoods all is quiet. We have to hope Kaz found somewhere safe."

"Yeah," I said, happy to grasp at that straw. "He knows how to take care of himself. But I hope he didn't get caught in a crossfire or picked up by the Krauts. Our papers aren't the best."

"That doesn't matter, sadly enough," she said, as Paul continued with his playing. The notes echoed in the courtyard, an odd serenade of serene beauty in the midst of terror and death. "Anyone picked up by the Germans is taken away. They sent another trainload of prisoners to Germany early today. The last, I hope."

"Listen, Diana, I'm worried about Kaz, but I have get moving. Do you know anything about our mission?"

She didn't, so I gave her a quick run-down of our pursuit of Marcel Jarnac, code-name *Atlantik*. I whispered, even though the pace of Paul's playing had picked up, and I could tell he was paying more attention to each note than to either of us.

"So, I grabbed the kid as leverage," I said, gesturing to our orchestra. "His brother has a soft spot for him, and I aim to use it."

"But hasn't *Atlantik* had time to get to the *Abwehr*?" Diana asked. "It's probably too late for leverage."

"Well, there's a slight chance he could have been delayed due to fighting and roundups, but I'm not counting on it. My idea is to trade Paul for a renunciation," I said.

"He could say he found out his information was faulty or from a plant," Diana said, grasping the idea right away.

"Yeah. Can you keep Paul here? Even if he wants to leave."

"I'm sure we can keep him occupied," she said with a sly wink.

"For twenty-four hours?"

"He's young," Diana said. "And there are restraints on the higher floors, if needed. But tell me, how are you going to contact *Atlantik* and prove you have Paul?"

"I was loosely held prisoner by the FFI," I said. "They didn't know what to make of me after Jarnac's denunciation. I think they believed it was all a mistake. I asked their leader, a young woman named Nicole, to put the word out I wanted to speak to Jarnac in the morning to straighten things out. I'm betting he'll show, since it's a good opportunity for him to tie up a loose end."

"Where?"

"At some barricades near the opera house on rue Volney. I need to get back there while it's still dark," I said, fighting the urge to yawn and failing miserably.

"It's very dangerous, Billy," Diana said, edging closer. I guessed my earlier comment had been forgiven. "I think I may be able to help. I'm going to talk to someone in the next room. Give me a minute."

She rushed off, the soft silk of her dress trailing behind her. Paul played on, the music rising and falling, rising and falling.

"Billy, wake up. Wake up!" Diana shook me by the arm, hard. I pried my eyes open, my eyelids heavy and my brain sluggish. I rubbed my face as it dawned on me the music had stopped.

"Where's Lambert?" I asked, sitting up from where I'd collapsed on the couch.

Standing behind Diana, visible in the light of the single lamp, was a German officer, tall in his shiny boots, a Knight's Cross at his collar. I wondered if I was dreaming, and wished I could wake up all over again to the languid strains of Lambert's violin.

But this wasn't a dream. I noticed his hand resting on his holster. Good. He didn't have a gun at Diana's back. My little .32 wasn't worth much, but two or three slugs to the chest would do the trick at this range if I could get to it in time.

"No, Billy," Diana said, moving between us. "He can help."

I stood, moving in front of Diana in case this Kraut decided to be unhelpful. Then I saw his face clearly. A face I knew well enough.

"Colonel Erich Remke," I said. "It's been a while."

I'd run into Remke before. First in North Africa, when I was stuck in a Vichy French jail. Then in Sicily, when we both were trying to get on the good side of a mafia boss, a side that was damned hard to find. But the last time, in occupied Rome, had been different. Remke was part of the German resistance against Hitler, and he'd funneled information to us about the extermination camp at Auschwitz. Diana had been part of that SOE operation as well. He'd told us about assassination attempts in the works and asked that we get word to the Allies about their plans. So, we were on the same side, sort of. Except for all the shooting.

"Captain Boyle," he said, giving his heels a little Prussian click. "Miss Seaton has told me of your mission."

"What?" I stared at Diana, wondering what the hell had gotten into her. In my dealings with Remke, I'd found him to be honorable enough. Hell, anyone who wanted Adolf dead was a pal in my book, but he was still an enemy soldier. And a member of the *Abwehr* to boot, the very guys we were trying to pull a fast one on.

"We have common ground," Diana said. "Let's sit and talk this through."

"Where's Paul?" I asked, catching a glimpse of his violin case. I knew he couldn't be far if he'd left it behind.

"I had one of the girls take him to the kitchen. He's in good hands. Now sit, and I'll pour some drinks. It's the main thing I do here," she said, with a quick glance in my direction.

"Miss Seaton is in great demand as a hostess," Remke said, pulling up a chair and setting his service cap on the table. "The One-Two-Two is as famous for its salon as for these rooms. They serve champagne and caviar along with gossip and secrets." Remke knew Diana and I were an item, and I had the sense he was trying to put my mind at ease. Maybe that was wishful thinking. Maybe he wasn't the worst enemy in the world.

"Which is why you were sent here," I said to Diana.

"Yes. The clientele is mainly German officers and their Vichy guests. The chatter after a few glasses of champagne is quite revealing," she said. "Well worth the price of wearing this ridiculous getup."

Remke avoided her eyes, probably thinking the same thing I was about her dress, and kept the conversation on track.

"I saw Miss Seaton here two weeks ago and recalled our previous dealings," Remke said, nodding his thanks to Diana as she handed him a glass of cognac. "At the time, I was dealing with some difficulties with the Gestapo and in need of a place to hide. It was mutually beneficial for me not to reveal her presence here to my colleagues in return for her assistance."

"You were part of the July 20 bomb plot?" I asked. Last month's failed attempt on Hitler's life had been big news. Plenty of GIs had thought it might mean an end to the war. A lot of them were dead by now.

"Some of us were to arrest the SS leaders in Paris once Hitler's death was announced," he said with a heavy sigh. "We did so, only to learn the announcement was premature. The SS was chagrined at being taken so easily without a fight. Therefore, the whole thing was quickly forgotten by all parties."

"But someone talked," I said, taking my own glass and downing a gulp. The sharp aroma lingered in my nose as the liquid warmed my throat.

"Someone always talks when the Gestapo starts in on them,"

Remke said. "It could have been anyone, simply giving them names to make the pain go away. I received word that a team of Gestapo agents was being sent to Paris, as the local men were no longer trusted. Since then, I have been a guest of the One-Two-Two."

"I'm glad the Nazis didn't string you up, Colonel, but what does that have to do with me?"

"*Atlantik* is my man," Remke said.

I finished the rest of my drink. I looked at Diana, figuring she must have had a good reason to spill the beans to Remke.

"It's all right, Billy," Diana said.

"Has he contacted you?" I asked, still trying to figure out what Remke was after.

"He arrived at the Hotel Lutetia last night," Remke said. "He's given his report to my aide, who is planning on meeting me at the Hotel Meurice in a few hours."

"The Hotel Meurice is the headquarters of General von Cholt-itz, the German commandant for Paris," Diana explained.

"You're going there with the Gestapo looking for you?" I asked Remke.

"The men who were looking for me left a few hours ago, according to my aide. They gave up and departed before they were pressed into service to do any actual fighting. There are no Gestapo at the general's headquarters, and I will remain there for as long as necessary."

"What are you going to do with *Atlantik*'s report?" I asked. "It gives you quite an advantage."

"On the contrary. It poses a problem, one you may be able to solve," Remke said.

"I don't get it. If Jarnac was a double agent of yours, isn't this the kind of thing you'd get a medal for?" I asked.

"It comes at the worst possible time," Remke said. "Before I could secure the report, too many people at headquarters had heard of it. It is imperative that we discredit Jarnac, or force him to recant, as you have suggested."

"Wait, I'm confused," I said, rubbing my eyes and trying to make sense of this. Maybe having that cognac wasn't such a good idea.

"Billy, here's the part you don't know," Diana said, her hand on my shoulder. "General von Choltitz has orders to destroy Paris. Thoroughly."

"Jesus. We ran into an engineer unit on our way here, loaded down with explosives," I said. "I wondered what they were up to."

"Demolition specialists have been arriving for days, and some of them have already wired buildings and monuments for destruction. However, von Choltitz is resistant to the idea of destroying Paris," Remke said. "He's playing for time, hoping the Allies enter the city as soon as possible. He'd prefer to surrender it intact."

"But not to the FFI," Diana said. "General von Choltitz and many within the *Abwehr* want to stop the destruction of the city, but they insist on surrendering to uniformed troops. I've sent radio messages to SOE telling them this, but they haven't answered."

"Not all of our interests coincide, but I am sure you will agree in the matter of Paris we are in accord," Remke said. "I have no wish to see Paris and its people destroyed, nor for our troops to fight a losing battle in its ruins."

"But you can't simply ignore Jarnac," I said.

"Unfortunately, no," Remke said. "Too many people have already heard about his intelligence coup, and word may have reached Berlin. We cannot take a chance on orders coming direct from OKW to re-arrange our defenses, such as they are."

OKW was the *Oberkommando der Wehrmacht*, and they called the shots. Literally.

"I didn't see a lot of troops between Rambouillet and Paris," I said, standing and walking to the window. I parted the curtains, looking out into the courtyard and the blacked-out windows across the way. This was a house of pleasure, and perhaps pain, but I doubted anybody else was debating the fate of one of the world's great cities.

"No," Remke said. "The units retreating from Normandy are shattered. It will take time to regroup farther to the east. But we do have anti-aircraft defenses ringing the Paris area. So far, von Choltitz has not ordered them moved to directly oppose your attack from the west. But if the *Acht-acht* guns were repositioned along the route of the French armor, it would be enough to stop them for a day or two."

He was dead right. The German 88 was an effective anti-aircraft weapon and an even more deadly anti-tank gun. If massed along the approach of General Leclerc's armored columns, the lead tanks would be blown off the road.

"Two days, even one, could force the general's hand," Diana said, standing next to me and taking my hand. It was like an electric shock, the warmth of her skin against mine. I gripped her tightly to mask the shakes. "Explosives have already been set throughout the city. If von Choltitz gives in and follows his orders, or is replaced by someone else, Paris will become a field of rubble."

"We cannot allow a delay," Remke said. "I will be expected to give a report on Jarnac's claims this morning. It would be best if there were good reason to disbelieve it. Unfortunately, his information has been quite reliable in the past."

"Well, if he took the bait, he'll be at the rue Volney barricade anytime now," I said, glancing at my watch. Dawn wasn't too far off. "I'll take Paul's violin. That's the best proof I can offer Jarnac that I have him. The kid would never willingly let it be taken."

"He will be kept safely out of sight," Diana said. "Call here when you have news of Jarnac. Remember to ask for Malou." She rattled off an eight-digit number and had me repeat it. By the third time I got it right.

"Do you have any coffee?" I asked. I needed something to blow away the cobwebs. Seeing Erich Remke standing over me when I woke up had gotten my blood moving, but that had worn off, and all I wanted to do now was lie down and deal with Jarnac tomorrow. But Paris might not be here tomorrow, so I stayed upright, maybe swaying a bit.

"You can get anything at the One-Two-Two," Diana said. "Some of Colonel Remke's *Abwehr* colleagues have been running a black-market operation out of the back rooms."

"A profitable enterprise, but sadly we do not have time for coffee," Remke said, brushing back his sleeve to check the time. "I have a car scheduled to pick me up at the front door in less than ten minutes. I can take you close to rue Volney and save you the trouble of evading our patrols."

"Sure," I said, still a little wary of any Kraut offering me a lift. But the thought of sprinting through the darkened streets was too much, and I put aside my natural battlefield caution. "I could use a ride. I'm bushed."

"Bushed? Tired, you mean? You certainly look it. These will help," Remke said, taking a small container from his pocket and handing it to me. "Pervitin. One or two of these will keep you wide awake."

"What is it?" I asked, shaking the metal tube and hearing the rattle of pills.

"It is a methamphetamine compound," he said. "It was first developed for pilots on long flights. Now it's issued to every soldier at the front. I used it myself to stay alert and watch for the Gestapo. The medical people claim it's harmless, but I would not take too many. Or use it for long."

"I only need a few hours," I said, removing the cork and rolling a white pill into my palm. There were seven left, more than I needed. I popped the pill and tilted my head back, letting it roll down my gullet. "Thanks."

"I will wait downstairs," Remke said. "Join me in five minutes, no longer. A single German vehicle waiting at the curb can become a target very quickly. Miss Seaton, you know how to contact me at the Hotel Meurice." With that, he gave another click of the heels, a bow in Diana's direction, and left.

"You're full of surprises, Malou," I said, going for a laugh and falling onto the couch. "If you've got anyone else hiding in that room, don't tell me, okay?"

"Billy, I'm worried about you," she said, sitting next to me and holding my hand in hers, cradling it as she brought it to her lips, kissing my fingers and leaving a trace of red. "You look worse than exhausted."

"I'll be able to sleep in a few hours, I hope," I said. "I'm pretty sure Jarnac's weak spot is his brother. Other than that, he's a callous bastard. I figure he won't be able to resist getting back at me for taking the map."

"Be careful," Diana said. "He sounds vicious. And smart, to have survived this long as a double agent. You must stay alert, but these pills are dangerous. I've seen men come here begging to buy more on the black market once they've gotten the habit. If you want another jolt, take these." She opened a drawer on the side table and handed me a round tin. It was marked *Scho-Ka-Kola* and contained wedges of dark chocolate. "They contain caffeine. They're standard issue for *Luftwaffe* aircrew."

"Thanks," I said, pocketing the chocolate. "But I'm more worried about you than my chances with Jarnac. Does any German other than Remke know what you're doing here?"

"No, I don't think so," she said, standing and brushing her hair back behind her ear. "Oddly enough, I do trust the man. Billy, you must leave now. Remke meant it about the car not waiting."

"Okay," I said, reluctant to leave, knowing she was right. Still, I hated the thought of leaving her alone. "What about the people who run this joint? Can you trust them?"

"I trust them to act in their own self-interest. They were eager to help, since there are bound to be reprisals once Paris is free again. They made a lot of money catering to the Nazis. Now they can claim they were servicing the Germans as a cover for SOE. They'd have little reason to betray us."

"Us? There are others here?"

"The usual. A three-person team with a hidden radio. But you don't need to know about them. Just convince Jarnac to recant his story, then get back to me. We will drink champagne, sleep, and wait for the liberation."

"I like the sound of sleep," I said, picking up the violin case and letting her lead me to the door.

Diana leaned in and kissed me, a long, soft caress of her ruby lips. She smelled of flowers, cognac, and fear, and at that moment I never wanted to leave her. Not in this place where betrayal and death were as likely as liberation.

No spy is ever safe.

"Go," she said, her forehead pressed to mine, her hand at the back of my neck. "And come back."

CHAPTER TWENTY-SIX

I DESCENDED THE stairs slowly, munching on a piece of chocolate, the bittersweet taste mingling with the perfumed traces of Diana's lipstick. The red imprint from where she kissed my tremoring hand was still faintly visible. Would it be there by the time I got back? If all went as planned, this thing might be finished in a few hours. I had to even the score with Jarnac for his murders, but that would have to wait until Leclerc's columns rolled into town.

"Shall we go, Captain Boyle?" Remke said, fitting his service cap on his head at a jaunty angle. The doorman let us out, glancing up and down the street before signaling us to go. A German soldier jumped out of the Citroën Traction Avant idling at the curb and opened the door. He snapped to attention as I followed Remke into the back seat and in seconds we roared off into the night. It was pitch-black, silent, and the streets glistened with rain.

"Have you told anyone else about Diana?" I said, keeping an eye on the sidewalk for any hint of an ambush. "How safe is she?"

"I have told no one," Remke said. "I have one man I trust with my life who knew where I was. The fact that the Gestapo did not raid the One-Two-Two proves his loyalty. As for safety, that is a hard thing to guarantee these days, but I will not be the one to be a danger to her. You have my word."

"Thanks," I said, stifling a yawn. "Are all the Gestapo gone from Paris? I heard they'd pulled out recently."

"The administrative staff, yes. But there are still agents at eighty-four avenue Foch, their headquarters. I imagine they are occupied with burning files and covering up evidence at this point."

"Let's hope," I said, the yawn finally breaking through.

"You will not be tired for long," Remke said, laughing and leaning forward to speak to the driver in German. He was so damn cheerful I wondered if he was still taking these happy pills. "We will be there shortly. A side street between the opera house and rue Volney."

"Good. Now tell me, since we're pals, what's going to happen after the surrender? You can't go back to Germany, not while the Gestapo is still sniffing around for you. I can help, you know. My boss, Colonel Harding, would love to chat with you."

"Samuel Harding, yes. I have quite a file on him, and it would please me to make his acquaintance. But surrender is not in my soul. There is still work to be done. A few in my resistance circle are still alive, and we must try to end this senseless war. So, give Colonel Harding my regards and tell him another day, another city."

The car pulled into a narrow lane, a crooked cobblestone road of shadows and closed shutters.

"Go up this road, take your second left, and you will come to rue Volney shortly," Remke said as the driver braked to a halt. "*Viel Glück.*"

He held out his hand. We shook.

"Good luck to you too," I said. "We're all going to need it."

I exited the vehicle, violin case clutched in my hand. I walked to the second left and headed for the barricade, wondering at my reception. It was after four o'clock. Deep into the night but still far from dawn. I didn't know how organized Nicole and her rue

Volney group were, but I was willing to bet the lookouts would be out of the damp and dozing. Their street wasn't a strategic point, and I figured the Krauts could easily go around them. The Germans weren't spoiling for a fight, especially not the men who'd had soft garrison duty here. The beaten and battle-hardened troops escaping from Normandy were another story.

I was close enough to the street to make out the name on the blue enamel sign on the building. I pulled my beret from my pocket and slipped it on, wanting to look like every other French guy in town. I softly whistled a tune to signal I wasn't a threat. "I'll Be Seeing You," a sad song for lovers separated by war. There was something in the lyrics about the spell of Paris, so it seemed appropriate.

I carefully climbed over the barricade, wincing as a cobblestone tumbled out from under my foot. It clattered to the ground, landing with a thud. No one came running. I eased myself to the ground and stayed in the shadows as I made my way to the café where Roger and I had eaten. When was that? My mind was hazy and the zipped-up chocolate and the Pervitin hadn't kicked in as far as I could tell.

I made my way upstairs, quietly, hardly believing I might have a chance to sack out and grab a couple hours of shut-eye. In the darkened hallway I edged along toward the room where I hoped Roger was still lying by the door. I was ready to step over him and curl up on my bit of floor. As I passed the last door before the room, I heard the creak of hinges behind me.

I felt a chill as the barrel of a pistol pressed against my neck.

Hands grabbed at me and pushed me into the room. Someone kicked at the back of my knees and I went down, the gun barrel shoved against the back of my head.

A small lamp cast a soft yellow glow over Marcel Jarnac, sprawled in the easy chair, a pistol in his hand and a snarl creeping across his face.

In the corner, Nicole was tied to a straight-back chair, a gag in her mouth and her eyes wide with fear. Roger looked a lot worse. Curled up on the floor, his face bloodied and swollen, he tried to rise only to get a kick in the head.

"No one betrays the Saint-Just Brigade," Jarnac said. "Where is the map you stole? Or have you already turned it over to the *boche*?"

I didn't speak. I saw the game he was playing, transferring his crime to me and trying to get his hands on the map at the same time. He'd surprised me by getting here this quickly, fast enough to work over Roger and threaten Nicole in case they had any idea what I was up to.

"*Frappe le,*" Jarnac said, glancing at the guy behind me, telling him to smack me.

"*Attendez,*" I said, raising a hand. Jarnac did the same, telling his muscle to wait.

I lowered my hand, patting the violin case. Jarnac had been so intent on his act that he hadn't taken notice of it. I tapped the hard leather with both hands, beating out a tune. Back to "GI Jive" this time, man alive.

I laughed. Not that there was anything funny going on, but at the realization that I felt good. Wide awake and ready to go. Which was a problem since men with guns wanted me right here.

"Open it," Jarnac said, his bluster suddenly gone. I popped the snaps and lifted the cover.

"*Italien,*" I said, remembering Paul's description. "From the last century."

The guy who'd kicked Roger shot a glance at the thug threatening the integrity of my skull. Kind of a what-the-hell-is-going-on-here look. Jarnac twisted in his seat, waving his pistol at Roger and Nicole, shouting orders at his men. They untied Nicole, lifted Roger up, and dragged them both out of the room.

That left Jarnac, me, and the fiddle. Plus a pistol and my head full of zing. Man, I felt good.

"Mind if I sit?" I asked, taking the violin and tossing it in his lap. I placed the case on the floor and grabbed the chair Nicole had been tied to, rope still hanging from the back. Convenient if Jarnac decided to have me trussed up. I turned it around and straddled it, resting my arms on the back.

"Where is he?" Jarnac said in a low growl. He was over his shock now and back to playing the tough guy.

"Somewhere safe. Someplace he'll never forget, ooh-la-la," I said. I had to remind myself not to give too much away. My mind was racing, and words had a way of tumbling out without too much in the way of thought beforehand. "Nice kid. I heard him play. Some Beethoven concerto. He's not going to be happy when he finds out I swiped his violin, but I figured you'd want proof."

"I want *mon frère*, and I want him now," Jarnac said. "This is a foolish game you are playing."

"Better a witty fool than a foolish wit," I said. "According to Shakespeare, anyway. And Sister Mary Gabriel. She was my English teacher back in Boston and loved the Bard. She quoted that line so many times I've never forgotten it. I was the foolish wit, of course, but that was back in high school. I've learned a few things since then, *Atlantik*." Jeez, I needed to calm down, but I was on a roll. Too bad it was downhill. Too bad I couldn't stop myself.

"Where is Paul?" Jarnac said, his voice measured and low. So was his pistol, about six inches from a part of my anatomy that I held in high regard. The wooden chair slats weren't going to do much to protect me.

"Don't shoot," I said, lifting the case from the floor and holding it on my lap. "Wouldn't want to damage the goods." I thought this was pretty funny and began laughing at my own joke.

"Stop!" Jarnac shouted. One of his men peeked in only to retreat after a few curses from his boss. "Who is this *Atlantik*, and why have you taken Paul?"

"Ah, I getcha," I said, leaning forward and balancing the chair on two legs. "Gotta keep the help from connecting you to the *Abwehr*. Wouldn't do for them to hear your code name."

"You must be drunk," Jarnac said. "Perhaps this will not hurt so much, then." He moved the muzzle of his gun to my kneecap and stared me down. I was already one step ahead of him.

"Colonel Erich Remke," I whispered. "If you shoot me, I'll scream his name. If you kill me, you'll never see Paul again."

The light in the room flickered, went out, then the bare bulb lit up again. I wondered who controlled the electrical power stations in Paris, and then lost interest in that as Jarnac tapped my knee with his pistol.

"I am not surprised you know the name of an *Abwehr* officer, given that you have turned your coat, as they say." Jarnac was keeping up the pretense that I was the traitor in the room, which was okay with me since he'd inched his pistol away from my moving parts.

"Time to get down to brass tacks, Marcel," I said. He looked confused. "It's an expression. Let's cut a deal. Come to terms. Shake on it. No more beating around the bush."

"You want a deal? Bring Paul here," he said, tapping the barrel against my knee. Such a subtle reminder.

"No, no way. But you can have him back before noon if you do one thing," I said. "One little thing and Paul will be plucking these strings instead of a harp."

"What thing?" Jarnac asked. I don't think he picked up on the harp strings. Too bad, it was a good line.

"Go to the Hotel Lutetia and see Remke's aide. The guy you reported to," I said, whispering with my hand on the side of my mouth. "Tell him you've found out the map was phony. A ruse, part of a deception plan. Then call Remke at the Hotel Meurice and confirm it."

"Not that I will do any of this, but if I did, what would happen then?" Jarnac said, his own voice a whisper. The deal was being cut.

"I get word from Remke that it's done, and I bring Paul to you. Brother and violin are reunited. No one needs to hear any details," I said.

"He is with your Polish friend, the baron?" Jarnac asked.

"It doesn't matter who he's with. He's safe and will be returned to you intact once you keep your side of the bargain."

"You have miscalculated, Captain Boyle," Jarnac said, leaning close and whispering in my ear. "You may be brave, but you are not a killer. Not the kind of killer who executes a young boy simply because I do not agree with your plan. You would kill me, certainly, but Paul, no."

"Two things to think about," I said. "One, I find that war makes cold-blooded killers of many men. Poles, especially, since they have endured so much butchery. Two, killing Paul would kill you. He's the only shred of decency left in your miserable world. Without him, you are less than nothing." There was some truth in what I'd said as far as Kaz went. He'd been casual with death and with life, but that had changed since he'd found out his sister was still alive. I actually didn't think he'd pull the trigger on Paul, but brother Marcel didn't know that. Or that I had no idea where Kaz had gotten himself to.

"I left decency in Spain," Jarnac said. "At my wife's grave."

"Is that what this is all about? Revenge against Lucien Fassier? Faucon, the Falcon?"

"He was known as Harrier in Spain," Jarnac said, nearly spitting out the name. "An executioner for the NKVD. Anyone the Stalinists wanted killed, he obliged."

"Your wife?" I asked. I hadn't thought much about Jarnac's motive, but this matched what Olga had told us.

"Yes. Renée was an anarchist. We were not always in agreement, since I was a fervent Marxist. But our love was great. Harrier killed her. His orders said she was an enemy of the people, a death sentence in Spain," he said. For the first time, Jarnac sounded like a man in pain. "He tied her up like an animal."

"But why kill all the others, if you wanted Lucien Fassier?"

"Ha! I was glad to find him that day and mark him for death," Jarnac said. "I had not seen him since Spain and thought I never would. He died slowly, I will tell you."

"But why steal the map? I understand revenge against Fassier, but why take the map?"

"When I left Spain, I vowed to hurt the Communists. Hurt them as badly as I could. It was only when this war came that I saw how to do that. You call it betrayal. But they betrayed me. And Renée. I wanted to make them pay. Dearly."

"So, you became a double agent for the Nazis," I said.

"The enemy of my enemy is my friend," he said. "And the Communists are my bitterest enemies."

Machine gun fire rose up from the street, followed by explosions. Grenades. More gunfire. Jarnac's men stormed into the room, weapons drawn.

"Yes, damn you," Jarnac hissed into my ear, proving he loved his brother more than he hated his worst enemy. He threw me to the floor and signaled for his men to leave, placing the violin in its case. Then he stopped, his lips pursed as he thought it through. He snapped his fingers for me to come along. He had to keep me alive. Terrific idea in my book.

They bundled us out of the room, two in front and one on our six, pistols and submachine guns at the ready. I thought about pulling out my little .32 but didn't want them to fall down laughing. Downstairs, medics were carrying in a wounded woman while another tended to Roger, cleaning his face and bandaging his ribs. Probably broken. I flashed him the "V for victory" sign and he gave a feeble wave back, like he was being polite but wished he'd never laid eyes on me.

The FFI fighters were at the barricade, mostly ducking under cover as German machine gun fire chewed up the masonry and shattered windows, showering the street with grit and glass. Nicole was in the fight, tossing German potato masher grenades into the street. Jarnac's men shoved him across the street, into the door that led to the rooftop escape.

Nicole caught my eye as she threw her last grenade. A mingled look of pity and disgust played across her face, and I wondered if she blamed me for bringing the wrath of the Saint-Just Brigade down on her group.

I saw the grenade as it sailed through the air in a high arc, headed right for her. My thoughts were still careening inside my skull, but everything else was in slow motion. I pushed Nicole down as Jarnac's man grabbed at me, pulling me into the doorway after his boss. I shook him off and caught the grenade by its wooden handle, flicking it back over the barricade. Zing zing.

It exploded before it hit the ground, a sharp cracking burst that dislodged stones and sent them tumbling down from the barricade. One of the fighters fell, clutching his face as blood flowed between his fingers. I picked up his rifle and climbed the barricade, got a good footing, and took aim.

I fired off two shots before every Kraut in Paris seemed to have me in his sights. I ducked, seeing Jarnac in the doorway yelling at me. I couldn't hear a thing, my ears still ringing from the explosion and the shooting. He sprinted to me, running low as his men worked to shield him.

"Ten o'clock, at the *Jardin des Tuileries*, directly across from the Hotel Meurice. I want Remke there as well. I will do as you ask, but if you are lying or if Paul is hurt, I will kill you," he said, his hand grasping my shirt.

"Get in line, pal," I said and rose to fire again. One shot, and a Kraut crumpled. The street was filled with trucks and half-tracks. The tracked vehicles mounted heavy machine guns, which were keeping up a steady fire. I ducked, covering my head as debris rained down on me.

A truck had smashed into one of the trees lining the road. Bodies were scattered around it, and I wondered if one of the FFI had opened up on the convoy without thinking things through. This wasn't a routine German patrol. These guys weren't wearing clean uniforms. They were filthy and worn, their helmets decorated with camouflage. The half-tracks still had fir branches tied to the sides. Combat troops from Normandy, hardened fighters who just wanted to get the hell through this town. But now they were distracted by their dead comrades, ambushed by civilians they considered to be terrorists. This wasn't going to be pretty.

I popped up again and fired, joining in with the FFI and their varied armory. A couple of Sten guns, some old French rifles from the last war, captured Kraut pieces like mine, pistols, and one shotgun. The Krauts had gotten smart and regrouped behind the armored half-tracks, letting their heavy machine guns do all the work. I tried to fire back but as soon as I moved slugs zipped over my head and smashed into the stacked cobblestones.

Nicole was shouting over the racket, signaling for everyone to fall back. One of the FFI guys tugged at my sleeve, beckoning me to retreat as a couple of kids wearing red crosses carried off the wounded.

Maybe it was the hop in my head, but I felt like I was hitting on all eight cylinders, so I went for another shot. I settled in on my sights as the half-track closest to me was targeting the other end of the barricade and fired at the machine gunner. I saw him jerk backward as the firing stopped. Another Kraut pulled him aside and got on the gun. I worked the bolt and fired again, a miss this time.

Something smashed against the hood of the half-track and bright flames leapt up and spread out on the road. The driver jumped out, his tunic on fire, and rolled in the street. Others vaulted over the back of the half-track as they ran for cover.

Another burst of flame spread out over the cobblestone street. Molotov cocktails, coming from the rooftop opposite us. Shots came from the rooftop as well, targeting the Germans who'd escaped the burning vehicle. FFI fighters returned to the barricade, firing at the *boche* who were searching the rooftop for their tormentors.

A Kraut officer, his own tunic smoldering and blackened, signaled to his men to pull back. The one remaining half-track kept up fire on the rooftops as soldiers jumped on trucks that sped past the barricade as they took parting potshots at us. The half-track trailed them as a final firebomb crashed to the road, barely missing it.

Cheers rose up from the barricade, the buildings around us, and from across the street. Nicole dashed to the top of the barrier, checked both ways, and gave the all-clear sign. Half a dozen men and women ran out to collect arms and ammo from dead Germans. I dropped my rifle and ran after them.

"*Vite alors*," I shouted, pulling an ammo belt off a Kraut corpse. They needed to hurry up if they wanted to be back behind the barricade when the fire started cooking off all the ammo in that half-track. I pointed to the crackling flames and hoped they got the idea.

I moved on to the next body, grabbed a rifle, and rolled the *boche* over, ready to unbuckle his belt.

He groaned and murmured something in German. His eyelids fluttered as he raised his hand and grasped my sleeve. He had a chest wound below the right shoulder, and with each breath blood bubbled up. There was an exit wound low on his side, and by the angle it looked like he may have taken a slug from the rooftop. It was messy as hell but at least it had missed his heart.

I told him it was going to be okay, checking him for any hidden weapons as I spoke soothingly and removed his helmet. I never liked prisoners wearing helmets—the damn things were basically a steel bludgeon—but I checked his helmet liner, and there it was. The usual photograph of a girl, this one holding a baby. I stuffed it inside his tunic pocket and grabbed him by the leather straps attached to his cartridge belt, then pulled him to the barricade. He winced in pain, which was a good thing. If you're conscious enough to feel pain, the shock might not kill you. Loss of blood was another thing. He bled the whole way, leaving a glistening red trail behind.

Explosions rocked the half-track, grenades probably. Then the ammo went off, lethal firecrackers of machine gun rounds in the turret popping off in all directions.

"He's alive," I said to the girl in the white coat who came running to help lift him over the barrier. We got behind cover just as the gas tank went up, a fierce fireball mushrooming up and settling into a column of black smoke. "*Vivant.*"

"*Oui,*" she said, pulling his tunic open to check the wound. I recognized her from yesterday, or last night, or whenever the hell that was, when I helped with the wounded kid. "Let us keep him that way."

Two other medics ran up with a stretcher, and I backed away as they went to work, cutting away his shirt, cleaning the wound, and applying a compress. The Kraut's eyes opened, and he gaped in fear at the French civilians leaning over him. His hand went to his head, looking for the helmet. I took his hand in mine and patted his pocket with it.

"It's here," I said, then explained to the girl. "A photograph of his wife and child."

"*Dein Foto,*" she said, packing another compress on top of the first. "*Deine Frau und dein Kind.*" The wounded German relaxed, his hand cupped over his tunic pocket. The medics wound bandages over his wounds and lifted him onto the stretcher and dashed off.

"Think he'll make it?" I asked.

"*Oui*, if he has not lost too much blood. We have a hospital set up in the Louvre Metro station. He will be brought there with our wounded," she said. "Roger is being taken there as well. Come, we must wash."

"You can't use a real hospital?" I said, glancing at my hands, sticky with drying blood.

"There are too many *boche* patrols and roadblocks," she said. "But we have decent facilities there, and it is safe underground. The Germans have left it alone since they know we help all the wounded."

"So that Metro station is the closest hospital to this area?"

"*Oui, monsieur*. Is there someone you seek?" She led me inside the café, which seemed to serve as the headquarters for this block.

"Yes," I said. I introduced myself as we cleaned up in the kitchen. Her name was Suzette, and she was a second-year medical student. I told her I was looking for a friend and that we became separated yesterday not far from here. "If he'd been hurt, that would have been the closest place to find medical care?"

"*Certainement*," Suzette said, wiping her hands dry. "If he was injured badly. I hope you find him."

I thanked her and wandered into the main room with the map, where Roger had shown me the local layout. I ran a skittering finger across the map, spotting the nearby opera house and the barricaded rue Volney. The Louvre was close to the river, and I traced a shaky line from where I was to the Metro stop by the museum. It was only a few blocks from the *Jardin des Tuileries*, where I was due to meet Jarnac in a few hours. It looked close, but it didn't look easy. The Resistance held the Louvre while the Germans maintained a strongpoint at the Hotel Meurice, opposite the gardens.

General von Choltitz himself could watch me walk along the

road, if he could spare a moment from thinking about turning this city into a fancy pile of marble and granite.

"Do not take the avenue de l'Opéra."

I jumped, not realizing Suzette had followed me into the room. I felt my heart rocket and the zing rip through my brain.

"Sorry, I didn't hear you come in," I said, working to calm myself down.

"Are you not well? You are perspiring."

"It's been a long night, that's all," I said. "What's the best route?"

"The *boche* let our vehicles go, for the most part," she said. "But a man alone would be stopped, or perhaps shot without warning. You would be easily seen on the avenue, so take to the side streets. Here. And here," she said, pointing to the map. "Then take the rue de Montpensier. It is very narrow and not much used by the Germans. It will bring you to the Louvre Metro station. Ask for *Docteur* Durand and tell him I sent you."

"Thanks, Suzette," I said. I took the tin of chocolate out of my pocket and opened it, nearly spilling them as I twisted the cap. "Here, take these. They're supposed to keep you alert." I took one and bit into it.

"They have much *caféine*, perhaps too much for you, yes?" Suzette said. "But thank you. I hope you find your friend. *Au revoir*."

There couldn't be too much as far as I was concerned. I had a lot to do and not much time to do it. I was running on fumes, and I needed to stay sharp. Plenty of time to sleep later. I studied the map, trying to memorize the streets I'd take to avoid the main thoroughfare. I finished the chocolate and ran my finger along the route one more time. My hand shook so much my fingernail beat a staccato rhythm on the wall.

Damn. The shakes still went into hiding when the shooting started, but I had no idea how long that was going to last. If my luck held, there wouldn't be much more shooting and the Fritzes would all march out of Paris, and there'd be a helluva party while we waited for Leclerc's cavalry to show up.

I laughed out loud, and I can't say why. I went into the kitchen, scrounged some stale bread and washed it down with a glass of water, fast, before the liquid sloshed over the side. I drummed my fingers on the zinc counter while my leg tapped out a beat. It would have been nice if there was any music playing.

I downed another Pervitin. I had the shakes, okay, but I was still feeling tired in my bones and like I had cobwebs strung across my brain. I couldn't risk a cloudy mind over the next few hours, so what the hell. I needed to be sharp. I needed more zing.

The lights flickered and then went out.

I decided to follow suit, and left by the rear door, laughing at my own joke. It wasn't that amusing, I knew, but I was beginning to find everything damn funny. I followed the alleyway to a side street and darted across the avenue. The sun was working its way over the horizon, sending out advance scouts of red rays to brush away the darkness. Dampness from last night's rains rose from the pavement, tiny swirls of fog burning off around my legs. I ducked into a deep doorway as I heard vehicles approaching in the distance. I had time to cut down a side street off the avenue de l'Opéra, but I was curious.

A half dozen trucks escorted by a couple of motorcycles sporting sidecars rolled down the road. The vehicles were muddy and worn, the canvas covers on the trucks tattered and flapping in the wind. More fugitives from Normandy. Krauts in the sidecars held machine guns at the ready, searching for an ambush.

I backed up deeper into the shadows, not wanting to put the old line about cats and curiosity to the test. The convoy passed me. The last truck had its canvas cover rolled down, and the Germans crammed in the back had their rifles pointed at the buildings.

A single shot echoed in the street. One of the Krauts in the last truck fell back, struck by a bullet. His pals grabbed him before he tumbled out, and then the shooting really got going.

I tried the door behind me. Locked. I pounded on it, but no one came to open up, a wise precaution with the lead flying everywhere. I peeked around the corner and saw soldiers getting out of their trucks, rifles leveled at windows and aimed at rooftops. There was no more return fire, only the angry crack of rifles from soldiers sick of being shot at.

I couldn't stay in the doorway; they'd be on to me in a minute if they headed this way. And I couldn't run away from them since the end of the block was half a football field distant. So, I did the only logical thing. I ran at them.

There was a zip in my step as well as in my head, but even so a few bullets hit the granite wall near my head as I rounded the corner, only a few yards away. I took it so fast I almost fell, but righted myself and ran like hell, hugging the side of the building as I made for the next street. More shots rang out and the *thrum* of bullets flying by my ear told me I needed to hustle before these guys improved their aim.

I skittered around the corner, arms flailing and lungs gasping as I put solid stone between my backside and the swarm of angry Krauts. I kept running, not wanting to waste a second looking back to see if anyone was following. After a few twists and turns, I stopped in a narrow side street and caught my breath. Which took a while. I could feel my heart slamming against my ribcage as if it wanted to be set free.

There were no shots or footsteps, so I leaned back against the cool granite stone and gulped in fresh morning air. Across the way, lights glowed in windows as early risers dressed and made their breakfasts.

The lights blinked out all at once, the electricity killed along the whole block. No warm breakfast for these folks. I pushed off and made for the next street. I didn't recognize the name. I checked the road I'd just left and drew a blank on that one. I'd run too far or in the wrong direction, and now I was all mixed up. I thought about knocking and asking for help, but I'd probably sound like a crazy man. Which might be the case, the way thoughts were bouncing around inside my head. I had to be nuts to think this scheme would work. But then again, if I was nuts, then it might work.

Made perfect sense to me.

I kept walking. I found myself on the rue Saint-Honoré, a boulevard that made me nervous. Too open. I ran to the next street, passing a café where the proprietor was sweeping the sidewalk. He took one look at me and scampered inside. I heard the click of a lock, and figured I looked like trouble. Probably the blood from the wounded Kraut on my blue shirt. Or the smell of my sweat. I almost knocked to beg for directions, but then I thought maybe he was a collaborator, and he might be tele-phoning the Germans right now. So, I moved along, taking the next turn.

There it was, a blue enamel plaque telling me I was on the rue du Louvre. But which way to go? Dumb luck had brought me here, but I couldn't tell if I should take a left or a right.

Then the light dawned. As in light bulb. The electricity came back on and illuminated a green neon sign hanging above blue double doors. The neon flickered a few times and finally settled down, spelling out LEDUC DETECTIVE.

A sign from heaven. A detective had to be a kindred spirit. If he was at work yet, he'd help. He had to.

I ran to the doors, glancing over my shoulder to see if I was being followed. No sign.

I rapped on the door. Nothing. Harder. Still nothing. I felt naked standing still, making a racket out in the open. I craned my neck to look up at the windows on the second floor, hoping for a glimpse of a friendly face.

"*Qui êtes-vous?*"

I jumped, not for the first time today, as someone snuck up on me. Well, he'd walked from across the street, but it amounted to the same thing. "Who are you?" I countered, caught off-guard. I knocked on the door again, ready to give up.

The guy facing me was well dressed in a light gray summer suit with a white snap-brim fedora. He was about my age, with thick black hair, a strong chin, and dark, glinting eyes that darted up and down the street.

"*Américain?*" he asked, his eyes wide at this early morning surprise.

"Yes," I said. "Do you speak English?"

"Come, you fool," he said, demonstrating a good grasp of the language and my situation at the same time. He grabbed me by the arm and opened the door with an old iron key. Inside, he locked the door behind us and pushed me up the stairs.

"Are you *Monsieur* Leduc?" I asked as we entered his office.

"Sit there and be quiet," he said, going to the arched windows and checking the street. "Were you followed?"

"I was chased by the *boche* for a while, but that was several blocks away," I said, taking a chair opposite his desk. "They weren't following me, exactly. More like using me for target practice. Almost hit me too." I tried to be quiet, but the words just spilled out until I finally zipped it.

"Very well," he said, after another minute of watching at the window. "What are you doing in Paris? Why have you come to my office?"

"I can't say what I am doing here. But I am an American officer, and I need your help," I said. "I know this sounds strange, but I'm a detective myself. I was a cop before the war. A *flic*. I thought a fellow detective would give me a hand."

"A hand? Ah, yes, I understand. But how am I to know you are who you claim to be? You sound like an *Américain*, but why should I trust you? You could be working with the *boche*, or the *flics*." He tossed his hat on his desk, sat, and studied me over steepled fingers.

"Aren't the police fighting the Germans?" I asked.

"Now they are, yes. But mere days ago they were doing their bidding. They are fighting hard, indeed, but it will take much blood to wash away the memory of what they have done to those French men and women who have resisted *boche* rule. Not to mention the roundup of the Jews."

"Are you with the Resistance?" I asked.

"That is a dangerous question to ask," he said. "What is your name?"

"Captain William Boyle," I said, extending my hand to him. "You can call me Billy."

"Claude Leduc," he said, grasping my hand. "You may call me *Monsieur* Leduc. Now, tell me what you require."

"I have to get to the hospital the FFI has set up in the Louvre Metro," I said. "I'm looking for a friend who may be injured."

"Another *Américain*?" Leduc asked.

"No, he's—not American," I said, my brain catching up with my mouth as I realized I still didn't know which side this guy was on. No sense telling anyone I was looking for a Pole. "I was on my way there and got lost running from Fritz. I tried to talk to a guy opening his café, but he got spooked and locked his door. Probably didn't like the bloodstains on my shirt. German blood, but how could he know? Then I saw your sign, and figured it was worth knocking and asking for directions."

"Are you nervous, Captain Boyle?"

"No, not at all. Why do you ask?"

"I could feel the unsteadiness in your hand, you talk too much, are perspiring, and seem uncomfortable. These are the things which betray a liar," Leduc said. He opened a drawer and withdrew a revolver. A nicely polished French army model 73. It made me embarrassed to be carrying a cap gun in my pocket. "Now place your pistol on the desk. Do so with great care."

"Sure, sure," I said, taking out the little .32 and setting it before him. "I'd be glad to trade."

"Very amusing," he said, taking my piece and giving it a sniff. "It has not been fired recently."

"Thank God," I said. "I'd be outclassed by a good stone if I had to use that thing."

"Now you are telling me the truth," Leduc said, almost laughing. "Please continue with more of it. Why have you come to me?"

"First, I'm not lying. But I am a little jumpy, you're right. It's the Pervitin. I took a couple of pills to stay alert. It's been a while since I slept. I had the shakes already, just not as bad. I'll tell you this, it's doing a damn good job of keeping me wide awake."

"Slow down, Captain Boyle. Where did you get the Pervitin?"

"From a guy," I said. "At a black-market joint." True enough. I didn't want to admit the guy was an *Abwehr* officer and the joint was a collaborationist brothel. There was an innocent explanation alright, but I didn't have time for that.

"Pervitin is a German drug, issued to their troops. They call it the *Stuka-Pille*, since their pilots use it. Or the *Panzer-Pille*, in the case of their army."

"Yeah, I can see why. I feel like I could fly," I said. "So, will you help me get to the hospital?"

"One thing I find interesting is that a fellow like you, who evidently does not speak much French, found Pervitin on the black market in the first place. It is quite rare, for two reasons. First, the *boche* love it, at least until they stop taking it. And secondly, there is very little market for it among Parisians. We are too hungry to waste money on such a drug. So, before I help you, tell me more about this *mec* who sold it to you."

"Listen, I'm sorry to have wasted your time," I said. "I'll just pick a direction and take my chances." I stood, only to see my little pistol aimed right at me.

"Sit down," Leduc said. "This little Ruby automatic is a nice accessory for a lady's purse, but it is capable of causing a good deal of pain. And it is not terribly loud, unlike my revolver. So, take a seat, speak the truth, and let us avoid bloodstains on my Aubusson carpet."

"Okay," I said, sitting down again and grasping the arm of the chair. That quieted the tremor in my hand, but it shifted to my leg which started doing the jitterbug on his fancy rug. "I'm an Allied agent. Two of us were sent into Paris to track down a killer. My partner is missing and I'm trying to find him. We had a contact who provided the Pervitin, but I'm not going to tell you any more than that."

"A killer? This is a city full of killers. Who? And what has he done?"

"Listen, *Monsieur* Leduc, for all I know you could be a Vichy sympathizer. A member of the fascist militia, or an informant for the Gestapo. I'm not going to tell you anything I wouldn't want the Germans to find out."

"Then we are at an impasse," Leduc said.

"No, we aren't," I said, standing again. "I have to find my friend. Shoot if you must, but I'm leaving. If you're a decent shot, give me a few steps to get off your carpet, and I'll bleed on your wood floor." I walked to the door, tensing as I stepped off the carpet.

Leduc laughed.

"I will help you, Billy Boyle. A man who risks a bullet to find a friend is worth trusting. You may even have your little pistol back," he said, handing it to me after he walked around his desk.

"Thank you," was all I managed. "You believe me?"

"*Oui*. You seem *très américain*. I will escort you to the Metro. It will be safe once we get there, but we must watch for *boche* patrols. But first, you cannot walk about in that shirt. And you have an odor about you."

"I can imagine," I said. He opened a file cabinet and produced a folded white shirt and a pair of socks. Clean socks.

"Here. I keep some clothing for emergencies. Take these and wash yourself," he said, pointing to a door at the far end of the office. He didn't have to tell me twice. I scrubbed myself in the tiny sink and put on the new socks and shirt. Leduc was a little bigger than me, but it was a good enough fit.

I came out a new man. Fresh clothing, a new pal, and a head full of zing. What more did I need?

CHAPTER TWENTY-SEVEN

LEDUC WENT LEFT, and I was immediately glad he'd decided to take me. I'd planned on going right. He motioned for me to stay behind him as we walked to the corner, where he leaned against the wall and checked for anyone watching before removing his fedora and craning his neck around the side of the building.

"All clear," he whispered. The guy knew what he was doing. Not like some private eyes I'd known back in Boston. Clumsy fellows who used brawn and bribes to get by. Sure, there were some good eggs, but they were rare. Maybe Paris fielded a better brand of detective, or maybe I'd gotten lucky.

I ran after Leduc as he darted across the street.

"It is not far," he said on the other side. "But we must take the longer way through the back streets. It is much safer."

As if to make his point, shots sounded ahead of us, impossible to pinpoint as they echoed off the granite buildings. It sounded like a moving gunfight headed our way. Leduc grabbed my arm and pulled me into a small bar, the red diamond-shaped sign above the door reading TABAC. He waved to the barman, who nodded as if he knew him and was not surprised to see Leduc make for the back door with a stranger in tow.

"You are with the Resistance, aren't you?" I whispered, as we took to the alleyway that connected to the next street, away from the sound of rifle fire.

"Why deny it?" Leduc said. "Tomorrow our ranks will triple. By the time the Allies come, everybody will be a *résistant*."

"I'm supposed to see a Doctor Durand at the FFI hospital," I said. "Do you know him?"

"*Oui*," he said, stopping as we came to the street. "Not his real name, of course. He organized the hospital, such as it is. He will find your friend, if he is there."

Shouts arose from down the street, and Leduc pulled me back into the shadowy alleyway. Sounds of heels hitting cobblestones filled the air as a crowd of young men and women ran by. Running away, or running to somewhere? It was impossible to tell.

"We will wait a minute," Leduc said. "In case." Of what, he didn't need to say.

"Tell me," I said, slumping down against the cool stone. "Have you heard of the Saint-Just Brigade?"

"What? The *Brigade Saint-Just*? Is the killer you seek one of them?" I should've picked a dumber detective. Leduc didn't miss a beat.

"Let's just say I'm very interested in them."

"Do not let them know," he said. "They are very dangerous."

"Good fighters?" I asked.

"*Bien sûr*," he said. "The Communists all fight. Ever since Moscow told them to. I grant them their courage, but many are slaves to their masters in the Soviet Union. You know of the FTP, yes?"

"Sure. The *Francs-Tireurs et Partisans*," I said.

"Yes. Many of them are working people who believe the promises of Marx. I do not agree, but I understand them, and know they are not afraid to strike at the *boche*. Even the police have FTP within their ranks."

"But the Saint-Just Brigade is different?"

"Oh, they fight, have no doubt," Leduc said, stepping out into the street and cocking his head for any sound of trouble. "But they brook no disagreement with Moscow. If Stalin orders it, it is done."

"Marcel Jarnac," I said, deciding to trust this *mec* who'd given me his shirt, if not off his back, from his desk drawer.

"Jarnac? Is that who you seek?" I nodded. "He is a man with blood on his hands. Much *boche* blood. The blood of *collabos* as well, such as the Vichy militia and right-wing politicians. But he has been linked to the executions of fellow Communists. Several who are not sufficiently pro-Soviet have been found recently floating in the Seine. Their hands were bound behind their back and they'd been shot in the head. A trademark of the *Brigade Saint-Just*."

"How do you know all this?" I asked, as I watched him scan the street once again.

"I know people who know things. That is how a detective works, *n'est-ce pas*? Come, there is no one following. Those young people were probably heading for the barricades along the rue de Rivoli."

We ran across the street, veering right and taking an arched passageway through a large apartment block. We emerged into a courtyard to see French tri-colors and what looked like homemade American flags hanging from the windows. We cut through the main entrance, out onto the street, where the residents were more circumspect. It was mainly laundry hung from balconies, along with curious residents leaning on their railings and shouting questions to people below.

"They want to know if anyone has seen de Gaulle yet, and if the Germans have attacked the barricade at the end of the street," Leduc said. In answer to one of those questions, a burst of machine gun fire sounded from the next block. Leduc quickened his pace, drawing his revolver from his waistband. People came out of their buildings, a few of them armed, a few of them wearing red cross armbands, but most of them bearing nothing but gleams of apprehension and anger in their eyes.

By the time we got to the barricade the lead was flying fast, the machine gun firing at those who dared show themselves and at the windows overhead, shattering glass and sending shards of stone spinning like shrapnel into the crowd. Those who were hit and those who didn't want to be backed away to the safety of doorways or their homes. Everyone who was armed found a spot at the barricade. Leduc, who seemed to know many of the fighters, directed several young men and women into a building to take up positions overlooking the Krauts. They were armed with captured German rifles and submachine guns. One guy carried a sack of Molotov cocktails, the deadly bottles of gasoline and kerosene clanking as he ran.

I chanced a look over the barricade as the machine gun fire drifted higher, aiming for the top floor facing the street.

"Shit!" I said, ducking.

"*Merde!*" Leduc echoed.

A Panther tank sat in the middle of the intersection, its hull-mounted machine gun spitting fire as the turret traversed, seeking targets. Next to it a burning truck lay on its side, dead Fritzes scattered around it.

"I thought this was the safe route," I said, covering my head as more debris showered down over us.

"No, I said it was safer," Leduc said. "Those words are different, are they not?"

I was about to say the safest thing would have been not to run to the barricade, but it seemed like Leduc was a part of this, and I couldn't expect him to skip out on his friends to babysit me.

"Listen, just tell me where to go from here," I said. "I can't help much with my little Ruby. Stay if you need to."

"I must," Leduc said. Then the tank fired.

The cannon shot blew a chunk off the corner of the building

to our right, the one the fighters had entered. The whine of the turret sounded as two bottles crashed to the street, Molotov cocktails thrown from the roof. They fell short, the bursts of flame pluming in front of the tank, a shimmering wall of fire.

The Panther fired again, higher this time, the cannon shell bursting near the top floor.

The FFI fighters at the barricade fired, even as Leduc screamed at them, waving his arms to warn them to get down. From what I could see, it was only the tank shooting at us, and there was no sense in wasting small arms fire on that armored monster.

The Panther lurched slightly closer, its machine gun raking the windows where the firebombs had come from. The turret swung again, and this time the muzzle of the cannon fixed on the barricade.

Leduc tapped my arm and ran off into the wrecked building as a shattering explosion hit the barricade behind us. I followed him up the staircase, realizing what he was up to. That sack had contained half a dozen bottles, but only two had been thrown.

We got to the top floor and saw why. The shell had exploded beneath the roof, collapsing it into this room. Bodies were tangled in the debris, the scent of gas thick in the air.

"Broken," I said.

"No, look," Leduc said, pulling a bag out from under an upturned couch. The flooring gave out from underneath him, sending furniture and debris sliding into the street. I held onto his arm, pulling him back into the hall.

The sack held two intact bottles.

"Got a light?" I asked.

"Yes, but the Panther is still too far away. If we miss, we are *fini*."

I didn't like the look in his eye. I stepped back into the shattered room and leaned out, spotting the tank as it fired again. He was right, it was a long shot from up here. The good news was I didn't spot any Kraut infantry.

"Okay," I said. "Lead on."

Leduc took me up the final flight of stairs, which led to the roof. We crossed over to the neighboring building and dropped through an open skylight, onto a table set up beneath it. It looked like a well-traveled route. Then down the steps and out a side door, up to the edge of the building where we had a fine view of the Panther. A side view, which was much more pleasing.

"No *infanterie allemande*," he said, pointing to a thick-trunked tree near the burning truck. I nodded, and we took off, each of us carrying a Molotov cocktail and pumping our legs like madmen, which wasn't far from the truth. Homemade firebombs against the heavily armored Panther was a fool's errand, and I sure was the right man for the job.

We slid to the ground behind the tree, which gave us a perfect view of the Panther's ass end. "We've got to hit it on the rear panel," I said. "The exhaust fans and air intake go right to the engine."

The Panther fired again, the explosion punching a hole through the barricade.

Leduc set his bottle on the ground and offered me a box of matches.

"No, you light them," I said, worried about the shakes, even though I couldn't feel them right now. He struck the match and lit the two kerosene-soaked cloths corked tight in the neck of each bottle. With a nod, we ran for the tank, hearing the clank of its treads as it began to move, over-confident about vanquishing the feeble opposition. With a burst of exhaust, it began to pivot on one track.

Ten yards away, I skidded to a halt.

"Now!"

We threw the bottles with their burning wicks. Mine hit the

rear low, sending a blossom of flame beneath the tank. Leduc's hit the rear of the turret, and the flames erupted across the engine compartment. The back end of the tank was a sheet of fire, but it was still moving, still pivoting on its treads, turning to face this new threat.

We ran back to the tree, hiding behind it and the smoke from the burning truck. The Panther lurched toward us, leaving flames licking the pavement where my throw had fallen short. Its forward machine gun fired wildly, searching out any target, blindly striking back.

The turret swiveled, the cannon fixed on our tree, a linden, which suddenly seemed terribly small.

The driver's hatch door popped open, followed by the commander's hatch on the turret. Black-clad tankers tumbled out as flames from the engine compartment burned brightly. One of them pulled a pistol from his holster and fired in our direction. Leduc took aim and fired twice, the Kraut spinning and clutching his side. I joined in with my Ruby, figuring any amount of noise might scare them away.

The five crewmen ran away, headed for the street opposite the barricade. I was shocked that we'd driven them off, but then the fuel tank went up, sending columns of fire out every opening. They'd been wise to run.

"The ammo's next," I said, not waiting for Leduc to reply. He was hard on my heels all the way across the street and back into the safety of the building. Explosions rocked the burning tank as the stored shells cooked off one after another.

When it was over, fighters emerged from behind the barricade to strip the bodies of weapons and ammo. We did the same, and I got a nice Walther P38 automatic from a Kraut lieutenant who had no further use for it. I took the belt and holster, along with several clips of 9mm ammo.

"Here," I said, handing Leduc the Ruby. "A souvenir."

"Thank you, Billy. A private detective needs a well-hidden pistol now and then," Leduc said. He spoke with one of the fighters, adjusted his fedora, and gestured for me to follow. "On to the Louvre."

"We were lucky, *Monsieur* Leduc," I said, as we left the celebrating FFIs behind. Smoke swirled from the smoldering vehicles, rising against the ruined buildings. Fighters were rebuilding the barricade, and there were bodies to be buried. Still, they cheered themselves on. Liberation was a heady drug. Almost as good as the Pervitin surging in my brain.

"Please, call me Claude," he said. "Now we are comrades. We have taken down a *boche* tank together."

"Sure, Claude. But we were still very lucky. My firebomb wouldn't have stopped them. Yours did."

"Of course," Claude said with a laugh, slapping me on the shoulder. "Did you think that was my first Molotov cocktail?"

CHAPTER TWENTY-EIGHT

CLAUDE AND I made it to the Louvre Metro station without encountering any more Panther tanks. There were plenty of people, many of them armed since the museum and the makeshift hospital were both strongly defended. A truck pulled up in front of us, and the wounded were unloaded. Kids, mere boys and girls, wearing FFI armbands and hastily applied bandages. An elderly woman, a mother cradling a crying child wrapped in a blood-stained blanket, and one German with bandaged eyes and a blackened face.

I prayed von Choltitz wouldn't order the plunger to be pushed. There was enough carnage in Paris as it was.

Claude took me down the steps, under the ornate Metro sign. Belowground, every space was given over to cots, beds, and blankets as white-coated medical personnel scurried from patient to patient. Claude asked for *Docteur* Durand, and a harried young woman greeting the new arrivals pointed down the hall.

"He is on the next platform," Claude said. "They are using the cars as a surgery. You will find him there. *Adieu*, Billy, I must go."

"Good luck," I said as we shook hands.

"*Bonne chance* to you," Claude said, setting his white fedora at a rakish angle and dashing up the stairs.

I made my way through the wounded to the platform entrance.

Beds were set up along the wall, and the Metro cars had their doors open, each one turned into a cramped operating theater or recovery room. The patients here were more severely injured than those in the entryway. None of them looked like they'd be out of bed soon.

"Durand? Doctor Durand?" I asked as a nurse headed my way, looking like she wanted to shoo me out.

She pointed farther down the platform, unleashing a stream of French that I didn't understand except for the tone, which communicated the fact that she was busy, and I was on my own. I went in that direction, passing the last of the beds and coming to an alcove. There was a table, two chairs, and one tired-looking surgeon. He was unshaven, his smock was splattered with blood, and he drew on a cigarette as if it were life itself.

"Doctor Durand?"

"*Que voulez-vous?*" he said, barely looking at me.

"Do you speak English?"

"*Anglais? Un peu*," he said, looking at me more closely. "You are *américain*?"

"Yes. I'm looking for a friend. A Polish fellow, about my age."

"The *américains* are here?" Durand said, kicking his chair back and standing.

"No. Not yet. Just *moi*. I'm looking for my friend. Suzette said if he'd been injured he might have been brought here," I said, speaking slowly and trying to calm him down.

"Suzette? She is well, *oui*?"

"Yes, I saw her at the rue Volney barricade. Now, do you have a Polish *mec* here? Slim, wears glasses, and has a scar?" I traced a line down my cheek. It was a hard scar to forget.

"Ah, yes, the baron," Durand said.

"He's here? Is he hurt badly?" I rested my hand on the holster at my belt, trying to steady the increasing shakes. I didn't know what I'd do without Kaz.

"He is resting, come," Durand said, grinding out his cigarette and beckoning me to follow.

"Where was he hit?" I asked. "Is it serious?"

"Hit?" Durand asked as he hustled down another platform, this one filled with less-serious cases. No one here was going to be doing the foxtrot tonight, but they were all conscious, at least.

"Wounded," I said. "By a bullet or shrapnel."

"Oh, I see. He was not wounded, *mon ami*. He has the *crise cardiaque*."

"What?" I said, grabbing him by the arm and stopping so I could look him in the eye.

"Here," he said, patting his chest. "*Attaque cardiaque*. You understand?"

"A heart attack? Kaz had a heart attack?" I couldn't believe it.

"*Oui*, come. You can see him."

I fell in behind Durant, trying to come to grips with what he'd told me. All of a sudden it made sense. Kaz had been tired lately, but I'd thought it was not enough sleep and too much war. And those headache pills. Maybe it wasn't a headache at all.

"Here," Durant said, his hand extended to a cot at the end of a row.

Kaz sat propped up by pillows, damp hair plastered to his head, a handkerchief held to his lips as he tried to stifle a coughing fit.

"Billy," he said, bunching the handkerchief in his hand and trying for a smile.

"Kaz," I said, going for the same and having a hard time of it. I'd caught a glimpse of the red-flecked handkerchief and was shocked by that as much as how white his skin was.

"What of the mission?" Kaz asked as I knelt by his cot. I looked up at Durand, a million questions swirling through my mind.

"I must return," the doctor said. "To *la chirurgie*. I spoke to the baron of his condition. My *anglais* is too poor to tell you, *oui*?"

"I will explain, *Docteur*, thank you," Kaz said with a smile.

Durant departed and Kaz dropped the grin like a heavy weight. "I will tell you everything, Billy, but first, what is happening?"

"Hang onto your hat, pal," I said, and laid it out as quickly as I could, beginning with when we got separated after running into Jarnac. How I'd made it to the rue Volney barricade where the fifis were sort of on my side, not buying Jarnac's claim that I was a *traître*. My late-night jaunt to grab Paul Lambert and how I hustled him and his violin to the One-Two-Two.

"And get this," I said. "Who does our contact Malou turn out to be? Diana."

"We should have anticipated that possibility," Kaz said, his brain obviously working better than his ticker.

"Maybe," I said. "But you'll never guess who she had stashed in there. One Colonel Erich Remke."

"Surprise upon surprise," Kaz said. "Was he there as a client of the club?"

"No. Hiding out from the Gestapo, he claims. Said they'd uncovered his role in the plot to kill Hitler."

"That does sound like *Herr* Remke," Kaz said. "Both his involvement and choice of hiding place." I filled him in on Remke running *Atlantik* and the common ground we found in not wanting the City of Light to be lit up like a bonfire. Plus, the bit about spreading the word I wanted to meet Jarnac at the rue Volney barricade, although I glossed over how they'd gotten the drop on me.

"So, here's the deal," I said. "I'm meeting Jarnac at ten o'clock opposite the Hotel Meurice. Remke is there now—he heard the Gestapo team sent for him has hightailed it for the safety of the Reich—and Jarnac has agreed to recant his story about Leclerc's approach route in exchange for Paul's safe return."

"What did you threaten to do?" Kaz asked.

"Kill Paul. Jarnac didn't believe me, but I got his attention when I told him you would do it," I said.

"So glad to be of assistance," Kaz said, as the patient in the next bed began to moan. His head and leg were wrapped in white gauze with a decidedly pinkish hue, and his hand shook like he had the palsy, which made me damned uncomfortable. "Jarnac agreed, really?"

"Yeah. He wants Remke at the meet. Now I need to figure out how to get in touch with Remke to let him know. I can't exactly stroll into the hotel lobby."

"The telephones are working, you know," Kaz said.

"Right, and I have Diana's number at the One-Two-Two. I can call her and have her deliver the message."

"Or I can make the call," Kaz said. "I am not crippled, Billy."

"First, give it to me straight. I know you've been feeling lousy for a while. It finally dawned on me what those pills were for after the doc told me about your *attaque cardiaque*."

"Nitroglycerin tablets. For chest pain," Kaz said. "I thought my heart problems were behind me, but I started having pains again." When I'd first met Kaz back in '42, he'd been pretty skinny and weak. He'd built himself up with exercise and had turned into a tough and wiry customer.

"You didn't tell me," I said.

"I did not want to let you down," Kaz said. "It became bearable with the tablets, for a while. And then this mission came up, and I knew you'd need me along, at least to point out the sights."

"Tell me what happened after we got separated."

"I went up to the rooftop ahead of you and crossed over to the next building. I found a gable window open and climbed in. Simple, except I had no idea where you had gone. I went out into the street and followed a group to a nearby barricade. Then I could feel my heart beating oddly. Rapid and fluttering. Then pain. Terrible pain. The next thing I recall is being bundled into an automobile and driven here."

"What did the doctor do?"

"Other than tell me to rest, nothing. He said I should avoid intense physical activity and any kind of stress."

"Which has pretty much been our life for the past couple of years," I said.

"Yes. I intend on seeing a specialist as soon as we return to London," he said. "Doctor Durant seems to be a fine surgeon, but he is not a cardiac specialist. I daresay the medical community in occupied France is somewhat behind on recent advances."

"But did he say if your condition is treatable?"

"Not that he knew of. His guess was that I have something called mitral stenosis. Something to do with a heart valve not pumping blood properly, which causes fatigue and shortness of breath. He said it is common among those who had one of several diseases during childhood. I did have rheumatic fever when I was eight or nine, which according to him can bring this condition on later in life."

"Okay, let's hope some sawbones back in England can fix you up," I said.

"One thing, Billy. You must promise me you won't reveal this to Colonel Harding."

"Kaz, you're in no condition to return to duty," I said.

"Of course. I shall request leave while I seek treatment. But I can't risk Colonel Harding discharging me on health grounds."

"But what about Angelika? You need to keep yourself alive for her sake," I said, as the patient next to us groaned loudly and thrashed about. Two nurses came running, and I got out of their way.

"Yes, of course. I promise, I will see a proper doctor in England, immediately. If he says there is no hope, then I will resign, or return to office duty if it is allowed. But I must stay in the field if possible, if only on the slight chance I can help Angelika or find her somehow. Please, Billy, promise me."

The moaning in the next bed stopped. The patient's arm, raised in mid-air, dropped to his side.

"*Mort*," one of the nurses murmured.

"Sure, Kaz. I promise." In the face of so much pain and death, what could I do but offer hope?

CHAPTER TWENTY-NINE

THERE WAS NO keeping Kaz down. He swatted away my proffered arm as we made our way through the narrow aisles and the scurrying doctors, nurses, and medics. We passed a few Germans who looked relaxed in spite of their wounds. Most Krauts feared being captured by partisans, who weren't bound by any rules of war—not that the Nazis paid much attention themselves. But these Fritzes had been well-treated, cared for, and now their war was over. I was jealous.

"Do you have any idea what's going on in the streets?" I asked as we stepped around a stretcher, empty except for a pile of blood-stained bandages.

"Each side seems to be entrenched in their strongpoints," Kaz said. "The Germans attack barricades and buildings, but without sufficient force to make a difference. There are rumors of Leclerc every hour. He is ten miles from the city, he is almost here, he is here, there, and everywhere. The FFI fighters seem euphoric, but there is desperation as well. What if Leclerc is delayed, and the Germans reinforce the city? It could be a slaughter."

"If there's a delay, let's make sure it's not our fault," I said, holding up my hand as we stopped to let a stretcher pass by.

"Your hand is no better," Kaz said, grabbing me by the wrist.

"About the same," I said, eager to change the subject. "Comes and goes. You sure you're okay?"

"I *had* a heart attack," Kaz said. "But I am not *having* a heart attack. I will be fine unless you want to race me to a telephone."

"Where are we going to find one anyway?"

"At a bar or *tabac* shop," he said, as we entered the main passageway leading to the stairs. "Or, perhaps in there." Kaz pointed to an open door I hadn't noticed before. It was a small office, barely wide enough for two people to pass. Probably for the stationmaster or whatever they called the head ticket-taker. The only problem was it was crammed with people, one of whom was shouting into a telephone with a hand pressed over one ear. It looked like a long line.

"We can't wait that long," I said. "Besides, those guys might not appreciate a phone conversation about calling German headquarters."

"True," Kaz said, heading for the stairs.

"Are you sure you can make it?" I asked, as he took the first step.

"May I borrow your pistol, Billy?"

"Why?" I asked, staying right by his side in case he faltered.

"So I may shoot you with it if you ask me that again," he said, pulling himself up the railing. I didn't say anything since I wanted him to save his strength for the steps.

Once at the top, we stopped to catch our breath. Both of us, since it was a long climb. People flowed by, excited groups of Parisians dressed for a hot summer day. Armed fifis wearing Cross of Lorraine armbands swaggered confidently, preening in delight as they displayed their allegiance and their weapons in a manner unthinkable a day or two ago.

Gunfire echoed from every direction, not the sound of a major battle, but the reverberation of short, sharp encounters throughout the city.

"We ought to find out about getting you to the *Hôtel-Dieu* Hospital," I said. "The way may be clear by now."

"No, for two reasons," Kaz said, wiping the sweat from his brow. "First, there is still fighting around the bridges leading to the hospital and the *Préfecture de Police* and too much open ground to cross without taking fire. Second, I don't intend on being a patient anywhere, at least not right now."

"Kaz, you've got to go back," I said, my hand tapping my holster.

"Why are you so jumpy, Billy?" he asked. "Your whole body is trembling as badly as your hand did at first."

"I took a pep pill," I said. "I needed to stay awake. Remke gave me these." I showed him the tin of Pervitin, not seeing any reason to tell him I took two, plus all that caffeine-laced chocolate.

"Methamphetamine," Kaz said. "Don't take another, it may put you in the cot I just vacated. And don't lecture me, you are not exactly the picture of health yourself."

"All I need is a good-night's sleep," I said.

"Hmm. That is the same thing I said when you first noticed my symptoms. We can talk about this later, right now we need to find a telephone." We walked away from the crowded Louvre Metro stop, and soon came to a small plaza. Kaz spotted Le Royal Bar and we strolled toward it.

"How did you come by that clean shirt, by the way?" Kaz asked as we neared the door. I told him about Claude Leduc and his detective agency.

"I am in dire need of a change of clothes myself, not to mention a bath," Kaz said. "I am certain I shall find both at the One-Two-Two."

"How are you going to get all the way over there?" I asked, as I opened the door. The interior was dark, only a few faint lights illuminating the long bar, but it was enough to spot the barman eyeing us, or maybe it was me and my pistol. A good bartender can see trouble before the door slams shut behind it.

"I will find a way. If Jarnac's men had not taken our cash, I would simply check in at the Ritz. But given my appearance, I doubt they would trust my credit," Kaz said.

We leaned against the bar. The barman approached, a cigarette dangling from his lips and a towel tossed over his shoulder. He and Kaz went on for a while with some sort of give and take.

"Billy, give this gentleman your pistol and belt," Kaz said after they'd shaken hands.

"Why?" I asked, as the barman brought over a telephone and set it down in front of Kaz.

"For the use of his telephone, two coffees—the real thing, he claims—and a supply of *francs*. All of which we need more than that *boche* Walther."

Coffee got my attention. I handed over my piece as Kaz swept up the *francs* like winnings at a poker game. He held out some for me, and I took a few of the bills, not even sure what I'd do with them. I recited the telephone number Diana had given me, and Kaz dialed the One-Two-Two. He asked for Malou, and in a minute he happily greeted Diana.

His face went cold.

"What? Slow down, Diana. When?"

"What?" I mouthed, grabbing his sleeve. He waved a hand, concentrating on what she was saying. He held up a finger, telling me to wait.

"Very well," he said. "I'll tell Billy. But please call our friend from Rome. Tell him Marcel wants to meet him along with Billy outside his hotel at ten o'clock. Yes, he's agreed. Yes, this morning. There's not much time. *Au revoir.*"

"What's wrong?" I asked, before he set the phone on its cradle.

"Paul Lambert has escaped," he said.

"Damn! When?"

"Less than thirty minutes ago. Diana had to meet with a Resistance contact and didn't want Paul to see him. She left him with one of the girls and locked the door. He apparently pleaded hunger and got her to take him to the kitchen. He knocked the poor girl unconscious, tied her up, then escaped out a kitchen window."

The barman brought our coffees. I probably didn't need any more caffeine, but it smelled great. I took it in my steady left hand, draining the small cup while I thought about what to do.

"Hey, should you be drinking that joe?" I asked.

"Billy, a cup of coffee is not going to kill me. Be glad your pistol is no longer in reach. Now, what does this mean for your plan?"

"Nothing, I hope," I said, glancing at the clock. "There's no way Paul can know where his brother is right now. Jarnac must be at the Hotel Lutetia or on his way to the Meurice. We have to assume he'll go back to his apartment or hide elsewhere."

"He has already performed his role in this charade," Kaz said, draining the last of his coffee. "As long as he does not communicate with his brother in the next hour or so, it should not be a problem."

Gunshots sounded from the street. People ran by the bar, some of them darting in for a moment, then walking calmly out as the shooting died down. Just another Parisian morning.

"You know, there's something odd about hearing Lambert tied up that girl," I said.

"Billy, such things are not unknown at the One-Two-Two," Kaz said with a bit of a smirk.

"You didn't meet him. He seemed pretty meek. The exact opposite of Marcel Jarnac. I'm actually surprised he went with one of the girls. He was intimidated by the place."

"So were you, Billy, admit it."

"Yeah, I was," I said, turning around to rest my elbows on the bar and stare out the front window. "Maybe he was all worked up over losing his violin. He was really attached to it."

"Well, if he's a classical musician, that makes sense," Kaz said.

"But still, escaping out a window. I didn't think he'd be capable of that." I started to pace along the narrow bar, back and forth, the possibilities playing themselves out like lightning bolts in my mind.

"What is it?" Kaz asked, his brow furrowed.

"Call back. Tell Diana to get out. Now. Her and her team. At once."

CHAPTER THIRTY

I'D MADE A big mistake. I'd underestimated Paul Lambert. I had assumed he was a meek musician who was the total opposite of his brother, and that it would be easy to keep him under wraps. I failed to take him seriously. He'd played a role, and I'd fallen for it completely.

I cursed myself as I made my way through throngs of people who seemed to be going in the wrong direction. I needed to get in position well before the meeting time, ready to spot any trick Jarnac had up his sleeve. I'd left Kaz to make the call to Diana, trusting he'd get word to her in time. The barman had already donned an FFI armband and was wearing his new pistol proudly, so Kaz decided to trust him and arranged to leave a message for me at Le Royal Bar, letting me know where he'd be.

Rifle fire rippled through the morning air. Not an all-out battle, but a steady series of shots coming from the direction of the Seine. Kaz had told me to head straight to the river and take the Quai du Louvre, bearing right to head into the *Jardin des Tuileries*. It was a big fancy garden along the Seine, full of trees, flowers, and plenty of places to hide behind well-trimmed shrubbery. The gardens were bounded on the far side by the rue de Rivoli, with the Hotel Meurice smack in the middle, facing the gardens.

It wasn't far, but I had to elbow my way through the crowd heading away from the river. As I got closer, I saw why. Krauts were lining the wall along the quay, firing across the Seine and down at the boat-shaped island in the river, where the *Prefecture de Police* sat like a fortress. Trucks rolled up and down the quai, *boche* taking potshots at the FFI across the water. No Germans came down these side streets, where the possibility of ambush lurked in the narrow passageways, but on the quay, they held sway, swarming to the wall and firing wildly.

They were trigger-happy, and beholden to no law when it came to shooting civilians in a city rising against them. I edged back to the corner of a building and surveyed the wide road. A few nervous Parisians, curiosity overcoming their common sense, did the same. Germans in front of us fired across the river as shots came from buildings on the far side of the Seine. Bullets chipped masonry over our heads, sprinkling the gathering with stone chips and a healthy dose of fear.

I moved back, away from the river. Within a block, life was almost normal except for the echoing gunfire. People sat in cafés, clustered in groups on the sidewalk, their newspapers open for the latest news. *L'Humanité* and *Combat*, two of the underground papers of the Resistance, now circulated openly. It was strange how the city contained so many things seemingly at odds. Death and struggle, along with a sunny morning at a neighborhood café.

I walked around the Louvre to the edge of the Tuileries gardens, trying to find a route to the Meurice. The rue de Rivoli was swarming with Germans, sandbagged emplacements at every corner, and armored vehicles clanking down the thoroughfare. No chance of strolling to the hotel lobby and asking for Colonel Remke.

The gardens were full of Krauts as well. A few officers sat on benches, smoking and enjoying the view while they could. Soldiers marched by, rifles shouldered, and not looking friendly. I did see a few civilians, but I didn't trust they weren't Jarnac's men, or maybe even plainclothes *Abwehr*, in place to nab me once I showed my face. It didn't seem likely, not if Jarnac was keeping his end of the bargain. But if little brother Paul had gotten to him, all bets were off.

I paced in the plaza by the west wing of the Louvre, spotting FFI men on the roof. They could have fired on any number of Germans, and vice versa, but maybe there was an informal art lover's truce. The absence of flying lead was fine by me.

But I was starting to feel conspicuous. A Frenchman of military age hanging around the German commandant's headquarters was bound to be noticed sooner or later, which could mean a bullet, a beating, or a ride on a boxcar full of slave laborers headed for the Reich. I needed to find a way in.

There he was. A gardener, going about his daily routine as if a battle wasn't about to lap against the borders of his beautiful *jardin*. Dressed in the standard blue cotton worker's jacket, he pushed a wheelbarrow along a row of shrubs while hoes, rakes, and other tools rattled as he moved. No one paid him any mind.

I trotted over, whistling to get his attention. He stopped, set his wheelbarrow down, and studied me through narrowed eyes. He had a couple of days' gray stubble growing and wore a cloth cap pulled down over his eyes. He glanced around, suspicious, or maybe just careful. He studied the German officers on the bench for a moment, then gave me a sharp nod as they ignored us. I decided to take a chance.

"*Américain*," I whispered. He drew on his cigarette as if Yanks strolling through the *jardin* was a routine event. Another nod.

I took the *francs* from my pocket and pointed to his jacket and tools. He looked at the money, then me. He waved away the cash, withdrew a crumpled blue pack of Gauloises from his pocket along with a small box of wooden matches, and removed his jacket. He handed it to me along with a hoe and a pair of shears. Apparently, he didn't want to part with the wheelbarrow, which was okay. At least now I looked like I belonged.

I shoved my arms into the jacket, one hand still clutching the cash. He held up a finger as I went to stash it. He selected one note very carefully, looked around again, and made a drinking motion with his hand. We both laughed and went our separate ways. Me, toward the Meurice. Him, away from me.

Smart guy.

I put the hoe over my shoulder and walked with the amiable gait of a gardener who liked being paid by the hour. I inspected the plantings, which all looked a bit worse for wear in the August heat. I worked the hoe between the manicured shrubs, scraping away at the few weeds that dared invade this fancy garden. I eyed the route ahead as I smoothed out the soil. To my right I saw Kraut guards out in front of the Meurice. A couple of civilians on the sidewalk strolled along with a Kraut officer. Gestapo, maybe, or collaborators trying to figure out the best way out of town.

To my left, a squad of Germans in their field gray trooped along the quay, headed for the shooting gallery a block away. But no one seemed to be watching me or watching for me. I glanced at my watch. Ten minutes to go.

I left the hoe between some bushes and moved closer to the street, snipping at the greenery as I went. Two officers on a path came within a couple of yards, but they were too busy arguing to pay me any mind. Tempers were on edge everywhere.

I worked my way behind a hedge and gave it a trim, making my way to the road. I was almost opposite the entrance to the hotel and the sand-bagged guard posts in front of it. The door opened, and Colonel Remke walked out, glancing up and down the street. I ditched the shears, walked around the hedge, and checked the street. Remke gave a brief nod of recognition. I waited.

In a second, I spotted Jarnac. He was waving papers at a guard at the corner who finally relented and let him through the checkpoint. He wore a suit jacket and an open-necked shirt. Odd attire for a hot day, and I'd bet he had a pistol stuck in the waistband of his trousers. A sentry close to Remke eyed me and unslung his rifle, taking a couple of steps in my direction before Remke called him off.

The colonel set off across the road, Jarnac hustling to catch up with him.

"It is done," Remke said to me in a low voice, his face turned away from Jarnac's approach. I didn't respond. After all, Jarnac wasn't aware we knew each other, only that I was aware Remke controlled the Frenchman as his agent.

"Where is my brother?" Jarnac spat out at me as soon as he was close enough.

"He's safe, and he'll be with you soon," I said. "Have you kept your side of the bargain?"

Jarnac looked to Remke, his mouth twisted in a hateful grimace. "Tell him. Then tell me how he knows of our connection."

"*Monsieur* Jarnac has confirmed his original intelligence about the advance on Paris was wrong. Likely a deception by the enemy," Remke said, his stern gaze fixed on Jarnac. "As for how an Allied agent knew of our work, I can only guess it was poor security on your end. The French are a vociferous people, after all."

"It was not me," Jarnac said, his mouth set in a grim line.

"Perhaps you were not careful enough during your visits to Paris," Remke said. "Whatever the reason, it no longer matters."

A pair of officers, two heavily perfumed women on their arms, walked by, chattering away as if the world was not quite ready to collapse around their ears. We kept silent for a minute, our only common language too dangerous to be overheard.

"What do you mean?" Jarnac said.

"You are compromised, and the front is moving quickly away from your base of operations," Remke said. "It should be obvious."

"We still have work to do," Jarnac said, hands clenched at his sides, his voice shimmering with rage. "The Communists cannot be allowed to win. France must not become Red. You must crush them now that they are out in the open."

"Do not lecture me, Jarnac," Remke said. "Out of consideration for our past association, I have agreed to let this officer go so he may free your brother. Otherwise, I would hand him over to the Gestapo, gladly."

"You want him to succeed?" Jarnac said, taking a step back as if he'd been punched.

"I don't want the Reds to rule France any more than you do," Remke said, stepping into the space Jarnac had vacated. "Don't you see the best way to avoid that is a column of General Leclerc's tanks?"

"You have betrayed me. Both of you. God help me, I swear on the soul of my wife I will kill both of you if Paul is not safe. Where is he?" Jarnac put his hand on one hip, pushing away his jacket like a gunslinger ready to slap leather.

"Do not," Remke said. "You will be shot in seconds. And Paul will die."

"You should be attacking the Reds instead of protecting this agent," Jarnac said, jutting his chin forward in aggressive anger. But he moved his hand off his hip. "Give him to me. I will keep him until Paul is returned."

Remke paused, giving it some thought. Either he was a damn fine actor, or I was about to find myself face down in the Seine.

"No," Remke finally said. "I will take him into custody and interrogate him. Telephone my aide at the Lutetia once you have Paul back."

"And then you'll let me go, right?" I said. I didn't need to act worried. I was.

"We shall see," Remke said, resting one hand on his shiny leather holster. Now it was his turn to hint at hardware being drawn. "*Monsieur* Jarnac, you know how to get in touch with me, and I believe you have received your final payment. Our business is concluded."

"You wait, Remke. You wait until the Soviets are at your door. When they kill everyone you hold dear, then think of me. Think of what you could have done here in Paris to wipe out the Reds. Instead, you wait for the Americans and their pet Frenchmen to take you prisoner. You don't deserve to live," Jarnac said. With that, he turned on his heel, spat into the gutter, and strode off.

"Come, let us have a drink," Remke said. "I don't know how long I have left to enjoy the bar at the Meurice. Take off that jacket. I haven't seen a man who's done an honest day's work in the Meurice bar for some time, except the barman, that is." I removed the blue jacket and draped it over a neatly trimmed bush, hoping its owner would find it after his drink. My newly acquired white shirt was still presentable, even alongside the impeccably attired Colonel Remke.

"You were pretty convincing," I said, as he clamped his hand on my arm and steered me across the street. In case Jarnac was looking, I told myself.

"Deception is a game that must be constantly played, Captain Boyle. Otherwise one forgets which lie is today's truth."

The fact that I understood him made me glad we were headed to the bar.

Inside the lobby, smartly uniformed officers scurried across the marble floor in their gleaming boots and fancy uniforms. Nothing like a Kraut in a dress uniform to put the doorman at the Copley Hotel to shame. Guards in more everyday field gray were positioned by the door, and at the head of the stairs was a full-scale machine-gun nest, sandbags and all.

The bar was less militaristic. Remke ordered champagne, and we took a small table by the window, but well away from the few others imbibing at this early hour. A solitary officer, a Wehrmacht *leutnant*, stood near the bar, hands clasped behind his back.

"Do you need to inform Miss Seaton?" Remke asked, glancing around the room and keeping his voice low. "For the release of Jarnac's brother?"

"No, I don't. He got away. Apparently, he wasn't the meek violinist I thought he was," I said, and told Remke about his escape.

"*Mein Gott,*" he said, shaking his head as a waiter brought the champagne in an ice bucket. When the flutes were filled, and we were alone, he raised his glass. "To your Irish luck, Captain Boyle. I assume you no longer carry that Irish passport. If you had it, I could arrange safe passage for you."

"No, just a *Milice* identity card for Charles Guillemot, who bears a slight resemblance," I said. When I'd last encountered Erich Remke in Rome, I'd been traveling as a priest from neutral Ireland. We clinked glasses and I drank the champagne. Cool and dry, it tasted like a velvet breeze on a spring day. A few streets away, people were killing one another, and here I sat drinking with my enemy.

"I will give you a pass," Remke said, removing a document from his tunic. He filled in my phony name and handed it over. "It is good for twenty-four hours. Return to Diana and find a place to hide. It should not be long now."

Diana? A minute ago it had been Miss Seaton.

"Does she need to hide?" I asked. "I thought the Gestapo had pulled out."

"Administrative staff, yes. But there are several teams rounding up prisoners for a final transport out of Paris. They are looking for any high-ranking members of the Resistance among those who have been captured, and of course Allied agents would be quite important to them."

Agents like me. Maybe he was planning on turning me over and keeping Diana to himself. No, that didn't make sense. That had to be the Pervitin talking.

"Thanks," I said, taking the pass, the paper fluttering in my hand. "I'll tell her."

"She should stay off the radio. There are still direction-finding vans driving through the city, at least in the areas where it is safe to do so. Tell her to wait and she can talk with her SOE handlers directly."

"Sure. But that's what you would want, isn't it? As a German officer? For her to cease communicating with SOE?" *Shut up*, I told myself. *You're not making sense. All he did was call Diana by her name.* But my brain wouldn't stop thinking the worst.

"If I was acting purely as a German officer, I would have had her arrested, and the Gestapo would be knocking your teeth out right now. Instead, here we sit. Have some more champagne and calm yourself, Captain." He poured another glass and I didn't hesitate.

"I'm a bit jumpy," I admitted. "The Pervitin and lack of sleep."

"Be careful," he said. "It works best if you are well rested to begin with. It may take a while for the effects to wear off."

Outside, a platoon of Remke's pals ran through the street, headed for the river. The firing had grown more intense, and several officers stood on the sidewalk, watching their men and shaking their heads. Their world was upside down. I knew the feeling.

"Maybe the Gestapo will pick up Jarnac," I said, half musing and half suggesting.

"No, it will be best for all of us if he is not caught. He has information to trade for his life. Information we both want kept quiet," Remke said.

"Right, right," I said, letting the bubbles slip down my throat. "Tell me, could you have delayed Leclerc with the information Jarnac gave you? I'm wondering if all this was worth it."

"Delay? Certainly," Remke said, draining his glass and smacking his lips. "As you well know, our anti-aircraft guns are also excellent anti-tank weapons. An armored dash along known roads would be susceptible to ambush by well-concealed 88mm guns. But stop the advance? No, not with all the air power at your disposal. All the delay would have accomplished was more time for the Communists to seize control. Or for General von Choltitz to be forced to implement the destruction of Paris, or be replaced by an SS general who would not hesitate."

"And if the Communists won the battle for Paris, there'd be a civil war when de Gaulle and Leclerc's tanks rolled in," I said. Maybe it was worth it.

"It is a certainty. There are many among the Communist-led Resistance who are simply following the most effective Resistance leaders. But some are pure Stalinists, and they'd fight other Frenchman gladly to gain the upper hand and keep de Gaulle from power."

"Like Jarnac's Saint-Just Brigade," I said. "He chose his cover well, running a hardline Red faction."

"Yes, he is clever," Remke said. "He never revealed to me his reason for collaborating, but he obviously hated the Soviets along with anyone calling themselves a Communist."

"You know he fought in Spain?" I asked. Remke nodded. "His wife was an anarchist. She was executed by the NKVD. That was his motivation for revenge. A few days ago, he spotted the killer at a gathering of Resistance leaders."

"The affair at General Patton's headquarters?"

"He told you about that?" I said.

"Yes, he hoped to pick up new intelligence there, and succeeded," he said. "But he told me nothing about his wife, or her killer."

"He left a trail of bodies and took his revenge on the man who killed her. It wasn't pretty."

"He may be continuing his efforts here in Paris," Remke said, with a glance at the officer who'd been standing by the bar. The other Fritz arrived at the table in a second, nodded as Remke whispered, and turned on his heel without a glance in my direction. "You may have answered a question that has puzzled me. My aide will return with some files in a moment. It is best that you not be seen upstairs. Too many bothersome questions."

"Fine by me," I said, helping myself to some more bubbly. A guy could get used to this. "What are your plans for when Leclerc arrives?"

"As I said, I prefer not to surrender to anyone. For now, my orders are to remain here at my post. Which I will do until the situation becomes untenable. I have a plan to escape along with my men, but it will have to wait until the last moment."

"Colonel Harding would be happy to see you again if you decide otherwise," I said, twirling my glass on the white table-cloth.

"Give him my regards. Perhaps another time," Remke said, a not unpleasant smile gracing his expression. "Until then, it is my duty to defend my nation, from enemies within and without."

"I'll drink to that," I said, as Remke's aide laid a stack of file folders on the table, then retreated to his previous position.

"There has been a rash of killings throughout Paris," Remke said. "Mostly known Communists. We thought at first it was the Gestapo, but this is not their style. They prefer to hide their corpses or ship their prisoners off to Germany." He opened a folder and showed me the contents. I couldn't make out the writing in German, but the photographs told the whole story. Closeups of hands bound behind the back with wire. Same for the feet, the thin wire cutting into the skin above the ankles.

I looked at one more file.

"Two bullets in the head, right?"

"How did you know?" Remke said, his eyes darting to his aide who appeared at his shoulder.

"This is how Lucien Fassier killed Jarnac's wife. The wire bindings were his trademark. That, and the two shots to the skull.

Jarnac's using the Saint-Just Brigade to extract his revenge, right up to the last minute."

Remke collected the files and handed them to his aide.

"You have been of great assistance, Captain Boyle," he said, standing. "Open warfare among factions of the Resistance will only complicate an orderly withdrawal. I must see if we can communicate this to the police. A somewhat delicate matter since we are now firing on them."

"Good luck, Colonel," I said, getting up and shaking his hand.

"We could all use some luck, Captain. This officer will show you to a rear exit. It will be simpler."

"No bothersome questions, right?"

Remke smiled briefly, tucked his cap under his arm, and conferred with his aide. While they were talking I took out my pill case, popped a Pervitin in my mouth, and swallowed it with a champagne chaser.

One for the road.

CHAPTER THIRTY-ONE

I LEFT BY the back door, which was only a bit less fancy than the front door, but at least it didn't open straight into the shooting war. I stepped into a narrow street, the buildings on both sides four stories tall, all creamy stonework and looking peaceable. I got my bearings and set off toward Le Royal Bar, where I hoped to find Kaz.

Still breathing.

I stuck Remke's pass and my *Milice* identity card inside my shirt. Easy to get to and easy enough to hide from a cursory FFI search. I made my way across a couple of barricades quickly enough. I stepped into a doorway as two truckloads of Germans rumbled by. The shooting gallery along the river was still popping along, but it had lessened in intensity, almost as if the combatants were getting tired of the whole thing.

Or, the FFI was running low on ammunition.

As the trucks turned a corner, I darted across the street and ran down a passageway, following a sign for the Louvre Metro. It felt good to run. I had to run. I didn't know what else to do with the energy in my legs and brain. Running was effortless, like floating. I was in another world, zipping across the shadowed cobblestones, the street at the other end a pinpoint of light.

Close to the end of the road I put on the brakes. Something

was wrong. I heard the harsh revving of motorcycles and saw people running, their shouts turning to screams as the vehicles drew closer.

Three shots echoed against the stone buildings. I edged closer, the crowd jammed up tight as they stampeded toward me. A few people made a quick turn into the alley and kept going, flowing around me like a rush of water. At the corner I saw six Kraut motorcycles, each with a sidecar, working their way up the road, which was jammed with carts and gazogene cars parked on either side. In the lead motorcycle, an officer in the sidecar had his arm raised, firing off rounds, screaming at the people in his way to move.

The Krauts were wearing goggles and helmets with foliage camouflage, their tunics thick with road dust. More troops from the front, a motorcycle detachment that had taken a wrong turn, perhaps, and was feeling threatened by the tight lane and the crowds of people no longer meek in their presence.

They were scared and about to turn vicious, their snarls and commands in German hovering on the brink of madness as they worked their machines closer to the open plaza. Another shot in the air, the officer shouting and waving his men forward. They were almost there.

A burst of machine-gun fire ripped through the air, hot white muzzle flashes sparking from the weapon mounted on the sidecar of the second motorcycle. The rounds scythed through the last of the Parisians making for the plaza, bodies cascading to the cobblestones. Others clung to their terrible wounds, in too much shock to even cry out as the motorcycles roared past, the bottleneck finally broken like a dam of twigs in a spring rain.

I stepped into the road as the sound of the heavy motorcycles faded away. Blood seeped around the cobblestones as the wounded began to shriek and moan, their anguish outdone by the living who cradled loved ones in their arms. Half a dozen dead on the eve of liberation.

I couldn't stay. I couldn't help. I had to keep going, find Kaz, find Diana, get them both to safety, and hide out until the tanks rolled in. Find Jarnac. Make him pay. Everything was jumbled up in my head, but I think I had the order straight. A hand reached out to me, clasping my arm, begging me to do something. A man, older than me, cradled a woman's head in his lap, his eyes full of shock and welling tears. I knew what he wanted, but no one could breathe life back into her shattered body.

I shook him off, feeling miserable, feeling invincible.

They'll never get me.

I ran to Le Royal Bar and barged in like a madman. The barman I'd sold my pistol to wasn't there. Maybe he was out getting his *boche*. A girl swept the floor as an older gentleman worked the bar, slowly wiping it down. They both stared at me. I wasn't sure what to say.

"A message? Do you have a message for me? Billy Boyle?"

The old man moved away, making believe he hadn't heard. I was getting the impression that four years of German occupation had made people very cautious. The girl, maybe twelve or so, rail thin with light brown hair done up in braids, beckoned me with a crooked finger. I followed her to a door at the rear of the bar which opened to reveal a steep, narrow staircase.

"*Parlez-vous anglais?*" I asked.

"*Non*," she said, then pointed at me. "Bill-lee."

"Okay, I get it," I said, nodding for her to continue. She scampered up the stairs and stood before one of the doors in an ill-lit hallway.

"*Le baron*," she said, smiling as she knocked on the door and opened it slightly. Then she was off. Kaz had obviously won her heart.

"Billy, what happened? Did Jarnac show up?" Kaz asked. He sat in an overstuffed easy chair near a large open window overlooking the plaza. The room was small, with a couch, table, and a threadbare but clean rug. Kaz looked small too, pale, and nearly swallowed up by the soft cushions.

"Yeah, it all worked out," I said. "He had no idea Paul had escaped, so he kept his side of the bargain."

"What was all the shooting?" Kaz asked as he looked out the window. A truck with a red cross splashed on its doors pulled into the plaza, the dead and wounded out of his line of vision.

"A column of Kraut motorcyclists came through a side street and shot their way out of a traffic jam," I said, looking out the window, the faint breeze sending white curtains to dance at my side. Medics with stretchers ran down the street as onlookers helped the less badly wounded to the truck.

"What do we do now?" Kaz asked, sighing as he removed his spectacles and rubbed his eyes. He dropped the newspaper he'd been reading. *Combat*, one of the Resistance papers. TOUTE LA VILLE AUX BARRICADES read the banner headline. The whole city to the barricades. As a rallying cry, it wasn't far from the truth. As the wounded were loaded into the truck, the plaza below me quickly reverted to a pleasant city scene, with plenty of people strolling by and taking their seats at the outdoor café. Buckets of water were splashed over the blood, sluicing it away in thin pink rivulets.

"Remke said I should get back to Diana and have her hide out until the Allies show up. There's still Gestapo teams roaming the city picking up FFI leaders, plus running those direction-finding vans. He thinks she shouldn't radio SOE at all." I plopped down on the couch, drumming my fingers on my knees.

"Diana insisted a message be sent to Colonel Harding," Kaz said, his glasses still dangling from one hand. "To tell him about Jarnac withdrawing his claim about the plan. Once that was done she'd leave. She said to see the doorman if she left before you got there. He can be trusted."

"Yeah," I said, standing and pacing some more. The room felt small and suffocating. I was worried. I knew it took a while to encode any message and make contact. "Okay, one coded message, and we'll hunker down somewhere. How about you?"

"I am content to remain here," Kaz said, putting his glasses on. It seemed to exhaust him. "Berthe brought me soup a while ago. Her father—the fellow you gave your pistol to—has been active in the Resistance and was glad to help. This is his apartment, and he insisted I stay here."

"Can you trust Berthe to keep quiet? And the old man at the bar?"

"The old man is her *grand-père*. He still has *boche* shrapnel in his leg from the last war. Berthe is old enough to know what is at stake. Now go to Diana. Unless you need to eat first?"

"No, no," I said. "Not hungry."

"Billy, you are quite the bundle of nerves. The Pervitin?"

"No," I said, shaking my head with more vigor than required as I held the curtain aside and scanned the plaza. "See? Steady as she goes." I held out my hand.

"Wonderful. Now show me your right hand."

"Never mind that, I've got to leave," I said, letting go of the curtain and stuffing my hand into my pocket. It seemed to be spending a lot of time in there. "Take it easy, Kaz. A couple of days, no more, and we'll be back at the Dorchester. Soft beds, good food, and the best doctor London has to offer."

"Make sure I am the only one who will need a doctor, Billy. Don't take any more of those pills," Kaz said. "Now, I am going to take a nap. Give Diana my best and find a quiet corner of Paris for yourselves. Montmartre, perhaps. A little garret. A bottle of wine."

He closed his eyes. I waited until I saw the gentle rise and fall of his chest as he breathed. Kaz had more heart than any ten men I knew. I hoped it was enough.

Outside the sun was high and the cafés were full. There was

wine and laughter even as the last of the blood was washed away. I hoofed it north, making first for the rue Volney barricade. It was a good landmark to steer by, and I felt I ought to apologize to Nicole and Roger for all the trouble I'd caused them.

I spotted Roger at the barricade, bandages and all. I hailed him as I drew closer.

"Sorry about bringing Jarnac down on you," I said, climbing over the cobblestones and glancing around for Nicole or Suzette to translate. He stood behind the barrier, a German MP40 submachine gun at the ready. He kept the weapon pointed right at me.

"*Nicole a été prise*," he said, a grim look on his face.

"Nicole is what?" I asked, spotting Suzette in her bloodstained white coat.

"Nicole has been taken away," she said. "By the FTP. The *Brigade Saint-Just*, to be exact. For crimes against the people."

"Jarnac," I said. Another thing I should have seen coming.

"He was not here, but his men were. Nicole is a good Marxist, but since she helped you, she has been charged by them."

"How can they do that?" I asked, still nervous about Roger and his gun.

"There is no law to protect us, not with all this fighting. We thought they were here to help, but instead they tied her up and took her away," Suzette said, her eyes still red from tears, exhaustion, or both. "Less than an hour ago."

"Tied? With wire?"

"Yes. How did you know?"

There was nothing I could say. I went back over the barricade, almost wishing Roger would pull the trigger.

CHAPTER THIRTY-TWO

I RAN. ACROSS the wide boulevard, heedless of a line of German trucks headed right at me. I sprinted to the sidewalk as the vehicles rumbled by, shoulders tensed against the possibility of gunfire. I skidded around a corner and flattened myself against brickwork. Nothing. Maybe they were headed out of Paris. Why else would they ignore me when Krauts were shooting people at every street corner?

I took off again, heart pumping from exertion, fear, and *Panzer-Pille*. The street was a straight shot past snooty shops, bistros, and apartment houses with tiny balconies fronted by fancy iron scrollwork. Not a barricade in sight. Five more minutes of running and my lungs burned, my legs ached, and my mind raced with possibilities and terrors. Did Paul find Jarnac, or vice versa? Would Jarnac raid the One-Two-Two?

No, I told myself. He wouldn't. It had the protections of a stout locked door, a Kraut clientele, and a tough-looking bouncer.

I came to an intersection and stopped to get my bearings. I thought I was close to the café where Kaz and I had stopped after we got off the train. When was that? Yesterday? Three days ago?

There. I recognized a wedge-shaped building sitting by itself, a line of trees offering cool shade. I made for the green cover, easing up as I walked the length of the structure. I worked to get my breathing under control and to calm my racing mind. Gasping for breath and dreading the worst didn't make for quick thinking. *Calm down*, I told myself. *Don't let Diana see you all panicky.*

I took a few gulps of air and rested for a minute with my hands on my knees. Better. I turned the corner and stepped into a doorway, staying out of sight while I eyeballed the street. It was quiet along the rue de Provence, still too early in the day for their business to be booming. No one was on the street in front of the One-Two-Two, no vehicles passed by. Deciding to be cautious, I doubled back along the tree-lined street, so I could cross the road and approach the One-Two-Two from the other side, giving me a look down a side street. As I walked, I kept my eyeballs swiveling, checking for anyone suspicious keeping watch on the place. I didn't see a person, just heard the soft rumble of an engine not too far away.

I stopped at the side street, the club less than half a block away. A couple of automobiles were parked there. One of them, a Citroën Traction Avant, had its engine running. The model, with its trademark chevron on the front grille, was distinctive. It was also the Gestapo's favorite vehicle.

I eased back, keeping an eye on the vehicle as I moved. I counted three men, two up front and one in the back seat. They hadn't seen me. The driver had his eyes glued to the rearview mirror, watching and waiting for something. The passenger had his head craned out the window, scanning the building opposite him.

Gestapo. On a stakeout.

For me? Or for Diana?

A shiver of fear settled in my gut. Sweat rolled down my back as my hand tremored. I laid it flat against the cool granite. They were here for Diana. There were probably more of them up the street, watching the rear exits. What were they waiting for? More goons, probably. A truckload of *soldaten* to bust in and search the place. It would be too big a job for five or six Gestapo agents.

I didn't have much time. I gave another quick glance around the corner before moving. The rear window rolled down. It was Paul Lambert in the back seat.

Quiet little Paul, the concert violinist, had gone to the Gestapo.

I ran, fast as I could, faster than I thought possible, cutting up the next street and trying to work my way around to the rear of the club, remembering the layout of the courtyard and hoping I could get in. I watched for the other Gestapo men I was sure were watching the back as well. I saw them. Two guys in a car, facing away from me, eyes glued to the back of the One-Two-Two. I spotted a trash can by an apartment house door, a folded-up newspaper on top, the best camouflage I could come up with. I grabbed it, stuck it under my arm, and walked straight ahead like any other guy on his way home. I didn't look at the car, the same way any Parisian would avoid eye contact with the *boche*. They let me pass, and I kept on, looking for some sort of way into the building. There was a door, but they'd see me take it. I kept walking, glancing up to see if anyone was looking out a window.

No one, but I couldn't risk drawing attention to myself. I walked on, going around the block. I'd have to take my chances at the front door and hope the team with Lambert stayed put. I ditched the paper and kicked into a run as soon as I turned the corner, my eyes darting to pick up any other watchers. I slowed by a small café, scanning people at their tables, seeing no one who looked like a plainclothes *boche*.

At the corner, I stole a look at the front door, once again about a half block away.

Damn. One of the agents was leaning against the wall at the far end of the block, using a newspaper prop himself. The front door was out. I backtracked to the café, Le Mistral, and walked inside. If there was a time to take chances, this was it.

"*Le toit?*" I asked the barman. He gave me an odd look, and I wondered if I should repeat myself. Maybe I had the wrong word for roof, or my accent was so bad he couldn't understand me. He nodded in the direction of the room behind me and pointed surreptitiously to the mirror behind the bar.

Two Kraut officers sat with their dates, partially obscured by a partition. They were too busy whispering and clinking champagne glasses to notice me, at least not right away. The place was fancier than it looked from the outside, and in my sweat-stained shirt I wasn't dressed well enough to be the busboy.

The barman headed for the kitchen. I followed, all the way to a back room filled with cases of wine and leafy vegetables in burlap bags. He looked back to be sure no one was watching, opened a narrow wooden door, and gestured for me to enter. With that, he was gone. He'd just risked his life, as if fugitive Americans came through every day.

I took the stairs, the wooden steps old and creaky. Up four floors, where I found the exit to the roof. After a small, flat platform, the rest of the way was along the slanted gray zinc roof. To one side was the pavement, four stories down. On the other, a flagstone courtyard. I moved slowly, inching along, my good hand gripping the peaked edge, the other nearly useless. I made it to the One-Two-Two roof, climbing over a low barrier that separated the two buildings. The pitch of the roof here was more severe, and I hoped I could make it to what looked like a skylight about twenty yards away. I needed both my hands, but the shaky one wasn't cooperating. My heart was jack-hammering, keeping a maniacal beat with my trembling right hand. I laid flat on the roof and pulled myself along as best I could, hoping the Gestapo didn't have anyone watching from inside.

And praying Diana or one of her SOE team was.

My hands were slick with sweat. My feet barely kept their grip on the slanting metal roof. I pulled myself along, fingernails sounding a drumbeat on the zinc.

I heard the squeal of brakes, then an engine gunning. Shouts from below. A truck rolled around the corner, braking again at the front door of the One-Two-Two. Krauts vaulted out of the truck as the Citroën sped out from the side road and pulled up next to it.

I froze. There was no way to get to the skylight in time. As the troops pounded on the door I waited for the skylight to open, for Diana and her people to flee.

A flurry of shouts rose up from below, and the Germans were inside. Two shots rang out from behind the One-Two-Two, then another volley. Someone tried to escape, only to run into the Gestapo waiting for them. I prayed, I pleaded with God to let Diana join me on the roof. We could run away, be safe, wait for the Allies to show up. We could have another day. Another night.

The skylight remained shut.

Shrieks and cries rose from the open windows. I looked below and saw Lambert waiting by the car, leaning against it, gazing at the windows as if he were enjoying the shock, fear, and terror the Gestapo raid spread through the house. I wanted to reach out and strangle him, if only to wash away the guilt I felt for bringing him here.

This was all my fault.

They came out. Soldiers first, then a Gestapo man.

Then Diana. Clothed in a long white dress, a second Gestapo agent clutching her arm. She didn't resist. There was no point, except to seek a bullet. She was followed by a man I hadn't seen before. Maybe her radio operator, since one of the Krauts carried a suitcase that was the size of an SOE radio case. He struggled, but it was useless. Maybe he wanted the bullet.

I didn't want to think about that. Or about where Diana was going. I had to think of something to do.

There was nothing I could do.

Doors slammed. The Kraut *soldaten* got into their truck, the Citroën roared off, leaving Lambert standing in the street. I started to scramble back, thinking I might be able to get at him. But the second Gestapo car came from around back, pulled up, and let him in. They drove off in the opposite direction, heading uphill to Montmartre. Giving the collaborator a ride home. How thoughtful.

I edged back the way I'd come. Took the stairs down into the kitchen of Le Mistral, palmed a small paring knife, and left by the back door.

I ran.

CHAPTER THIRTY-THREE

IT WAS UPHILL all the way, but when you've reloaded Pervitin a few times, the hills don't seem to matter as much. I didn't let up, despite the pain in my thighs, despite gasping for air, despite my heart thumping against my ribcage.

There were still things I could do. Get back to Kaz, contact Remke, work a deal of some kind. Exchange myself for Diana, anything to get her free of the Gestapo. I didn't have much time, but I had some, and I'd spend it on Lambert.

I didn't go around the front, remembering his escape out the rear window. I hustled down the back alley and stood behind the old building that housed Lambert's tiny apartment. Windows were wide open, and I could hear the soft strains of his violin floating through them.

The last person to have the violin was Jarnac. Had he returned it to his brother? Was he inside, listening to the serenade, celebrating the revenge they'd taken on Diana? I grabbed a garbage can and pulled it over to the low roof of the cottage abutting Lambert's building, reversing the course he'd taken when he tried to get away from me. I got on it, almost fell off, finally grabbed the rain gutter, and hoisted myself up. I got to Lambert's window, the violin louder as I drew closer. I snuck a look into the kitchen. No one there, no sound other than the musical notes and the scrape of the horsehair bow over strings.

I eased through the tall window, letting myself down onto the kitchen floor as quietly as I could. The knife came out of my pocket. I stood still, quieting myself, listening for sounds or voices.

The music. Shuffling footsteps from the next room down a high-ceilinged hallway, sweaters and jackets hanging from hooks along the wall. I took two steps closer, listening for any reaction. Nothing changed. A few more careful steps, and I was at the door, looking into a sitting room. Lambert was alone, standing by the window, eyes closed, violin tucked under his chin, delicate hands fingering his precious Italian instrument from the last century.

I was going to kill him. He was a collaborator by any definition, an informer, the lowest of the low. Any Resistance member would shake my hand for it. He'd gotten two agents captured, the third killed. He'd taken away what I loved most in this world when he threw Diana to the wolves.

Fair's fair.

I half turned and took two steps, the look on his face dream-like as I approached.

I slashed his hand. The bow dropped to the floor, blood splattered across his chest. His eyes opened in shock, his mouth gaping in surprise. He didn't feel the pain. Not yet.

I cut his other hand as it gripped the neck of the violin. Straight across the knuckles.

He gasped.

I had to hand it to him; even as he backed away, he managed to hold onto the violin, clasping it to his chest as his blood coated it.

"Sit down," I said, pushing him into an armchair. I took the violin as the pain ate through the shock and he winced, rocking back and forth, cradling his bleeding hands. I tossed him a shirt that had been hanging on a chair and took a seat facing him.

"Please, don't," Lambert said, doing his best to wrap his hands. He cringed as I leaned closer. "No more."

"Tell me why you did it," I said, setting the violin on the floor. "You didn't have to."

"Please, be careful with my violin," he said, his crazed eyes darting between the knife in my hands and his prized possession on the carpet.

"That fiddle is the least of your worries. Answer me."

"You tricked me. That woman too. Marcel said I should inform the authorities," he said, his eyes squeezed shut against the pain.

"The Gestapo, you mean. Weren't you surprised your big brother told you that? He's on the other side, isn't he?"

"Yes, yes, but he said it wasn't right, what you'd done," Lambert said. "Please, let me go to the doctor."

"Wait," I said, seeing how things weren't adding up. "When did you speak to him?"

"An hour ago, when he brought my violin back," he said. "He knows how I value it."

"No, that wouldn't have given you enough time. It sure wasn't enough time for the Gestapo to set up the whole raid on the One-Two-Two. You had to go to them right after you got away. I really did underestimate you, Paul. You're in this with your brother, aren't you?"

"No, no," he said. "Marcel is a patriot, a good Communist."

"We both know that's not true. And we both know you went to the Gestapo all by yourself. My guess is that Marcel was delivering information to the *Abwehr* and passing the same dope on to you to give the Gestapo. That way you double your money, right?"

"What is dope? I do not understand you. Please, it hurts." He clutched the shirt as best he could, clumsily wrapping it around his hands. Blood welled up, overflowing the split flesh. No matter how hard he tried to staunch the flow at one slash, another ran red rivulets down his arm.

"You understand enough, you bastard," I said, slapping him hard. "Did I just miss Marcel? Did he come by to congratulate you?"

"*Oui*," he spat, the first glimmer of hatred showing in his eyes.

"But he will not miss you. He will finish you. And that *boche* officer, both. You will not live to see the Allies in Paris, believe me."

"He's killing other Communists," I said. "Using the Saint-Just Brigade to murder those who don't measure up to their definition of a good Red. Why are you part of that?"

"He is my brother," Lambert said, wincing as another wave of pain washed over him.

"There's more," I said, holding up the blade. "Tell me. Or else."

"I will, I will," Lambert said as he wept. "Marcel came back from Spain broken in spirit, yet he still raised me, took care of me. *Ma mère* died giving birth to me. *Mon père* was a pig of a man who beat me. Marcel rescued me and did everything for me, even in his terrible pain. So, I do everything for him. If he wants to kill *le Bolchevik*, then that is what we do. Better even to have them kill their own, to Renée."

"That's quite a sob story. You love your brother," I said.

"*Oui.*"

"And you love music. Playing the violin," I said.

"Do not damage the violin, please," he said, his eyes caressing the instrument at my feet.

"I'm going to tell you something, Paul. I am going to kill Marcel. Today, tomorrow, whenever and wherever I find him. You will never have your brother again." I rose, stepping out into the hallway and grabbing some of the clothing hung on hooks. "I'm sure those cuts hurt, but not as badly as you might imagine. Do you know why?"

"What? It hurts, please, I need a doctor."

"You do," I said, wrapping a coat around his torso and pulling it tight, tying off the sleeves at his back. I took a belt from a raincoat and tied one ankle to the leg of the heavy armchair, then did the same to the other leg with a cord pulled from the curtains. Satisfied he wasn't going to run away, I went into his bedroom and returned with a sheet.

"Please, bandage my hands, call a doctor," he said. I began to rip the sheets.

"I don't see a telephone," I said.

"The *tabac* down the street," he said, a glimmer of hope in his expression.

"You really need stitches," I said, pulling the bloody shirt away and stuffing it into his mouth. Blood oozed from the deep cuts, welling up like witch's tears. "I knew a cop who was cut like that, from the thumb across the back of his hand. Did it to himself with a razor-sharp knife on a fishing boat when a swell hit. Should've paid attention, but he had his eye on storm clouds moving in fast. Took them a while to get in since they were tossed around a bit. He'd bandaged his hand, but said he wasn't worried because it didn't hurt too much. By the time he got to the hospital the next morning, the doc told him there'd be permanent nerve damage. It's the radial nerve. Runs up the back of the hand into the thumb and forefingers. His hand was numb, he just didn't realize it."

Paul mumbled something through the gag as he studied his hands, both with the same arcing slice.

"Yeah. It's dawning on you, isn't it? Don't worry, you're not going to bleed to death. But by the time you get out of here, it'll be too late to heal those nerves. Probably is already, but I want you to have a lot of time to think about it. Your life is ruined. But cheer up, Paul. There's good news."

He raised his head to follow me as I used the strips of bedsheet to bind him to the chair even more tightly, hoping it was all a charade, that I was going to call a doctor, that he'd be okay, that his music would once again fill the air.

"The good news is, I'm not going to destroy your violin," I said. I picked it up and set it carefully on a chair in front of him. "Look at it. I want you to think about what you've lost."

CHAPTER THIRTY-FOUR

I LEFT A whimpering Paul Lambert behind, my rage at what he'd done unabated. It felt better than doing nothing at all, but it didn't feel great. Whatever happened, at least I wouldn't have to think about him living free and easy while Diana suffered. Or died.

I grabbed his bicycle from the landing. First stop was the *tabac*. It was crowded, with people pawing at a fresh stack of *Combat* newspapers. The headline was something about French troops and Paris, but all I cared about was whether this was a friendly place to ask a favor.

"Telephone?" I said to the *mec* at the counter.

"*Téléphone?*" he answered, his brow furrowed as he took in my accent and the rosy spray of blood on my sleeve. I explained as best I could that I was an American and needed to make a call. This set off a flurry of cheers, hugs, kisses, and a bottle passed around to the delight of all, the blood forgotten or perhaps assumed to be *boche*.

Everyone was celebrating, except me. I wanted to make a damned telephone call. I said something rude, and the men crowding me understood the tone, backing away, and muttering. Bad move. I needed a friendly favor, not an argument.

"*Désolé,*" I said, holding up my hands to all present. "*La guerre.*"

That put me back in everyone's good graces, and I toasted de Gaulle when the bottle came my way. Our comradeship cemented, I managed to get across that I needed to call Le Royal Bar on the rue Saint-Honoré. A telephone book was thumbed through, a few customers telling the *mec* to hurry up, which he responded to with a few choice words.

In a minute he put the call through and handed me the receiver. He waved for everyone to be silent as I heard a faint voice answer.

"Berthe?" I asked. It was. "*Le baron? C'est* Bill-lee."

"*Oui. Un moment.*" I heard the telephone clatter as she set it down. The crowd gathered in close, and I gave the thumbs up. A muted cheer arose.

"Billy?" It was Kaz. "Where are you?"

"Montmartre," I said. "They've taken Diana. The Gestapo."

The mention of the dreaded secret police drew a gasp. A few people moved away.

"When?" Kaz said, staying cool. "At the One-Two-Two?"

"Yes. Less than an hour ago. It was Paul Lambert, but that doesn't matter. Call Remke, see if he can do anything. I'll be there as soon as I can."

"Dear God. Yes, yes, I will call the Meurice immediately. Come quickly."

I left amid cries of *bonne chance* and *vive de Gaulle*. I waved as I hopped on the bicycle and pedaled away, but my heart wasn't in it. I wasn't sure what Remke could really do. The Gestapo was a law unto itself.

But there was a chance. There *had* to be a chance. I coasted down the hills, thankful at least for an easier trip out of Montmartre than in.

Bells began to ring. A few at first, and within seconds it seemed as if every church bell in Paris joined in and didn't let up. It wasn't marking the hour, this was something else, something joyous. Good news for someone, but not the news I needed. I realized I hadn't heard church bells ringing at all while in Paris, and now they were unleashed and making up for lost time, the peals sounding from every direction.

I skirted the One-Two-Two club. I couldn't look at it. Didn't want to be reminded of how helpless I felt watching Diana being taken away. Going around the One-Two-Two got me lost and dumped me into a roundabout that brought me around the back of the opera house, decorated with swastika banners. The administrative headquarters of German forces in Paris was right across the street with its own banner in black Gothic letters. I couldn't turn around, it would arouse too much attention. I pedaled on, playing the Parisian.

The sentries ignored me. They were looking at each other, craning their necks to determine where the bell-ringing was coming from, and shaking their heads. I think they knew what it meant. There was only one thing that would wake all those silent bells.

Allied tanks. Leclerc.

As loud as the bells were, it took me a moment to realize there was no shooting. A ceasefire? Or perhaps the Germans were repositioning what combat troops they had left to oppose the armored advance.

Maybe no one wanted to die when the outcome was about to be made certain.

Whatever the reason, I decided to take my chances on the avenue de l'Opéra, a straight shot to my destination. I could have chosen a better way to put that, but I prayed I hadn't jinxed myself and bent over the handlebars and pumped like hell.

The avenue was deserted. A few people, some of them armed, stirred at street corners and ventured out a few steps. No marching Germans, no truckloads of retreating troops from Normandy.

Maybe the front was moving on Paris faster than the Krauts

could retreat from it. Perhaps they'd gotten out all the combat troops they could. I slowed myself and braked in front of Le Royal Bar, hopping off the bike and dashing inside. Kaz sat at the bar, the telephone in front of him, chatting with Berthe's *grand-père*. At the end of the bar, three young men and a woman sat cleaning an assortment of weapons. A couple of pistols, two German rifles, along with several Sten guns. Twenty-four hours ago, it would have been unthinkable to do that in any public place. Things were moving quickly.

Berthe ran up and asked me something, pointing outside.

"She wants to know if that is your bicycle," Kaz said, his voice weary and low.

"She can have it," I said, knowing how valuable bikes were when people weren't allowed to purchase petrol. "The owner won't be needing it."

I sat at the bar while Kaz translated for Berthe. She skipped outside, happy enough. Liberation and a new bicycle. Through the window, I could see her working to remove the small yellow license plate, required by the Germans on all bicycles. Good. There was no reason for her to be linked to Lambert's place.

I looked to Kaz, my question unspoken.

"I got through to Colonel Remke," he said. "He promised to call back."

"But what did he say?"

"That he would check with the Gestapo. But it may be difficult since most of them are gone, and the rest are packing up whatever they can steal. He offered to say she was his informant, and that he'd like her back."

"There was another member of the team taken," I said, nodding my thanks to the old man who set a glass of beer in front of me.

"Billy, it will be a miracle if he gets Diana back. A miracle," he repeated.

"If they haven't left yet, maybe we can stop them," I said. "Gestapo headquarters is on avenue Foch, right?"

"Yes, past the Arc de Triomphe, about an hour's leisurely walk," Kaz said. "Faster with a bicycle, of course. But what could you do there? Think about it, Billy. Any action you take will get Diana killed in a moment."

"If there's not many of them, maybe I could surprise them. Sneak inside."

"Billy, slow down. Listen to yourself. There are only the two of us. As you pointed out, I am in no condition to engage in a fight with anyone. You are suffering from lack of sleep and too much Pervitin, both on top of a bad case of nerves. Don't deny it. You are perfectly poised to make a terrible decision." His eyes bored into mine, and I knew he was right. I had to look away.

"I already made a terrible decision, back when I took Lambert to Diana. It's my fault, Kaz. She's in a Gestapo cell and it's my fault." I drank down the beer and rolled the cool glass against my forehead. I didn't know what to do.

The telephone rang.

"*Allô? Ja, ich verstehe.*"

No one paid any mind to Kaz's shift from French to German. The barman poured a small glass of brandy and set it down in front of Kaz, who nodded his thanks as he listened. Everybody loves a baron.

I couldn't follow the conversation at all. It was mostly Kaz responding with a *yes* or *no* and asking a few quick questions. I figured Remke wanted the conversation in German at his end, since English was obviously out of the question and French might raise suspicions.

Kaz hung up. And sighed.

"Colonel Remke contacted the remaining senior Gestapo agent in Paris and explained he wanted an informant released. He was told there would be no further need for informants since Paris would be destroyed before the Allies could enter, and that all political prisoners were being transported to the Reich," Kaz said. He took a sip of the brandy.

"He's got to be able to do something else," I said, wracking my brain to think what that could be. I watched the four FFI fighters gather up the weapons and leave, their faces lit by determination and long pent-up rage.

"He tried, Billy. He sent his aide with a written order demanding Diana's release. The aide and his driver were ambushed by the FFI before they got halfway there. His aide was killed, and the driver wounded. He regrets there is nothing else he can do."

"He's probably too busy packing," I said, the words bitter in my throat even as I knew them to be unfair.

"The colonel will not be leaving," Kaz said. "He has been ordered to remain by his *Abwehr* superiors and report on conditions until the last. A useless task, he said, and one that was probably aimed at keeping him safe from an investigation into his role in the July 20 plot once he returned to Germany."

"I bet his bosses were worried he'd talk and implicate them," I said. Which only made me think about Diana being interrogated by those bastards. I tried to stop thinking about it.

"He said a small detachment of Leclerc's tanks has crossed into the southern suburbs. German troops are being pulled back, and it may only be hours before the Allies are here in force," Kaz said, taking another drink. "He thought the Gestapo would pull out at dusk to take advantage of traveling in darkness."

"How many of them?" I had to ask.

"They have a platoon of soldiers for an escort and some of the Vichy militia still left in Paris to guard three truckloads of prisoners," Kaz said. "The avenue Foch runs through a wealthy part of town. There are no barricades there, nothing to stop them, and more German troops bivouacked in the nearby Bois de Boulogne. It is an impossible situation, Billy."

"I can't just sit here," I said, running my fingers through my hair, feeling like ants were crawling over me. Despair ate at my gut, and I thought I might be sick. "I have to go."

"Where?" Kaz asked, but he already knew. "Go then, Billy. I will be here," he said, drawing a city map closer. It was marked with German positions. "Stay a block north of the Champs-Élysées, there are German strongpoints along the way. See?" I did. "Then stay on the right side of the Arc de Triomphe and go straight up avenue Foch. There are trees on either side that should give you cover."

I studied the map for a moment, stood, and placed my hand on his shoulder. "Thanks. You should get some rest. Go upstairs."

"No. Colonel Remke said he would call if there was any unexpected development. I am perfectly fine, Billy. Go."

I squeezed his shoulder and stopped myself from telling him what a terrible liar he was.

I WALKED OUT, taking a route that skirted the Hotel Meurice and kept me on the far side of the Champs-Élysées. Every shop I saw was closed, either looted of anything valuable, or waiting out the final battle. The cafés were open, busy as hell with people gathered for a drink and the latest news. A couple of FFI trucks rolled past, fighters shouting out to people on the street, notes of joy and defiance mingling with the grinding of gears and blue exhaust fumes.

Shots sounded, tiny far-off *pop pop pop*s that could have signaled celebration or mayhem. I couldn't do much of either. No weapon and no friends other than a Kraut colonel who couldn't do a damn thing and Kaz, who was wise enough to know there was nothing to be done.

Smoke rose in the sky from somewhere across the river.

One loud explosion sounded, close, but the echoes bounced around, and I had no idea where or what it was.

I saw the Arc de Triomphe in the distance and cut through a side street thronged with people celebrating, a barricade topped by laughing children. People started slapping me on the back, and a woman kissed me, her lipstick tasting of raspberries and blood. I pushed away a bottle of wine and elbowed my way through the crowd, leaving a few choice words in my wake.

I hated seeing the Arch. It was the kind of spot I wanted to stroll by with Diana on my arm, in a Paris free of Nazis, on a breezy summer's day like this. Instead, she was in a prison cell. I spat on the sidewalk and hurried on.

The avenue Foch was bordered on either side by a green strip of grass and trees, a thin park along the thoroughfare. Kaz was right, it was easy to dart between the trees and hide in the deepening shade.

I crouched behind a tree trunk as two trucks drove by, full of Fritzes headed home. Kaz had been right about the neighborhood too. Big, fancy mansions lined the road, sort of like Beacon Hill without the hill and more room to spread out. I came close to the end of the avenue where most of the homes had their curtains drawn, as if proximity to the Gestapo bred a desire to see nothing of the outside world, and for the world to see even less of you.

I spotted trucks lined up outside number eighty-four, a couple of houses ahead. Kraut sentries stood behind a tall wrought iron fence, beneath red swastika banners hanging limply in the afternoon sun. More trucks were parked behind the fence, and I saw soldiers loading boxes inside them. Smoke drifted up from the rear of the building, probably burning files, the kind of documents that would incriminate the Nazis and their Vichy allies.

I faded back into the trees, working my way closer until I had a good view of the main entrance. A line of hedges gave me good cover as I knelt next to a tree and leaned against it. My legs ached, and my insides felt hollow. When was the last time I had eaten? I had no idea. No idea what day it was, no idea what I could do other than be here and hope Diana somehow knew. Knew I stood witness, knew I would find her. Somehow. Someday.

My body went limp with fatigue. My mind was still racing, still full of zing, but I felt like melting into the ground and resting there forever, even if I couldn't shut down the thoughts pinging around inside my head. Or the guilt I felt in my heart.

I couldn't afford to nod off. I took the tin of Pervitin out of my pocket and shook the pills into my hand. Three left. I took one and dry-swallowed it. The last one, I promised myself. After this one wore off, there'd be no need, no reason to stay awake. I thought about taking the other two, just for a minute, and opened the tin again. I threw them away.

I settled in, waiting, turning the tin over and over in my hand, the red and blue label mesmerizing as I twirled it. I looked at my watch. A few hours left until dusk. I watched the Krauts behind the fence loading the trucks and tying down the tarpaulin covers. That left the two trucks on the road for the prisoners, unless there was another I couldn't see. I'd have a good chance of seeing Diana if they brought them out front.

The Pervitin kicked in, and I had a hard time sitting still. I twirled the tin as fast as I could but fumbled it with my shaky hand. I picked it up with my steady left hand and twirled it in the opposite direction. I pressed my cheek against the rough bark of the tree, trying to feel something other than shame and despair. How could I have been so stupid? Why did I leave Lambert with Diana, thinking he was harmless? This is war, and fresh-faced kids were killing one another every day.

I wanted to rage, to scream, to cry out Diana's name.

But I kept quiet, hiding behind the shrubbery.

Time passed. Kraut guards walked around the trucks a few times. They carried their rifles slung on their shoulders, laughing and joking the way idle soldiers do. On the doorstep of the infamous Gestapo headquarters, they had no reason to be afraid. Fear was their weapon.

A couple of them stopped on their circuit of the parked vehicles to lean against a truck and have a smoke, out of sight of their officers. I began to think about what I could do to damage those trucks, but I didn't even have that paring knife anymore. I had nothing but an empty tin.

I stared at it. Bright red and blue with white lettering. The colors of the French flag. The British and American colors as well. I twirled it some more and got up from my crouch, moving slowly behind the tree, watching carefully.

The *soldaten* ground out their cigarettes and walked back to the wrought iron gate.

I weighed my chances. Could I make it to the back of the closest truck? There was only a fifty-fifty chance they'd put Diana on that one, but it gave me the best line of approach. If any one of the guards took a few steps in my direction, I'd be dead.

I waited, hoping for a break, knowing it was useless, crazy at best.

Minutes later, the call came. A voice hollered out something, and I heard the shuffle of boots. Something about *essen*, which I knew was the Kraut word for chow. It made sense. If they were about to hit the road, they'd feed their men. Maybe they were overconfident, leaving the trucks on the road unguarded, but I doubted they'd be that way for long.

I ran low along the hedge, went through a gap and stayed down as I sprinted across the street. I placed the tin on the truck bed, right in the center, an arm's length in. The bright colors stood out even in the gloom beneath the canvas top. I darted back to my spot, feeling foolishly hopeful.

Would Diana see the pitiful gesture? Would she know it meant I was close, that I would do whatever it took to get her back? Would she know I was sorry?

Or would she be hustled into the next truck, taken away, and disappear?

I didn't have long to wait. The guards must have wolfed down their black bread and sausage, since doors slammed open minutes later amid shouts and commands, the starting of engines and the grating sound of iron gates being opened.

A double line of prisoners was marched out, each one with their hands bound. First in line was the man captured along with Diana. An officer trailed him, carrying the suitcase radio used by the SOE. Odds were they'd keep him alive for a while and try to force him to radio London with phony information.

Then I saw Diana, her white dress standing out like a beacon. It was still clean. No bloodstains.

The two lines were marched to the waiting trucks. A guard waded in between them separating the prisoners with his rifle butt, directing the line Diana was in to the first truck.

The one with the tin.

The man in front of her was the first one up, and he extended his arm to help her.

She took it, then froze. For a second or two, that's all. I saw her fall, her hand going down to the truck bed as if to steady herself. She looked back, scanning the street, her eyes searching, but a guard forced her in, jabbing at her with his rifle.

She'd seen it. She knew.

Maybe it gave her some small hope.

It was foolish, all right, but it created another connection between us, that little tin carrying the weight of our desires. To survive and be together again. Or to die and be together again.

I watched the convoy roll away, the canvas tops tied down tight, marking the beginning of the prisoners' journey into darkness.

I stood up, brushed myself off, and started walking back.

The bells were still ringing across the city.

CHAPTER THIRTY-FIVE

THE SKY WAS darkening as I walked along the deserted avenue Foch. Distant explosions sounded from across the river, faint glows from fires marked by columns of black smoke. Occasional rattles of gunfire broke out, rising quickly into chattering crescendos and ending as abruptly.

I took my time, wandering down side streets. I stopped to gaze out over the Seine, flowing peacefully as the city waited for its liberation, and Germans waited for death or captivity. I didn't see any more trucks or half-tracks crammed with escaping troops. The front was nearly here, and most of the Fritzes still in town were stuck for the duration.

There were plenty of them out in front of the Hotel Meurice, where General von Choltitz held sway over the ever-diminishing German real estate in Paris, and where Erich Remke was marooned. For them, the war was nearly over.

Allied tanks were drawing closer. And Paris was intact. Some solace there, for this grand city, but I couldn't feel it. I knew it, but there was no joy in the knowledge.

I approached Le Royal Bar as Berthe was drawing the blackout curtains. I doubted any German patrols would be coming around to enforce the regulation, but years of habit are hard to break.

"*Monsieur Bill-lee, vite, vite,*" she said, waving her arms as soon as I was through the door. Worry was etched on her young face, and I followed her to the rear of the bar. "*Le baron*."

Kaz was on the floor. He didn't look good. He lay on a blanket, another one rolled up under his head. His face was pale, and his breath came and went in ragged gasps.

"Kaz," I said, taking his hand. He didn't respond. I looked to the half dozen people standing there, most of them armed and some of them sporting bloody bandages. "Does anyone speak English? What happened?"

"*Il est tombé*," said a young woman with a German MP40 slung over her shoulder. I had no idea what that meant, which she must have understood from the look on my face.

"*Téléphone*," Berthe said, tapping the bar and keeping it simple. "*Boche*." Then she made a falling-down motion with her hand.

"The German called and he fell down?" I put my hand to my face like a telephone and did the same falling routine. She nodded and knelt to point at Kaz's head. I felt behind his ear and found a nasty bump. It was bad enough that he'd had another heart attack, but he'd smacked his head as well.

"Doctor?" I asked.

Everyone shook their head.

"*Beaucoup blessé*," Berthe said, pointing to each of the wounded. Yeah, I got that. Many wounded. Too many for the doctors at the makeshift hospital. I noticed the bandages and medical kit on a table and realized the bar was functioning as an aid station, patching up the slightly wounded to lighten the workload down at the Metro station. Weapons and ammunition were stacked up against the rear wall, perhaps from the more badly wounded. Since the underground doctors hadn't done anything for Kaz except give him a cot, this stretch of floor would do just as well.

Pointing to my wristwatch, we worked out that the call had been about fifteen minutes ago.

"*Merci*," I said to Berthe and the others. "*Merci*."

I sat on the floor next to Kaz, willing his eyes to open. Berthe brought a damp washcloth and dabbed it on his forehead. He didn't respond.

What had Remke said?

Was it good news, or something so terrible it gave Kaz a shock?

It couldn't really be either, I thought. Diana was in a truck headed to Germany. What good or bad thing could have happened quickly enough for Remke to call about?

"Snap out of it, Kaz," I whispered. "Don't you leave too."

I put my hand on his chest. I could feel his heart beating. I'd once held a bird between my cupped hands as it fluttered against my palms. That's what it felt like.

I moved my hand and rubbed my eyes, feeling the bone-deep weariness hiding behind the shivers of drugged energy running through my body. I needed to rest, but it was impossible to still my jangly nerves. I wanted to stop thinking, to stop wondering and worrying about Diana and Kaz, but they were the only things on my mind.

Except for Remke's message.

I had to find out what it was.

I got up, went to the bar, and took a long drink of water. Berthe brought bread around to the wounded and ripped off a chunk for me. I ate, knowing I had to. I drank some more, then checked the weapons in the back. I took a Sten gun and several magazines of ammo.

No one said a thing. I caught a glimpse of myself in the mirror behind the bar as I left.

I wouldn't have said anything to me either. Unshaven and grim, with pinpoint dark pupils and a haunted look, the image seemed to be of another man. A man on the edge with everything to lose.

About right. I headed for the Hotel Meurice, to the sound of heavy firing across the Seine.

Hurry up, you bastards.

I made for the Tuileries Gardens, trying for an easy view of the hotel. If the tanks got here soon enough, and if the German top brass wasn't going to fight to the last bullet, there'd be a lot of *Hände hoch* going on right outside the front door. That would be my chance to collar Remke and find out what his call was about. And maybe make good on my offer to take him in to Colonel Harding, who'd be glad to get the inside story on the German Resistance.

Plus, the Meurice would be one of the main targets for Leclerc's force, which meant ambulances and army doctors wouldn't be far behind.

Something for everybody at the Meurice.

As I edged through the gardens, I dropped flat at the sound of a revving engine and tank treads. Through the darkness, I saw two monsters advancing through the gardens, chewing up the landscape and settling in about fifty yards away.

Panthers. Heavy German tanks. Somebody was ready to put up a fight.

I backtracked, moving away from the Panthers and closer to the Louvre. Across the Seine, the sky glowed eerily red. Explosions sounded off to the west, but as the shelling stopped, another sound murmured and echoed from within the buildings on the Left Bank. It rose and fell several times and was unmistakable. It was the sound you heard even blocks away from a ballpark when some slugger hit a home run.

Thousands of cheering voices.

Thousands of Parisians cheering on *la libération*.

I listened all night.

At first light, I crawled under a bush and hid myself as best I could. Unlike the rest of Paris, where crowds surged in and out of fire fights as if it were a crazed circus, the rue de Rivoli was deserted.

Deserted if you didn't count the Germans behind anti-tank

roadblocks and sand-bagged emplacements in front of the hotel, and the steel beasts stationed in the gardens. I'd hoped for a faster advance, but now it looked like there'd be a showdown right in front of me before too long. I thought about going back to check on Kaz, but I didn't want to get cut off from my ringside seat. There was nothing I could do for him, but plenty Remke could do for me.

An hour passed, with more sounds of fighting across the river. The dawning light filtered in between buildings, sending sharpened sunrays advancing like ghostly soldiers into the city. The growl of engines and tank treads grew from the direction of the Arc de Triomphe, and I shuddered to think of what more German reinforcements might mean for the fight shaping up.

The Panther closest to me let out a high-pitched *whirr* as its turret traversed the approach. I listened again, and heard the sound of tank treads coming our way. Not from behind, not more Krauts. A distant *crack* split the morning air and a shell hit the Panther, exploding but not stopping it. Finally! Leclerc's tanks were on this side of the Seine and moving in. The Panther fired, and within a second was hit again, this time with greater effect. Smoke billowed and the crew bailed, jumping out from every hatch and running for the hotel.

The Sherman tanks moved closer, firing on the other Panther. One Sherman stalled, pouring smoke. The others kept on, hitting the Panther again and again until it exploded, sending spouts of flame out every blown hatch.

It was over damn quick. No long last stand, just burning hulks of steel and running Fritzes.

I stood and ran to the edge of the garden, watching as another column of tanks approached from the opposite irection. That meant they'd broken through to the *Prefecture de Police*, probably last night. That might have been the cheering I heard.

I dove for cover as German machine guns behind a sandbag

emplacemcent fired on the tanks headed for the roadblock. The tanks drove on, unleashing high explosive shells and blowing a hole through the defenses. The surviving Germans hightailed it for the hotel, and I spotted infantry moving in. A German half-track pulled out from a side street and fired on the French GIs, cutting several down. A flamethrower team ran forward, spraying fire at the half-track, engulfing it in seconds. They moved on to torch other German vehicles parked along the road, sending thick black smoke billowing. Every Kraut in sight was dead or running for cover.

The tanks moved slowly forward, lobbing a few shells toward the Meurice. Infantry ran up the sidewalk, ducking between columns and returning fire. I ran closer, stopping when I spotted a German in a second-story window aiming his rifle at the troops. I sprayed a few bursts from the Sten, and he disappeared inside.

I waved, jumping and yelling like an idiot, caught up in the rapid advance, the heady scent of victory, and the grim thrill of revenge. The soldiers waved back, then moved closer. I paralleled them, watching for any Krauts still hidden in the gardens. I knew enough to steer clear of the infantry squads working their way up a city street. They had their own rhythm and pace, born of closeness and combat. A stranger in their midst would only be in the way.

They quickly advanced on the hotel lobby and tossed in smoke grenades. Gray clouds billowed from the entrance as they ran inside, firing. More shots seconds later. And then quiet. Sherman tanks roared up, pivoting and turning their guns outward.

The battle for Paris was all but over.

CHAPTER THIRTY-SIX

I TRIED TO go inside, but a French officer stopped me. I pretended I understood what he was saying and walked out into the street, where a bunch of French tankers and infantry were gathered around a Sherman, passing around a bottle. In minutes, the empty street had filled with civilians, cheering and celebrating with Leclerc's men.

I accepted the bottle, took a long swig, and passed it on.

One of the tankers chattered at me, and I explained I was an American.

"Excellent," he said in strangely accented English. "We are all internationalists here, comrade."

"Sorry?" I said, not getting this at all.

"We are *La Nueve*, the 9th Company. Made up of Spanish volunteers. Many of us fought in the Spanish Civil War and continue the fight against fascism with General Leclerc. You have heard of us in America?" He took a long drink of wine and smacked his lips as even more civilians gathered around. I noticed his tank was named Guernica, after the Spanish town the Germans had leveled with their bombers.

"No, I hadn't," I said, wondering how many more times I'd hear about the Spanish Civil War. I did give him all the names I'd run across in the investigation. Only when I mentioned Lucien Harrier did his expression change.

"Many of us were anarchists," he growled. "Every good anarchist knows of his crimes. He is dead, you are certain?"

"He's dead, and it didn't come easy."

"Good." He gathered his men and told them the news. They were grim-faced, not unhappy to hear it, but unhappy to relive the memory of what he'd done to their comrades and loved ones. I knew how they felt.

They all patted me on the back, welcoming me as an honorary member of *La Nueve*, since I'd brought them welcome news of an old enemy. Soon they got orders and pulled out, waving aside the growing crowds as they rumbled off.

Meanwhile, a column of trucks pulled up to the hotel entrance. For the prisoners, I was informed by a young lieutenant. Because to march them through this growing throng would be a death sentence, not that he had any problem with that.

I positioned myself near the trucks so I could spot Remke, although how I'd separate him and keep him in once piece I hadn't yet figured out. I looked around for a red cross, but no ambulances were in sight.

The hotel door opened.

A few young German officers with a lot of fancy braid and tailored uniforms came down first, guarded on either side by French troops. Behind them was a portly fellow. General von Choltitz himself. He looked stunned. He must have known what was coming, but it looked like the reality of it had punched him in the gut.

The crowd roared and jeered, hurling insults, shaking their fists, letting the pent-up fury of the past four years out in volley after volley of spitting invective. Hands reached between the guards, striking Germans as they made for the trucks. Right behind von Choltitz was a German sergeant, carrying a suitcase. The general's, undoubtedly. A long arm grabbed it and pulled the suitcase into the crowd to much laughter and derision. Uniforms and underwear flew into the air, ripped apart in seconds. The sergeant looked like he was about to faint. The crowd pressed closer, squeezing the lines of guards closer together, threatening to break through on either side.

The first truck was full and pulled away from the curb, people pounding on its side in unrestrained fury. Guards herded the prisoners to the next truck, cries and taunts increasing as more Germans were marched out.

I saw Remke. He came down the steps, tall and erect, a knapsack over his shoulder. We made eye contact and I moved closer. It was impossible to speak and be heard. I waved, signaling him to come forward.

Remke was within an arm's length, only a guard between us. The throng pressed forward again, jeers and curses filling the air. I reached out and grabbed his sleeve.

"What did you tell Kaz?" I shouted. "I'll help you, but please tell me now."

He clasped my hand, held onto me, and began to answer.

A gunshot exploded from behind me, just over my shoulder. Then another at my side. Remke fell to the ground as screams rose up around us. Two more shots went off, but I was on the pavement with Remke, our hands still clasped.

His eyes fluttered. Two wounds in his chest spread blood across his dress uniform like a flame burning through parchment.

"*Geh zu den Schweden,*" he gasped, a look of shock on his face as he tried to focus his eyes on mine.

"What?" I asked. "I don't speak German, what are you saying?"

"Ilse," he said, but he was no longer speaking to me. His eyes gave a final blink as he spoke her name once again with his final breath.

"Goddamn!" I roared and stood, forcing my way through the pressing crowd. "Which way did he go?" I shouted, although I doubted anyone in this baying horde cared about one dead German more or less.

I saw him. Paul Lambert, easy enough to spot with his

bandaged hands, pumping pinkish white as he ran steps behind his brother, who was holding the pistol he'd shot Remke with.

I ran, clutching my Sten, thankful for the load of zing in my head that was doing a good job of fooling my legs into running this fast. Of course he'd have to kill Remke, he was the one man who could prove Jarnac to be a traitor.

Had they even seen me in the crowd? Maybe not. It might give me an edge.

I stayed on their heels through the Tuileries, jumping shell holes, and weaving around the still-smoldering Panther. Only when we neared the bridge spanning the Seine did Lambert turn around. From the look on his face I knew he hadn't expected to see me. I'd been right. They had no idea I'd been next to Remke, their eyes focused on their quarry, waiting for the right moment.

Lambert shouted to Jarnac, who turned quickly, his face twisted in rage. He pushed his brother behind him, raised his pistol, and fired. Then he knelt and steadied his aim for another shot.

It happened in a split second. I saw the blood seeping down my sleeve. I didn't feel a thing. I felt my finger steady on the trigger, hardly heard the burst, hardly heard the clinking of smoking shells as they bounced off the cobblestones.

Jarnac was down, but not dead. His legs moved as if he wanted to rise but couldn't get the rest of him to cooperate.

Paul Lambert was down. Dead, with a bullet in the head.

Jarnac groaned, stitched up with bullets from the gut to the shoulder. He didn't have long.

"Your brother is dead, Jarnac," I said, walking to stand over him. "If you'd stayed upright you would have taken that slug. But you wanted to kill me so badly, you gave your brother a bullet to the brain."

He tried to speak. He moved his mouth, but no sound came out.

"You started this, Jarnac. What begins in blood ends in blood."

He didn't hear a word I said.

CHAPTER THIRTY-SEVEN

I WALKED BACK through the gardens, avoiding the gaze of the charred tanker who'd made it halfway out the turret hatch before the flames consumed him. He looked surprised. Maybe it was the empty eye sockets that gave him that expression. Or maybe everyone's surprised at the end, even a bastard like Jarnac. Moments after murdering a prisoner and trying to kill me, he probably couldn't imagine breathing his last next to the corpse of his brother. But there he was, his blood running between cobblestones, another body to be forgotten in the midst of jubilation. Maybe he'd be remembered as a hero. That would be a fine joke.

People poured into the streets and flowed into the Tuileries, dead Germans only adding to their joyous celebrations. Cheers, singing, church bells, laughter, and the steady clanking of tank treads rose in a crescendo of celebration, louder than anything I'd ever heard short of an artillery round hitting next to my foxhole. The air felt compressed, as if it couldn't contain any more noise, the joyous racket bearing down on me like a blanketing fog.

I looked at my right arm, puzzled. A red gash showed through torn fabric, Claude Leduc's white shirt soaked in red from the elbow down. Funny, but my hand wasn't shaking.

Across the Seine, throngs of civilians and soldiers massed

along the embankment, making for the bridges, the tanks carrying FFI fighters armed with flowers and bottles of wine along with rifles and Sten guns.

I stumbled through the crowd, heading for the Meurice. When I got there, German prisoners were loading their own dead into trucks under the watchful eye of French soldiers who were protecting them from the onlookers as much as guarding them. I couldn't spot Remke. I don't know why I even looked, maybe to find a death worth mourning. Maybe because I felt a kinship of sorts. He was a military man who knew when to follow orders and knew when disobedience was the better course.

Maybe I'd hoped for inspiration.

Geh zu den Schweden.

What the hell did that mean? I repeated it over and over, making sure I'd get it right to tell Kaz.

Kaz. He had to be okay.

He had to.

The small plaza in front of Le Royal Bar was a mass of people. American GIs were mixed in with Leclerc's men, and all of them were being kissed by every Parisian who could lay their hands on a piece of khaki and pull the guy close.

Everyone was delirious with joy. Tears coursed down cheeks, the grimy unshaven cheeks of tankers and the creamy pink cheeks of young girls. It seemed the whole city was on the brink of madness. The bitterness of the past four years expelled by the struggles of the last few days and the undeniable might of the armored columns storming into the city and shattering the last remnants of the hated Nazis, leaving only charred corpses and cowed prisoners.

The bar was jammed, filled with GIs, FFIs, and more of the slightly wounded. Berthe took hold of my hand and guided me to the rear, where a medic took my weapon, ripped my shirt sleeve off, and cleaned my wound. As she applied a compress and wrapped it, I studied Kaz.

His head was bandaged. He was still pale, but his breathing seemed a little steadier. He was propped up against the wall, and I prayed he'd open his eyes. If all the racket inside and out didn't wake him, I didn't know what would.

I got the medic to understand I wanted my bandage wound tight. She made a sewing motion, and I nodded. Yeah, I knew it would need stitching, but right now I wanted it to hold together so I could get Kaz out of here. American GIs mixed up in this big party meant that it wasn't Leclerc's forces alone that had barged into Paris. Those GIs wore the ivy leaf shoulder patch of the 4th Infantry Division, the unit that had been near Rambouillet a few days ago. Which told me Colonel Harding and Big Mike would be with them and out looking for us.

"Kaz," I said, kneeling once the bandaging was done. "Kaz, can you hear me?"

I took his hand and repeated his name.

Nothing.

Berthe joined us, shaking Kaz's shoulder.

"Baron, *s'il vous plaît*," she said, her tiny voice insistent.

Kaz squeezed my hand.

Berthe saw it and clapped for joy. She kissed his cheek, and his eyelids fluttered open.

"Kaz, can you hear me?"

Another squeeze.

"We've got to go. Can you walk? Never mind, I'll carry you."

"Billy," he said, his voice a ragged whisper. Berthe scooted off and was back in seconds with a glass of water. She put it to Kaz's lips and he drank, releasing a great sigh. His eyes opened wider, and he gave me a nod. Let's go.

"*Geh zu den Schweden*," I said. "Remke said that. What does it mean?"

"The Swedes," Kaz managed. "Go to the Swedes. He told me . . ."

"Told you what?"

He tried to say something else, but it was too much. His eyes closed and he was out. I felt for his pulse. It was there, but it didn't seem right, fluttering like a butterfly in the wind.

Time to go. I took Berthe's hand and explained, as best I could, that we had to leave. I knew she didn't understand, not the words anyway, but I thanked her for being Kaz's friend. I told her she was brave, then I scooped Kaz up, struggled for a second to keep my balance, and gave Berthe a nod goodbye.

She'd been silent the whole time, her lower lip betraying a quiver. But when she spoke there were no tears.

"*Merci pour le vélo*," she said. That I understood. Thank you for the bicycle.

I turned away as people parted to let me through, keeping my head down and avoiding their eyes. Of all the things I'd seen and heard in Paris, why did it take a child's simple thank-you to bring me to tears?

I stumbled through the surging multitudes, making for the rue de Rivoli and the Hotel Meurice. It was slow going, but I kept Kaz close to my chest, his dangling legs taking a few hits from oblivious celebrants. We made it to the steps of the Meurice, which were being kept clear by sentries who looked like they'd much rather be out in the streets drinking wine and kissing girls. I backed up to the wall next to the steps and slid down, still holding Kaz. He felt like a child in my arms as I cradled his head with my hand.

Still steady.

I watched the world go by. Swirls of brightly colored dresses, khaki, and white shirts almost as grimy as mine. A troop of French soldiers marching in formation, maybe to show who was now in charge. Chants of *de Gaulle, de Gaulle* rose and fell. Five young women, stripped to their undergarments, their heads roughly shaved, were paraded down the street as examples of what collaborators of the horizontal persuasion could expect. I wondered what the fate of the girls at the One-Two-Two would be. I wondered if the French men who made a bundle off the black market operating out of the club would ever get their heads shaved.

I tried not to think about Diana.

I worked on what the Swedes had to do with all this and came up with nothing. Maybe it was a code. Maybe when my brain evened out and stopped zinging all over the place, I'd understand.

Maybe Kaz knew.

I patted his head. Kaz knows everything.

I wished I could sleep. Someday.

I tried to close my eyes. I couldn't seal out the light, but I did feel my eyelids heavy with grit and shuttering like a screen door latched too loosely in high winds. Once, they closed completely. Then I was back on this sunny Paris boulevard with the giant block party and the bells and the tanks and all the pretty girls.

THE WALL HAD softened. No, it was a blanket, and I was lying down. Where the hell was Kaz? I tried to sit up, panicking as I called out for him.

"Hey, Billy, it's okay. We got you."

I blinked.

Big Mike, hovering over me. Where the hell were we?

"You okay?" Big Mike asked.

"Kaz?" was all I could manage.

"Right here," Big Mike said, crooking his thumb toward a stretcher behind him.

I looked around. It was an ambulance, the half-moon windows at the back filtering in light through green leaves as we drove.

"Hospital," I said, trying to sit upright. "We got to get him to a hospital."

"Relax, Billy, that's where we're headed right now. Kaz has been checked out, he's stable. You relax, okay?"

"No, in England. He needs a specialist. Mitral something or other, I can't remember." There was something else I had to remember, but my mind was as thick as molasses. I looked around the ambulance as if there might be a clue somewhere. Kaz was covered with a wool blanket, asleep. Or unconscious, I wasn't sure. He needed a real hospital, not some army forward aid station.

"Billy, look at me," Big Mike said. "Look at me." More insistent, so I tried to focus.

"What?" I didn't feel right. No zing. Everything was hazy, heavy, and so confusing.

Beneath my own wool blanket, I felt the quiver come back, like an old friend you'd outgrown, but who still hung around your house uninvited.

"Did you hear me, Billy?" Big Mike shook me.

"No, what? Spit it out, willya." He was beginning to get on my nerves.

"This *is* England. We found you and Kaz three days ago in Paris."

"Three days?" Nothing was making any sense. Big Mike didn't make sense.

"You've been out of your head for three days, Billy," Big Mike said. "We were worried."

"Yeah, well, I was worried about Kaz. But at least you're getting him to a hospital," I said, not certain why it had taken so long.

"Not just Kaz, Billy. You too, buddy. You're not doing so great," Big Mike said.

"I'm fine," I said, trying to rise. I was stopped by the straps across my chest. "Get these things off me!"

"We're almost there, Billy," Big Mike said, looking away, staring out the half-moon windows instead of looking me in the face. "Almost there."

"Are the Swedes there?" I asked as I closed my eyes, not knowing why I'd asked, but knowing it was important.

The sunlight played on my lids, leaving dancing, flickering images of light. It was like watching a film in the middle of a dream. Vague, haunting images burning themselves into my mind, trying to warn me, or remind me, of what I needed to know, or already knew.

Sweden. It was Sweden in my dreams, even as I pressed against the restraints.

HISTORICAL NOTE

THE FAMOUS STAND of the Polish 1st Armoured Division on Hill 262, also known as Mont Ormel ridge, helped trap many of the Germans surrounded by Allied forces near the town of Falaise. Mont Ormel, with its commanding view of the area, sat astride the only escape route open to the retreating enemy. Their three-day ordeal ended when the Poles pushed back the last German attack after close-quarter fighting. The division sustained 1,441 casualties including 466 killed in action.

The phrasing General Eisenhower uses in Chapter Nine to describe the slaughter that took place inside the Falaise Gap is taken from his memoir *Crusade in Europe* (1948), in which he likened it to a scene out of Dante. "It was literally possible to walk for hundreds of yards at a time, stepping on nothing but dead and decaying flesh."

The Battle of the Falaise Gap was a tremendous defeat for the Germans, made possible in large part by the Polish stand on Hill 262. Estimates of German causalities are imprecise, but it is generally agreed German forces suffered about ten thousand dead and fifty thousand captured, in addition to tremendous losses in equipment.

It was indeed the policy of the Allies not to liberate Paris immediately. As supreme sommander of Allied Expeditionary Forces, Eisenhower did not consider the liberation of Paris to be his primary objective. The goal of the American and British forces was the destruction of all German forces in order to end the war in Europe as quickly as possible and then concentrate military resources against the enemy in the Pacific.

In addition, the Allies had estimated that thirty-six hundred tons of food per day would be required to feed the population of Paris after Liberation. Utilities would have to be restored and transportation systems rebuilt, all of which would take significant amounts of materials, manpower, and engineering skills needed elsewhere for the war effort.

The deception plan in this novel is my own invention. But the notion would have made strategic sense, and the purpose behind Colonel Harding's plan mirrors Eisenhower's strategic thinking.

As for the poem "Hellish Night" by Arthur Rimbaud, several mistranslations have come to us from the original French. The line:

grand le clocher sonnait douze . . . le diable est au clocher, à cette heure

Translates properly as "the moonlight when the bell struck twelve." But somewhere along the way a translator changed "bell" to "hell," perhaps through keyboard proximity or some other unintended error. With apologies to Monsieur Rimbaud, I found the mistranslation incredibly powerful and chose to go with "when hell struck twelve" for the radio message that plays a key role in the story.

General Charles de Gaulle did not share Eisenhower's thoughts on the French capital. The uprising in Paris began without his help or encouragement, spurred on mainly by the Communist resistance groups led by the charismatic Colonel Rol. Once the fighting began, de Gaulle pressed for French forces to be sent into the city. As a Frenchman, he did not want the rebellion to be crushed with great loss of life and the possible destruction of Paris. As a politician, he did not want the Communist-led uprising to succeed without him. He got his way, and General Leclerc's tanks, along with American GIs who were added to the attack as it became bogged down, took Paris in time for de Gaulle to make a grand entrance as the President of the Provisional Government of the French Republic.

The Saint-Just Brigade represents the extremist wing of the Communist-dominated *Francs-Tireurs et Partisans* resistance group. There were many purges of party members who did not properly conform to the Soviet line. A shadowy FTP group operated a secret prison within Paris after the Liberation at what is now the George Eastman Dental Institute. They used it as a torture and execution site, eliminating everyone from captured fascist collaborators to Resistance members and some unfortunates who were simply in the wrong place at the wrong time. The murder files that Colonel Remke shows Billy describe exactly how their victims were disposed of.

Pervitin was mass-produced and millions of doses were given to German forces. It was called Pilot's Salt, the Stuka Pill, and the Panzer Pill. The drug was wildly popular, until supplies began to run low and soldiers had to deal with their addiction to this meth-amphetamine.

The gathering of war correspondents at Rambouillet was real enough. Ernie Pyle, Andy Rooney, Bruce Grant, and others were there waiting to enter Paris. Besides the Germans, they had one other enemy—Ernest Hemingway. As described in this narrative, he did take over the one hotel in town for the ragtag group of *résistants* who followed him. Hemingway did play fast and loose with the regulations concerning war correspondents, but he claimed to have gathered useful information. Andy Rooney's opinions of Hemingway are actual quotes, which he gave later in his life. He was not a fan.

ACKNOWLEDGMENTS

I AM ONCE again indebted to first readers Liza Mandel and Michael Gordon, for their able scrutiny of this manuscript. It is so helpful to have careful readers who can look at the story with fresh eyes as it nears completion; they are a tremendous help.

My wife, Deborah Mandel, works on editing and proofreading these stories with amazing diligence. She reviews chapters as they are written, then the final draft multiple times, making significant improvements with each pass. She also puts up with cranky writer syndrome with great patience.

I am very grateful to Cara Black for allowing Billy to venture into the universe of the Leduc Detective Agency, and to meet Claude Leduc, the *grand-père* of her *détéctive très chic*, Aimée Leduc. If you haven't read her Parisian mystery series, you are in for a treat.

The entire staff of Soho Press is amazing. They make this hard work quite bearable, and their creative support is a tangible joy.

Continue reading for a preview of the next
Billy Boyle Mystery

THE RED HORSE

CHAPTER ONE

SOMETHING WAS WRONG.

The wind bit at the back of my neck, and I hunched my shoulders as gray clouds scudded across the sky, outpacing me as I trudged along the gravel path. I stuffed my hands into my pockets, thankful for the warmth.

Thankful I could hide the tremor in my right hand.

Because they were watching.

I couldn't let them see how bad it had gotten.

My boots scrunched on crushed stone, the wide walkway stretching out before me. It looked like a straightaway, but the low wrought iron fence on either side curved slightly to the left. It was a circle. A long circle, but all the same, circles lead nowhere.

Which was where I was, evidently.

I don't know why. I haven't figured it out yet. All I know is that beyond the ornate fence, painted a gleaming jet black and hardly higher than my hip, there is another fence. In the woods, about ten yards in. A serious fence. Ten feet high and topped with coils of barbed wire. Patrolled by British soldiers who watched from the other side, silently staring me down.

I pushed on, trying not to attract their attention as they moved through the shadows beyond the wire. Two days ago, they'd let me outside. Not the soldiers, but the doctors, or nurses, or orderlies, or whatever they were. They said I could walk, that it might help me sleep.

But I can't sleep a wink. Maybe that's why I'm a little confused. Sometimes it feels like I can't stay awake, either. Or move, for that matter. I didn't want to go outside, but they insisted, so I started walking.

Two days I've been walking this circuit. My eyes are gritty with fatigue, but every time I stop to sit on a bench, my lids stay open. There's a haze over everything—the woods, the guards, the massive stone structure constantly off to my left, its towers and turrets visible above the treetops and across the lush green lawns. My memory is hazy too. I don't remember how I got here, although I recall waking up in an ambulance.

Before that, all I remember is France. Paris, to be exact. But everything is jumbled up, like in a dream, where things look familiar but nothing makes sense. I know this place isn't a dream, because nothing looks familiar and nothing makes the slightest bit of sense.

It isn't a dream or a nightmare. No, it's worse.

Why?

The answer to that one was coming up ahead. The gravel walkway sloped downhill as it curved around the rear of the scattered buildings. I hadn't even counted them all. There was the main building, four stories of sandstone set down in front of a green lawn, with a tall clock tower at the center. Wings extended off either end at right angles, like giant arms, encompassing a smattering of smaller buildings, all covered in the same sooty stone, soiled by the chimneys spouting coal smoke into the gray skies.

A service road cut across the path ahead. The gate was set in the woods, part of the security fence guarded by soldiers. I'd caught a glimpse of them a few times as they opened the gate to let in trucks bringing supplies. Their forest-green berets marked them as elite Commandos. I didn't look in their direction anymore. They might think I was planning an escape.

Which might not be a bad idea if I knew where to go.

I quickened my pace as I passed the stone pillars that once had marked the entrance to the grounds. I could see the old metal sign that had greeted visitors; it was rusted and pitted by age, but still clear enough to announce what this place was.

Saint Albans Pauper Lunatic Asylum.

I was sure I'd been here before. I hadn't seen the sign back then, but I'd driven through a back entrance to visit a British major. I hadn't stayed long, but I knew this was the same joint. Except everything was different. Maybe because they'd let me leave that last time.

So, I know I'm at Saint Albans. About an hour outside London, if I remember correctly, not that my memory's all that good right now. I do know I'm not a pauper. But there are some strange people here, and the place is surrounded by barbed wire and guards, so I guess it is some sort of asylum.

Lunatic? As I walked the path, I eyed the other residents. Or patients, probably. I tried not to make eye contact, not being up for a friendly chat. I saw the whistling man, an American who strolled the circuit regularly as he whistled a tune. The same tune. All the time. We passed each other, his eyes focused straight ahead and a little toward the sky, as if he were waiting for angels to swoop down and take him away.

I came to a Brit sitting on a bench. His wool cap was pulled down, covering his eyes. His arms were crossed and his legs jittered, boot heels keeping time. I'd seen him around. He was one of the mutes. Never spoke. There were a few of them here, all wearing the British battle dress uniform.

But that was all I could tell about them. Everyone was in uniform, but the rule at Saint Albans was no rank or unit patches. No identification, except for the color of your uniform. Last names only. It made sense, in a way. If the place was full of lunatics, it wouldn't do for a crazy colonel to start issuing orders to loony lieutenants.

I picked up the pace as the path took me closer to the south wing. That was the medical area where people wore pajamas, bandages, and casts. They spent their time in bed, rolling around in wheelchairs, or limping about on crutches. I hadn't run into any mutes or whistlers among them.

But I hadn't been in the south wing in a couple of days.

I couldn't handle seeing Kaz.

Lieutenant Piotr Augustus Kazimierz, that is. Kaz and I work together. We had some trouble in Paris and ended up here. I'm walking around and he's not.

Bad heart. Really bad. My brain is sort of scrambled, but his ticker is shaky. He always had some sort of problem with it, which is why he ended up as a translator working in General Eisenhower's headquarters. Kaz had been given a commission in the Polish Armed Forces based on his brains, not his brawn. But he'd built himself up, strengthening his body and using his brilliant mind as part of Ike's Office of Special Investigations.

Until Paris.

Everything had fallen apart in Paris. Kaz's heart, my mind, and, well, something else.

I can't think about that now.

I pressed on, head down, not looking at the medical ward windows for fear I'd see Kaz looking at me. Wondering. Worried about his future and my sanity. I didn't want to think about that either. Or that other thing clawing at the edges of my mind.

I walked faster, staring at the façade of the main hall now that I'd turned the corner. A few faces gazed out at me from the offices at the front of the massive building. Bored typists, doctors in their white coats, a few uniformed honchos, Yanks and Brits who gave the orders around here.

I made for the entrance, glancing up at the tall clock tower dead center. Ten minutes of five, but that time was only right twice a day. The thing was busted.

I stopped, uncertain if I wanted to go inside or take another tour of the estate. I stood there, rooted to the spot, paralyzed by the simple task of deciding if I wanted to go indoors. This sort of thing was happening all the time, and I didn't like it much. Like I said, something was wrong.

I stood still, unable decide which way to go.

Which is why I saw the two men up in the clock tower. The door to the tower was usually locked and off-limits. They were nothing but blurs of brown uniform, heads and shoulders barely visible above the crenellated stonework as they scurried around, circling the white flagpole with the British Union Jack flapping at the top.

Then there was only one man, and he was flying.

CHAPTER TWO

HE MUST HAVE been a mute, because he made no sound.

Until he hit the ground.

The sound of boots pounding gravel snapped me out of my stupor. I ran toward the body as the front door slammed open and people tumbled out. White coats, uniforms, and suits. Behind me, a couple of guards were making a beeline for the body.

I got there first. I pushed aside a Yank in his unadorned khakis and a Brit major in his service dress uniform.

"Don't touch anything," I said. "I'm a police officer."

Why the hell did I say that?

I knelt by the body, my mind a jumble of thoughts as I studied the dead man. Sure, I'd been a cop before the war. I'd even made homicide detective before I traded blue for khaki. But why did I announce myself like that?

Maybe it was the situation. People had a habit of rushing into a crime scene and obscuring what evidence there might be.

"Sure, you're a policeman," one of the guards said, his hand grasping my shoulder. "Now come along."

"Wait a minute," I said, shaking his arm off and raising my hand. He stepped back, and I could see his palm resting on the butt of his holstered pistol. It was a typical pose, putting enough space between us so he could draw his weapon without me grabbing it. I took my time, studying the corpse, committing everything I saw to memory. I may have had a few screws loose, but I knew what was what when it came to murder. Or suicide, maybe.

"Okay," I said, rising and taking a few steps back, my hands raised slightly, apologetically. I didn't want to risk being pistol-whipped.

"Get these patients away," the major snapped, sparing a moment to frown in my direction. He was a thick-faced guy with a brown mustache and a stiff gait that seemed to pain him. Or he didn't like his mornings ruined by patients falling from great heights, I couldn't really say.

I gave the guard a friendly nod to let him know I wasn't going to cause any trouble. I let him pull me back a few steps as his partner gathered the other Yank and an older Englishman in his darker khaki wool serge. As the major stood over the body, one of the white coats knelt and felt for a pulse. Purely for the record.

One other white coat stood aside, watching me. Maybe I was paranoid, or a lunatic, or both, but it was odd that he spent more time looking at me than at the guy who'd taken a swan dive onto packed gravel. Beneath his white jacket he wore captain's bars on one collar and the caduceus of the medical corps on the other. He wasn't a stranger. Captain Theodore Robinson, US Army psychiatrist. Blond hair, glasses, and an athletic build. Track star in college back in Wisconsin, he'd told me. We'd had a few chats, which consisted mainly of him yakking because I didn't have much to contribute. But the army paid him anyway, he said, so I sat and listened. I'd been bored, but the army paid me too.

Robinson's gaze finally wandered to the body. Mine went up to the clock tower. Nobody was leaning over, distraught at not being able to stop this guy from falling. I looked at the main entrance, where by now, the second man would have burst through, telling his story of trying to talk the jumper out of his fatal leap.

Nothing.

"What do you think?" I heard the major say.

"We've been worried about Holland for a while, haven't we, Dr. Robinson?" This from the British white coat. Older than

Robinson, gray showing at his carefully trimmed temples, dark bags under his eyes, and a thin, sharp nose that made him look like a sparrow hawk.

I didn't hear Robinson's response as the guards ushered us inside. I thought about saying something about the other person I'd seen up in the tower, but I was low man on the totem pole around here, and I could end up in a padded cell if I spouted off to the wrong person. Like the guy who'd tossed poor Holland to his death.

Or, I was imagining things, and then they'd put me in a strait-jacket for sure. My best bet was to clam up and keep my head down. I let the guard shove me inside, resisting the impulse to unleash a smart- aleck wisecrack and give him a chance to kidney punch me when no one was looking. He wore sergeant's stripes and a mean grimace splashed across a face in need of a shave. A private trailed us, Sten gun at the ready, looking angry enough to squeeze off a few rounds for the hell of it.

"You guys been at it long?" I asked, once we were inside and the door slammed shut behind us.

"At what, Yank?" the sergeant said as his companion stood by the door.

"Guarding this place. Patrolling the perimeter, that sort of thing." I was going for polite conversation to learn anything about their routine, but the grizzled non-com wasn't going for it. "Have you been on duty all night?"

"Yes, while you've been dreaming of Betty Grable, we've been tramping through the woods to keep you safe, lad. Now go on, leave the business outside to the major. He knows how to handle these things."

"Okay, Sergeant," I said. "I didn't catch your name."

"Didn't give it, but since I know who you are, Boyle, seems only fair you should have it. Sergeant Owen Jenkins," he said.

"Well, Sergeant Jenkins, I'm flattered. What do you know about me besides my name?" I asked, wondering if it might be something that was news to me.

"You like to walk," he said, taking one step forward and fixing his dark eyes on me. "And you're not friendly, not the way a lot of Yanks are. Most of you lot talk too much and too soon, if you don't mind my saying so. Not you, though."

"The conversation in here isn't to my liking," I said. "Maybe if we met in a pub we'd get along better. What's the best watering hole around here? Or are you new to the area?"

"New?" Jenkins said. "Why'd you say that?"

"With all the fighting in Normandy, this must be like a rest area for you fellows," I said. "What do they do, rotate you in for a few weeks of easy duty before you head back to the front? You can't be stuck here permanently, can you?"

"Next time I see you, Boyle, best walk the other way," Jenkins said, his finger stabbing my chest. So much for making polite conversation. I didn't think a tough British sergeant would be so sensitive. "Or you'll be here, permanent-like."

"Come on, Sarge," his private said, walking to a window and glancing out front. "He's tetched in the head, remember? Pay him no mind. They're taking the stiff away, so let's go have a smoke."

"Bastards," Jenkins said, apparently taking in me and everyone else in residence at Saint Albans. "Living easy while our lads are fighting and dying. Leastways you and the others without any wounds. It's one thing to be shot up, but where's your wound? You're nothing but a coward in my book."

He turned on his heel and marched out the door, slamming it against the wall.

"Don't say anything, sir, willya?" asked the private, glancing at the open door as he whispered. "Sarge is a bit on edge, is all."

"Don't worry, kid," I said, looking more closely at him. His wool field service cap was pulled low over his eyes, but it didn't disguise the fact that he had no worries about a five o'clock shadow. "Who would believe a nutcase like me anyway? What's your name?"

"Fulton, sir. Private Martin Fulton."

"Okay, Fulton. Now tell me something and I'll keep this all under my hat. How did your sergeant know my name? Are you watching me during the day? Keeping tabs on me?"

"No, that's not our job. Sarge asked that big fella who was here the other day, the Yank sergeant. He said you were a captain and that we should watch out for you, that's all."

"So you are watching me. Thanks, Fulton, now get back to your bully-boy pal and stay away from me. Get it?"

Private Fulton's face worked itself into a twist, as if he couldn't understand plain English. He shook his head and walked away, muttering. Watch out for me, he'd said. Spy on me, more like. Jenkins, Fulton, and others, I bet. I'd have to watch them.

And have a talk with Big Mike. There was no reason for him to go around spreading rumors. He was supposed to be my friend. Some pal.

I heard a flurry of voices from outside. It sounded like Robinson and the others were at the door, about to enter the foyer. I darted into a hallway, not wanting to draw attention to myself or answer any questions. My bootheels were loud on the tiled floor, and I scurried as quietly as I could to a small alcove in the center of the hallway. On a stairway, the walnut banisters gleamed brightly, polished by countless hands over the decades. Next to the stairs was a door, an engraved sign proclaiming it to be the entrance to the clock tower. NO ADMITTANCE.

The door was wide open.

It was as good as an invitation.

I shut it behind me and walked up the narrow staircase. The stone steps were worn, and my footsteps echoed as I made my way, wondering what was going through Holland's mind as he took his final steps. How had he gotten in? I knew the door was kept locked or was supposed to be.

Perhaps someone had been working on the clock, or doing some other repair job, and left the door open. I stopped to catch my breath, took a gulp of air, and kept going. I could picture a workman panicking as he saw Holland at the top of the tower. Maybe he tried to bring him back down and Holland fought back. Maybe it was an accident. If so, the workman might have hightailed it, trying to avoid any blame.

Or, was Holland murdered? Was that what Jenkins meant when he said I might find myself here *permanent-like*?

I came to the top of the stairs. I opened the access door and stepped out. The Union Jack snapped loudly in the breeze above my head, startling me. The space was smaller than I'd imagined, taken up by beams that held the flagpole in place and the thick stonework of the battlements. I walked around, looking for a trace of evidence as the wind whipped at my face. Up here, the breeze would carry away any loose bit of fabric or paper.

Had Holland left a note? Probably in his pocket. That's where jumpers stashed them sometimes. I leaned over the edge, looking down at the spot where he'd landed. A small darkening stain and scuffed stones were the only vestige of Holland's final act upon this earth. Who was he anyway? What demons delivered him here? And down there?

From this vantage point, I could see the attraction. Vault over the wall and in seconds you'd have not a care in the world.

I could also sense the fear. The trembling fear of being pursued, unable to speak, his voice tamped down into the darkest corner of his mind, cornered and pushed against the hard, cold stone.

Hands grabbing him and hoisting him over.

The scream silent inside his head.

"Boyle."

I jumped. Not like Holland, but I jumped, my heart thumping at the surprise.

"Step away from the wall, Boyle," Robinson said. "Let's go to my office and have a chat."

"Sure," I said, walking around the flagpole, keeping my distance. I'd learned one thing, anyway. Dr. Robinson was light on his feet.

Other Titles in the Soho Crime Series

STEPHANIE BARRON
(Jane Austen's England)
Jane and the Twelve Days
  of Christmas
Jane and the Waterloo Map

F.H. BATACAN
(Philippines)
Smaller and Smaller Circles

JAMES R. BENN
(World War II Europe)
Billy Boyle
The First Wave
Blood Alone
Evil for Evil
Rag & Bone
A Mortal Terror
Death's Door
A Blind Goddess
The Rest Is Silence
The White Ghost
Blue Madonna
The Devouring
Solemn Graves
When Hell Struck Twelve

CARA BLACK
(Paris, France)
Murder in the Marais
Murder in Belleville
Murder in the Sentier
Murder in the Bastille
Murder in Clichy
Murder in Montmartre
Murder on the Ile Saint-Louis
Murder in the Rue de Paradis
Murder in the Latin Quarter
Murder in the Palais Royal
Murder in Passy
Murder at the Lanterne Rouge
Murder Below Montparnasse
Murder in Pigalle
Murder on the Champ de Mars
Murder on the Quai
Murder in Saint-Germain
Murder on the Left Bank
Murder in Bel-Air

LISA BRACKMANN
(China)
Rock Paper Tiger
Hour of the Rat
Dragon Day
Getaway
Go-Between

HENRY CHANG
(Chinatown)
Chinatown Beat
Year of the Dog
Red Jade
Death Money
Lucky

BARBARA CLEVERLY
(England)
The Last Kashmiri Rose
Strange Images of Death
The Blood Royal
Not My Blood
A Spider in the Cup
Enter Pale Death
Diana's Altar

Fall of Angels
Invitation to Die

COLIN COTTERILL
(Laos)
The Coroner's Lunch
Thirty-Three Teeth
Disco for the Departed
Anarchy and Old Dogs
Curse of the Pogo Stick
The Merry Misogynist
Love Songs from a Shallow Grave
Slash and Burn
The Woman Who Wouldn't Die
Six and a Half Deadly Sins
I Shot the Buddha
The Rat Catchers' Olympics
Don't Eat Me
The Second Biggest Nothing
The Delightful Life of
  a Suicide Pilot

GARRY DISHER
(Australia)
The Dragon Man
Kittyhawk Down
Snapshot
Chain of Evidence
Blood Moon
Whispering Death
Signal Loss

Wyatt
Port Vila Blues
Fallout

Bitter Wash Road
Under the Cold Bright Lights

TERESA DOVALPAGE
(Cuba)
Death Comes in through
  the Kitchen
Queen of Bones

Death of a Telenovela Star
  (A Novella)

DAVID DOWNING
(World War II Germany)
Zoo Station
Silesian Station
Stettin Station
Potsdam Station
Lehrter Station
Masaryk Station

(World War I)
Jack of Spies
One Man's Flag
Lenin's Roller Coaster
The Dark Clouds Shining

Diary of a Dead Man on Leave

AGNETE FRIIS
(Denmark)
What My Body Remembers
The Summer of Ellen

MICHAEL GENELIN
(Slovakia)
Siren of the Waters

MICHAEL GENELIN CONT.
Dark Dreams
The Magician's Accomplice
Requiem for a Gypsy

TIMOTHY HALLINAN
(Thailand)
The Fear Artist
For the Dead
The Hot Countries
Fools' River
Street Music

(Los Angeles)
Crashed
Little Elvises
The Fame Thief
Herbie's Game
King Maybe
Fields Where They Lay
Nighttown

METTE IVIE HARRISON
(Mormon Utah)
The Bishop's Wife
His Right Hand
For Time and All Eternities
Not of This Fold

MICK HERRON
(England)
Slow Horses
Dead Lions
The List (A Novella)
Real Tigers
Spook Street
London Rules
The Marylebone Drop (A Novella)
Joe Country
The Catch (A Novella)

Down Cemetery Road
The Last Voice You Hear
Why We Die
Smoke and Whispers

Reconstruction
Nobody Walks
This Is What Happened

STAN JONES
(Alaska)
White Sky, Black Ice
Shaman Pass
Frozen Sun
Village of the Ghost Bears
Tundra Kill
The Big Empty

LENE KAABERBØL & AGNETE FRIIS
(Denmark)
The Boy in the Suitcase
Invisible Murder
Death of a Nightingale
The Considerate Killer

MARTIN LIMÓN
(South Korea)
Jade Lady Burning
Slicky Boys
Buddha's Money
The Door to Bitterness
The Wandering Ghost
G.I. Bones
Mr. Kill
The Joy Brigade
Nightmare Range
The Iron Sickle
The Ville Rat
Ping-Pong Heart
The Nine-Tailed Fox
The Line
GI Confidential

ED LIN
(Taiwan)
Ghost Month
Incensed
99 Ways to Die

PETER LOVESEY
(England)
The Circle
The Headhunters
False Inspector Dew
Rough Cider
On the Edge
The Reaper

PETER LOVESEY CONT.
(Bath, England)
The Last Detective
Diamond Solitaire
The Summons
Bloodhounds
Upon a Dark Night
The Vault
Diamond Dust
The House Sitter
The Secret Hangman
Skeleton Hill
Stagestruck
Cop to Corpse
The Tooth Tattoo
The Stone Wife
Down Among the Dead Men
Another One Goes Tonight
Beau Death
Killing with Confetti
The Finisher

(London, England)
Wobble to Death
The Detective Wore Silk Drawers
Abracadaver
Mad Hatter's Holiday
The Tick of Death
A Case of Spirits
Swing, Swing Together
Waxwork

Bertie and the Tinman
Bertie and the Seven Bodies
Bertie and the Crime of Passion

JASSY MACKENZIE
(South Africa)
Random Violence
Stolen Lives
The Fallen
Pale Horses
Bad Seeds

SUJATA MASSEY
(1920s Bombay)
The Widows of Malabar Hill
The Satapur Moonstone

FRANCINE MATHEWS
(Nantucket)
Death in the Off-Season
Death in Rough Water
Death in a Mood Indigo
Death in a Cold Hard Light
Death on Nantucket
Death on Tuckernuck

SEICHŌ MATSUMOTO
(Japan)
Inspector Imanishi Investigates

MAGDALEN NABB
(Italy)
Death of an Englishman
Death of a Dutchman
Death in Springtime
Death in Autumn
The Marshal and the Murderer
The Marshal and the Madwoman
The Marshal's Own Case
The Marshal Makes His Report
The Marshal at the Villa Torrini
Property of Blood
Some Bitter Taste
The Innocent
Vita Nuova
The Monster of Florence

FUMINORI NAKAMURA
(Japan)
The Thief
Evil and the Mask
Last Winter, We Parted
The Kingdom
The Boy in the Earth
Cult X

STUART NEVILLE
(Northern Ireland)
The Ghosts of Belfast
Collusion
Stolen Souls
The Final Silence
Those We Left Behind
So Say the Fallen

(Dublin)
Ratlines

REBECCA PAWEL
(1930s Spain)
Death of a Nationalist
Law of Return
The Watcher in the Pine
The Summer Snow

KWEI QUARTEY
(Ghana)
Murder at Cape Three Points
Gold of Our Fathers
Death by His Grace
The Missing American

QIU XIAOLONG
(China)
Death of a Red Heroine
A Loyal Character Dancer
When Red Is Black

JAMES SALLIS
(New Orleans)
The Long-Legged Fly
Moth
Black Hornet
Eye of the Cricket
Bluebottle
Ghost of a Flea

Sarah Jane

JOHN STRALEY
(Sitka, Alaska)
The Woman Who Married a Bear
The Curious Eat Themselves
The Music of What Happens
*Death and the Language
  of Happiness*
The Angels Will Not Care
Cold Water Burning
Baby's First Felony

(Cold Storage, Alaska)
The Big Both Ways
Cold Storage, Alaska
What Is Time to a Pig?

AKIMITSU TAKAGI
(Japan)
The Tattoo Murder Case
Honeymoon to Nowhere
The Informer

HELENE TURSTEN
(Sweden)
Detective Inspector Huss
The Torso
The Glass Devil
Night Rounds
The Golden Calf
The Fire Dance
The Beige Man
The Treacherous Net
Who Watcheth
Protected by the Shadows

Hunting Game
Winter Grave

*An Elderly Lady Is Up
  to No Good*

JANWILLEM VAN DE WETERING
(Holland)
Outsider in Amsterdam
Tumbleweed
The Corpse on the Dike
Death of a Hawker
The Japanese Corpse
The Blond Baboon
The Maine Massacre
The Mind-Murders
The Streetbird
The Rattle-Rat
Hard Rain
Just a Corpse at Twilight
Hollow-Eyed Angel
The Perfidious Parrot
*The Sergeant's Cat:
  Collected Stories*

JACQUELINE WINSPEAR
(1920s England)
Maisie Dobbs
Birds of a Feather